I0762482

BY SAMANTHA SALDIVAR

Play You for It

RUNNING HOME TO YOU

RUNNING HOME TO YOU

SAMANTHA SALDIVAR

DELL
New York

Dell
An imprint of Random House
A division of Penguin Random House LLC
1745 Broadway, New York, NY 10019
randomhousebooks.com
penguinrandomhouse.com

A Dell Trade Paperback Original

ISBN 979-8-217-09261-1
Ebook ISBN 979-8-217-09262-8

Printed in the United States of America

1st Printing

BOOK TEAM: Production editor: Michelle Daniel • Managing editor: Saige Francis • Production manager: Ali Wagner • Copy editor: Alicia Hyman • Proofreaders: Jill Falzoi, Alissa Fitzgerald, Catherine Mallette, Nicole Ramirez

Book design by Alexis Flynn

The authorized representative in the EU for product safety and compliance is Penguin Random House Ireland, Morrison Chambers, 32 Nassau Street, Dublin D02 YH68, Ireland. https://eu-contact.penguin.ie

For Mom and Dad

RUNNING HOME TO YOU

PRESENT DAY

The metallic pop of bat meeting ball greeted Abby as she stepped out of her car into the wind, and while not visible from the parking lot, she detected the play by sound alone. Off-speed pitch, hit flaccidly to the shortstop, a routine grounder to first base. The PA announcer confirmed as much above the half-hearted thrum of fans. "And that's a groundout from Jenkins to short. Gladstone on the play to wrap the top of the fourth. The Eagles lead the Wildcats, 6–3."

Abby stretched the drive out of her neck and rolled another flight from her shoulders. Her job kept her on the road two hundred days a year, living out of suitcases and hotels, zigzagging across state lines in search of baseball's next messiah. Today that search had lured her through the Columbia River Gorge, winding up the bends and hills to a high ridge where Insley University sat with Mount Hood looming behind.

Like the other scouts who'd made the trek, Abby had come to watch Kayson Cannon—a promising shortstop on an unprecedented hitting streak. But unlike the other scouts, walking across the parking lot electrified the hair on the back of her neck and, despite the wind, sparked a fire in her chest. She stopped to gather her breath because this wasn't just a scouting trip. This was her homecoming.

She'd never intended to come back. Just as she never intended to veer from the baseball diamond that afternoon, bypassing the game for the smaller, empty ballpark a short distance away. Abby couldn't say for sure if muscle memory, nostalgia, or self-loathing brought her there—probably some horrible combination of all three—but she stopped at the backstop of the softball field like it had always been the destination. One that had eluded her for nearly a decade.

Abby braced herself on the chain-link fence. The place had hardly changed. She recognized the same dips and bald spots in the grass. The same maroon paint peeling off the dugouts. And the smell—dirt, the not-so-distant river below, and something scholarly, like stale books from the library. One inhale transported her back, tightened invisible cleats on her feet, sprouted sweat beneath her nonexistent jersey, and miraculously restored her knees to scarless and springy. She'd played and scouted on a hundred different fields, in a dozen different countries, but would go to her grave certain that this beaten down diamond was the most beautiful.

But then a gust punched through the gorge, rustling her dark hair and flapping the championship banner on display in the outfield. The one she'd never seen before. A last straw she couldn't bear. Another hit echoed from the baseball field, and Abby turned her back on the memories before they swallowed her whole.

Rather than stand with the other scouts, Abby plopped down into the bleachers. She preferred to be inconspicuous. It allowed her to see how the fans reacted to a prospect—intel she considered just as valuable as radar guns and sabermetrics when it concerned who her employer might invest millions in.

"Didn't think you were going to make it." A shaggy-haired man with chewing tobacco bulging his lower lip slid in next to her. Tanner worked for the competition, but Abby enjoyed his camaraderie on the road. Unlike the older, crusty men who still took notes with pencil and paper, fumbled with their cellphones, and refused to lug a laptop, he thought nothing peculiar about her femininity.

"I miss anything good?" Abby asked him.

He grinned. "Thirty-eight hits for the kid."

"The streak continues."

"Shhhh." Tanner brought a finger to his lips and narrowed his brow at her. "You know better than that."

Abby rolled her eyes at him and the nearby fans who flicked her glares. She'd encroached on one of the game's many superstitions. Don't step on the foul line. Don't cross the bats. Don't say "streak" or "no-hitter" unless you wanted to cruelly end it right then and there.

"I don't believe in that shit," she said.

Tanner chuckled. "Oh, come on. We all believe in it a little."

The Wildcats' hitter knocked a line drive to left field, spurring light cheers from the opposing team while he rounded first. Abby set her gaze firmly on the action, despite Tanner blabbering beside her.

"You've never seen a bad case of the yips?" he asked above the PA announcer. "Or gotten in a slump so bad you swore you were cursed?"

Abby shoved a hand into her sweatshirt pocket, fingers trembling until they brushed the plastic coin in her pocket. The one she clutched when the air got too thin or her mouth too dry as if pleading for the elixir she'd left behind. As if reminding her of the bridges she'd burned, the missteps and meltdowns, the reasons she'd never allowed herself to return.

"There's no such thing as curses," she said, though the words wobbled.

"Right. Tell that to the Red Sox and the Cubs."

They watched the next batter hit a skipping grounder to Kayson. Abby trained her eyes on his feet, clocking his reaction time to discern whether he saw the ball or heard it first. In that short millisecond, in the twitch of his shoulders, she knew it was sound. His footsteps landed light but mechanical. Rigid but perfect form. As his throw sliced across the field to the first baseman, a smile broke across his face. Not a cocky, victorious smile, but something airy. Like he belonged in that exact moment. A love for the game that Abby searched for in stadiums and creaking bleachers. Of course it was here. It was always going to be here.

Tanner nudged her as the inning ended. "You played here, right?"

Abby nodded, still clutching that coin in her pocket. "Yeah. A long time ago."

"That's exciting." Tanner beamed. Abby imagined he was the kind of guy who still showed up to bother his high school coach once a year. "Any of your old squad still around?"

"I don't know," Abby lied. She knew exactly where everyone landed after that last game. Another reason she'd dreaded this trip, and the same reason she took it.

"I'm going to go," she said.

Tanner's mouth fell. "You just got here. Kayson's got another at bat coming up."

"Yeah, I know. I just can't."

She couldn't manage a solid excuse. All she knew was that it was too soon or too late or maybe the timing would simply never be right. But before she could run away once more, she heard her. A voice that cut straight through the game and the anxious rhythm filling her ears.

"Abby?"

She didn't dare turn. She didn't move or breathe as heavy footsteps thudded down the bleachers. It was too late to run now. Instead, she clutched the coin in her pocket, closed her eyes, and surrendered.

EIGHT YEARS EARLIER

JUNIOR YEAR

Professor Cruz asked her to lunch after two weeks of staring each other down. Abby didn't doubt she was the worst student in her class, hadn't wanted to take it in the first place, but they'd been hurtling toward this encounter since she arrived at Insley University. Longer than that. They'd been building toward this meeting her entire life.

That first day, Abby had arrived late and slipped into a desk at the top of the slanted rows, maintaining as much space as possible.

"And we'll take a deeper dive into the varying levels of scrutiny applied to the Fourteenth and Fifteenth Amendments, so that by test time, you're able to apply those to hypothetical . . ."

Professor Cruz trailed as her eyes landed on Abby. Despite the distance separating them and never having met before, the exchange radiated reunion rather than discovery. The pause dragged so long that a student in front spoke up.

"Professor, are you okay?"

A few students shifted to find what distracted her. Their beady eyes made Abby squirm, but she didn't dare look away first.

"Right. What was I saying?" The professor pivoted from her audience and fiddled with the clicker to jump ahead a few slides on the projector. "Right, let's start with strict scrutiny."

After class, Abby scrambled to the exit, not prepared for anything beyond a shared stare. The professor didn't seem to be either, as no new text messages came. It almost prompted Abby to drop the class altogether, but curiosity won out. For the next few weeks, while everyone else studied Gender and the Law, Abby studied Isla Cruz.

She analyzed the way she gestured, the way she paced, and the way she spoke. Abby thought they might look alike, but it was hard to know for sure. She'd only seen photos before. Isla's hair was more chocolate than Abby's black waves, her skin lighter but warm. She was slender, where Abby was wide hipped and broad shouldered, taller, muscles teeming on her frame despite six months of disuse.

For those first few weeks, at the end of every class, Abby disappeared, putting a safe distance between them. Until one day Isla followed her into the hall.

"Hey, Abby, can you wait a minute?"

She shut her eyes as students streamed past on either side of her. She considered merging in and pretending she hadn't heard her, but they couldn't play strangers forever.

Abby turned. "Hey."

Isla's eyes scaled her up and down. Abby might've found it off-putting if she wasn't doing the same.

"Do you want to get lunch?"

Rather than converge at one of the campus dining halls, they went into town. Insley University lay just outside of Hood River, a community of fewer than ten thousand, its heart a medley of small restaurants, mom-and-pop shops, and breweries. Tourists flocked for hikes and windsurfing, panoramic views of the river and mountains, wineries hidden in sprawling orchards among the hills.

They met at a bar called Sunny's. Insley sports memorabilia adorned the walls, beer residue stuck to the floorboards, and students lounged on the wraparound patio. When the waiter took their order, Isla asked for an iced tea while Abby ordered a double vodka soda. The professor's brow furrowed as Abby produced her fake ID.

"How are you liking Insley?" she asked when the server left.

"It's fine."

"Sorry about the situation with your classes," Isla said. "I worked with the academic advisors. There weren't a lot of spots left, and I figured I could open an extra place in my class. That way you can at least get some upper-level credits to start. I know pre-law isn't exactly for everyone. Or maybe it is. I didn't even ask what your major is. At least, I didn't notice one on your transcript. Not that it's a problem if you don't have one yet. Do you know what you want to do after you graduate?"

Their drinks arrived, a well-timed disruption to Isla's ramble, especially since Abby didn't have an answer to that dreaded question.

"Sorry, I'm talking too much." Isla's cheeks flamed. "This is just kind of weird."

Rather than find her annoying, Abby took pity. Maybe because she noticed their sameness. Her eyes, wide set and vibrant copper, peered out as if from a mirror. Her mouth was the same too, plump lips, the lower barely fuller than the top.

"Yeah," Abby said. "Yeah, it's definitely fucking weird."

"And you're doing okay? You're settled in at the apartment? Do you need help with furniture or money?"

"You don't have to do that."

"I want to."

"Why?"

Isla canted her head and extended a half smile. "Because you're my sister."

A younger Abby had fantasized of such a declaration. She'd first sought Isla after a few deep searches on the internet. Isla was away at college when eleven-year-old Abby called her house and Isla's mother promptly hung up on her. When Abby's mom caught wind of the bold attempt to track down her long-lost half-sibling, she took her phone and computer privileges away for a month.

She got her second chance during high school when Isla friended her online. They didn't exchange messages. It was a silent lifeline. A chance to peek into each other's worlds. A peek that would've satisfied

Abby's curiosity, just enough acknowledgment to bandage the wound of not knowing all of oneself.

This, sitting across from each other, was never supposed to happen.

"I'm sorry for everything you're going through." Isla's eyes glassed over, and Abby tore hers away. "Like I said, if you want to stay with me instead, I have room."

"No, I think that's too much." Abby traced the condensation on her glass. "But thank you. You've done enough already. I don't want to be a burden."

"You're not a burden. We're family."

"We share the same asshole father and a last name. I don't know if that's family. Plus, I'm twenty. I don't need another parent."

"Right." Isla nodded. "But can I ask you something?"

"Sure." She sighed. Summer had a late choke hold on September and the heat worsened Abby's hangover. She fingered the cigarettes in her pocket, debating if it would be rude to light one.

"Did he ever call you?" Isla asked.

Abby finished her drink. "No."

She lied. Her father, not that she made a habit of calling him that, called periodically over the years. A few birthdays. A few holidays. All dependent on his sobriety, who he was dating, where he was living, if it was a high year or a low. There wasn't a formula to it, though she tried to find one in the beginning. By her teens, she caught on to his bullshit and hung up whenever he called. When he rang six months ago, she didn't dial him back.

"What about you? Do you talk to him?"

"Occasionally," Isla said, averting her gaze.

"Well, you knew him longer and better than I did."

Isla scoffed. The scoff sounded like Abby's, and it made her smirk. "I'm not sure if that's true. And even if it is, I'm not sure it's a good thing." Isla stopped to flutter her thick lashes at their server. "Can we get two shots of tequila?"

Abby's mouth fell open as he darted off. "Wow, Professor."

"I don't know why I thought I'd be able to do this sober." Isla cocked a brow at her. "That's a nice fake by the way."

"Relax, I'm basically twenty-one."

"As an employee of the university, I'll pretend that's true."

When the shots arrived, they each shook out a pinch of salt, clutched limes, and held up their drinks.

"To long-lost sisters and second chances," Isla said.

Abby clinked her glass despite the toast ringing more sentimentally than she liked. They hissed through the liquor, their grimaces identical. She didn't know if she'd ever get used to seeing her reactions reflected on a stranger.

"Listen, I know you don't need another parent or something," Isla said. "And trust me, I'm not trying to be that. I hardly have my life together, to be honest."

"Really? You seem like super put together."

Isla's flawless curls, her ironed slacks and stilettos, jewelry, manicure, and makeup suggested a meticulous existence.

"Maybe on the outside. But our dad, or lack thereof, did a number on me. I don't know about your mom, but mine wasn't exactly parent of the year," she said. Abby's mouth unintentionally crumpled, and Isla winced. "I'm sorry."

"No, don't be. Honestly, it's kind of nice to know you've been through the same shit."

Isla frowned. "When I say I'm here, I mean as a friend. And if you need to call someone for something, anything, I hope you'll consider me."

"I will." Abby worked her answer past a tearful swallow. To her relief, she spotted their server across the way and subtly nodded at him for another round.

"Are you going to play this season?" Isla asked.

"I don't know."

"You should."

Abby bit her lip. She'd put the game out of her mind for months, avoided it like she avoided everything else that once instilled joy but now fell flat. "I'm not sure I want to or if the team will even want me."

"Coach Whitley would be thrilled. I've already talked to her about you."

She sighed. "You didn't need to do that."

"Just think about it, okay?"

"Why do you care?"

Isla shook her head, blinked and shifted as if embarrassed. "I don't. I was just trying to be helpful. But forget it. Only do it if you want."

Two more shots arrived, and this time Abby raised her glass to Isla's. "To our asshole dad, our messed-up mothers, and not having our shit together."

They clinked glasses, scowled through the booze, and chuckled. Abby clung to the warmth in her chest, ignited by the tequila, but fanned in Isla's presence. She'd lost almost everything that spring, but gaining a sister, no matter how strange the concept, gave her something solid, steady, real. Enough to consider returning to other aspects of her life, including the game that had once stood at the center of her world.

October crispened the morning air, turning leaves brittle on their branches. Kate Hutchins plunged into it with gusto, each breath on her run a cleansing bath for her lungs. She cut across campus, past the quad and athletic facilities, winding through town, until she jogged parallel to the water.

This was her year to be the strongest, fastest, best. She took care to lift in the offseason, building her core, pumping up her throwing arm, improving her flexibility. After two seasons of fighting for her spot against an upperclassman who despised her, Kate's position on the softball team was finally hers alone.

She arrived home to the blue house in time to shower before

morning classes, counting the hours until practice. Not only did she crave the game, but reuniting with all her teammates, meeting the freshmen, and seeing Coach incited the anticipation of a family reunion on an unofficial holiday.

"You know there's no extra credit for practicing before practice," Mick, her roommate and the team's catcher, said as Kate entered the kitchen. She hovered blearily over a bowl of cereal, her short straw-colored hair poking out at odd ends.

"It's not practice. I run because I like it," Kate said. "You're always welcome to join."

"Please, I have two good years left on these knees, if I'm lucky." Mick poured another helping of cereal. "I heard the freshman class is going to be shit this year."

"Can't be any worse than last year." T.K. stretched as she entered the cramped, barely held together kitchen and helped herself to coffee as though she lived there. "Have you seen my cleats?"

Mick glared as T.K. plopped into the seat beside her. "No. I'm not doing it this year."

"Doing what?"

"Keeping track of your shit and mine."

T.K., the squad's left-handed hurler, wouldn't know where the field was if the team didn't remind her. She missed practices, chased more than one game day bus, and lost three softball mitts last season. Mick functioned as T.K.'s keeper, the pitcher-catcher duo more like a disgruntled married couple than teammates.

"I'll help you look." Kate sorted through the shoes piled at the door. "But how'd you get in here?"

T.K. poured herself a bowl of cereal. "Shupe never locks the back door."

"Damn it, Shupe!" Mick shouted.

"What!" a voice shrieked from upstairs.

"You're going to get us robbed or killed."

"Have you seen my cleats?" T.K. shouted.

"What?"

"Have you seen my cleats?"

Jillian Shupe thumped downstairs, toothbrush foaming in her mouth, messy red curls fanning her face. She chucked a cleat at T.K., which she narrowly dodged. The next shoe came directly after, and Kate caught it before it smacked Mick.

"The fuck, Jill," T.K. said through a mouthful of cereal, milk dribbling down her chin.

Jill spit toothpaste into the kitchen sink. "Quit leaving your shit here. I tripped on those clown shoes in the bathroom and almost knocked myself out."

"You better not be calling me a clown, ginger," T.K. said.

"Well, the shoes literally fit."

"How about you quit leaving the back door unlocked, Shupe," Mick said.

"I didn't!"

"You're sneaking out to see Dylan again, aren't you?"

Jill's face flashed as crimson as her hair. "I am not."

"You two are back together?" Kate asked.

"Not that type of back together, Hutch." T.K. snorted as Jill shoved her. "Jill's just getting slipped the ol' Dill."

Kate cleared her throat and checked her backpack for the books she already knew were there, desperate to hide the blush overtaking her cheeks.

"T.K., return to your own house, eat your own cereal, and find your own gear," Mick said.

T.K. drained the milk from her bowl and flicked Mick behind the ear.

"Don't forget practice today. Pitchers and catchers at three o'clock . . ." Kate trailed as T.K. slammed the door behind her. "And she left her cleats."

Mick groaned. "Nope. I'm not doing it. Let her pitch barefoot."

After chasing down T.K. with her cleats, Kate walked to campus with Jill. As a political science major on a pre-law track, Kate spent most of her time at Cormac Hall. She sat in the first few rows of every lecture, and now, as a junior, knew most of the professors and peers within her major. But when she found her usual place that morning, a new face greeted her. The unfamiliar student made a point to stand up from the end of the first row to flop down closer.

"Hey," she said.

Kate furrowed her brow. "Hi."

"You play softball, right?"

"Uh yeah." Kate pulled out her notebook, making a point to look busy. "How'd you know?"

"Your jacket." She draped an arm over the seat between them. "I'm Abby."

Kate ventured a glance. She met amber eyes underscored by shadows. A stare that radiated fatigue, and yet Kate tilted her head, drawn in by something else. A flicker that screamed familiar. Perhaps she'd seen her before. It wasn't exactly a big school. But if she had, she'd remember the way her breath snagged in her throat. She'd remember how difficult it was to hold eye contact when she met her head-on. She'd remember that despite the instinct to draw back at Abby's forwardness and the faint trace of cigarettes wafting off her, she unconsciously leaned into the space between.

"I'm sorry." Kate cleared her throat. "Can I help you with something?"

"Maybe. You see, today is—"

Professor Cruz's footsteps interrupted. "Abby?" She raised a brow and set her briefcase on the lectern.

"Professor?" Abby said back.

Kate narrowed her gaze as she looked between them. The casualness in which Abby greeted the teacher, and the familiarity with which she responded, landed like a joke she wasn't in on.

"You never sit up here." Professor Cruz folded arms across her chiffon blouse, squinting as though amused.

Abby shrugged. "Trying something new. Is that allowed?"

"I guess. Just don't bother poor Ms. Hutchins."

"Morning, Professor," Kate said.

"I think it's too late for poor Ms. Hutchins." Abby smirked.

Kate bit her lip to avoid flashing a smile back. One that threatened to spring big and cheesy despite the unwanted attention. She didn't know this Abby character, didn't understand why she went out of her way to sit beside her, or why one of her favorite professors had a soft spot for the smoker who usually hid in the back of the lecture hall. Kate purposely ignored her for the rest of class, hustling out when it ended in case she tried to speak to her again, unaware that it wouldn't matter when she arrived at practice a few hours later.

As always, she showed up early. Her visor perfectly straight, ponytail tight against her head, her Insley Eagles T-shirt tucked into her gray softball pants. A few players clamored in the dugout, Mick among them, fastening her catching gear. But while they had time to spare, someone was already working out on the diamond, plunging Kate's heart into her stomach.

It was Abby, coasting with feline grace at shortstop. Dirt covered her thighs and stomach. A few wild pieces of black hair fell into her eyeline. Coach Whitley hit her a grounder, sharp and deep. Abby tracked it in a few nimble strides, scooped it in her glove behind second base, squared up in one motion, and drilled a throw to first. Kate shuddered at how loud it popped.

"Who the hell is that?" Jill asked in the dugout.

"Transfer student, I think?" Mick said.

"Fuck. She's good."

Abby dove for a line drive near third base, making a nearly impossible catch look like an easy stretch. The coaches roared in approval. Abby wasn't just at shortstop. She was in Kate's position. And she was good at it. She was great at it. Kate couldn't move.

"You okay, Hutch?" Mick asked.

"Yeah," she whispered.

Coach Whitley hit Abby a few more balls, all of which she handled effortlessly, every throw on target, her footwork light but precise, like a dancer's steps. She didn't muscle or force it either. Her arm stayed loose, flopping at her side like a limp noodle, and yet she wielded raw power. Kate could have watched for hours, absolutely hypnotized.

Abby jogged to the dugout afterward, wiping at a light mist across her forehead. She nodded at Kate but didn't say a word.

"Circle up." The group tightened around the robust, Australian-born Dana Whitley. This season marked her third at the helm, meaning she'd been with Kate's class from the start. "Welcome back."

The team clapped and shook each other's shoulders. Kate couldn't bring herself to smile.

"Today we have a few walk-ons trying out with us, but we're going to treat this like a regular practice. I also want to introduce a late addition." Coach Whitley gestured to the brawny player in the back. "This is Abby Cruz, junior transfer from UCLA. She plays shortstop and made all-conference last season, and we expect her to have a big impact here. Let's make her feel welcome."

Mick patted Kate's back and whispered, "Don't let it get in your head."

But it was too late. Kate clenched her teeth, overcome with freshman-like nerves. She incessantly drifted to Abby during warm-ups, eyeing her form while they threw, envious of her height advantage and wingspan, hating that her rolled-up sleeves revealed toned biceps and square shoulders.

All week, they took turns at shortstop. A grounder for Abby, a grounder for Kate. They ate up every ball, diving, scooping slow rollers and bounces bare-handed, grunting to launch a throw to Jill at first base. While Abby moved like an animal or dancer, fluid and lithe, Kate moved like a machine, rigid but consistent. Her crouch, her steps, her glove always found the right angle, always adjusted to the bounce, her throw a laser to Jill.

Every so often, Abby nodded at Kate's performance, a smile playing at her lips after a big dive or slide to make the play. It made Kate want to scream. It was as if she didn't realize they were competing, or worse, she didn't consider her competition. Kate punched the pocket of her glove and glared in return.

“What the hell is she doing here anyway?” T.K. asked after the third day.

Abby always vanished as soon as practice finished, and with the coaches gone, gossip stirred in the dugout.

“Looking for more playing time?” Jill tossed a ball to herself while she lay on the bench.

“She was all-conference. I doubt that was an issue,” Mick said. “I mean, who leaves the best program in the country for this shithole? She dropped a whole division coming here.”

“Exactly,” Courtney Seaborn, their senior captain, said. “I bet she got kicked off the team.”

“Why?”

“Who knows? Attitude issues?” Courtney shrugged. “But there’s something off. I heard she could only get in here because her mom or someone works for the school.”

Kate, who purposely eavesdropped but didn’t partake in the conversation, stiffened. She’d been so fixated on beating Abby that she failed to put the pieces together. She remembered Abby’s casual exchange with Professor Cruz. She didn’t seem old enough to be her mom, but they had the same last name and, on further reflection, looked alike. She kept the information to herself. No matter how much she begrudged Abby’s arrival, she didn’t want to fuel speculation. She’d beat her on merit alone.

By the end of the week, they were neck and neck. She counted only one more error than Abby in the field, and while Abby made unbelievable tags, snags, and double plays, Kate held steady. During conditioning and sprints, she outshined her. In fact, while Kate finished the timed mile first, Abby struggled in the back, coughing as she finished nearly last. Kate almost snarked something about the cigarettes she caught her smoking but bit back the taunt. Especially since the rumors grew more brutal by the day.

After Courtney’s charge that Abby must have been kicked off her last team, the theories on why turned cruel. Some believed she was suspended for fighting with her coach. Another rumor was that she had sex with her coach. Yet another was that she'd slept with two of her teammates, causing so much drama that she was forced out.

Usually Kate, the squad's unofficial moral compass, would put an end to the rumors, but couldn't muster it this time. Not as she tried to edge Abby out, though this side of her ambition, one without empathy, wasn't something she was proud of either. The best she could do was pray that Abby never caught wind of the gossip. She wondered if that's why she avoided the dugout and locker room, trudging off without a goodbye. It wasn't lost on Kate that her teammates only cheered for her during drills and scrimmages, never offering Abby a compliment.

"I got it." Mick jogged to join Kate, Jill, and T.K. in the outfield, while Abby smacked line drives off the pitching machine. "I figured it out."

"Figured what out?" Kate shagged a grounder that rolled into the grass.

"Abby," Mick said, catching her breath. Kate and everyone within earshot fell quiet. "An old teammate of mine was a year ahead of her at UCLA. Apparently, she got kicked off the team."

"No shit. Do we know why?" T.K. asked.

Mick's throat bobbed as Abby launched a ball over the fence. She brought herself to a whisper, forcing them to creep closer. "I guess she had a breakdown. Her mom died and Abby lost it. Bitched out her coach, skipped classes, started showing up to practice wasted from the night before."

Kate's heart clenched, and a wave of nausea surged in her gut. The rumors, her jealousy, and Abby's isolation no longer seemed a natural result of her unwelcome arrival but a shameful reflection of her own insecurity.

"And get this—her dad is Audie Cruz," Mick said.

"Who?" Jill asked.

"You know." Mick put on her best radio voice. "'Adios, Audie Cruz! It's outta here!'"

As if proving her lineage, Abby hit her deepest home run yet, the ball flying over their heads to the grass slope behind the fence. Kate, still processing the new information, stared in awe. She swore Abby scowled back as if she heard them.

"He's a Hall of Famer," Mick said. "The Padres retired his number last year."

T.K. raised an eyebrow. "Maybe that's why she got another chance here."

Abby roped a ball straight at the foursome. T.K. shrieked before Kate caught the line drive.

"Ladies, this isn't social hour! Break it up!" Coach Whitley shouted.

As they dispersed, Mick hit Kate's thigh with her glove. "You can beat her out, Hutch. We're all pulling for you."

"Thanks," Kate said, but she frowned once alone.

Abby stepped over home plate and lined up to hit lefty, because of course she was a switch-hitter. Kate sighed as she crushed ball after ball. She didn't want her spot handed to her, planned on working for it, had worked for it endlessly, but this seemed unfair. Even worse, now her resentment didn't seem justified.

She no longer envied Abby but pitied her, no longer saw a competitor but someone fallen. Only Kate, who often jumped in to help strangers with a kind word or a pat on the back, didn't know if she could do it now. It marked the first time, and certainly not the last, that Abby made her question everything she believed.

THE HAZING INCIDENT

Persistent showers shifted softball practice indoors. While her teammates slacked off in the musky confines of the retired basketball court, Kate dug in as determinedly as before. Coach Whitley promised she hadn't made a decision about shortstop, wouldn't until spring, and that she noticed her efforts. The small assurance pushed her harder.

She continued her morning runs, ate leaner, lifted heavier, and now, accustomed to Abby's presence, ignored her competition altogether. Despising Abby, comparing herself to her, wouldn't do Kate any good. She could only focus within.

That was the beauty—and simultaneously, the misery—of softball. At the heart of the team sport was an emphasis on the individual. Whether up to bat or in the field, despite your teammates surrounding you, you were alone. An island unto oneself.

Of course, despite her best efforts, Kate still observed the other shortstop. Abby never arrived at practice early, just barely on time, her uniform stained and untucked. She didn't smile and while she exuded poise when playing, her shoulders slumped otherwise, her stare downcast except to glare at anyone who might whisper in her vicinity.

Kate knew she should try to get to know her. They had a class together. They literally shared a position, but she never spoke up. In fact, so much time passed without talking to Abby that now it seemed awkward. So, she maintained the status quo, communicating only when necessary. Until the swim to Wells Island.

Every year, after Coach Whitley announced the final roster, the team partook in a little friendly hazing. The university outlawed such practices, but they kept it lighthearted. The swim to Wells Island wasn't even really a swim; calling it that was just part of the fun.

The upperclassmen blindfolded the freshmen, drove them to the dock, and told them to jump into the icy waves on the count of three. When the countdown ended, the upperclassmen would reveal it was a prank and that no one had to swim, but every year, some unlucky, overly eager freshman threw themselves into the river before the big reveal. Humiliating, yes. Harmless, for the most part. And, of course, an unintentional test of who was most gullible.

After the prank, the upperclassmen subjected the freshmen to a game of trivia. Wrong answers earned a spray from a hose on the dock, correct answers earned a shot of vodka, so that as the trivia progressed, it became more challenging.

While the tradition typically ended in laughs and memories, this year Kate approached it apprehensively. The senior ringleaders, Courtney Seaborn and Lauren DeHaven, insisted that along with the four freshmen, they haze Abby too.

"We've never done this to transfers," Kate said.

"We hardly ever have transfers." Lauren, their ace pitcher, rolled her eyes.

The team gathered in the parking lot after practice, minus the freshmen and Abby. The sun hadn't set and, fortunately for the newest Eagles, it was an unusually dry and mild day for October. Of course, that was thanks to Kate's secret planning, checking the forecast for weeks, subtly suggesting to Courtney and Lauren that they do it on this day in particular.

"Cruz thinks she's better than the rest of us. Let's bring her down a notch," Lauren said.

"You of anyone shouldn't have an issue with this, Hutch." Courtney patted the hood of her car. "Let's round them up and meet at the dock. You guys hit the dorms. We'll take care of Cruz."

Kate sank as she hopped into Jill's car with Mick and T.K. Abby was already detached from the team, and this would only make it worse. The regret anchored into her shoulders. She should've said something to her. Anything at all.

They made easy work of cornering the freshmen in the dining hall. Kate's group nabbed Riley Brookheimer, a promising left fielder. The other upperclassmen gathered the remaining newbies, giggling as they blindfolded them, a happy show even for the victims as their peers hooted and threw food at them on their way out of the cafeteria.

Lauren and Courtney held a blindfolded Abby's arms when they arrived at the dock. Ketchup stained the transfer's shirt. In fact, as she drew closer, Kate noticed mustard in Lauren's hair, an irritated scratch on Courtney's cheek, and a cut on Abby's lip.

"What the hell happened?" Mick asked as they led the freshmen down the dock.

"We found her at Sunny's," Lauren said. "Chased her into the kitchen."

"She threw a lit cigarette at me." Courtney scowled when Mick snorted. "It's not funny."

"You jumped me. What did you expect?" Abby asked.

"It isn't supposed to be like this," Kate said to no one in particular.

The wind dragged in clouds from the west and rocked the boats tied to the dock. Wells Island, an unoccupied speck in the middle of the river between Oregon and Washington, didn't appear far from their vantage point, but was at least a quarter mile away.

"Line them up!" Courtney jerked Abby around to face the water. The squad lined up the freshmen next to her. "Welcome to the Wells Island swim!"

Abby growled. "This is bullshit. I've already been a freshman. I'm not doing this."

"You've never been an Eagle, Cruz." Courtney clapped her back so hard that Kate flinched. "When we remove your blindfolds, we'll count to three, and you'll jump into the river. The first one there and back is off gear duty. You don't want to know what happens if you're last."

Kate gulped as she removed Madison Quong's blindfold. She didn't remember the tradition being so mean-spirited. Last year as a sophomore, no longer on the receiving end, she found it harmless and fun. Even as a freshman, preparing to plunge into the swells felt like a thrilling rite of passage. But it didn't feel right now.

"One . . ." Lauren started the count with a grin. "Two . . ."

Abby glanced over her shoulder at Kate like she knew she'd find her. Somehow, she always seemed to find her. And Kate always failed to give her anything in return. Not a hello, not a smile, not even a nod when she did something good at practice. But she wouldn't overlook her now. Kate offered a minuscule, nearly imperceptible shake of her head. If Abby noticed, she didn't make it known and turned back to the river.

"Three!"

Abby didn't fall for the bait, but Madison and Riley, on either side of her, twitched to jump. Harnessing the same speed and strength she wielded on the diamond, Abby grabbed both freshmen by their shirts and yanked them back as they started their leap. The remaining freshmen gaped at Abby, who shook her head at them.

"Looks like this might be our smartest freshman class yet." Lauren scowled at Abby. "Usually, we get at least one swimmer. Thanks for that, Cruz."

"Not too late for you to show us how it's done," Abby said. "I'd love to see you take a dive."

"Okay, that means it's time for trivia!" Mick clapped and cut in before another fight broke out between Abby and the seniors. "But first, claim your prizes."

The rest of the team had already been passing around a few bottles of liquor and poured shots for the hazing victims. While the freshmen winced, Abby tossed her drink back like water.

"That's right, Cruz, drink up," Courtney said with a sneer.

"Okay, it's time for round two of the Insley Initiation Games! I'm your host, Mick McMechan!" Mick procured a microphone and note cards from her letterman's jacket. "Shupe, if you'd be so kind."

Jill hit play on a small portable speaker and game show music echoed on the dock. T.K. bopped along, taking a happy pull from her bottle of vodka. She offered it to Kate, but she shook her head, too busy staring at Abby, who nodded at her and mouthed thank you.

"Our first question is for Ms. Izzy Palamino of Denver. What year was Insley University founded?"

"1863."

"Correct! T.K. will get you your prize," Mick said as T.K. poured Izzy a shot. "Next up it's the pride of Carson City, Riley Brookheimer. How many conference championships has the Insley Eagle softball team won?"

"Seven."

"Correct! Pour some booze for Brookheimer!" Mick turned to Abby next. "Now, for our favorite transfer student, Abby Cruz. Abby, who is Insley University's current president?"

Abby stared blankly, her mouth in a tight line. They warned the freshmen countless times to study up on school and team history, that a test was imminent, but Abby clearly hadn't. She probably assumed it didn't apply to her, though Kate also got the impression that she didn't study much at all.

"This is stupid," Abby said.

"How about a different question . . ." Lauren smirked. "Why'd you get kicked out of UCLA?"

Kate frowned as Abby's cheeks flushed.

"That's not on my cards, DeHaven," Mick said, still impersonating a game show host. "Abby, last chance. The president of Insley University is . . ."

"Kiss my ass?"

"Brilliant guess!" Mick boomed. "But it's the incomparable George Urgayle."

The team laughed, and Courtney sprayed Abby with sickening pleasure. The punishment usually entailed a quick splash of water to the face, but she predictably soaked Abby from head to toe until Mick finally shouted enough.

The next rounds passed in similar fashion. The freshmen class proved their competence, answering their questions correctly, even as the alcohol flowed. Meanwhile, Abby encountered the hose three more times, dripping and trembling in the wind. Kate tried to put a stop to it after the second round, but when Courtney suggested Kate receive the punishment instead, she shamefully backed down.

By round five, the freshmen wobbled, and Abby stood drenched. When Palamino staggered after her correct answer, nearly vomiting at the presentation of another shot, Abby drank it for her. She did the same for Brookheimer, who gratefully passed hers off with a hiccup.

"All right, Abby, I get the feeling this has never happened to you before, but you're oh for four on the day. Let's see if we can bump up that average as you show us how well you know your teammates," Mick said. "What is Kate Hutchins's hometown?"

To everyone's surprise, especially Kate's, Abby answered without hesitating. "Deer Park, Washington."

"Correct!"

But the hose came anyway. Courtney blasted Abby for a fifth time, and when it finally stopped, the team stood so still that only the river and obnoxious music cooed.

"Fuck you!" Abby moved for Courtney, but Mick blocked her.

"Daddy can't save you now, can he, Cruz?" Courtney scoffed. "We know Mommy certainly can't."

Abby lunged over Mick, swiping Courtney's hair, before Kate and T.K. dragged her away. Abby seethed, her chest galloping under Kate's hand. She braced for fists or tears, but neither compared to Abby's desolate, glistening gaze. It punctured a hole in Kate, deflated the integrity of her chest, sending the walls and roof caving in.

"What the hell is wrong with you, Seaborn?" Mick yelled.

"She needs to relax! It's a little water from a hose. Back before the university got involved, the freshmen really did have to swim to the island."

"I'd rather do that than this bullshit!" Abby shouted.

"Then do it!"

The dock fell quiet.

Abby nodded. "Okay, fuck it. We're going to have to pump the freshmen's stomachs and I'm going to get hypothermia anyway."

"Oh my God, you're dramatic. You won't do it." Courtney turned to the team. "She won't."

"Watch me." Abby snatched the liquor bottle from Jill and chugged.

Kate's pulse charged in her throat. People had jumped into the river this time of year before, but never after sunset, never after drinking, and never for a full swim to the island. "No, this has gone too far. The game is done."

"Nah, the game is just getting started." Abby hissed and smacked the empty bottle into Jill's stomach.

"That water is way too fucking cold, dude," Mick said. "Seaborn, call a truce."

"I'm not calling a fucking truce," Courtney said. "Let her drown."

"Court, stop it!" Kate shouted.

"Shut up, Hutch! I know you warned her about the swim." Lauren glared.

The team erupted in drunk hysteria, pointing fingers, inching into each other's faces, the seniors screaming at the juniors, the juniors screaming at the seniors. The inebriated sophomores chanted for Abby to swim. In the chaos, before anyone could stop her, Abby ripped off her soaked T-shirt, chucked it at Courtney's face, and dove into the river.

The water met her skin like a thousand knife tips. She kicked and reached through the initial shock, met the air, and gasped, before bobbing back under. The river's claws dragged her down like a monster of the deep. She flailed, grunted bubbles, and choked when she came up again. On the dock, her teammates screamed for her to return, but she floated on her back instead. Water sloshed in her ears. Her eyes met the lavender sky.

"Mom."

Abby didn't know if it came off the wind or from her frigid lips. Perhaps flirting with mortality conjured the lost word. Pictures flashed along with it. Her mother in the kitchen with the teal tile backsplash, hips swaying as she cooked, singing along to Springsteen in the summer. Laughter and encouragement, clapping from the bleachers and the beach.

"Swim, Abby," she'd say during those long summers. "Swim."

Abby swore the message arrived on the gusts plowing through the canyon, courtesy of an unmistakable ghost. There was no other explanation. So, she swam. Not back to the team, but forward.

The current fought her on the choppy swim. Her legs cramped and her toes stiffened. A contradictory pain that permeated the icy numbness it created. But if Abby was anything, it was stubborn. Durable. And while each stroke through the water hurt, at least now she controlled her own pain. For months she'd tried to with booze and poor decisions, but unlike those vices, the swim inspired her to fight for a life she didn't know she still cared about.

When she finally hauled herself up the shore, she struggled to breathe. Of course, she still mustered enough energy to flip two middle fingers at her teammates on the dock. Then she flopped down, huffed, and stared at the vacant island's treetops. She considered what it meant to evade drowning for one more day. If it would mean anything at all tomorrow.

"Did you swim out here?"

Abby popped up to catch the wind's message, certain it was another whisper from her mother. Instead, she discovered two men in a small fishing boat.

"It's dangerous! Can we give you a ride back in?"

She didn't really want to return but couldn't withstand the cold much longer either. They pulled her into the boat and gave her a towel. The ride back took two minutes, but she pathetically slumped into herself when they arrived.

"Holy shit," Mick said.

The fishermen lifted her up to the landing. In the team's frenzied, nonsensical bickering, Kate reached her first. She draped her coat around Abby and held her close as she swayed.

"You're insane," Courtney said.

Abby cracked open her frozen lips. "But-but-but I'm off-off gear duty, right? First one, first one there and back-back, b-bitch."

Jill chuckled. "That's technically right, Seaborn. You stated the rules loud and clear."

"Okay, everyone needs to get the fuck out of here before we're all busted. You take the freshmen back to the dorms. We'll take care of Cruz," Mick said. "Go!"

The team scattered in the dark, sprinting for the parking lot, and while out of the clutches of the Columbia River, Abby trembled harder by the second.

"Are you okay?" Kate asked.

Abby leaned into her as water dripped off her nose and hair. "Just fuck-fucking cold."

"Mick, she's turning blue." Kate pressed a hand to Abby's cheek. "She might have hypothermia."

"Should we take her to the hospital?" Jill asked as they reached her car.

"No hospital," Abby and Mick said in unison.

"Hospital means Coach finds out. Coach finds out, we're dead. I'm talking full fucking kangaroo," Mick said.

Abby convulsed as she slid into the middle seat, teeth clashing so violently that she worried a dislocated jaw might ail her next. Jill started the car, blasted the heat, and wiped a circle across the foggy windshield.

"She could die from hypothermia," T.K. said.

"She's not going to die. Let's just get her back to our place."

By the time Jill's car squealed out of the parking lot, the violent shaking and bone-chilling cold left Abby dizzy. She shut her eyes, uncomfortable enough that sleep tempted as a better option. But then a hand squeezed hers, and she jerked back up. It was Kate rubbing her fingers for warmth, and while the friction barely broke through the cold, Abby hissed thank you. Kate didn't acknowledge her, but hedged in closer, her shoulder propping up Abby's, unbothered by her weight or dampness.

Abby's heart hadn't stopped skipping from the adrenaline of the swim, so she didn't attribute it to Kate, but she couldn't ignore the way her breath caught. She hadn't been this close to someone in months. The loneliness mercifully lifted, and it took everything in her to not wilt into Kate entirely.

"If something happens to her, we're going to get kicked off the team, maybe out of school." T.K. scrolled through her phone. "People go to prison for hazing. I'm not going to prison!"

"Why don't you figure out how we can help her and then it won't matter!" Mick peeled off her jacket and handed it to Kate, who wrapped it around Abby. "How is she?"

"Cold," Kate said, still rubbing her hands.

"Isn't hypothermia where you're supposed to take off your clothes and use body heat?" Jill asked.

Kate turned rigid against her and Abby would have chuckled if shaking hadn't consumed her frail energy.

Mick scoffed. "Quit fantasizing, Shupe."

"I'm serious!"

"She's right." T.K. pointed to her phone.

"Stop. No one is getting naked," Mick said.

"Thank God," Abby muttered.

Jill glanced in the rearview mirror. "I have to admit, that was kind of badass, Cruz."

"It was dangerous," Kate said.

"Dangerous? We had to stop you from jumping in after her."

Abby's eyes widened at Kate, but she didn't respond.

Mick chuckled. "First picking a fight with the seniors, then jumping into the river. Do you have a death wish?"

Abby frowned but delivered her answer with the same performative confidence that sent her swimming. "Absolutely."

While everyone resumed their joking, Kate stopped rubbing her fingers. She stared at Abby wistfully, the longest look they'd ever exchanged since they met, and squeezed her hand. In what seemed like a miracle, for the briefest of moments, Abby stopped trembling and squeezed back.

She'd longed for such acknowledgment, though she couldn't pinpoint why. It started long before softball. Abby first noticed her in the front row of Isla's class, answering questions in a reserved manner that suggested timidity, but with a cutting weight that demanded one listen. When Abby spotted the softball patches on her letterman's jacket, she considered introducing herself but spent weeks eyeing the back of her head instead. And when she finally worked up the courage to put herself out there, meeting those ice blue eyes and freckles, Abby didn't even care that Kate dismissed her. She wanted to keep staring, wanted to keep teasing, wanted to know more.

Instead, they became competitors, and with the rest of the team equally threatened, Abby existed on the outskirts. But this simple hand squeeze, Kate's shoulder against her own, filled her with fleeting hope that they could be more than rivals.

At the house, Mick barked orders like she would in a game. "Jill—tea, Kate—blankets, I'll find you some clothes, and, T.K.—just don't make anything worse."

Abby fought drowsiness, dipping in and out of the house's lights and colors while she shivered on the couch. The girls milled in and out, handling her like a rag doll. She grumbled when Mick shoved her into the bathroom to take a hot shower. Jill forced her to take hold of a warm cup of tea, Kate tucked blankets around her, and even T.K helped, though Abby imagined the pizza she ordered wasn't simply out of the goodness of her heart.

"Did you really throw a cigarette at Seaborn?" Mick tipped back and forth in a rocking chair suited for a front porch. None of the furniture in the small house was sensible or cohesive, but its asymmetry was part of its charm.

"Yeah, she's lucky I didn't deck her. DeHaven grabbed me from behind, tried to throw a hood over my head. They chased me around the whole fucking bar and Seaborn tackled me in the kitchen," Abby said, provoking laughter from her captive audience. "A waiter tripped over us, spilled burgers and fries everywhere."

"I would've paid to see that." Mick snorted. "Don't worry about Seaborn. She's just jealous that you're going to be hitting cleanup this season."

She shrugged. "The manager blacklisted us, which sucks. I like Sunny's."

T.K. waved her off. "Give it a week. They've shredded like three of my fakes and still let me in."

"Court was out of line," Kate said from the spot next to Abby. "Sorry for what she said to you."

"It's okay." Abby didn't want to relive the low blow. Instead, Kate's remorse surprised her, just like her hand in the car. Just like her apparent willingness to jump after her, even if now she wouldn't look at her, picking at the threads of the couch instead.

She didn't remember falling asleep, but woke to the blue wash of the television a short while later. The rest of the living room was empty. Empty except for Kate. She clicked off the TV and draped another blanket over Abby in the dark. "Thank you."

Kate hovered, a dim outline in the nearby glow of kitchen appliances. "Are you feeling better?"

"Yeah," Abby said, though the telltale signs of sickness were emerging along her raw throat. "Thanks for letting me crash here. And for tipping me off about the swim. I know you don't like me very much."

"Little did I know you were going to jump in anyway," Kate said. The floor creaked as she pivoted to leave, but then she turned back. "That was nice. What you did for the freshmen. You didn't have to."

Abby shrugged. "It was nothing."

As her vision adjusted to the darkness, she noticed the crease in Kate's chin deepen with a frown.

"I don't not like you, Abby. You're just chasing something that I really want too."

Abby nodded, wishing she had something better to say than "I know." She considered apologizing, but she wasn't sure why. Maybe to continue their conversation. Maybe to erase the frown that hadn't left Kate's face.

"Well, get some rest," she said before shuffling out.

"Yeah. Good night, Kate."

Abby's eyes fluttered closed, and she sank into the deepest sleep she could remember, safe in the presence of her teammates, and the memory of Kate's hand on her own.

After months of resenting her arrival at Insley, Kate prayed she'd find Abby. The morning after initiation, she discovered a neat pile of blankets on the couch and nothing else. Her stomach hardened. More unbearably, the hollow place in her chest that had opened on the dock grew with regret, with empathy, and a loneliness she didn't understand.

She searched for Abby during class, swiveling each time someone entered, but she never showed. On the quad, she glimpsed every person she passed just in case. She prayed. She prayed that nothing worse happened. That she'd see Abby, confirm she was okay, and that exposed hole in her heart would close, allowing them to return to rivals.

Before practice, she hurried to the locker room, certain she'd find her. Still nothing. Just the team suiting up in unusual silence. Kate joined the juniors in their corner bank of lockers.

"Have you seen her?"

"No, but the seniors are MIA too," Jill said.

Kate sighed as she flopped down to the splintered bench and kept an eye on the door, not that Abby had ever shown up before. She hadn't even claimed a locker.

T.K. popped her gum while she braided Jill's hair. "You think she snitched to Whit?"

"Didn't take her as the type," Mick said. "But shit is tense."

Coach Whitley cleared her throat behind them. "Hutchins, can you come with me please?"

"I wasn't there," T.K. whispered as Kate passed her.

Dana Whitley's office had once belonged to the last men's basketball coach before they got a new gymnasium, and it was still furnished as such. Other than a computer, everything reeked of the seventies, from the squeaking banker's chair to broken filing cabinets. Coach Whitley commuted from Portland, so perhaps she considered refurnishing the office impractical. Plus, the team didn't have money even for small luxuries, trekking to most away games on buses and bunking five to a room in motels.

"Take a seat." Coach Whitley stepped behind her desk.

Kate discovered Abby already in a chair with the hood of her sweatshirt raised. Her gaze widened as Kate sat next to her.

"I heard about what happened at the dock yesterday," Coach Whitley said. Kate swiveled to Abby, whose mouth dropped. "Cruz didn't dob. You think I don't know everything that goes on around here?"

Coach Whitley wasn't an overbearing leader. She rarely yelled, didn't believe in using running as punishment, and usually let the players work things out among themselves. But right now, with her hands clasped on the creaking desk, Kate felt like a guilty teenager about to get chewed out.

"Kate didn't have anything to do with what happened. It was Seaborn and DeHaven. She tried to stop it." Abby sneezed. Her words escaped as though pushing through gravel. "She shouldn't be in trouble."

"This isn't about that, but I can assure you that Seaborn, DeHaven, and the other seniors have been dealt with," Coach Whitley said. "What happened wasn't okay. You put your life in danger and that's not allowed on my watch. Understood?"

Abby nodded. "Yes, Coach."

Kate's knee bounced. She still didn't understand why she'd been called into the office.

"On that note, it's not lost on me that you're struggling." Coach Whitley rotated her computer monitor around and Abby's cheeks flushed. Kate leaned forward to read the transcript of mostly D's and low C's. "I know you're skipping classes. In fact, you're barely making the grade in most of these. That doesn't fly on this team."

"Am I cut then?"

"Do you want to be?"

She shrugged, and it extended the trough in Kate's chest, much like Abby casually chuckling at her own death had her clutching her hand as if to keep her.

"Kate's the best student on our team. Besides attending every one of these classes and meeting with your professors, I want you to study with her."

Abby coughed. "That's not necessary."

"It is if you want to play here," Coach Whitley said. "Moving forward, Hutchins is going to be your partner for everything. Warm-ups, weight lifting, road trips, team dinners. You will attend, and she will make sure you are there." She shifted to Kate. "If you can't get her where she needs to go, I'm holding you responsible."

"What?" Kate clenched her teeth. She could handle tutoring Abby. She'd tutored plenty of teammates, though helping her rival stung. Letting Abby fail her classes and get cut might be in her best interest. But taking responsibility for her entirely struck her as excessive. Especially since what little she knew about Abby—her smoking, hanging out at bars, always unkempt, barely on time—suggested that she'd have her work cut out for her. "Coach, I'm not okay with this."

Abby flicked Kate a glare. "Me neither."

"Well, that's too bad." Coach Whitley paused. "Cruz, can you step out for a moment? In fact, get checked out at health services. You're not practicing today."

"This is . . ." Abby stood and peered down at Kate, who waited for her to say something. She searched her eyes for a semblance of hatred or despair, but found none. She couldn't quite figure out what Abby wanted before she shook her head and tore off.

"Why me?" Kate asked once they were alone.

Coach Whitley sighed. "Well, because frankly, I've been disappointed in you," she said. That was the secret to the woman's laid-back, nonpunitive leadership style. The D-word slapped ferociously. "You're the heart of this team. The girls look up to you and you left Cruz in the cold."

Kate sunk in her chair. "I didn't."

"You ignored her, and the rest of the players followed suit."

"I'm competing with her. I didn't say or do anything bad to her, but I'm not about to be her best friend when she's after my position."

"And that's where you're wrong," Coach Whitley said. "You know that this game is much bigger than where you take the field. More than that, you know Cruz's history, don't you?"

Kate nodded as a stone overtook her throat.

"She's not well. She's partying too hard and that stunt at the river wasn't just fun and games. That came from somewhere dark." Coach Whitley's mouth sagged. "Maybe I'm wrong, but I don't think kicking her off the team is the best thing for her. In fact, I think the team might be the only thing that can save her."

A tear budded at the corner of Kate's eye, and she swiped it away. An invisible war triggered inside. Helping Abby, keeping her on the team, threatened everything she worked for. She might as well hand her the coveted shortstop position. Yet in her heart, she knew helping was the right thing. More importantly, it was the only way to fill the hollow space gnawing at her heart.

"I know I'm asking a lot, but in the end, I don't think you'll regret this."

"Yes, Coach."

A few more tears streamed loose. She didn't know if they rolled for herself or Abby.

PARTNERS

Kate Hutchins didn't take no for an answer. Abby groaned when Kate showed up at her apartment, shoulders raised against the chill while she delivered a determined flurry of knocks to the door. She contemplated ignoring her until she gave up, but Abby also didn't want her to leave. Not when she spotted her through the peephole, her gentle features taut with determination, chestnut hair blowing in the wind, almost unrecognizable from the field.

She took an extra beat to study her, before finally cracking the door with a sigh. "I'm sick."

"That'll happen when you plunge into the river this time of year," Kate said.

"What are you doing here? Haven't you heard of a text?"

"You weren't answering those so Coach told me where to find you. I thought we could hit the library." Kate's brows drew together. "We have three weeks to get your grades up. I'm sorry, but we don't have a choice."

"You could just let me fail," Abby said.

Kate seemed to mull it over, staring at Abby for a beat, probably taking note of her raw nose and the bags under her eyes. "I'm not going to do that."

Despite the answer resounding with a hint of begrudged duty,

Abby was secretly relieved that Kate wasn't giving up on her. Even if she'd nearly given up on herself.

"Fine. Just give me a minute."

Abby didn't dare let her inside. She'd been at Insley for two months, but her mattress still lay in the middle of her bedroom floor. In the last few weeks, she'd stopped doing laundry, picking out her least smelly shirts for practice. Both the kitchen sink and her ashtray overflowed, while she'd let the refrigerator dwindle to empty.

She paused after throwing on clothes, lingering on a photo of her mother atop her dresser. She didn't know if it was sickness or the drama of the last few days, but Abby had been tossing and turning more than usual at night, consumed by nightmares and tears. Consumed with visions of the crash, the ring of that dreaded phone call with the news, stomach lurching when she wondered if her mom had died instantly or if she had felt the heat on her skin. If she was aware enough to fear the end or if she thought of Abby when she took her last breath with regret.

She swallowed the threat of fresh tears before charging outside and slamming the door behind her. She buried her hands in her sweatshirt, teeth clenched against the chill, as she walked ahead of Kate.

"Why'd you do it?"

Abby narrowed her gaze. "Do what?"

"Jump in the water," Kate said, catching up alongside her.

"Does it matter?"

"I guess not."

Kate bit her lip as if holding back more and Abby sighed. "What?"

"I'm just trying to understand. It seems like maybe you don't want to be here. At Insley."

Abby rolled her eyes as they crossed the quad. "That would be convenient for you, wouldn't it?"

"That's not what I'm saying—"

"I don't know. I don't know but I don't know what I'll do if I'm not here. If I don't play." Abby tried to gulp away the tightness in her throat. "It's the only thing I know how to do right now. I just keep waiting for it to feel normal again."

She stopped herself from the rest. That she kept waiting to feel anything at all. Just like that twisted baptism in the river when the ice hit her skin and confirmed she was alive. She kept waiting for the game to fill the hole in her heart and bring her back.

It'd worked plenty of times before. The one thing she always excelled at, understood, belonged to. That's what had stung in the weeks leading up to the dock. She didn't belong on the team. Maybe she didn't even belong on the field.

But she trudged through the motions, needing it, even if she didn't want it. That's what the game required. Getting up to bat after striking out again and again. An error in the field almost always guaranteed the next ball was coming to you. It promised as much letdown as triumph, and the rest loomed mundanely in between. In the waiting. Lately, Abby took permanent residence there.

When they reached the library steps, Abby paused and glanced at the phrase etched under the roof above the marble pillars. *Ad astra per aspera.*

"It says, 'To the stars through difficulty,'" Kate said next to her.

Abby's mouth fell. "You know Latin?"

"A little."

"Of course you do," she muttered as Kate barreled through the iron doors.

Abby trudged after her, passing the bookshelves and wide tables in the center of the room where groups of students huddled together. They found a spot on the second floor. Abby grumbled as she unloaded her backpack, carelessly tossing books to the table. "I don't know where to start," she said.

"Maybe the assignments and tests that count for the largest portion of your grade?"

Abby hunched over her laptop, searching for said priorities when Kate cleared her throat. "What?"

"Do you mind if I . . ."

Her eyes widened as Kate inched over, so that she hovered above the laptop too. Her hand reached for the touch pad, briefly brushing Abby's. While Kate clicked through her assignments, Abby stared at her cheek, freckled and a touch rosy beneath. And when she pulled back, their shoulders skimming slightly, the same warmth that once stopped her from shaking filled her stomach.

"How's your grade in Professor Cruz's class?" Kate asked as she returned to her chair.

"I uh." Abby turned red, uncertain if it stemmed from the graze of Kate's fingers or the reminder of her failings. "I think I have a C. I don't know. Maybe I'll get lucky, and she'll continue to have mercy on me."

Kate's lips quirked. "Is Professor Cruz your . . ." She stopped as if it was a secret.

"We have the same bastard father." Abby shrugged. "Isla's kind of the reason I transferred here."

"Are you close?"

"Not really. We met for the first time a few months ago."

"Do you have other siblings?"

"No, it's just—" Abby almost choked. "It *was* just me and my mom." She stared at the table.

"I'm sorry," Kate said.

Abby fingered the thick textbook next to her. "You're taking the LSAT?"

"Yeah, this spring."

"Of course you are," Abby whispered.

They spent three hours in the library, perhaps more than Abby ever had. School never interested her, and she typically managed only passing grades. She felt self-conscious in Kate's presence.

Kate, who arrived everywhere early, whose softball pants and practice shirts were always clean, tucked in, ponytail so sleek that light bounced off her chestnut tresses. Kate, who apparently wasn't just a talented athlete, the fastest and fittest on the team, a sure starter at shortstop if not for Abby, but also a high-achieving student. Kate, who everyone adored and looked up to, not because she was funny like Mick, or scary like Seaborn, but because she radiated kindness and calm.

Abby rooted in competing envy and admiration while Kate worked with blue intensity shooting from her gaze. She broke every twenty minutes to check in with Abby, to give her note cards to study for her exams, to suggest readings for her essay, to ask what she thought of the latest chapter in Isla's class that Abby hadn't studied, before summarizing it for her. Then she'd silently go back to her own work like some academic assassin.

Abby swore she stared as much as she studied, drifting to the hair Kate tucked behind her ear. To her pinched brow and perfect penmanship. She lingered on her hands. The ones that touched Abby that day after the river as though she were an egg or infant, something fragile and not yet broken.

"Are you okay?" Kate asked.

Abby jolted and recovered with a scowl. "Can we call it a night?"

Kate nodded. They packed up, and while she loathed studying, Abby didn't want it to end. Her shoulders sank as she trailed Kate through the maze of books, down the spiral staircase, and out to the dark quad.

"Let me know how your economics test goes," Kate said.

Abby nodded, savoring a last glimpse before returning to isolation.

"Hey, there you are!" A towering man cut between them and threw an arm around Kate. "You didn't text back."

"I was in the library." Kate's cheeks flushed. "This is my teammate Abby. Abby, this is my boyfriend—"

"Blake Davis." He offered a hand. Abby shook it, her teeth grinding together. "You're the transfer student, right? Katie says you're amazing."

"She does?" Abby darted her eyes back to her.

Kate slipped beneath Blake's arm and started down the sidewalk. "Come on, we should get going."

But Blake kept his feet planted, hands in the pockets of his letterman's jacket. A silver cross hung around his neck. "Have you found a church yet?" he asked her.

Abby laughed, but neither he nor Kate joined in. "Oh. You're serious?"

"We go to New Hope Baptist, if you ever want to join . . ."

"Let's go." Kate tugged his hand and barely spared Abby a glance. "I'll see you tomorrow."

"Nice to meet you." Blake smiled and she grimaced back as he followed Kate like a docile puppy.

Abby's sadness at their study session ending shifted to bitterness. Bitterness at being Kate's project, a charity case that she only took on because of Coach Whitley's demands. Bitterness at needing her tutoring and companionship because no one cared, and lately she didn't even care herself. But mostly, bitterness at not being the one to follow Kate across the quad with her hand as a steady guide.

She intended to put her best foot forward with Abby. Kate didn't approach a task with anything less; plus, she accepted their forced partnership as apt penance for her previous neglect. But after their first study session, Abby cooled to an impenetrable degree.

"How was your test?" Kate would ask.

Abby only shrugged. Kate grew to dread helping her with essays, correcting her work to an annoyed, "Really?"

"You know I'm just trying to help, right?" she asked as they slammed their books shut.

Kate didn't know what she expected. After the dock, after glimpsing Abby's deep-rooted sorrow, a part of her longed to understand, maybe even help, but Abby didn't let her. Not that Kate fully understood how. Not when her shoulders drooped, or her eyes cast to a far-off place, or she mindlessly scribbled in the margins of her notebooks. Not when she showed up to a study session, red eyed and sniffling, refusing to meet Kate's face.

"Are you okay?" she asked.

Abby's throat bobbed. "Yeah."

Kate frowned. "Is it . . ." But she always stopped, uncertain what to say, hoping it might be enough for Abby to meet her halfway.

"What?" She rubbed her eyes and hunched over her textbook. "I'm just having a shitty day, okay?"

"Okay."

She swore the closest she ever got to Abby was when she'd catch her stare across the table. It held a haunting sadness, and yet its intensity bore into her like she wanted something. It'd grow so heavy that Kate often blushed, spurring another grumble whenever she snapped Abby out of it by asking what she wanted.

Their partnership on the field didn't thaw either. Every practice they threw together, took grounders at short, lobbed pitches to each other for hitting drills. They spoke little, but in the silence, Kate admired and envied. No matter how doggedly she trained, she'd never swing as smooth or throw as crisp. Even sick, even sad, even scarcely trying, Abby was by far the best.

And just as Abby rolled her eyes at Kate's tutoring, Kate too grew annoyed at Abby's effortless skill.

"You're leaning out," Abby said as she tossed her pitches.

She gritted her teeth between swings. "No, I'm not."

"You're losing power because you're dipping out early like it's a slap." Abby threw her another ball and Kate whiffed. "Pulled your head on that one."

"I know," Kate said with a scowl.

There was no escape. Abby stopped avoiding the locker room, swiping the last dented cubby next to Kate's, the two of them silently tossing equipment and slamming doors before and after practice. The dilapidated, mold-riddled showers had two temperatures—ice cold and third-degree-burn hot—so the locker room only accommodated storage, changing, or socializing. Still, Kate averted her eyes, squared up to her own locker while she dressed, never quite comfortable in her own skin or at the sight of others'.

But with Abby, she failed to avert her gaze. Kate unconsciously suctioned to her as she sat in her sports bra and shorts on the bench, legs kicked out, arms bracing her as she casually leaned back. Kate didn't notice she'd stopped breathing until her chest tightened, nor realized she was staring until Abby's dark eyes flashed into hers.

"Dude, what do you think?" Mick flexed in front of a dirty mirror on the wall. "I'm trying to bulk this season. Cruz, you're built. How much are you lifting now?"

Abby just shrugged, her eyes not veering from Kate's. "I don't know. How much?"

Kate blushed, her voice barely there. "One-forty," she said, her jaw locking at another reminder of Abby's superior strength. She hated loading more onto the bar in the weight room, the two of them glaring as they spotted each other. The frustration boiled so hot beneath that it often left her outwardly trembling, much like it did now, as Abby smirked across the way. Kate turned back to her locker and huffed to catch her breath.

"You know what that means?" T.K. strutted in, swinging her makeup bag.

"What?" Jill asked from the locker next to Kate's.

"That you can lift me." T.K. raised an eyebrow at Abby. "Want to try?"

The team snorted and Abby shook her head. "Does that line actually work?"

"On half the basketball team so far," Jill said.

"What do you think about the dating scene here anyway?" T.K. asked. "I bet it sucks compared to L.A."

Abby shrugged, her eyes catching Kate's once more. "I don't know. The only guy I've talked to invited me to church."

Kate's brow hardened at the reminder of Blake and Abby's scoff at his invitation.

"Well, I'd go to church and get on my knees for some of those CAC boys," T.K. said.

"We don't actually kneel," Kate said.

"We know *you* don't," Courtney Seaborn said to a roar of laughter that left Kate bright red.

Jill leaned in to whisper, "She means . . ."

"Yeah." Kate cleared her throat. "I get it now."

She was used to being the last one to understand a dirty joke or sexual innuendo, sometimes looking it up later, and while she often covered with an embarrassed, hollow chuckle, she couldn't this time. Not with Abby quietly squinting at her as though she'd actually seen her naked in the locker room. In fact, Abby not joining their teammates' laughter made Kate more mortified than if she had.

"Are you even allowed to be within a hundred feet of a church, Court?" Abby asked dryly. "I thought they had a rule against hooves."

Courtney chucked her dirty socks at Abby's head, which she easily dodged.

"The church is fine," Mick said. "It's the holy water she has to avoid."

Kate slung her backpack over her shoulder and strode quickly for the exit. "I'll see you guys tomorrow."

"Oh, come on. It was a joke, Hutch!" Courtney called after her as the door slammed shut.

The night before their Gender and the Law final, the last before winter break, Kate teetered on the edge of breaking. She couldn't stand the stares and the scoffs or her own conflicting push and pull, in which she swung wildly between longing to help Abby and then just as quickly needing to escape her. That's why she invited her to the blue house, for the buffer of their teammates in case she snapped. And she did, while they sat at the rickety kitchen table, Abby rolling her eyes as Kate aced every term on the color-coded study guide she made for them.

"Did I do something to you?" Kate asked.

"No." Abby narrowed her brow. "Why?"

"Because it seems like you hate me."

Jill, who sat with them, glanced up from her accounting homework. Mick ate popcorn on the sofa while she iced her knees and peered over the cushions.

"I don't hate you," Abby said.

"Then what's with the silent treatment?"

Abby lowered her chin to her chest. "It's embarrassing to be babysat by you," she mumbled so quietly that Kate barely heard her.

Her mouth slackened. "It's okay to need help."

"Well, I think I liked it better when you ignored me." Abby returned to the study guide with a scowl.

"This wasn't my choice."

"Yeah, trust me, I know. I know you're only doing this because Coach made you. I'm just a charity case."

"That's not true."

"I'm sure you'd rather be studying to be a lawyer or playing with your perfect boyfriend."

Jill covered her mouth, eyes darting between them.

"What does Blake have to do with anything?" Kate asked.

"He doesn't!" Abby shouted.

The tension of the last few weeks burst to the surface. "Then why are you always mad at me? I'm the one who should be mad at you!"

"Guys, maybe no one should be mad," Jill said.

"Why should you be mad?" Abby asked Kate.

"How about for you coming here and gunning for my position? And now I'm expected to help you and you're not even grateful!"

Jill joined Mick on the sofa and reached for the popcorn. "Give me some of that."

"I am grateful!" Abby's eyes bulged. "I'm probably going to pass all of my stupid classes because of you!"

Kate's heart rattled up her throat. "Good!"

"Yeah. Thank you!"

"You're welcome!"

Abby stood, chair squealing on the hardwood as she swiped the study guide. "And thanks for this too. I'll see you in class tomorrow." She snatched her backpack. "Have a good winter break."

"You too," Kate said, roiling with confusion. She wanted Abby to leave and simultaneously wanted to yank her back down to stay, even if it meant screaming at each other. "Merry Christmas."

"Yeah, Merry fucking Christmas." Abby slammed the back door.

"What the hell was that?" Mick asked.

"I don't know," Kate whispered. She stayed planted in her seat, her chest heaving, skin burning despite a small portable heater being the only source of warmth in their thin-walled house. Kate didn't like the spat but despised the emptiness that replaced it. She stared at Abby's chair, rubbed her throat, and shivered.

The morning of the final, Kate glanced at Abby endlessly. In fact, she caught herself doing it so often that she worried Professor Cruz might accuse her of cheating. Her mind drifted to their bickering and what she'd say to Abby now. Should she apologize? Shouldn't Abby apologize?

Kate finished the exam first, even with the distractions, nodding briefly at Professor Cruz, who wished her a nice winter break. She paced in the hall, debating whether to wait for Abby. Her bus left in a few hours, so they could still talk, maybe grab coffee, though they'd never done that before, and Kate envisioned Abby rolling her eyes and saying no. She bit her lip, infuriated by the imagined situation, but even more deflated by the thought that they wouldn't speak at all for the next few weeks.

"Forget it," Kate muttered after ten minutes. She departed, unaware that Abby left the classroom a few seconds later, clenching her teeth to stifle a call after her.

WINTER BREAK

For the first time ever, Abby dreaded winter break. Probably because for the first time she didn't have a true home to return to. Isla did her best to fill in the gaps, inviting Abby to her condo, a glass tower too industrial and chic for its place in the trees.

"You really don't want to be with your family?" Abby asked, craning her neck back to admire the high ceilings.

"No, this is exactly where I want to be. Mom is on a cruise with number four."

"Number four?"

"Stepdad number four," Isla said on the way to her kitchen, all open shelves with terra-cotta cookware and an herb garden in the window. Abby followed before she disappeared into a walk-in wine cellar. "White or red?"

"Uh, whatever's fine."

While their ten-year age gap and separate upbringings left distance between them, Isla's home with its curated décor and artwork stretched those differences into something insurmountable.

Abby knew little about Isla's life—just the pieces she parsed out from eavesdropping on her mom's phone calls. She knew Isla grew up wealthy, and by the looks of the condo, was apparently still wealthy, but not because of their father. Isla's mother came from old

Hollywood money. She'd been a part of Audie Cruz's foray into new-found fame and fortune.

Abby at least gave their father credit for that. He'd come from nothing in Puerto Rico, playing his way out of poverty into big-league stardom. Isla's mother supposedly managed his early career, negotiating endorsements and contracts, but let him keep the money in the divorce—her prenup was still better. And Abby imagined, even if it wasn't true, she was happy to be rid of him with his road game antics, illicit affairs, and parties splashed across the tabloids.

Meanwhile, Abby's mother had tried her hand at Hollywood, but there was little money to speak of. A few guest appearances at prime time, typecast as the loud Italian friend in rom-coms. She'd lasted a few years on a bad soap opera when Audie entered the picture.

By the time he left, Abby and her mother saw little of whatever money he'd entered the marriage with. Though by what Abby scoured online—the vacation homes, his designer suits when he made appearances, the yacht and girlfriends—he wasn't suffering. Not while she and her mother lived in a cramped Los Angeles bungalow.

The money never really bothered Abby. Perhaps because while her mother struggled to make ends meet post-divorce, she didn't notice. Or maybe her mother just didn't let her. Not with their trips to the beach and surf lessons, softball camps and tournaments every summer. It wasn't until she grew older that Abby detected the strain. The burned dinners and nights sleeping on the couch. The missed days of work because she wouldn't wake up, usually following a surprise appearance by Audie. Abby stared off into that same place as she imagined shaking her, begging her to eat something, to say something, to get up so she wouldn't lose another job. She was lonely now without her, but God, she'd been lonely then too.

Isla popped the cork from a bottle of red, interrupting her thoughts. "What did you and your mom usually do for Christmas?"

Abby bit her lip. She hadn't talked about her mom with anyone in months. An inkling of shame came with it, as though she was single-handedly letting her memory fade away in a second, painful death.

"Not much," she said. "What about you?"

"Usually some stiff dinner with my grandparents. We celebrated Hanukkah for a few years thanks to number three. That was fun." Isla slid her a glass of wine.

Abby peered into the glass, hoping that the prickle might leave her eyes before it became a stream down her cheeks. "My mom's family was in New Jersey, but I never met them. So, it was just the two of us. The occasional neighbor or boyfriend, but no stepdads for me. We usually ordered Chinese and watched old movies."

When Abby sniffled, Isla didn't prod. She just squeezed her shoulder. "That sounds perfect. Let's order Chinese."

The differences between them ceased to be insurmountable after that Christmas. And despite Isla's distant nature, despite barely knowing each other, Abby found it easier to be around her than most others. She wondered if that's what it meant to be kin.

It wasn't just Isla that Abby connected with over break. A few days after Christmas, an unexpected number buzzed her phone.

"Yo, Cruz, what're you doing?"

Abby rubbed her eyes as she sat up in bed. "Is this Mick?"

"Dude, you're still at Insley, right? Come hang out with me."

The McMechan clan lived in Beaverton, a sprawling suburb outside of Portland, only an hour from campus. Five people made up the immediate family in a cinnamon-scented house that overflowed with noise. Mick's older brother and sister were as quick-witted and obnoxious as she was. Her mother, a round woman who rarely left the kitchen, offered snacks almost hourly, and hugged Abby like she'd always known her. Mr. McMechan held court in his recliner, arguing with the TV. He lumbered like a bulldog and laughed like a giant, so infectious that Abby suppressed chuckles whenever he opened his mouth.

The home functioned as a revolving door of cousins, aunts, and uncles with the same laugh. Friends and neighbors didn't knock. They strutted to the kitchen for Mrs. McMechan's cookies and gifted Mr. McMechan cases of Rainier. Abby didn't know how to handle the influx of people, so she followed Mick's lead, joining board games, sliding into a seat at dinner, drinking beer and playing Ping-Pong in the garage.

She stayed three nights at the McMechan house, sleeping on the top bunk of Mick's childhood bed. Her family treated Abby like the rest of the kids and Mick never prompted any deep conversations, talking only about softball and school. It was perfect.

On New Year's Eve, they attended a house party hosted by one of Mick's high school classmates. Abby didn't mind sinking into the background, sipping cheap whiskey, joining the occasional game of flip cup as Mick floated from conversation to conversation. After an hour, she stepped outside for a cigarette and tugged down her beanie in the frost. A group huddled around a firepit, blasting music, but Abby stayed back, contemplated the stars, and thought of Kate. The entire visit, her ears perked whenever Mick mentioned her name like her favorite song had come on the radio.

"God, it's cold." Mick exited the house behind her. "You know, if you quit smoking, you wouldn't have to stand out here." She nudged her and outstretched a hand.

Abby passed the cigarette, smirking when she took a drag. They stood for a while, sharing a smoke, Mick uneasy on her feet after drinking the brightly colored concoction the hosts served out of coolers. "Can I ask you something?"

"What?" Mick burped.

"Did Coach put you up to this?" Abby asked. "Inviting me to hang out?"

Mick punched her arm. "Shut up, Cruz, you're an idiot."

Abby chuckled, placated, though not entirely convinced. "Sorry, it's just with Coach making Kate keep tabs on me, I assumed."

"Well, don't," Mick said. "How's it going with Hutch, anyway?"

Abby shrugged and lit another cigarette. "Fine, I don't know. I probably shouldn't have argued with her."

"You pass your classes?"

"Yeah. She's a miracle worker."

She didn't mean it sarcastically either. Kate's tutelage not only pulled Abby out of her academic hole but motivated her. Abby studied and worked long hours at home after the library, fearful of letting Kate down or looking stupid. With Mick tipsy, Abby dared the question she'd pondered endlessly.

"What's the deal with her boyfriend?" She glared at Mick's grin. "What?"

"Nothing, I just didn't think you'd care," she said, still smiling.

Abby's shoulders hitched up to her ears. "I don't. It's a question, Mick."

"Relax, I'm fucking with you." Mick slid out a beer from her ski jacket and cracked it open. "Kate and Blake have been together since freshman year. He's fine. A real golden boy. You know, football player, baseball player, declaring for the MLB draft this year."

"I didn't know he was that good." Abby ground her teeth with the same unexplainable jealousy that overcame her when they met outside the library.

"Yeah, leave it to Hutch to date the best ball player in school history." Mick sipped her drink and handed it to Abby. "They met at CAC."

"What's that?"

"Collegiate Athletes for Christ. You didn't have it at UCLA? It's like a club for Christians. Church, Bible study, volunteering, and they sign a purity contract."

Abby choked. "Really?"

"You didn't know? Don't you two talk?" Mick looked at her incredulously. "Kate's family is super religious. She has like a million siblings and was raised really sheltered. She hadn't even been on a plane before our freshman season."

The information overwhelmed her. She suspected Kate a touch prudish but attributed it to her perfectionist ways. This left her head spinning. It didn't, shouldn't, matter to her. Just like it shouldn't matter that she was with Blake. Kate was her teammate, not even her friend. Yet Abby grimaced as though betrayed.

"She's not bigoted though, if that's what you're worried about. I mean, half the team is queer," Mick said, unprompted. "What's your deal anyway?"

Abby took a drag from her cigarette. "You know me. I'm a switch-hitter."

"I knew it. My gaydar is great, but my sense for bisexuals is off the charts."

Abby laughed. "What about you? Are you seeing anyone?"

"No. You interested?" Mick winked.

"God, no." Abby smiled.

Mick finished her beer. "Come on, let's find girls to kiss at midnight."

Abby followed her, disappointed for a reason she couldn't place, but simultaneously elated. For the first time since coming to Insley, she had a friend. While they failed to find a midnight kiss, Mick, staggering on the way home, her arm draped over Abby's shoulder, gifted her optimism for the New Year. "You're pretty cool, Cruz," she said.

"You too, Mick." Abby's dimples sprouted, so unused lately that her cheeks twinged.

Even after Mick's revelation, Abby counted the days until Kate returned from break. She arrived in the locker room early that first day back, knee bouncing until Mick arrived with her roommates in tow.

"What up, Cruzer?" Mick slapped her shoulder in a hug.

The other players observed bewildered. Jill nodded at her next, patted her back on the way to her locker, and then Kate appeared. Abby shuddered when their eyes met. She didn't recall her gaze shining so blue. The type of eyes that reflected storms and seasons. She cleared her throat. "Hi."

"Hey," Kate said, already suited up in her pristine practice uniform.

"I um." Abby stopped before blurting she missed her. Stopped before mentioning their fight and apologizing like she intended to. "How was your break?"

"Good. Yours?"

"Good."

They lingered. Kate bit her lip and released a small noise that resembled a laugh, but Abby couldn't be sure.

"Let's go warm up." Kate brushed past her, and Abby drew in a breath, struck with an ailment she didn't understand, but certainly knew the source of.

THE DECISION

"They're predicting nineteenth round." He grinned that boyish, eye-squinting grin that she knew she should return, but Kate couldn't. She just sat in their usual booth at the diner on the edge of campus and didn't move. "What's wrong?"

"Nothing." Kate swirled the straw in her water. "Nineteenth round. Wow."

Blake nodded, his smile drooping a little. "Yeah, I mean, it's not the top, but it's still a fat signing bonus. I don't think staying senior year is going to change much." He reached across the table to hold her hand. "I know it's scary, but we can do the distance, Katie. I know we can."

But it wasn't the distance that left her nauseated. His news made her so envious that she stewed under the vintage light fixture, the jukebox crooning behind them, hating that Blake wouldn't have to lose the game like she would. In less than two years, it would end for her. There wasn't a draft for softball players or a chance at a professional career. Every few decades, women's leagues rose and crumbled, and even if one did again, it wasn't enough of a paycheck to live off. Not even the Olympics was a guarantee, as the sport frequently got dropped from the summer games.

Kate forced a smile. "I'm happy for you."

But after they kissed, Blake narrowed his eyes. "You sure you're okay?"

"Yeah." Kate sighed. "Just tired from practice, trying to hold my own against Abby."

"Right." Blake gulped a too-big bite of his burger. "Has Whit decided yet?"

She shook her head and picked at his fries.

"Well, don't put so much pressure on yourself. Maybe you can split time at shortstop again this year." He shrugged and Kate resisted responding that it was easy for him to say. "You're competing with baseball royalty. She's got like a dozen golden gloves and home run derbies in her DNA."

"Big Blake!"

The baritone rumble signaled the arrival of Blake's teammates, who brazenly piled into their booth. When Blake apologized, Kate waved him off and dismissed herself. Her mind was already elsewhere, had been for weeks, months maybe—tied up with Abby Cruz.

They continued to study and train together through winter term. They still didn't exchange many words, but the stubborn lines loosened between them. Perhaps Abby befriending Mick helped things, or maybe it was that Kate spent winter break wondering what she was doing and who she was with. Or maybe it was that Abby stopped scowling whenever Kate helped her in the library, and while her stares didn't stop, Kate swore less anger brewed there, even if it still made her blush.

Of course, at practice, her desire to win, to be the best, tugged her back in the other direction. She'd set her mind to it, pushing to be faster, throwing harder, grunting and huffing while Abby glided. Kate ignored her rare compliments or suggestions, slamming her locker shut next to her, only to spend the night wishing for it to be tomorrow, when they'd see each other again.

She fought the same whiplash as she walked back to the blue house, Abby once again on her mind. She came over more often after winter break to hang out with Mick and the others, and each time

Kate pulled open the door, she secretly hoped to find her, though she wouldn't dare extend the invitation herself. Just as she didn't dare break out in the grin her mouth twitched for when she spotted her at the kitchen table with T.K. and Jill.

Kate cleared her throat as she closed the back door. "What are you doing here?"

"Helping them with their Spanish homework," Abby said.

"You speak Spanish?" Kate asked.

"Yeah, kind of." Abby shrugged. "It was my first language thanks to Audie. No wonder I suck at English."

"You don't suck at English. You just never do the assigned reading."

Abby rolled her eyes.

"How do I ask a man how much money he makes?" T.K. twirled her hair around a finger.

"That's not on the test," Jill said.

"It should be. I'm going to Spain this summer."

Abby cackled, and Kate realized she had never heard her really laugh before. Not sarcastic or half-hearted, but full. Her chest fluttered at how Abby threw her head back and glowed.

"Okay, try this. *Soy una prostituta. Estoy buscando un sugar daddy.*"

Kate snorted as T.K. repeated it with gusto. Abby chortled again too, deep and hearty, her gaze settling into Kate's. When the laughter ended, she longed for it to return, to move closer or stay, but she was still the competition. She still intended to win.

"I'm going to study upstairs. Night."

Abby's smile faded, but she nodded. "Good night."

By late February, a few rainless days allowed them to return to the field. They layered sweatshirts and fleece headbands as wind whipped through the gorge. The type of cold that made each grounder sting when it hit their mitts. Kate and Abby switched off at shortstop, huffing clouds into the frost, exchanging side glances and the occasional nod. Until it happened.

Coach Whitley paused infield drills. "Hutchins, move over to second. Cruz, stay at short."

It plunged an already freezing Kate into ice. She sucked in a sharp gasp. All the hard work meant nothing. Abby had finally won. Kate clenched a fist and shifted to the other side of the infield. She felt Abby's gaze on her cheek, a sensation she'd become accustomed to, but stared straight ahead.

"Let's turn two!" Coach Whitley shouted.

While second base wasn't much different than shortstop, with as much ground to cover, Kate found it uncomfortable, like using your nondominant hand. The crushing fury didn't help her focus either. She planted her feet on the bag as Abby flipped the ball. Kate fumbled it in her glove.

"Again!" Coach Whitley barked before smacking a rough hopper at Abby.

Abby handled it on the bounce and lobbed it low. Kate caught the toss but struggled to transfer it from her glove to her hand. She at least managed a throw to Jill this time.

"Too slow, Hutchins!"

Kate glared at Abby. "That was a low toss."

"Just barehand it," Abby snapped back and spit into the dirt.

The next ball zipped between shortstop and third. Abby dove and snagged it on her stomach. She twisted like a cat, tossing the ball to Kate from the dirt. She caught it as the practice runner slid into the base and clipped her ankles, sending her to the ground with a thud.

Kate clenched her teeth while she lay on her back and stared at the overcast sky.

"I'm so, so sorry. I'm sorry, Hutch. I didn't mean to."

The runner, Madison Quong, apologized profusely until Abby nudged her out of the way and hovered over Kate.

"You okay?" she asked, hauling her up.

Kate hated that her stomach swooped at Abby's concern. At how her hand lingered on hers so that she had to yank it back despite not wanting to. "You're going to get me killed."

"I'm not the problem," Abby scoffed. "Your timing is way off."

"You put me in the line of the runner."

Abby threw her head back. "It's not my fault that you're not aware of your surroundings."

"Well, this isn't my position!" Kate shouted.

"Okay, that's enough! Enough for today!" Coach Whitley encouraged the rest of the team to disperse as she joined them at second base. "Kate, we're just trying things out."

"No. I know what this is." Kate ripped off her glove and charged for the dugout.

Mick, Jill, and T.K. knew better than to go near her as she packed her things, but Abby didn't hesitate. Her heavy feet plodded down the dugout steps.

"I'm sorry," Abby said.

Kate refused to turn from her bat bag. "No, you're not."

Abby groaned. "Fuck it then. I'll play second."

"What?" Kate jerked her head up.

"I don't care. I'll do it if it means that much to you." Abby shrugged.

"Are you serious?"

"Yeah. I can play anywhere."

More insulting than her nonchalance was that it was true. The team couldn't afford to not have Abby in the lineup, and Kate knew there wasn't a position she couldn't master.

"If you don't care, why have you been trying for shortstop this whole time?"

Abby squinted as if it were obvious. "I always play there because I've always been the best at it."

"Exactly! You're the best at it, so don't give it to me out of pity!"

"Here we go again," Mick said to Jill as she unclipped her shin guards.

"Oh, like you've been helping me out of pity?" Abby roared back.

Kate shuddered. Her heart trilled the same way it did during their argument before winter break. "Why do you hate me for helping you?"

"The same reason you hate me for offering to play second base! Consider us even."

"No!"

Abby stood less than an inch from her, sweaty hair poking out from her stocking cap, eyes burning through Kate's. "What do you want from me?" she asked.

Kate's mouth dropped open for words that didn't come. The scrappy inflection short-circuited her brain, spilled currents down her spine, sparking a rush of heat across her skin. Her knees might've buckled if it weren't for Jill bumping in behind her.

"Okay, show's over, folks," Jill said. "Let's take a walk. Abby, go smoke a cigarette or something."

"She's not supposed to smoke," Kate said.

Abby gritted her teeth. "You're not my babysitter."

"Maybe I should be." Kate didn't veer her eyes from Abby's. Something inside warned that breaking from her gaze would be more unbearable than the discomfort she endured beneath it.

"Okay, I'll take Cruz." Mick jerked Abby away and nodded at Jill. "You got Hutch. We'll take this up again tomorrow."

Kate watched Abby stomp out of the dugout, ignoring Jill's assurances, inflamed with rage, and a senseless flutter. One she couldn't shake, even as she lost what she thought she wanted most.

Abby knocked on Coach Whitley's door two days after she named her shortstop. "You got a minute?" she asked.

"Of course." Coach Whitley waved her inside. "I actually wanted to talk to you too."

Abby gulped. "Oh."

"No, it's good." Coach Whitley leaned on the front of her desk. "Your grades are looking much better."

"Oh yeah?"

Abby's shoulders loosened. She'd certainly tried harder, and studying meant spending extra time with Kate. Of course, over the last few days, they'd returned to glares and quiet. Only this distance crushed her.

Abby thought they might be nearing friendship, but the latest fight sent them back to square one. They warmed up together, but Kate didn't bother with a hello. In return, when Abby spotted her in the library, she sat at a different table. She still stole glances at her so often that she didn't get anything done.

"Seems things might be getting better with the team too?" Coach Whitley asked.

"Yeah, I guess."

"And away from the field?"

Abby folded her arms across her chest like it might hide the truth. "I'm fine."

"You know, I lost my dad when I was around your age. If you ever want to talk—"

"Well, I did want to talk to you about Kate." Abby jumped in both to stop the conversation she didn't want—no matter how well-intentioned Coach Whitley was, Abby wasn't exactly welcoming a heart-to-heart—and to dive into the real reason she'd trudged into her office.

Coach Whitley's brow furrowed. "What about her?"

"I think maybe she should take shortstop."

"Why's that?"

Abby hadn't thought that far ahead. All she knew was that she hated how Kate despised her, more than she hated giving up her spot. "Well, it clearly means a lot to her."

"And it doesn't mean a lot to you?"

"I don't know."

It certainly did before. Now she wasn't so sure. Maybe it was Kate or maybe it was that she still couldn't feel it. That she kept playing out of habit, and the joy had yet to resurface.

"You know, you have a real opportunity here, Abby. You're incredibly talented." Coach Whitley smiled as if trying to rouse the same from Abby. "You could use this season to get back to the next level. Maybe even take a shot at Team USA."

Abby swiped a softball from Coach Whitley's desk and turned away. "Trying to get rid of me already?"

"Trying to make sure your potential doesn't get lost in the grief."

She squeezed the softball tighter, mirroring the walls of her chest. "What potential? There's hardly a future for me." Abby paused to clarify, more for Coach Whitley than herself. "A future for me in softball. I mean, you played for the Australian national team and still had to come all the way over here to coach?"

"Played in leagues around the world too. This game doesn't come easy. You have to chase it sometimes. But that's part of the beauty, don't you think?" Coach Whitley sighed when Abby turned back to her. "If you really want Hutchins to play shortstop, you two can work it out on your own, okay?"

"Okay."

Abby walked straight to the blue house. She grumbled on the uphill trek, one sneaker untied, sweat breaking out beneath her tattered hoodie. She charged for the back door and pulled, scowling when it didn't budge. "What the fuck?" She pounded the splintered wood. "Hey! It's me!"

"Jesus Christ." Mick yanked open the door. "What's wrong with you?"

"What's wrong with you? Since when do you lock the door?" Abby asked as she stomped inside.

"Jill and Dill must be on a break," Mick said. "What's up your ass?"

"I need to talk to Kate." Abby tensed when she spotted her over Mick's shoulder. "Can you give us some privacy?"

"Mm-hmm." Mick grinned before she slinked away, and Abby rolled her eyes.

"What's going on?" Kate asked.

"Maybe we can sit?"

Abby followed her to the couch. In the last few months, she'd grown comfortable in the house—its waft of old furniture and Jill's lavender incense, the bottle-cap-covered coffee table, and softball posters from seasons past. The weak warmth from the groaning heater never failed to thaw her chest. Except now, as she sat on the couch next to Kate. For as much as she'd grown accustomed to the house, as much time as they spent together, she hadn't quite grown comfortable with her. Not with their unending game of two steps forward and one step back.

"Everything okay?" Kate asked.

Abby rubbed the back of her neck, less confident than she had been in Coach Whitley's office. What seemed reasonable twenty minutes earlier, now seemed potentially condescending.

"I feel bad about how things went down. I'm sorry for taking your position."

Kate sighed and Abby worried she'd triggered another fight. She didn't understand why it happened so often. While she certainly had a temper, laid-back was Abby's natural state, and with everyone else Kate exuded calm and control. Perhaps they simply spent too much time together. Or maybe it was the tension beneath, the competing and jealousy, coupled with their forced partnership. Only it wasn't just a forced partnership. Somewhere along the way Abby began needing Kate. Enough that when they drifted, she scrambled to get her back.

"It's not like we can both play there." Kate tilted her head in a way that restored Abby's hope. "And you didn't take it. You earned it."

"I know how much you want it though. I wasn't trying to insult you when I said I could play second base instead. I should've probably just moved over there before."

"Why would you do that?" Kate's gaze flickered, as if prodding Abby to say something they both already knew.

"I don't want you to hate me."

"You care enough about me liking you that you'd give up your position?"

Abby grimaced. "It sounds really lame when you say that."

"Sorry." Kate uncrossed her arms. "I'm just surprised. I thought you didn't like me."

"I do. A lot." Abby lowered her volume like it was a middle school secret, though the way her cheeks warmed suggested that wasn't too far off. "I guess I feel stupid around you. I know I'm another assignment to you and you don't care—"

Kate's eyes widened. "Of course I care." Her bottom lip firmed against her mouth's falling corners. "I notice, you know? That you're sad some days. I know you've been through a lot."

Abby's heart contracted just once. Her throat tightened like it had in Coach Whitley's office, and at Isla's condo on Christmas, and on the dock, and any place that someone alluded to her loss.

"I don't pity you and you're not stupid." Kate shook her head, then chuckled. "Granted, any inferiority you feel is a small fraction of what I feel playing against you."

"You don't have to play against me. We're a team." Abby unconsciously shifted closer. "Play with me. Really, you can play shortstop, and I'll play second."

"That's ridiculous."

"Well, I care too. I notice you too." Abby's brows drew together. She gulped to steady herself before the rest. "You're the only reason I'm on the team, Kate. I was drowning. I mean, I almost really drowned that day in the river. And you were the first one to help me."

Kate's eyes rippled with something softer. A fragile shimmer that threatened to break. Abby only caught a glimpse of it before Kate cleared her throat and looked away. "You can't give up shortstop for me," she said. "I want to earn it."

"Understood." Abby smirked.

Kate smiled back. "And I'll give second base a shot."

"Good. Let's turn two then."

"Let's turn two."

TURNING TWO

Turning two, successfully completing a double play, requires the utmost trust and timing, especially when executed between the shortstop and second baseman. It's the closest thing to a ballet you'll see on a diamond. Whoever doesn't field the ball catches the toss at second base for the first out, then throws to first base to complete the double play. The opposing team's runner usually has sights on your ankles during the exchange, so add dodging spiked cleats to the list. It happens so fast that the second baseman and shortstop don't have time to look or speak. They simply trust the other person will arrive at the right moment.

The week before their first tournament, Abby and Kate focused on perfecting their timing. Granted, working as one instead of competing took getting used to. Not just because a hint of envy lingered when Kate eyed Abby at shortstop, but because their styles clashed harsher than before. Abby's wild feats and risky throws versus Kate's desire to do it clean, correct, and consistent.

To no one's surprise, Abby turned two like an art form. When receiving the ball from the second basemen, she floated. She'd brush the bag with her toes, fearlessly jump or twist out of the runner's path, and fling a bullet to first. On the reverse side, she never just threw the ball to the second baseman. She delivered it underhand, behind her back, flipped it out or on top of her glove, occasionally between her legs. While the team laughed, Coach Whitley yelled at the circus-like feats. "Quit faffing around, Cruz!"

More than once Kate would scoop a grounder and glance up to find Abby not covering the base. Instead of throwing, she double clutched, letting the runner breeze safely by.

"Why didn't you throw it?" Abby asked.

Kate's mouth dropped. "Because you weren't there!"

"I'll always be there! Just trust me."

"How can I trust you when you're not where you're supposed to be? Why can't you just do it right?"

Abby smacked her glove before turning away. "It's not going to be perfect every time, Kate!"

Their arguing became such a normal part of practice that Jill took to sitting on first base while they hashed things out. Once, they didn't even notice Coach Whitley dismiss everyone for a break, until it was just the two of them bickering on the empty infield. The problem was that they both staunchly believed that they were right. That and maybe they secretly enjoyed it. When Mick suggested as much, Kate shook her head and slammed her locker shut, but her cheeks flamed bright red.

Before Abby, Kate never yelled except to call a play or cheer for her teammates, never cursed or argued, never lost her composure or said an unkind word—so much of which was instilled in her as a child—but she unloaded on Abby daily. And Abby never flinched. Kate discovered unexpected freedom in it. In saying what she wanted. In the way she never had to apologize to Abby and Abby never apologized to her. In how it lit up her chest when Abby's vigorous eyes met hers and paused there, even with practice fluttering around them as if daring Kate to tear away first. Or daring her to stay. In the way it all made that perfect double play sweeter, because it was purely theirs. Pure Abby and pure Kate.

"Just try it from here." Abby grabbed Kate by the forearm to adjust her positioning at second base. That also became a common occurrence. Abby demonstrating better ways for Kate to throw or change her footwork, never hesitating to grab or graze her in the process. Kate always tugged her hand back, but she enjoyed Abby's closeness, the calluses on her palms, the rough but assured movements.

Kate shook her head. "If I do that, the runner's going to take me out."

Abby rolled her eyes. "Don't play so scared."

"I'm not!"

Kate peered into Abby's copper gaze, sweat on her forehead, and fought the unbearable urge to take her face in her hands and shake her. She wanted something to shout in return, to even the score somehow, so she shifted to her consistently unkempt appearance.

"You should tuck in your shirt," Kate said.

"You should untuck yours." Abby smacked the bill of Kate's visor, dropping it to her line of vision.

Kate's mouth fell. While she typically responded to teasing with a passive laugh or unbothered shrug, she sought retaliation in a rush of maddening desire. She lifted her visor and chucked her mitt at Abby, who chortled. When Kate stammered an apology, Abby closed in, grabbed her shirt, and untucked it from her waistband.

"Stop!" Kate pushed her.

Their teammates scrambled to break them up, but there was no need. Abby laughed, hands on her knees, howling so loud that everyone stopped. Kate's mouth broke into a beam, and then she laughed too. And when Abby returned her glove, grinning on her way back to shortstop, Kate forgot to breathe.

The day before they left for the tournament, they stayed late for additional practice. Mick hitting grounders, Jill at first base. They turned two at various angles, Kate so accustomed to Abby's tosses that she no longer required a glance. She lobbed the ball to the perfect position, knowing that Abby would magically appear.

In the privacy of their own practice session, Kate admired Abby's moves at shortstop, asked her how she did it, and in unparalleled glee, Abby scrambled to show her. They switched positions, Kate at shortstop, Abby at second. Kate mastered new tricks and flips, threw tosses behind her back, understood the thrill of playing without the need for perfection. Another new freedom found thanks to Abby.

"Okay, I'm calling it a night!" Mick said as the two of them slapped hands under the lights. "We've got a flight to catch tomorrow!"

"Want to stay a little longer?" Abby asked Kate.

She nodded. Even though she was tired and plenty prepared, she wanted more of the game. More of Abby too.

"You don't listen to the ball, do you?" Abby asked her when Mick and Jill left.

Kate furrowed her brow. "What do you mean?"

"You see. You know where it's going based on where it hits the bat. But the speed of sound is unbeatable."

"Actually, the speed of light is faster."

"Of course it is." Abby chuckled. "Here, let's try something." She peeled off her outermost layer, a baggy Padres T-shirt over her sweatshirt, and ripped it in half.

"What are you doing?"

"Just humor me." Abby tore the T-shirt into strips with her teeth. Kate's stare locked on to her mouth and fingers, and she swore the ground shifted beneath her feet, leaving her lightheaded. She cleared her throat and glanced away, as Abby chose the longest strip of fabric and stepped behind her. "You trust me?"

Her breath on Kate's neck, and her chest hovering at her back, sent her spinning again. She barely managed to mutter, "Yes."

Abby wrapped the fabric around Kate's head as a blindfold. Then her hands gripped her shoulders. "You think a lot. You're mechanical. Stiff." Abby rubbed Kate's biceps a few times, then squeezed her shoulders again. "Relax."

But Kate couldn't relax. The touch started a fire in her lower abdomen. She choked on a gasp as Abby's hands swept down the middle of her back. Her neck and chin unconsciously lifted as if trying to ascend somewhere higher. Somewhere she might understand the power of a simple graze.

"You don't have to be so perfect." Abby's mouth must have been close to her ear because Kate detected heat on her skin. "Let it go."

"Okay," Kate whispered.

Abby disappeared, leaving Kate blind and bothered. She buzzed inside like she needed something—or someone—to hold her down. Another new sensation courtesy of Abby, only this didn't feel like freedom. This threatened to keep her hostage until it decided to mercifully release her.

The metallic pop of ball against bat brought her back. Kate tensed, worried that it might come straight at her.

"I've got you! Just listen," Abby said, smacking another.

She steadied herself and adjusted to the darkness. The sounds sharpened. She sensed if the hit traveled to her right or left based on the ping of the bat. Soon she knew if it was a grounder or line drive. After a game of pointing to the correct side, she ventured a few steps, attempting to beat the ball before it skimmed the dirt. By the end, Kate didn't just understand the game, she heard it too.

When she removed the blindfold, Abby's smile greeted her, and Kate froze. They'd known each other awhile now, but she looked different. Different from just hours ago. Her eyes shinier, her features gentler, her broadness not a threat but a marvel that Kate could stare at endlessly. She didn't know why the difference emerged, but she thought it might be because Abby made her feel something real. Something free. Kate wondered if she looked different too. If Abby noticed Kate's heart hammering when she rubbed her back.

By the time they left the field, stars sprinkled the dark. Kate used the walk home to gather her composure. Abby stayed quiet too, but it was an easy solitude that filled the space between them, a welcome change from their stiff silences.

"It's almost unfair how good you are," she said.

"I'm not that good."

Kate scoffed. "You are that good. I wish I could play like you."

"I wish I loved it like you do." Abby's plump lips hitched between a smile and a frown.

Kate stared at her as their steps kept a peaceful rhythm on the damp pavement. "I think you do."

"Maybe." Abby kicked a rock down the road. "I just don't know if I can feel it anymore."

"You play like you do. Like it's part of you."

"It might be."

"If you were a guy, you'd go pro." Kate pictured Blake and shrank into herself. Tonight, the overwhelming excitement for someone else brought her pause. She'd done nothing wrong, but didn't know what it meant.

"If I was a guy, my name would be Audie Cruz, Jr., and I'd be a prick." Abby laughed. "We'd get divorced in like a month."

Kate's eyes widened. "Oh, we'd be married in this reality?"

Abby shrugged like it was nothing, but her ears flamed bright red. "I mean, we bicker enough. Match made in heaven."

"Or hell." Kate chuckled, desperate to make a joke of the entire thing. Desperate to hide that it unfurled wings inside her.

"Probably that," Abby said with a throaty laugh.

Kate diverted her gaze, thankful the February chill overpowered the heat threatening to burst through her cheeks. They walked the rest of the way in silence and stopped at the edge of the driveway.

"Well, have a good night." She started toward the door when Abby stopped her.

"I'm sorry if I've been overbearing."

Kate turned back. "I'm sorry for arguing with you."

"I don't mind." Abby smiled. "You look great over there, Kate. I know the change hasn't been easy. I know I don't make things easy. I guess I just feel like I can do anything with you."

"I feel the same way."

Kate slackened, but not with sadness or shame. The declaration breached the barrier she had long ago formed to keep Abby at a distance. The one built to thwart a rival. The one that stayed, even as their worlds grew closer, and prevented a friendship. But that night, Kate couldn't find it.

It dissolved beneath the gleam in Abby's gaze, not just sorrow and something unknowable, but soul. While Kate thought it new, she also understood that she'd seen it before. Seen it on the dock, in the library, in their arguing, in their competing and working together. Abby was alive, swimming and fighting against the grief, and Kate was what she latched on to.

The weight of it rocked her. She wanted to both shirk and sink in it. She wanted more of Abby, of her laugh, of her teasing, of her infuriating pushiness, of her soul. She'd call it friendship but knew as she peered into Abby with new sight, something deeper sprouted, leaving her chest and stomach tender but full.

THE SPRING TOURNAMENT

Thunderous clouds shifted above as Abby dug in at shortstop and T.K. wound up in the pitcher's circle. When the ball left her hand, a cellphone rang, the sound so penetrating that Abby stood straight up and missed the grounder whizzing past.

Her teammates, Coach Whitley, and the crowd screamed and booed, as the runner rounded first and flew to second. The ball sat in the outfield, but Abby didn't move. The ringing continued. It squealed from the sound system like jet engines. Abby asked Kate if she heard it, but she yelled at her too as more runners scored.

Abby sprinted off the field to answer the call. She frantically searched the dugout. Ripped down bat bags, tore them open, chucked gloves and helmets as she rifled for the phone. Abby shuddered when she finally found it, the game roaring behind her. She flipped it open, said hello, and her mother answered.

Abby lurched awake. A ding filled her ears, and the seatbelt sign flashed red.

"Flight attendants, take your jump seats," the pilot said overhead.

Next to her, in the middle seat, Kate seized both armrests, the color draining from her face. They'd taken off from Portland that morning for the spring showcase in Phoenix.

"How much longer?" she asked.

Kate shook her head, whimpering when the plane dipped.

"Are you okay?" Abby quickly dismissed her nightmare, far more concerned by Kate's trembling. "It's just turbulence."

"Do you think we're going to crash?"

Abby snickered. "I wish."

Kate's eyes flashed with such horror that Abby regretted her sarcasm. "That's not funny."

"Sorry," Abby said as the plane briefly dropped again. Kate yelped and clutched Abby's hand. Abby's stomach flipped, but she stayed steady as the plane leveled out. She didn't want to frighten Kate. More than that, she didn't want that hand to leave hers. "It's okay. Let's just talk."

"I think I hate flying," Kate said through the thickness of bottled-up tears.

"I think you do too." Abby tightened her grip as she laced their fingers together. Letting go never occurred to her. Not just because of how their connected hands alleviated the pull in her chest—one that begged for such closeness—but because she'd never seen Kate like this. Vulnerable. She was always stitched tightly together. Even when disappointed, she simply dug in, worked harder. But this unraveling made Abby determined to keep her from falling apart. "Mick says you have, like, a hundred siblings."

"I'm one of seven." Kate sniffled. The plane rattled through another bump. "Dear God, please let us live."

"Fuck, seven kids? For real?"

"Yes."

"What number are you?"

"Three."

"Lucky number three," Abby said. The plane swooped again, and she leaned closer, their shoulders brushing. Kate didn't pull away. Her weight settled gently against Abby, and while the turbulence diminished, her stomach jolted so hard that she nearly lost her train of thought. "I, uh, what are your siblings' names?"

"Rebecca, Hannah, R.J., Matt, Leah, and Gabriel."

"How'd your parents keep track of all of you?" Abby asked.

"They didn't."

"They come to a lot of games?"

"No." Kate's lips drooped. "My dad is busy coaching, and my mom isn't big on sports—or maybe just me playing them."

Abby's brow furrowed. "I'm sorry."

"It's okay. They don't say it, but they're upset I didn't go to their school. They work at Eastern Washington Bible College." Kate didn't stop even as the plane rattled, her stare fixed on Abby's. "But if I went there, I'd have to study theology or music. I'd probably just get married off at twenty, like my older sisters."

"That's pretty badass of you." Abby grinned. She'd misjudged Kate from what little she knew of her, unaware that coming to Insley required taking a stand.

The corners of Kate's mouth lifted. "I don't think anyone has ever thought that of me."

"They should." Abby squeezed her hand and drifted her thumb across it in a slow circle. Kate still didn't let go. "Are they supportive of law school?"

She shook her head, and additional empathy pitted Abby's chest. "It's so much time and too much money. They don't understand what I'll do after. They're far more interested in when I'll marry Blake and start having babies."

Abby stopped tracing her hand. "Yeah, when's that going to happen?"

"I don't know. I have a lot I still want to do. Who knows where he'll be after the draft." Kate's gaze didn't leave Abby's, but her frown resurfaced. Abby frowned back. In the silence, they became aware the seatbelt light no longer glowed red. Kate blushed as she pulled her hand away. "Sorry, I'm such a wimp."

"You're not," Abby said, resisting the urge to find her fingers again. "So, do you have a top choice for law school?"

Kate flipped open her LSAT book and didn't look up. "Berkeley."

"Wow, from Bible school to Berkeley. You really are a badass, Hutch." Abby smirked.

"Don't call me that," she said.

"A badass?"

"No, Hutch. I like that you call me Kate." Her eyes met Abby's in a shock of color.

"Okay, Kate," she whispered.

Abby dreamed of her mother again before their first game. She launched herself awake with a gasp. She wasn't sure if she'd been shouting as she had in her dream, but when she glanced around the hotel room, her teammates slept soundly. Mick and T.K. shared one bed; Kate and Jill were in the other. Abby slept on a rollaway, the springs digging into her back.

She checked her phone. A quarter to five. Their game wasn't until nine, but with her mother in her head, with her heart in a knot, tears building an army in her throat, she knew sleep wouldn't come. Instead, she got out of bed, slipped on a hoodie, and left the room as quietly as possible.

The team stayed at a hotel on the edge of the city, closer to the tournament fields than downtown. Abby worked in from the outskirts, slinking under dark overpasses, avoiding used needles and people sleeping on the sidewalk. She stopped only to buy cigarettes.

Not an hour passed before Kate called. Abby ignored it but texted her to avoid alerting Coach Whitley.

I'm fine. Don't worry.

Where are you?

I'll be back in a little bit.

Abby smoked and roamed. The Arizona landscape, flat and desolate, suited her mood. She plopped on a bench near Sky Harbor as the sun rose and planes glided to the runway. With each puff and landing, she contemplated taking the field.

She'd spent months practicing for this moment, but it never occurred to her that it wouldn't be the same. But of course it wasn't. She'd been going through the motions. She hadn't really felt the game since that terrible night almost a year ago. Since she lost sight of it in grief.

Abby returned to the field anyway, like a lapsed Catholic dragged themselves to Easter Sunday—it was simply what you did, no matter how much you'd changed. Even when you weren't certain you believed. In that way, the game had been her religion. The one thing she understood, not just physically, but in her soul. The last true and safe place. Now she wondered if simply playing could be enough. If she could bear to come back to the game but not herself.

She returned to the hotel room twenty minutes before team breakfast.

"Where the fuck have you been?" Mick asked. "We've been freaking out."

"I went for a walk," Abby said as the door slammed behind her.

"Are you okay?" Kate asked.

Abby didn't look at her. "I'm good."

"We need to be downstairs in ten," Mick said.

"I'll be ready."

While sleep-deprived and a touch anxious, she set her gears to autopilot. Fortunately, softball was part of her default settings. She didn't speak at breakfast, not in the van, or when she warmed up with Kate, but her vision sharpened, her body loosened, and the ballpark fizzled into focus as Coach Whitley read the starting lineup in the dugout.

"Hutchins, Aalberg, Seaborn. Cruz, McMechan, Hightower. Shupe, Crosby, DeHaven. Let's jump on them early. Hutchins, give us a good look." Coach Whitley patted Kate's shoulder before heading out to coach third.

The team clapped when the umpire shouted, "Play ball!" and Kate stepped into the box.

"Come on, Hutch! Get us started, Three!"

Kate roosted on the left side of the plate, nimbly perched, bat poised, shoulders so slackened that the three on her jersey stayed perfectly still. Leadoff hitter suited her. They typically weren't the biggest on the team, but the most consistent and fastest. The person you relied on to get on base so your power hitters could knock them in.

Kate didn't swing at the first strike. She took two balls, faked a bunt, then fouled off another. 2–2. Abby had observed her during practice but underestimated this part of her game. Disciplined in working the count, squeezing extra pitches to wear down the pitcher.

"Let's go, Kate!" Abby yelled.

She let another ball go, bringing the count full. Abby chewed her lip. Kate fouled off the next outside pitch. Not a good one, but close enough to fight off. The final pitch peeled inside, and Kate hacked it just to the right of second base, skipping into center field, a stand-up single. Abby raised her eyebrows and clapped.

Trish Aalberg bunted next, moving Kate to second. One out.

Courtney Seaborn launched a shot directly to the left fielder. Two outs.

The PA announcer buzzed in the speakers. "Now up for the Eagles, number twelve, the shortstop, Abby Cruz."

She chopped a practice swing. Coach Whitley feigned a few meaningless signs, the plan to hit away. Abby's heart rumbled. Usually, the box didn't faze her. The pitcher never scared her. But that was before. The game was different now.

"Strike one!"

Abby sighed. She swore she heard a phone chime and snapped her head to the bleachers.

"Strike two!"

She whiffed at a rise ball. She knew better.

The pitcher dug her toe in front of the rubber, whacked her glove against her thigh as she hurled another. Abby wanted to swing, moved her hips to swing, but kept her hands back as the ball dropped low.

"Good eye, Cruz!" Mick shouted.

Abby adjusted her batting gloves and helmet. She gazed at the field. The one she longed for in grief and belonged to since birth. She waited for it to wake something in her, to hear it, but nothing came. Her eyes shifted to Kate, ready to run on second base. She nodded at her, and Abby nodded back.

She committed to the swing before the pitch left the circle. Her bat connected high, and the ball traveled on a rise. She gritted her teeth as she ran to first, uncertain if it would be out three or drop. The shrieks of her teammates answered, and still wheezy from her morning smoke, she continued to second.

"That's Cruz with the double to score Hutchins. One–nothing Eagles."

Abby sighed in relief as a run glowed on the board. It confirmed what never stopped being true. No matter how fucked the outside world got, she knew how to play, how to compete, how to be the best. Even if it was just going through the motions.

On defense, the same rang true. She charged the first grounder that cracked her way, throwing to Jill with time to spare. She accepted Kate's high five, before the infielders whipped the ball around the horn.

"One out!" Kate called.

The only grin she managed that day was when it came time to turn two. She snagged the ball on a dive, flipped it out of her glove to Kate, who appeared not a second too soon, caught it bare-handed, threw and jumped over the runner in one motion. The team and crowd erupted. And while Abby finished the day with a triple, four RBIs, and an errorless outing at shortstop, Kate's glint after the play was her favorite moment of the game.

The Eagles won 9–4. The team celebrated, but Abby observed as if separated by glass. She nodded at their compliments, but her reactions strained as if bending iron. And as she glanced at the bleachers she knew why. Her mother wasn't there, not that many parents made the trip, but she wouldn't be a text or a phone call away either. No matter how bad things got, no matter how far the game took her, Abby's mother had always been that. Now she was just a phantom ring in her ears that stole her sleep.

They had a doubleheader the next day, and while she lay on the rollaway that night, she decided she didn't need it. Not like this. Ten minutes after Coach Whitley checked on them for lights out, Abby ripped off the covers and slipped on her sneakers.

"What are you doing?" Mick sat up in the dark.

Abby shrugged on a jacket.

"Abby, don't," Kate said.

If anyone could stop her, it would've been Kate. But Abby didn't want to be stopped. The game might have been hers, she might've crushed the ball, but she didn't feel it. She'd won, but it didn't make her believe. So, she left the room, slammed the door, determined to find another way to feel.

Every morning and every night, Kate prayed. She never forgot or missed. Usually, she prayed for simple things. She gave thanks, asked for health and strength, for her family, friends, Blake, and the team. She prayed for Abby too.

She prayed for her when she learned of her mother's death. She asked God to grant her peace. She prayed for Abby's safety when she jumped in the river. She prayed for her health when she looked extra haggard during their study sessions. She prayed she wasn't alone on Christmas. Lately, she didn't have a specific reason. She prayed for Abby so often that she became the last thing she thought of before sleep. She did it again now, nearly whispering as she paced the room.

Dear God, please watch over her, please keep her safe, please bring her back. Back to me. The request droned on like a tape in her head, while she stared at the door as if she might conjure Abby by hope alone.

"It's been three hours. I think we should call Coach," Jill said from bed.

Kate glanced at her phone. One o'clock in the morning. She'd called Abby thirteen times, left a voicemail, and sent ten texts.

"She'll come back." Mick sat at the hotel room desk and flipped through a dated travel guide.

T.K.'s snores rippled through the tension. She slept with a silk eye mask and noise-canceling headphones. She was slated to pitch in the morning and, despite Abby's untimely departure, insisted on her nine hours of beauty rest.

"Maybe we should look for her," Kate said.

Mick shook her head. "Let's give her one more hour. Bars close at two."

"How do you know she's at a bar?" Jill asked.

"Because it's Cruz."

Kate frowned. She regretted not doing something more. Abby clearly hadn't been in a good place that morning. Kate thought she heard her in her sleep, but Abby was out the door before she could ask. She barely ate. While she played flawlessly, she wasn't the same.

"I should've followed her," she said.

"No. Then we'd be worried about both of you," Mick said.

"At least we'd be together." Kate subtly clasped her hands, repeated her prayer, nearly moved her lips with it.

"She's not your responsibility."

"She actually is."

"I know Coach said that, but I think this is beyond tutoring her." Mick stood and stopped her pacing. "She'll be okay."

"I think we need to tell Whit," Jill said. "If something happens, and we didn't say anything, we'd feel horrible. Plus, if Coach knows about this, you'll get to start at shortstop, Hutch."

"I don't care about shortstop," Kate muttered.

Jill shrugged. "I'm just saying. I like Cruz too, but this whole time you guys have been duking it out, when all along she was going to self-destruct. I mean, some people are just wired that way."

"Don't say that."

Mick frowned. "We're both just trying to say that you can't hold yourself responsible. Abby is going to be Abby."

Kate hated such an assessment. Hated them talking about her like they knew her. They didn't know her like Kate did. Didn't see her like Kate did. Didn't care about her like Kate did. Like her chest might collapse or expand based on where Abby landed, on what she felt, on what she said at any given moment.

When the door beeped a few minutes later and the handle turned, the trio jumped to their feet. Abby stumbled in, steadied herself on the wall, and hiccupped.

"Where were you?" Mick asked.

"I'm just-just getting my cigarettes," Abby slurred.

"You're not going back out."

"Y-yes." She grabbed her lighter. "I am, Mickey."

"We have a game tomorrow," Kate said.

"No, no, no. *You* have a game tomorrow." Abby pointed at her. "That makes you starting shortstop. You're great at it. Waste to have you at second."

Her belligerence turned Kate's spine to stone. "Don't leave."

"You're sweet, but you need to let me go. You'll learn that eventually." She hiccupped again. Kate grabbed her arm and Abby jerked away. "Don't."

Mick snatched Abby's other arm. "Don't do this, dude."

"Stop." Abby grunted, somehow staggering despite their efforts to restrain her. "Guys, come on. Let me go!"

"Stop it! Shupe, help!" Mick wrapped herself around one of Abby's legs. Kate clung to her torso as Jill secured an arm. Despite Jill being the tallest, Mick the heaviest, and Kate the fittest, it took all three of them to wrestle Abby to the carpet. T.K. never stirred.

"God, she turns into the Hulk when she's drunk." Mick heaved as they piled on top of her.

"Get off!" Abby bellowed.

"What do we do with her now?" Jill asked as she pinned Abby's arms.

"I think she needs to cool off," Mick said.

Kate's mouth dropped. "Mick, don't."

"Yeah, come on." Mick and Jill hauled Abby off the floor and dragged her to the bathroom.

"Let me go! Let me fucking go!" Abby shouted hysterically. "I don't want to be here, I don't want to be here, I don't want to be here anymore!"

Kate's throat constricted. "Guys, be careful."

Jill turned on the shower as Mick tore off Abby's shoes.

"Just let me go. I can't do it. I can't. I can't." Abby slackened out of Mick and Jill's hold as water splashed into the tub. She released a mournful cry. "Just let me go. I don't want to be here anymore."

The three of them stood stunned. Despite her melancholy, Abby always appeared stoic. Never a tear. Never a word about what she'd been through. Perhaps it was because of how she played, but this crumbling didn't seem possible.

"Hey, dude, it's okay." Mick widened her gaze at Jill and Kate. "We won't put you in."

Abby slinked to the corner until she hit the wall with another sob. "I should've been there, you know?"

"Been where?" Jill asked.

Kate cautiously eased to Abby, who swayed but didn't run. After all their time together—the studying, the competing, the bickering, the silences, stares, and rare smiles—she felt like the only one who could. "It's okay," she whispered. Her hand trembled as she touched her shoulder. "Abby, it's okay."

"I can't. I can't stop hearing it. I just want it to stop. Please. I can't."

Abby covered her ears, clamped her eyes shut, and cowered at something none of them could see. Unlike Mick, who backed away, and Jill, who blanched, Kate inched closer. She whispered assurances that Abby likely couldn't hear but said them anyway beneath her incoherent pleas. And as Abby shielded her ears and rocked, Kate reached out and covered those same hands with hers. She didn't tell her that there wasn't a sound to be heard. She helped Abby cover her ears, not in understanding, but faith. To not only whisper it to her, but show, "I'm with you."

"Please make it stop. I want it to stop." Abby sniffled.

"I know." Kate cupped the sides of her head. "I know."

And then Abby's eyes opened. They welled, shiny and inebriated, but Kate recognized that flicker. That soul. That gravity. Kate didn't want Abby to hurt, but she knew this was what always stood between them. This was what Kate always wanted to understand, and now that she did, she couldn't imagine ever being angry, ever being jealous, ever being anything but this close to her again.

Abby uncovered her ears long enough to burrow into Kate. She startled at first, not only because Abby nearly knocked her over, but because they'd never hugged before. Still, when Abby clutched on, Kate held her back tighter, refusing to let go even as her legs grew unsteady. Mick and Jill helped her bear the weight, the four of them lowering until they all sat on the bathroom floor.

"You got this?" Mick asked.

Her eyes glistened and for the first time, Kate realized damp tracks of tears streamed down her own cheeks too. "Yeah."

Jill sniffled. "Is she okay?"

"I don't know, but I won't leave her," Kate said.

She held the back of Abby's head while she hid in her neck long after Mick and Jill retired to bed. She hushed her until the sobs dwindled to cries, the cries to whimpers, and finally the whimpers to sniffles.

And in between, she prayed. She thanked God for Abby's return, but mostly for this understanding, no matter how painful. It intensified the mysterious swelling in her chest. She longed to explain it. She wondered if it might soothe Abby or herself, but she didn't know what to say, except maybe, *if you only knew how often I talk to God about you.*

"I miss her." Abby sniveled.

Kate's chest rocked. "I know." She kissed the top of Abby's head, held her lips there, and closed her eyes.

Blacking out successfully rid Abby of nightmares, but it came at the price of her worst hangover yet. The agony radiated through her skull when she opened her eyes. The coolness beneath her cheek provided at least some reprieve until she discovered it belonged to the bathroom floor. A sheet draped her shoulders, and curled up nearby, sleeping beneath a comforter with her head on a pillow, was Kate.

"What the fuck?" Abby whispered.

Before she could investigate, her gut churned, her mouth salivated, and her throat filled with bile. She crawled to the toilet, threw her head into the bowl, and puked. Not long after the initial heave, a hand rubbed her back. She cringed at Kate's comfort, which, despite little memory of the night before, she knew she didn't deserve.

"Just go," Abby said between retching.

But the hand didn't leave. She tried to recall the night. She remembered going to a bar and slamming shots. She didn't know how she got home.

T.K. bulldozed in. "Oh my God, gross."

"Get out." Abby coughed.

"I have to do my skincare routine," she said.

Kate sighed, still rubbing Abby's back. "Can it wait?"

"I need to start now if I'm going to be on time. Who knows how long she's going to be doing this."

"T.K., you better be joking." Abby groaned.

"I can't pitch if my pores are clogged. It's not my fault you got hammered last night."

She, of course, expected no less from T.K., who started every week with a fresh manicure, accessorized her game day braids with matching bows, and dyed her hair a new color every few months. It was currently gothic black and down to her waist.

"Jesus, can we stop yelling? We all slept like shit." Mick snatched her toothbrush from the counter.

"I think I'm dying." Abby flushed the toilet and rested her head on her forearms.

"We need to pull it together," Mick said. "Someone wake up Shupe and I'll throw Cruz in the shower."

"No, just leave me." Abby moaned as Mick and Kate yanked her to her feet. "I can't play. Tell Whit I'm sick."

"Oh no, you're playing. I don't care if you puke all game." Mick confronted her like a vengeful parent. "What the hell were you thinking?"

Abby turned her cheek as the catcher buffaloed into her space. "Back off, Mick."

"No, dude. You can't keep doing shit like this." Mick glanced at Kate. "Do you know how bad you scared her?"

"Mick, it's fine," Kate said.

"No, it's not. You scared all of us." Mick clutched Abby's shirt when she tried to slink away. "We can't cover like that for you again. Do you understand? We won't."

Abby dropped her head. "I get it, okay? I'm sorry."

"Say it to Hutch."

She dragged her eyes up to Kate's. Abby hated herself for disappointing and scaring her, then receiving her goodwill when she wasn't deserving. "I'm sorry, Kate."

She frowned, but nodded. "It's okay."

"We care about you. All of us. Don't forget it, idiot." Mick patted Abby's cheek, somewhere between a slap and caress. "Let's go, we're going to be late."

Abby showered off the bar stench, hurled again, and somehow scraped together her uniform. At breakfast, she cautiously sipped water, plagued with regret as Kate, Mick, and Jill gazed over with bags beneath their eyes.

For as long as she could remember, Abby had acted only at her own behest. Growing up with her mother required early self-reliance. She never worried about the consequences for others. She assumed the group helped her after the hazing incident simply to cover their own asses. But last night, they didn't have to cover for her. They could've easily gotten her kicked off the team, Kate could've taken shortstop, and they would've been done with her. Instead, they saved her. And maybe all along, bringing them into her life was how the game was saving her too.

Granted, as she battled a hangover beneath the Phoenix sun, Abby thought the game might kill her instead. She dragged through warm-ups with a migraine. When she missed more than one ball, Coach Whitley took notice.

"You okay, Cruz?" she asked.

Mick held a finger to her mouth, demanding Abby's silence, doubling down by dragging the same finger across her throat.

"I'm good." Abby bit back a sour mouthful.

By game time, she struggled to balance, the dirt transforming into choppy waves beneath her unsteady feet. The first batter whizzed a shot between her and Courtney. Usually, she would've lunged for the out but stayed back on her heels.

The next batter hit into a perfect double play. Kate scooped the ball and flipped it to her. Abby strained to catch it, clipped second base with her toes for the out, but didn't attempt a throw for the double play. She braced herself on her knees to avoid vomiting.

"Come on." Kate smacked her glove in frustration. "We had that."

Abby drew a hand across her clammy forehead. "Sorry."

When T.K. struck out the next two batters, she could've kissed her. On the way to the dugout, Mick ripped off her catcher's mask and bared her teeth. "Get it together."

"Fuck off," she hissed.

The problems continued at bat. She intended to hit a ground ball and make herself an easy out so she could retire to the dugout. Instead, she somehow finessed a shot to the outfield and groaned when it rolled to the fence. Rather than run to second base, Abby stopped on first and nearly retched.

Mick got up next and Abby swore she smiled as if plotting revenge. She launched a hit past the right fielder forcing Abby to sprint for second, then third, her stomach gurgling every step.

"Go!" Coach Whitley waved her on toward home plate. "Take a turn!"

Abby moved at half-speed but also couldn't pump the brakes. Her strides kept cycling, momentum building, as the catcher called for the ball.

"Back! Back!" Coach Whitley yelled.

But Abby charged onward, tripping toward home plate. The catcher blocked her path while she waited on the throw. With no other option, Abby lowered her shoulder as the ball flew in. She knocked into the catcher, and they tumbled behind the plate. Abby dragged her hand through the dirt in search of the coveted marker.

"Safe!" the umpire barked.

Abby rolled onto her back and groaned as the Eagles cheered. In the dugout, her teammates jostled and smacked her back. She shrugged them off, pushed their hands away, ripped off her helmet, and threw up in the nearest trash can. They darted back in disgust.

"What the fuck," Lauren said.

Abby flipped her off with her head still in the trash can, and when the inning ended, she didn't dare move.

"What's going on?" Coach Whitley asked.

"Something I ate," Abby said.

Coach Whitley turned to Mick, who shrugged. "Fine. Cruz, you're out. Hutchins, take over at shortstop."

Abby's heart stopped. Not because she cared about getting benched or losing her position, but because Kate got to take it. She lifted her head to see her take the field. When she settled her cleats into the dirt, popping bright against the green outfield, white foul lines, and boundless blue behind, Abby swore it's where she'd belonged all along.

She spent the doubleheader lying on the bench with a towel covering her eyes but sat up to watch Kate at shortstop. She observed her footwork, her steady crouch, her zip of a throw. While Abby had once criticized Kate for being stiff and mechanical, from the bench she witnessed something she never quite mastered herself. Abby exuded freedom within the game, but Kate exuded love. While the softball lived inside Abby, a natural part of who she was, Kate worked for it with a tenacity that could only come from the heart. She played like she believed in it. Like she might restore Abby's belief too.

That night, the group adjusted sleeping arrangements so Abby couldn't leave, though she promised profusely not to. Jill slept on the rollaway, blocking Abby's end of the bed, while Kate took her side, guaranteeing that she would literally have to crawl over them to escape. Not that she wanted to. Rather than dread another nightmare, rather than itch for a drink, she sank into the pillows. She eyed Kate in the dark next to her, lulled to sleep by her breathing.

Abby recovered for Sunday's games and welcomed Coach Whitley's change in the lineup. "Hutchins, stay at short. Cruz, let's try you at second."

"Yes, Coach." Abby grinned as she caught Kate's smile.

While Abby certainly preferred shortstop, she played second base brazenly. Playing second ensured Kate rightfully shined at short. They locked down the defense, a ball never breaking their fortress, the two of them errorless through the doubleheader, diving, sliding, whipping outs to Jill.

The final out of the tournament sent Kate diving across the dirt. She twisted and flung the ball off target to Abby, but it didn't matter. She tagged the runner behind her back and threw to Jill for the final out, the win, and a roar. It wasn't just going through the motions either. Abby could feel it again.

When Kate came at her for a high five, she crushed her in a hug and lifted her off her feet. Organically, either to Kate, the softball gods, or the unknowable magnetism that drew her back to the field, Abby whispered into her neck, "Thank you."

Kate's gaze glistened when she released her, a pure blue that knotted Abby's throat. She didn't fully recall her night of debauchery or breakdown, but something in her knew it then. Kate was her anchor. A whisper, a hug, a pair of lips to the top of her head in the harrowing noise. She waited for her to respond, saw her mouth open, but then the rest of the team tightened around them. Abby held her stare for as long as possible, wanting her to know what she knew. That it wasn't the game that saved her. It was Kate.

Thunderstorms in the Midwest delayed their flight home. Most of the team lounged across chairs at the gate, slept on their duffel bags, studied, or scrolled. Abby found Kate at a table in the nearby food court. She'd apologized at least a dozen times for her drunken behavior, been forgiven just as many, but the urge to say it struck again.

"I'm—"

"Don't," Kate stopped her, never glancing up from her reading.

Abby smirked. "Okay." She leaned back in her chair. "What are you studying?"

Kate winced and revealed her Bible. "Book of Job."

"Oh." Abby didn't know if she should change the subject, but didn't want to dismiss her either, especially with the way Kate shrank into herself, like it was something she usually hid. "What's it about?"

"A man trying to understand why God has allowed him to suffer so greatly."

Abby's ears perked, courtesy transforming to curiosity. "Does he get his answer?"

"Not entirely. Just that God is beyond our understanding."

"And you find comfort in that?"

Kate pursed her mouth. "I don't know if it's meant to comfort us. Maybe it's just supposed to remind us of how small we are. That we're not entitled to understanding."

"Stupid me. I thought the Bible had all the answers," Abby scoffed, but then frowned at Kate's blush. "Sorry. I wasn't really raised religious."

"Do you believe in God?"

If it was anyone else, Abby might have rolled her eyes, dismissed them as a Jesus freak or religious fanatic attempting to evangelize her. But she didn't detect moralizing in Kate's question. "I want to."

"What do you mean?"

Abby sighed. "Because if there's a God, then maybe there's a heaven. And if there's a heaven, maybe that means my mom is there."

"She is," Kate said with such certainty that it almost convinced her.

Abby's throat tightened. "You can't be sure though. Can you?"

"No, not entirely." She tilted her head. "That's why they call it faith."

Abby's knee bounced beneath the table as if the months of lonely grieving lay in wait for this moment. She'd tried to rid herself of it with booze and risk, taking control of her own hurt. But that's all it was. More hurt with nowhere to go. Except now, maybe it did have somewhere. Right here with Kate. She'd been there from the start, showing up every day when no one else did. And while Abby didn't know if she believed in God, she knew after that weekend, she believed in Kate.

"Did you know it was a car crash?" Abby's voice resounded low and unfamiliar, but perhaps that was only because she'd never spoken of it before.

"I didn't."

"They called me that night. The police. She'd been drunk, was drunk when she got behind the wheel." Abby cleared her throat, the story stinging on its way out like a thorn extracted from skin. Kate placed a hand on top of hers, stopping the trembling that Abby hadn't noticed. "It wasn't just then. She struggled with it for years. I could never get her to stop."

"How could you? You were a kid."

The first round of tears started in her throat. She trained her gaze on the Bible, though she didn't know if its promise of an afterlife meant her mom was stuck in some other realm or if it was just a crock of shit, and she returned to the nothing that Abby now carried with her.

"I don't tell people how she died, because I'm sure some might think she got hers. That she deserved it. It's like I carry her shame with me instead. Like a curse."

Kate squeezed Abby's hand tighter. "No one deserves that. Not you. Not her either."

Abby shifted her eyes up, not bothering to hide the tears in them. The same inkling as earlier that day assured that Kate knew them, understood them, could take them.

"She was—" Abby considered stopping as the memories fell upon her. The fights, the empty bottles, the picking her up from the bar, the putting her to bed, the staying out to cope, the relief that came from leaving for college, and the accompanying dread. "I—" She sighed and shook her head.

"It's okay. You don't have to," Kate whispered.

"I used softball as an escape. A way to never have to think about it or go home. But maybe I shouldn't have." A droplet slid to her chin, and she wiped it away. "I knew something bad would happen, and I didn't stop it. Sometimes I even wonder." She exhaled and shut her eyes. "I wonder if she did it on purpose and if I might have missed my chance to help her." Abby choked on a cry. "I miss her. I miss her so badly, but then there's also a part of me that's relieved that I don't have to worry anymore."

When Abby opened her eyes, she discovered Kate's tears. And while she cherished her assurances and the comfort of her hands, this empathy meant more than words, though she knew just what to say too. "Nothing is your fault."

Abby nodded but crumpled, fighting to keep her whimpers quiet, unsure if the confession or that gentle declaration finally freed her.

"I know this might not be the right thing to say and some people hate it, but I pray for you all the time." Kate sniffled as she drew circles on the back of Abby's hand. "I guess when I say that, I mean, I think of you. My heart thinks of you."

Abby's chest rocked, but not with her usual burdens. "My heart thinks of you too."

Kate glimpsed down at their interlocked hands. The brief shift regrettably brought the airport back into focus, as though they'd been in their own bubble until then.

"Flight 534 to Portland, good news. We're ready to start your boarding process," the gate agent announced.

Abby didn't move from her chair as Kate gathered her things and turned for the gate. She stayed seated, uncertain how she might leave their conversation behind.

"Hey." Kate reappeared and wrapped an arm around Abby. She rested her chin atop her head, and Abby's heart shot into her throat. "Let's go home."

Abby's eyes widened as Kate grabbed her hand and pulled her to her feet. She nodded, still in a daze. "Let's go home." She couldn't remember the last time she'd said or meant it, but knew she'd never have to wonder where it was again.

WAITING

Abby started going to church after the spring showcase. It wasn't exactly a spiritual awakening that led her there, and she never actually went inside, but every Thursday evening, she stood at a safe distance from New Hope Baptist's doors, waiting for Kate to emerge.

She didn't know when the waiting started. She only knew that they'd spend every day of that school year together, but it wouldn't be enough. So, Abby waited for Kate, and Kate waited for Abby. No more meeting in the library or locker room. Not when they could meet each other after classes, on the walk to campus, the field, or home.

Everything changed after the spring showcase, though they never discussed it. Abby knew it from the way they studied side by side, occasionally brushing shoulders or thighs. She knew it in the way she held her breath until Kate withdrew, then spent the remainder of their time in the library desperate for her to return. Desperate for Kate to gently tap her on the back and pull her attention away from their books.

She knew it on the field too when they weren't just together, but moved as one. When they turned two, with Kate at shortstop and Abby at second base. When Kate hit first, and Abby knocked her in for a run. An extension of the other.

That's why Abby awkwardly waited for Bible study to end. If she was honest though, she didn't exactly mind it. Not when Kate came through those church doors. She'd flash Abby a smile, sometimes a brief wave when she saw her and something about it felt like faith. That if she waited long enough, Kate would appear, and the rest would fall into place.

Of course, she wondered if Kate noticed the skeptical glances as she left her church group behind to join her. She made quite the Jezebel for the faithful, puffing cigarettes with her shades on, the hood of her sweatshirt raised in the sun. But if they ever said anything to Kate, or she caught wind of the disdain that Abby recognized from the distance, she never mentioned it. Just as she never forced Abby into the pews.

Blake Davis was a different story.

"What am I going to have to do to get you to join us?" He always pleaded with a grin, like it might be the day that David beat Goliath. Like if anyone could convert her, it would be him. He seemed to be the king of New Hope Baptist and Collegiate Athletes for Christ, always with a small entourage in tow. And again, if Kate noticed, or if it bothered her, she never showed it. She trailed at a distance, chatting with a friend on her way to Abby.

"Maybe an exorcism." She blew smoke over her shoulder, though she considered fumigating him with it. "Oh, wait, that's the Catholics, right?"

He feigned a chuckle. "I really think you might like it."

"Thanks, but I'm good."

"Right, well, maybe next time."

The little flock of followers behind him whispered among themselves and glared. Kate dawdled down the church steps, but when she spotted them together, her pace quickened.

"You know, I was hoping you could help me with something." Blake fished a baseball card out of his pocket. "Audie was one of my favorite players growing up. I can't imagine him being my dad."

Abby gritted her teeth. "Yeah. Me neither."

Blake just kept smiling. "Do you think you could have him sign it?"

"Blake, don't." Kate slid between them, eyes widening at the baseball card, then at Abby.

"Why?"

"No, it's fine." Abby took the card. "I'll see what I can do."

"Thank you." Blake clapped her shoulder, and she barely withheld a growl. "If he ever comes to a game, I'd love to meet him."

"Sure, but he's really busy. I doubt if he'll make any this season."

"We should get to the library," Kate said.

They scrambled to leave, but not before Blake pecked Kate's lips goodbye. Abby rolled her eyes behind her sunglasses and squashed her cigarette into the pavement, grounding her shoe into it far longer than necessary.

"Sorry about that," Kate said, as they walked to campus.

"Don't worry about it." Abby adjusted the backpack on her shoulder. "How's he supposed to know about Audie?"

"When was the last time you saw him?"

She bit her lip and considered not answering. Kate would have let her get away with it too. Let her light another cigarette and stew. Which is probably why she told her anyway. Why she always ended up telling her.

"I was eleven. He showed up at one of my softball tournaments. Cheering louder than everyone." Abby kicked a rock down the sidewalk. "He and my mom got into a screaming match in the bleachers. I wanted him to see me play, but not with how upset it made her." She shoved her hands in her pockets. "He was around sporadically before that, but I never really knew him. And the blowups my parents would have . . . that was far worse than missing him."

"What about now?"

"He called after Mom, but I didn't answer. It's been ten years. I don't need him."

They strolled in easy silence. The one that belonged just to them.

"You never try to make me go in," Abby said after a beat.

"You don't want to."

Abby stared at the pavement, searching for another rock to kick. "You don't think I need saving?"

"Do you?" Kate asked.

She shrugged. "I think it's a work in progress."

"It usually is." Kate smiled before handing her a stack of laminated note cards. "Quiz me?"

Abby smiled in return, but a smidge of shyness held it back, like if she grinned too big, Kate might detect how much she adored her. "You know, at this rate maybe I should take the LSAT too."

"You should," Kate said, and Abby knew by her cheerful lilt that she meant it.

"How'd you know you wanted to be a lawyer?" she asked as they crossed the quad.

"I guess I've always been passionate about fairness. That we all deserve an equal shot." Kate's gaze shined brighter at the topic. Just like when she played shortstop. Like her entire heart lived in it. "When I was little, I never understood why my brothers got to play on my dad's field and I couldn't."

Abby nodded. "That's right. He coaches baseball?"

"Yep. Two decades now. He calls it God's game."

"Oh, how American of him. I always imagined God would be more of a soccer fan though. More global appeal."

Kate released a peeved, stifled laugh that Abby knew meant she didn't want to admit she found it funny. She shoved her ever so slightly, and Abby chuckled before nudging her back. And for a few perfect, heart-stopping seconds, Kate left herself leaning against her shoulder.

"I think it pushed me into playing harder," she said gently. "Holding on to the game tighter. And now, making sure no one is left out. At least that's what I hope to do."

Their gazes met as their steps slowed. Abby hated that Kate drew back. Hated that she stopped talking. Hated that they'd reached the library steps.

"You'll make a great lawyer," she said.

"Thanks." Kate bit down a smile and cleared her throat. "Now, quiz me already."

She lingered as Kate climbed the steps, chattering without realizing Abby wasn't following behind her. While they were together, Abby realized she was still waiting. For what, she couldn't say for sure, except maybe more.

The windsurfers and boats in the river bobbed like distant bathtub toys from the condo's perch on the ridge. Kate didn't know how much money professors made, but Isla's curated home suggested a certain air of wealth. Everything about her did, even with her bare feet and oversize button-down billowing in the breeze as they ate dinner on the deck. It made Kate even more self-conscious to join the professor off campus, but when Abby invited her, she didn't dare say no. Lately, Kate would've blindly agreed to just about anything for another minute with her.

"Thank you for everything you've done. Ever since Abby started spending time with you, she's been getting better. Lighter even," Isla said when Abby left the table.

"She does seem better." Kate glanced at her untouched wine. "But I don't think it's because of me."

Isla angled her chin to the side. "Seriously? Give yourself credit. You're really special to her."

"She's special to me too." Kate considered her wine and wondered if it might settle the jitters she hadn't shaken since Abby picked her up. She'd gotten used to enduring the giddiness in the brief moments they touched, in a gaze held too long, in the anticipation of their next meeting, but never had it consumed her so fully that she struggled to touch her dinner.

"You're not talking shit about me, are you?" Abby plopped back into the seat next to her.

"No." Isla winked at Kate. "I was just telling her I know a great civil rights attorney she should intern with in the fall."

Kate shook her head. "No. I wouldn't want to impose, and you've already done too much," she said. Isla insisted on writing Kate a letter of recommendation for law school and connected her with her vast network of attorneys and professors to help beef up her applications.

"It's not imposing. Luca would be lucky to have you."

"See, babysitting me might pay off." Abby sipped her wine.

Kate frowned. "Don't say that."

She spent so much of dinner trying not to look at her too long that when she allowed herself a glimpse, it surprised her all over again. Abby's inky hair, long and wavy, her tan skin visible beneath a tank top, shorts, and tired leather sandals. A stark contrast to the Abby on the field or in the classroom. A starker contrast to winter Abby, who trudged through the cold in layers of faded hoodies, well-worn flannels, and tattered jeans, never without a beanie. This Abby, sun-kissed and languid as if she belonged on the beach, was so natural it was as if Kate witnessed her return to herself with the change of seasons. And perhaps that's what made it more beautiful—that she'd seen her through the winter. Just like when she smiled or laughed, it struck deeper knowing that she'd once seen her broken.

Never on trend or fashionable, Kate had tried on a dozen outfits before dinner, finally settling on white jeans and a chambray shirt. Upon picking her up, Abby beamed and told her she looked pretty. Kate could barely mutter thank you. Just as she barely picked up on the conversation about her possible internship with her focus fully absorbed by Abby's lips.

"So, this attorney doesn't happen to be the one you moved here for, is it?"

"Is this the moment you decide to become an annoying younger sister?" Isla tossed her napkin at a snickering Abby. "I didn't move here for him."

"He lives here?" Kate asked.

"No. No, he's in Portland." Isla swirled her wine. "He did his undergraduate at Insley and recommended me for the job here. But yes, he is my ex, and yes, he just happens to live forty-five minutes away."

"You *really* haven't seen him since you came back here?" Abby asked.

Isla bit her lip and stared out at the water. "No."

Abby bumped Kate's knee beneath the table and raised a brow at her. Much like on the field, Kate didn't need her to explain. She wanted her to ask Isla for more details, so that she couldn't rebuff Abby as a pesky sibling.

"Why not?" Kate asked, though she didn't truly wonder. Not as she obsessed over Abby's leg leaving hers, and the pleasant static it left behind.

"It was a tough breakup. It was my fault really." Isla paused for a drink. "We met at law school, and I adored him. He wasn't like the rest of the Yale crowd. To this day he acts embarrassed to mention it." She smirked and then frowned again. "My mom wasn't a fan. She wanted me with someone who *was* like the rest of the Yale crowd."

Kate's parents suddenly flashed through her mind. They certainly didn't require a Yale man, but a devout, honorable Christian was required. They already beheld Blake like Moses himself, and each time she called home they asked about him, unsubtly following up with the importance of marriage and children.

Usually, it didn't bother Kate. She always deflected with law school, but now it put a wrench in her stomach. She was overcome by a wave of nausea as she glanced at Abby—one she wouldn't allow herself to ponder too deeply.

"She's not why I ended things though. I mean, maybe a little. Luca wanted marriage, and with my parents' track record, I'm not inclined to throw my hat into the ring." Isla shrugged. "So, I went into family law like I always planned, settling big, nasty New York divorces, hating myself even though I thought it might make sense of the ones I witnessed as a kid. I tried dating someone in the Yale crowd, even brought him back to San Diego. Until one day I woke up and realized I hated every part of my life. I couldn't go to work, I couldn't get up, I could barely explain it to my boyfriend or my colleagues or myself. Now I think it's because I was always lonely, and it finally caught up with me."

For the first time that dinner, Kate could see how clearly Abby and Isla were kin. In how despite her hunched shoulders, the glimmer didn't leave her gaze. In how easily they teased each other, despite only knowing one another a few months. Kate had six siblings, but never talked to them with such openness or depth. Instead, they'd grown up side by side like silent parishoners. And while she'd spent her childhood surrounded, Kate related to Isla's loneliness, as if she too had been kept from family.

"Then I saw the job posting here, at this little school that I only knew of because of Luca. It felt like a sign. I asked him for a recommendation and here we are. Hiding out in the hills." Isla smiled at Abby. "But for the first time in a long time, I don't feel lonely."

"Well, cheers to that." Abby raised a glass and the three of them clinked for a toast. "You know, maybe the timing was just wrong with Luca. I bet he'll be happy to take your call about Kate's internship."

"That's not why I was offering." Isla shook her head.

Abby nudged Kate's thigh beneath the table. "Now you really have to do it. Love is on the line."

"Well, I certainly can't deny love." Kate pressed her leg back into Abby's and let the grin reach her eyes.

By the time Abby dropped her off at the blue house, Kate's body hummed as if overflowing with the longing she'd suppressed during dinner. They stared, Kate in the passenger seat, Abby behind the wheel, like they'd reached the end of a date, taunted by the anticipation of a kiss. And Kate wanted it. Wanted it so badly that she squirmed. Desperation and fear gathered in her throat.

Abby eased in. Kate gasped and froze. Rather than lips, Abby's forehead found hers and rested on it. Their breaths mingled, hot and close, so that she didn't know where her exhales ended, and Abby's inhales began.

"Sometimes I wish I could have more of you," Abby whispered.

Kate quivered, shut her eyes, fought a desire she didn't know existed in her. One that shouldn't exist in her. She drew back, rested a hand on Abby's cheek. Her amber eyes shimmered in the dim light. "Good night." Kate slammed the car door and didn't turn back.

Mick and Jill lounged on the couch, but she charged upstairs. An unbearable pulse thrummed in her, turning every speckle of skin into a current, the most powerful of which surged salaciously low. She locked her bedroom door and panted.

Kate rarely touched herself, had only attempted a few times without reaching climax, out of curiosity rather than arousal. During a singular puberty talk, her mother correlated it with the devil. When her friends mentioned masturbating or sex, she pretended to scroll on her phone. But this heartbeat begged for touch. The swollen sensation that often filled her heart expanded between her thighs.

Kate dropped to her bed, scrubbed hands down her clammy cheeks, and fought to ground herself. She needed a cold shower. She needed to text Blake. She needed to pray. But her chest rocked, her stomach smoldered, and the throb wasn't just persistent, but pleasant. It demanded chasing.

With one hand clutching her winded throat, she trailed the other down her abdomen, and dared to plunge beneath the waistband of her jeans. She closed her eyes and sighed in relief at the brush of her fingers. She discovered not only that pulse, but wetness along her opening, so plentiful that it drenched her fingers. She writhed at the slipperiness. She'd never been so needy for touch, never been wet, never been turned on to the point that she considered no other option but to free herself in it, to press and rub and lust for more.

She pictured Abby's lips. Pictured her hands on her chest. Imagined her whispers. Imagined all three of them on her neck, on her skin, between her legs. She mouthed her name, as if saying it aloud might be a worse transgression than her fantasies alone. She saw nothing else, wanted nothing else, couldn't stop if God himself demanded it. She came in silence, vibrating, gasping until the static returned to calm.

And that's when she fully understood the nausea at dinner. The daily fluttering that never freed her. The guilt. She desired Abby not just on the field and in the library and every minute in between, but like this too. She took a cold shower, prayed for forgiveness, and vowed after a sleepless night to never do it again.

Fortunately, Abby never mentioned their exchange in the car. They practiced without awkwardness, too deep in the season, chasing a conference title, to allow anything to stand in the way. And with only a few months left together at Insley, Kate turned to Blake.

Even during the earliest, most enthusiastic points of their courtship, they struggled to make time for each other. Blake's baseball schedule often interfered with Kate's softball commitments, and he trained as obsessively as she did. Now he also juggled the pressure of scouts and agents as the MLB draft drew near, and Kate felt guilty for not being more supportive.

Any other girl at church or CAC would drop everything to help him. They fawned over him, told Kate how lucky she was, waved signs for him at the games she couldn't attend, and found excuses to talk or pray with him. Kate always nodded along unbothered—similar to the way she found their vow of celibacy a relief rather than a challenge. But now she realized her complacency might've been because her affections drifted elsewhere.

"I can't believe this is it," Blake said as he stopped his Jeep at their favorite viewpoint, a tree-lined cliff they often hiked. They gazed out at the expanse of plateaus that rolled beneath the pink horizon. "I always thought we'd leave Insley together."

"You could still stay." Kate couldn't meet his gaze when she said it. She stared at his hand, wrapped around hers instead, wishing she knew what would fix the guilt gnawing at her gut—him leaving or him staying. "Finish senior year. Finish your degree."

"And risk getting hurt? It'd be a waste." He scoffed. "Plus, if I go now, grind it out in the minors a few years, I could get called up before I'm twenty-five. That'd be great for us." Blake flashed a grin. "You could come with me. I know you have enough credits to graduate early. You could take a year off before law school, we could get married—"

"And miss my last season here?" Kate furrowed her brow, taken aback at him even suggesting it.

"Right. No. Of course not. I'm just going to miss you." Blake's eyes softened. He pecked her hand with his lips. "I'd marry you now if I could."

Kate's frustration faded at how gently he said it. At how fully she knew he meant it and how she wasn't ready to give it. "We can't."

"Actually, we could."

She pulled her hand back. "Is this a proposal?"

"Do you want it to be?"

"Not right now." Kate chewed her lip. "How about we see how you feel after you get drafted?"

"You don't believe me?"

"No," she whispered. "I do."

She kissed Blake more vigorously that night, cradled his stubbled cheeks, allowed his tongue to enter her mouth without flinching. She let him touch her chest and waist, hoping to rouse the same pulse and wetness, because she needed him to be able to. She needed them to not blossom only for Abby.

When Blake grinded against her, Kate didn't push him away at first, maybe because he was leaving, and maybe because she thought it might make up for how completely she wanted someone else. But it didn't. Her back tensed, and her lips stopped working, and the rest of her went numb, because all she wanted, all she could think of was Abby in the car. Of how much different it felt. Of how it made her feel everything and this made her feel nothing.

"Stop. Can we stop." Kate dragged in a ragged breath, and Blake scrambled off her. "I'm sorry."

"No, I'm sorry." He shook his head. "I just got caught up in—"

"It's okay." Kate rubbed his shoulder and swallowed a sob. "I'm just not feeling well."

She found surprising comfort in saying it because she wasn't lying to him or herself. Though she hated how rare those moments were beginning to feel.

THE END OF JUNIOR YEAR

Despite not making the national tournament, the Insley Eagles posted one of their best softball records that junior season. For the first time in a decade, the team won the conference championship and made a historic run through regionals. Individually, Kate and Abby won top honors. Abby broke school and conference records for home runs and RBIs, Kate made academic all-American for the second year in a row, and they both secured first team all-conference honors.

It gave them plenty to celebrate at the spring awards banquet. Each year, the softball, baseball, and lacrosse teams, tennis stars, and track athletes gathered at the Columbia Crest Golf Club. It was a rare night of opulence for a school that hadn't updated uniforms or fields in five years, but a generous booster had a connection with the country club and a nephew who ran hurdles, so the Eagles dusted themselves off for a night of hors d'oeuvres and chandeliers.

The junior fivesome of course had mixed views on the event.

"It's a crock of shit," Mick said as she lounged on the couch the week before.

T.K. rolled her eyes. "You just say that because you hate wearing dresses." She spun around in a yellow ball gown, flipping hair off her shoulder. "How about this one?"

"That's the one," Abby said.

T.K. glared. "You said that about the last three."

"Yeah, because I want this to end."

Kate couldn't resist a laugh, glancing up from her book to meet Abby's smile. She gulped from the beanbag in the corner. A deliberate choice, like every one as of late, to keep space between them. And while it was easier with classes over and the softball season finished, it was also harder because Kate missed her. When Abby showed up at the blue house that afternoon, she was so thrilled that she had to steady herself on the doorframe.

"What are you wearing?" T.K. asked.

Kate pulled her eyes away from Abby, who she swore hadn't stopped staring since she arrived. "Who? Me?"

"Yes."

"I have a black dress."

"The one you wore last year?" T.K. asked.

"And the year before," Jill said before striking a pose in the flowing lace high priestess gown she planned to wear.

Kate blushed.

"Here. Try one of mine." T.K. pulled her dress off, never self-conscious, and chucked it at her.

"No thanks," Kate said.

"Fine, be boring."

Even if Kate cared about clothes, she rarely had extra money to spend on them. Usually, she wouldn't have been embarrassed by it if it weren't for Abby. Though that quickly went away too, when she caught her smirking, as if it were an admirable quality and not inherent lameness.

"Mick, we need to find something for you," T.K. said as she reappeared in a short tube dress that looked better suited for a club.

"I don't want to." Mick threw her head back like an angry child.

Abby groaned. "Then don't. Just wear what you want."

Mick furrowed her brow as if it never occurred to her as an option. The four of them stared at her, and Kate swore they witnessed the wheels churning: the moment when Mick, who'd come out long ago but never quite settled into her own skin, rejected everything that no longer aligned with her. Chopping off most of her hair that year had been a start, but this felt different. Or maybe it was just Kate who noticed, while she too wondered if everything pressed upon her still aligned.

"What do you want, Mick? A suit and tie? Your uniform? Your stupid pajamas?" Abby leaned back on the couch and laced her hands behind her head like she couldn't care less. "Just let me know and I'll wear the same, idiot."

And that's how Abby and Mick ended up in slacks and shirts instead of dresses that night. Mick wore a bow tie—which would become her signature for years to come—while Abby sported a necktie so loose it looked like she'd stumbled out of a bar after a ten-hour day on Wall Street. It was typical Abby—casual, cool, and uncaring. And yet Kate knew what she'd silently done for Mick *was* caring, which made it all the more endearing. All the more attractive too, though Kate didn't think it possible.

She couldn't stop staring through the ceremony. While she sat with Blake and other CAC members, her gaze constantly drifted to Abby sitting with the upperclassmen. It distracted her so fully that she nearly missed her own name as the athletic director took the small podium at the front of the ballroom to announce an award she didn't expect.

"It is my great privilege to give this to a young woman who embodies kindness, spirit, and generosity, not just on the field but off it. She puts her teammates first, constantly pushing them to not just be the best softball players but the best versions of themselves. She is a top shortstop not only in the conference but in the country, a future team captain, and one of our brightest students. This year's Rich Aldren trophy for sportsmanship goes to Kate Hutchins."

While the room erupted with applause, Kate instinctively searched for Abby, whose grin made her forget about the award, the crowd, Blake, and the rest. She just wanted to hug her. She just wanted her.

"What are you doing? Go get it." Blake nudged her from her seat, squeezing her arm as she passed.

Kate tried to recover, but to no avail. Not when Abby accepted a plaque for her broken records, sheepishly nodding at the athletic director and hurrying back to her table as quickly as possible. Even as Blake accepted his Insley Male Athlete of the Year award, Kate veered to her. And every time, Abby's stare waited to receive her.

After the trophies, accolades, and speeches, the softball team gathered together. Kate joined them as Blake met up with his own teammates.

"Okay, enough of this country club shit." Mick grinned. "I think it calls for a little celebration."

"Sunny's?" Jill asked.

"Hell yes."

"I thought half of you got blacklisted." Kate glanced at Abby, Courtney, and Lauren.

"I'm friends with the bouncer." T.K. wiggled her tongue suggestively.

"Ew."

"Okay, let's go." Mick clapped her hands. "Come on! Move, move, move."

Kate bit her lip and glanced over her shoulder at Blake.

"You coming?" Abby asked her.

"I don't usually go out," Kate said.

"It's one night." Abby followed her gaze. "I'm sure he'll be okay."

Kate turned back to her, heart banging unbearably. She couldn't possibly say no.

A line of people snaked around Sunny's when they arrived, but T.K. made good on her dalliance with the bouncer, who allowed them to slip under the velvet rope and into the overflowing bar. Students elbowed to order drinks. Rotating rainbow hues illuminated the dance floor where people danced and shouted in corners. Kate, Jill, and T.K. stood at a slick table while Abby and Mick got drinks.

"Everyone get in here!" Mick distributed tequila shots. Lauren, Courtney, and the other graduating seniors joined as well. Abby squeezed next to Kate, wrapped an arm around her waist to hedge in close. "To our best season yet. Thank God DeHaven and Seaborn are out of here, so we have a shot next year."

"Fuck you." Lauren ruffled Mick's hair.

They clinked their drinks and tossed them back. Kate winced. She rarely, if ever, drank.

"Are you okay?" Abby leaned in, still hooked around Kate's waist, her mouth perched at her ear. Kate nodded, heat rising in her stomach, loosening her shoulders, like she'd waded into a hot tub, sending her subtly slackening against Abby's chest.

"Yo, Abby! Abby!" Mick shouted. "We still on?"

Abby rolled her eyes. "Do you really need my help?"

"Yes. You're on friend duty, so I can land this thing."

Kate glanced between them. "What are you talking about?"

Jill stopped sipping on the dangerous looking fishbowl of booze she shared with the on-again Dylan Farrelly. "Mick asked Haley Stewart out."

"The intern? From the athletic trainer's office?" Kate shouted over the music.

Everyone nodded, and she battled the familiar feeling that she'd been left out of their secret club. The club of dating and sex.

"I noticed Mick getting her wrist taped for no reason." Abby grinned. "And ice baths after every game."

"It's for my knees!" Mick shouted.

Courtney and Lauren returned with a second round of shots, and Kate grimaced.

"Anyway, that's when I knew something was up," Abby said. "So, I told her to ask Haley out or I would."

"You would?" Kate asked.

Abby shrugged. "I had to set a fire under Mick somehow. And it worked." She tossed back her drink, and Kate regretfully did the same.

"Well, we'll see." Mick eyed the door as people squeezed inside. "That's where you come in and put this thing in Cruz control. Distract the friend, get me some alone time."

Abby chuckled. "Only if she's cute."

"She?" Kate muttered.

"Trust me, she's cute," Mick said.

Kate sank. She knew it shouldn't matter if Abby flirted with someone else, if she was interested in someone else, or if someone else was interested in her. But it strangled her insides, so every butterfly that had previously flapped died.

An hour of drinks passed before Haley's arrival, and by her second cocktail, Kate wavered. The only positive of her tipsiness was Abby's watchful gaze, always ready to steady her, to brush her back, to whisper in her ear. The claustrophobia of the bar provided ample excuses to stand closer, to bump into each other, to rest with their bodies touching a second longer, shielded by the crowd and the team's growing drunkenness.

"You know, I might miss you, Cruz," Courtney slurred, throwing an arm around her.

Kate laughed at Abby's snarl.

"Don't get sappy, Seaborn. You're just a sloppy drunk."

"Oh, fuck you. Maybe I should chase you into that kitchen for old times' sake."

"Sure, let me go light a cigarette first."

Abby nodded at Kate and led her away from their giggling friends. Kate tried to stop her from getting more drinks, pulled her back by the tie like she'd longed to for hours, but then released her and apologized before their faces came dangerously close. And in the brief minutes apart, Kate ached for her to return, surviving off glimpses of her from the corner.

"I don't know if I can drink any more," Kate hiccupped when Abby returned.

"It's club soda." Abby winked.

Kate sighed in relief. "Thank you."

"To turning two."

The lights cast her skin and gaze in a golden hue. She locked eyes with Kate as if up to bat, choosing the perfect pitch, driving that record-breaking swing.

"To turning two." Kate clung to the pleasant weightlessness, surely the result of the booze and having Abby to herself. Something she hadn't allowed herself since Isla's. "And to next season."

"Already on to next season?"

"Isn't that half the allure of softball? Looking forward to the next chance?"

Abby chuckled. "Maybe. I don't know if it's a blessing or a curse."

"Definitely a blessing," Kate said.

Their eyes met again, and Abby cleared her throat, leaning closer to speak above the music. "Is this miserable for you? Slumming it at Sunny's?"

"It's fine." She sipped her club soda, hopeful but unconvinced it would sober her. She braced herself on the table to not sway, and when she glanced at Mick, she frowned. "Are you really going to hit on Haley's friend?" Her delivery landed more hostile than intended.

Abby smirked. "I don't know. Would it bother you?"

Kate's mouth fell. "No."

Abby inched closer. "I know we didn't talk about it, but I'm sorry about what happened after Isla's."

"It's fine." Kate glanced away, as if a single look might reveal that Abby's affections that night resulted in her first climax.

"I know I made you uncomfortable." Abby twirled the thin straw in her bourbon. Kate's heart pounded as Abby brought her mouth to her ear, her words vibrating into her cheek. "I just feel something when I'm with you."

Kate nearly dropped her drink. She didn't fully know what Abby meant, but her gaze said the rest. The same as in the car. *Sometimes I wish I could have more of you.* "We can't."

Abby sighed. "Because of Blake."

"And because I'm not—" Kate couldn't finish the sentence. She wasn't afraid to say it, but in light of recent events, she didn't know if she meant it.

"Right." Abby nodded, a faint frown pulling down her mouth.

Kate didn't know if the booze or their closeness inspired her, but she blurted a confession as if she might drown beneath it. "I feel confused when I'm with you."

"Good confused or bad confused?"

"It depends." Kate paused. "It feels good, but it scares me. I'm not supposed to."

"Not supposed to what?"

"Want you." Kate shuddered. She felt lightheaded. Someone bumped into her, and she nearly toppled over before Abby braced her.

"What if I wanted you too?" she whispered with hands around her forearms.

Kate bit her lip. "It wouldn't matter."

Abby opened her mouth to speak when Blake interrupted. "'*Adios, Abby Cruz! It's outta here!*'" He topped off his unwelcome arrival with her father's catchphrase. "Get it? It's like Audie but it's Abby."

She released Kate. "I'm not drunk enough for this," she muttered.

Kate frowned. "Don't get too drunk."

"You seem a little tipsy yourself." Blake wrapped an arm around Kate and kissed her. When their lips parted, she caught Abby as she scowled and tossed back the rest of her drink.

What had the potential to be a great night, a night with Abby's undivided attention, transformed into an awful one. Kate wished to disappear, wished she hadn't come at all. Especially as Mick joined them with Haley Stewart and her friend.

"Hey, guys!" Mick bounced on her toes, hands twitchy as she gestured. "You know Haley, right?"

"Good to see you again." Kate smiled for Mick's sake. Her friend stared at Haley like she'd pinned the moon in the sky. And Haley shone as if she had, eyes reluctantly breaking from Mick.

"Good to see you too." Haley nodded at the group, rested a grin on Kate, Abby, and Blake. "Congrats on the season. And on the draft, Blake."

"Thanks! They're projecting eighteenth round now. Brewers are interested." He grinned.

The blonde at Haley's side cleared her throat and Mick scrambled to introduce her.

"This is Haley's friend Zoey." Mick hastily pointed out Kate and Blake, but nearly shoved her at Abby. "Zoey, this is Abby."

Kate tensed as Abby shook her hand.

Zoey's crimson lips curved with a smile. "Mick was saying you broke some school record?"

"Was she?" Abby smirked. "She's my biggest fan."

"The biggest." Mick clapped her shoulder. "Maybe we should get some drinks?"

"Please." Abby darted her eyes at Kate, the look reminiscent of the unknowable glares that had leveled her at the beginning of the year. Kate narrowed her brow back.

"You want to go?" Blake asked when they left.

Kate shook her head and stared at the group at the bar. Stared at Abby whispering in Zoey's ear, much like she had hers. "No, let's stay."

She observed Zoey from a distance. Her chest was fuller, her dress more revealing, her legs thinner, golden curls bouncier, her giggle daintier. Kate suddenly hated her own modest dress, her bulkier muscles, and the way everyone around her treated her like a square. She hated that when she told Blake she couldn't drink any more alcohol, he brought her a beer because that's what he was drinking. She hated that no matter how hard she tried not to, she never stopped looking for Abby.

"I think she's got it in the bag!" Jill yelled with Dylan's arm around her waist, drink sloshing to Kate's feet. Mick and Haley swayed together on the dance floor. "Can you believe it?"

"No," Kate said, but she stared at Abby, leading Zoey outside by the hand. She kept watching as Abby lit a cigarette for her, smoked one of her own, laughed, trained eyes on her, leaned too close for comfort. When Zoey kissed Abby's cheek, Kate's chest spasmed as if struck. She turned away before witnessing more.

"Can we leave?" she asked Blake, who was in the middle of telling a story.

"Yeah, hold on, babe."

"I need to go."

Kate started for the door without him, bumped haphazardly through the crowd, and chanced one last glance against her instincts, in time to see Abby's mouth on Zoey's. She rubbed away a tear, more aware than ever why she couldn't finish her sentence that night.

Abby woke in the blue house living room to mark the end of junior year. She stirred beneath a quilt, a beanbag chair sagging beneath her. Her head pounded as she stood and flopped to the couch. She had her first day of work that afternoon and already regretted subjecting herself to summer classes and a part-time job. Just as she prepared to steal a few more hours of sleep, footsteps creaked on the stairs, and Kate rounded the corner.

She popped her head up from the cushions. "Hey."

Kate froze. "I didn't know you slept here."

Abby almost replied, *Me neither,* but shrugged instead. "What are you doing up?"

"I was just going on my run." She tightened her ponytail and kept her gaze on the floor. She wore an INSLEY ATHLETICS sweatshirt and running tights. Abby thought her irresistible at the banquet, the simple black dress a magnet she couldn't resist. But seeing her like this, without makeup, bleary with sleep, much like on their road games, never failed to melt her.

"Did you have a good rest of your night?" Abby asked.

The downstairs bathroom door squealed open, and Zoey slinked out.

"Oh hey," Zoey said. She was a pale, mascara-smeared vision of unwell.

"Morning," Abby said.

"I'm just leaving." Zoey straightened out her dress. "Thanks for everything."

"Yeah." Abby didn't move as the front door shut, awaiting Kate's reaction.

"Nice," she said, jaw clenched.

"Hey, nothing—" Abby paused.

Last night, after Kate's rejection, she'd encouraged Zoey's advances, as if jealousy might change her mind. She wanted Kate to realize that wanting each other mattered, that every graze, every glance, the light touch of a forehead, mattered more than anything to Abby. She wanted her to know that the next three months loomed torturously because she wouldn't get to see her every day, hear her voice, or search her eyes to discern her mood.

Worse, however, than how much she wanted to scream and shake Kate until she understood, was Abby's fear of breaking her. She recognized Kate's terror when she confessed to wanting her. She knew it went against the faith she staked her character on. It made it impossible to know which was crueler: professing her love or keeping it from her.

"Nothing happened. Mick and Haley came back here, so Zoey wanted to too. I slept on the beanbag."

The sloppy make-out session was unsatisfying and short-lived. It didn't take long for Zoey to start talking about her ex. Abby listened through a few drinks, patting her shoulder when she cried, certain but not sorry she wouldn't see Zoey again after that morning.

"I saw you kiss."

"It was nothing." Abby hated the way Kate refused to look at her. Hated that she wanted to beg for forgiveness despite doing nothing wrong. "Kate. Come on. Are you mad?"

"No."

Kate didn't reverse her frown, but flicked her eyes up. She sat next to Abby and rested her head on her shoulder. Abby's heart stilled. She survived off scraps, off hovering, grazes, a rare handhold, dipping her toe in and out, like a game of how much she might pilfer. But this beat all.

Abby wrapped her arm around her, rested her cheek to her chestnut locks, relished her aroma of soap and rain. Kate released a heavy, trembling sigh. They didn't speak for several minutes. Abby ignored the drum in her chest, so accustomed to its rhythm now that she knew it was simply a song for Kate.

"When does your bus leave?" Abby asked.

"Two o'clock."

Abby rubbed her arm and Kate leaned in deeper. "I'm going to miss you." She forced a chuckle. "I don't know how I'll get through summer classes without you."

"You'll be fine," Kate said.

"Are you sure it's safe where you're going?"

"I'll be safe," she said. "I'm more worried about the flight. I don't know how I'm going to handle a day in the air without my turbulence buddy."

"I guess you'll have to find a new one," Abby whispered into her hair. She dared to set her lips there for a beat, didn't purse them, but settled for another scrap of close but not quite.

"I wish I didn't have to." Kate shifted and cupped her cheek, placing a thumb at the corner of Abby's mouth with such beautiful regret that it warranted tears. Her forehead came next, gently bumping against Abby's for a rest. She held Kate's shoulders and closed her eyes, wishing to stay there for longer than they'd ever allow themselves.

"Good thing it's just a few months." Abby reluctantly opened her eyes.

Kate nodded as she withdrew. "I'll miss you." This time they hugged, long and tight.

"Send me a postcard," Abby said. "And a map. I'm not sure where Zambia is."

Kate smiled. "Don't get into any trouble while I'm gone."

"I'll try not to." Abby stayed seated as she stood to leave. "Have a good summer, Kate."

"You too, Abby."

She waited until Kate left, and then she groaned, certain that the only thing worse than scraps would be summer.

SUMMER

Dear Abby,

Greetings from Zambia! I hope this reaches you as right now you seem impossibly far away. It makes me homesick to think of, so I try not to. Luckily, my days are busy. We're working with a local church to rebuild a school. The language barrier is difficult, but it reminds me how much you can say without words. I suppose you've given me ample practice in that area. We spend a lot of time playing with the children here, though sometimes I wonder how much new soccer balls and baseball bats make up for not having parents and the poverty they endure. Our pastor encourages me to pray for answers and for the children, and let God take care of the rest. For some reason it leaves me unsatisfied. Enough about me though. How's your summer? Are you going to your classes? I hope you're not lonely. Write me if you find the time. It would brighten my day.

Kate

P.S. You'll be glad you weren't my turbulence buddy this flight. I got sick so many times they made me sit with the flight attendants.

• • •

Kate,

You'll be happy to know Insley is as boring as ever and your letter might be the highlight of my lame summer. I'm relieved you're safe and I'm sorry about the horrible flight, but I wish I'd been next to you, holding back your hair, if only to return the favor.

I'm going to class but it's hard to focus with summer teasing me outside. I'm working at a water-sport shop on the river. It's mostly handing out kayaks and kites to ill-prepared tourists, but on the plus side, I get free rentals and essentially live in a wetsuit. I'm learning how to windsurf. It's not as satisfying as freely catching waves, but equally therapeutic. Letting the breeze take over, trusting the water, reminds me of that sweet spot on the field where you feel more than play. I'm not sure if that makes sense. Do you ever feel that?

I'm sorry you feel your mission is coming up short. I agree it probably takes more than baseballs and Bibles to make a real difference, but you should know your kindness is a gift of its own. Having been on the receiving end of it, I can admit you pulled me from a dark place when no one else could. I'm not sure if I believe in blessings as much as I believe in timing, but if I did, I'd certainly consider you one.

I think of you often.

Abby

P.S. I'm house-sitting for Isla while she's on a weird wellness retreat for future cat ladies. I think you're going to have to play cupid with Luca.

• • •

Dear Abby,

Thank you so much for the letter. I could imagine your voice while I read it, and it made me smile. Your reassurances help. I'm giving what parts of my heart I can here and when the kids smile and seem to forget about everything except playing or running without worry, it makes it worth it. I hope this doesn't sound strange, but in those same moments, I see you. In their laughter or dimples or a pair of eyes. I think I miss you so much that I search for you in others.

I'm glad to know your summer is going well. I get the feeling you're windsurfing more than studying, but you've always been much cooler than me. I understand what you mean about feeling more than playing. It reminds me of that phrase everyone throws around: "Let the game come to you." You can't control the waves any more than you can control what happens on the field. You can only feel and react. I think accepting that is surrender. I've always enjoyed that part of softball, taken comfort in it. Maybe because in many ways it's reminiscent of faith. Surrendering to the unknowable.

Clearly, I've spent too much time alone out here. I'll be back stateside in a few weeks. Then it's off to Colorado to be with Blake for the draft. We're almost done fixing the school's roof. I honestly go to bed so sore and tired that it's easy to sleep. It reminds me of the farm in Deer Park. Is it bad that I don't miss it as much as I miss Insley?

You're my blessing too.

Kate

P.S. I'm sorry to disappoint you, but I doubt my matchmaking abilities. In fact, after your success with Mick and Haley, so chivalrously "distracting" Zoey, maybe you should play cupid instead.

• • •

Dearest Kate,

Is that jealousy I'm detecting in your postscript? You know I would have rather been distracting you.

I've thought of that night a lot. You looked stunning, and I forgot about everything else—Blake, the team, the bigger questions. I've never experienced what I have with you, with anyone else. There's a word for it, one I think we've both considered, but I'm not sure it's right to say. Not when I mean it so completely. I guess it's cowardly of me to write this in a letter, when you're on a different continent, but I'm afraid of hurting you with a confession more than I fear your rejection. Maybe pen and paper can soften the blow.

If faith is surrender, then I think playing softball is the closest I've ever been to God. It must not be a coincidence then that I found you there too.

I think it's okay to not miss Deer Park as much as the rest of your life. Home is a feeling too. You know what I just thought of? The ballpark is the only place where you must return home to win. Maybe that's why we always find our way back there.

Praying this letter gets lost in the mail.

Abby

• • •

Dear Abby,

You can say love. I love you too. Friends can love each other. I'm just not and can't be in love with you. Especially not when I'm committed to someone else. Though that may be presumptuous of me. You didn't say you were in love with me. Either way,

I wish we would've said it to each other in person before we went our separate ways. But maybe it's just one of those things we've been saying without words. It makes me sad that you correlate love and hurt. Surely you don't believe that your love could hurt me. Or that love may hurt you?

If we're sharing secrets, that night at Sunny's made me jealous. I often wish to have you to myself. Sometimes I feel like I do. When we're turning two, when we're studying and I catch you looking at me, when we had dinner at Isla's. Those moments keep me awake sometimes. They put something foreign in my chest and stomach, like I might explode from the inside out. Maybe it's good in that case to only have you in moments.

One more week here. Six until I see you.

Love,
Kate

P.S. How are classes? Have you chosen a major yet?

• • •

Kate,

I love you too. I agree, I should've said that a long time ago, but it feels good to write it now. Of course, I didn't mean to make you say something that you didn't mean.

As far as love hurting, maybe I'm just projecting. No matter how much we might love, or think someone loves us, we hurt each other, don't we? My mom loved me, but not enough to not hurt me or herself. I worry that may be in me too. Worried that Audie might also exist somewhere deep, but I don't know him well enough to be sure. I think that's why I resent them sometimes. It feels like the only thing they gave me was a curse.

Does it make you feel better that I get jealous too? I'm even jealous that you're on your way to see Blake. He's a good guy, decent third baseman, but horrible timing, am I right? I'm wishing him and you luck with the draft.

Yours always,
Abby

P.S. Like all overachieving students, I've decided to be a general studies major. Why restrict my talents to something simple like one subject, when I can just generically kind of know all of them? If I send you my philosophy midterm, will you write it for me?

P.P.S. Mick says hello. She and Haley are obnoxious. I'm talking five-hour phone conversations. They might as well start writing each other love letters. I swear everyone is madly in love this summer except for me.

• • •

Dear Abby,

You may not have been able to hold my hand, but you certainly got me through the flight home. I must have reread your letters a dozen times. The last one had me laughing, but also left me aching for you.

I hope you know I meant it. I'm no expert, but I know love doesn't free us from hurt. I'm sorry for the pain your parents caused you, but I don't believe you're destined to repeat their mistakes. You're not cursed. You're full of such goodness that I can't imagine you hurting anyone you love. I hope you know I never intend to hurt you either.

But I have to be transparent with you. Since the draft Blake's been more obstinate about marriage. He hasn't officially proposed, but we've had serious discussions. I've told him I'd like to wait until after law school, which he'd rather I delay, or as I suspect, put off altogether. The Reds are likely going to send him to play Single-A ball in Florida and he wants me to come as soon as I finish at Insley. I haven't told my parents. I don't think they'd understand. In fact, I haven't told anyone else except you.

You've probably realized by now, I'm in Fort Collins. I know I could technically call or text, but something about these letters feels like I'm closer to you than when we talk. You're not obligated to keep writing of course.

I'm playing with the collegiate summer series next month. I'm nervous. Coaches for the national team are supposed to be there. I wish you'd come. You'd make the national team easily and I always play better with you.

Love,
Kate

P.S. General studies is fine, as long as you graduate. And absolutely not. Try Marcus Aurelius for your midterm. I think you'll like him.

P.P.S. No summer love? I find this hard to believe knowing you . . .

P.P.P.S. Let them enjoy their phone calls. Love letters aren't for the faint of heart.

• • •

Kate,

Congratulations on being engaged to be engaged to a Cincinnati Red. He made the front page of the *Insley Inquirer*, which is quite a feat. There's a picture of you too, celebrating with him. I've sent a copy.

I think you're right to follow through with law school, and not because I selfishly would hate for you to go to Florida, but because you're too damn smart and have worked too hard to throw it away. Even if you are going to be Mrs. Blake Davis, you deserve to have dreams too. You're going to make an excellent lawyer. Besides, what does Aurelius say? "Your worth is no greater than your ambitions." You are as great as your ambitions, Kate, and worthy of pursuing all of them. If your parents or Blake can't understand that, then maybe they're not fully understanding you.

I know you'll play great in the summer series without me. Don't be nervous. Just breathe. Surrender. And try not to be so perfect.

Love,
Abby

P.S. I don't know if I'd associate love with my summer relations.

• • •

Dear Abby,

I'm counting the days until Insley. I'm excited to see you. I'm also in the worst hitting slump of my career. I think maybe I just wanted this one too badly. Nothing feels right. I'm tense. I'm distracted. I think knowing our last season is ahead, that the game ends here, is getting to me. I thought maybe if I made the national team, I might keep softball in my life a little longer. I remember that there's always another game, another chance, but time is moving faster than I'd like. Decisions about the future, about Blake, about law school. And what about you? I haven't even asked where you might end up or what you'll do after we graduate. I can hardly function on the field without you. How will I do the rest?

I hope you're well.

Love,
Kate

• • •

Dear Kate,

You haven't lost anything yet. I'm excited to see you too. Keep breathing.

Love,
Abby

P.S. I know I could've texted this, but it felt right to end the summer with one last letter.

SENIOR YEAR

Abby windsurfed as revenge. With Kate a confusing stitch in her heart, she vigorously took to work, and when Lonnie, a sandy-haired windsurfer who flirted with her at the shop daily, offered her lessons, she accepted. She missed surfing, missed her teammates and Isla, missed sex, but most of all, missed Kate. So, she spent long afternoons and sunlit evenings when she didn't have class or a shift with Lonnie on the river.

And then the first letter came.

Abby ditched Lonnie so abruptly that he showed up at the shop, certain something horrible had happened to her. When she shrugged, told him to relax, they were just having fun, he knocked over a rack of kayaks. One of the kayaks cracked a window, which would come out of her paycheck, but she didn't care. She was too busy composing a letter to Kate in her head. Too busy debating whether to sign it with *Sincerely, Abby* or *I miss you* or *Love, Abby.*

She floated between correspondences, an eye on the gorge, the gap between state lines reflective of the valley in her chest. When she wrote Kate, she wrote it to the canyon and the water too, alluding to love and jealousy, uncertain if it would return. But it did. Kate said *love* first. She also said *friends* and *can't* and *Blake.*

Abby rode the wind with abandon after that letter. She indulged the various tourists, offered pointers, agreed to give lessons to more than one attractive woman, agreed to drinks after, and sex next. It was better than her typical propensity for self-destruction. She preferred that Kate didn't know. Preferred that she continued signing her letters with love, even if it didn't include the ardor Abby wished for.

The week before Kate's return to Insley, Abby couldn't sleep. She anxiously considered what might be different between them. She worried she might have said too much, that Kate might keep distance from her after their conversations of wanting.

She soared across the water during her last work shift, leaning into the wind, muscles clenched against the sail, thighs and feet straining to balance. She cut across currents, picked up speed, launched off waves for a little air and a crash, just to climb up and do it again. She plowed water and splashed the windsurfers she recognized, rode until her legs and lungs burned.

Abby admired the view of Hood River's tiny city center crawling up the hills as she coasted in and dismounted with a plunge. She lugged her board and sail through the shallow waves, when a shout echoed from the pebbled shore.

"Do they really pay you to play all day?"

Kate's bare feet sank into the sand, chestnut tresses a flag in the wind, her eyes a glowing lighthouse from the breakers.

"What?" Abby fumbled her gear as she charged through the water, unable to move fast enough, like the end of a dream. "What are you doing here?"

Kate smiled. "I came a few days early. Mick told me you were at work and the shop told me you were here."

Abby dropped her board and stood gaping in her wetsuit. "I'm so glad to see you." She started for her, but then stopped. "I'd hug you, but I don't want to get you wet."

Kate flung herself into her arms anyway. Abby squeezed back, nestled into her shoulder, and fought the sting of tears.

"I missed you too," Kate whispered into her neck.

They chuckled at nothing in particular when they released each other, just giddiness on Abby's part, maybe the same on Kate's. Abby studied her for the familiar and for the changes that naturally emerged during time apart. More freckles peppered Kate's cheeks, her chestnut waves a little longer, face a little firmer. She could have sworn her cerulean gaze deepened in her absence, richer and gentler, but lively. Loving. Or maybe Abby had just missed her so much that she projected everything that long-awaited look made her feel.

"You cut your hair," Kate said.

Abby snapped out of her trance and raked a hand through her drenched locks. "Oh yeah. I got tired of messing with it in the water."

"I like it." Kate cleared her throat. "Seems like a rough summer gig."

"The worst." Abby winked. She hefted up her board and sail and led Kate to the grassy slope bordering the waves. Her heart thundered, but it didn't unsteady her. In fact, it jolted as if knocked back into place, as if the entire world was knocked back into place. The gorge became more gorgeous, the sherbet sunset sweeter, even the seagulls sang instead of squawked.

"You're pretty good." Kate nodded out at the water.

"I had a lot of time to practice."

Abby unzipped her wetsuit, shimmied it down to her waist, and let the wind dry her in her bikini top. Kate's eyes roved across her skin, pausing on her right shoulder blade. She traced the tattoo with a finger and Abby gasped, her shudder and raised skin surely noticeable to Kate, but she didn't retreat. "I didn't know you had this."

"It's for my mom." Abby stared down at the grass. "Honestly, I don't even remember getting it. How fucked-up is that?"

Kate carefully outlined the sun pressed in ink. "I thought of you so often," she whispered.

Her fingers left the tattoo and crawled upward, exploring the back of Abby's neck. She closed her eyes, sighed at the touch, then simultaneously resented the touch, roiled, and writhed at the impossibility of those perfect fingers.

"How's Blake?" Abby asked.

Kate withdrew and cleared her throat again. "He's good. He's with his new team in Florida."

"Good." Abby searched Kate's eyes, but they darted away from her. "I'm happy for you. Getting married and all."

"I wish you wouldn't say that."

"Why?"

"Because it's not like that. Nothing's changed." Kate frowned.

Abby bit her lip. They eyed the horizon, the water reflecting every shift in the sky, waves topped white like whipped cream on a sundae.

"This year is going to be excruciating, isn't it?" she asked, certain that Kate knew what she meant.

"No." She smiled. "It's going to be the best one yet."

"Maybe for you." Abby chuckled at Kate's ability to still sparkle in her shade.

"For you too," she said. "It's our last one together. I mean, you know, as a team. Though it's seriously messing with my head. I don't know what's wrong with me."

"There's nothing wrong with you." Abby stood and offered Kate a hand. "Want to get dinner? I'm supposed to meet Mick and Haley. It'll be nice to have you, so I'm not third wheeling with two horny lovebirds."

Kate laughed as Abby helped her up. "Do I have a choice?"

Abby embraced her again, firmer than before. "I miss our letters," she whispered.

Kate rubbed her back. "Why? Isn't this better?"

Abby released her. "Yeah, but there was something safe about writing. It doesn't seem right to say those things here, does it?"

"Not quite." Kate tilted her head to the side, her chin quaking just once. "But it doesn't mean it's not still true."

Abby nodded. "Let me put this gear away. I can drive us." She turned and sank at the confirmation she didn't want. Summer letters were over, and the stamp of love, gone with them.

After her fifth straight game without a hit, Kate accepted she'd fallen into a slump. It'd taken root over the summer, when she returned to Washington to finish a few final tournaments with her club team. She'd hit into an easy out nearly every at bat, squandering any shot at an invitation to try out for Team USA. She'd hoped returning to Insley, her safe place, surrounded by her favorite people, might cure it, but during their exhibition games that fall she struck out a dozen times.

"Hutchins!" Coach Whitley waved her over to the home dugout after practice. "Step into my office."

Most of the team had cleared out, except for the usual suspects who always left in a pack. Jill, Abby, and Mick tangled with each other in a typical Three Stooges routine, half running, half wrestling each other around the bases in a game that no one quite understood the rules of, while T.K. talked loudly on her phone in right field.

"What's up, Coach?" Kate asked.

"Just wondering how to harness all that energy for a national title." Coach Whitley chuckled as the stooges tripped over each other. "How are you, Kate?"

"I'm good."

Coach Whitley narrowed her gaze like she didn't believe her. "School's good?"

"Yeah. Yeah, just working on my law school applications." Kate swallowed. It wasn't just the applications, but the internship and letters of recommendation too, and while her LSAT scores were above average, Berkeley was far from guaranteed.

"And everything else? The boyfriend, home—"

"All good," Kate said, growing impatient. "What's this about?"

Coach Whitley frowned. "I know you're struggling up at the plate and I'm just wondering if something else might be going on."

"Nothing's going on." Kate adjusted her visor, unable to stop her gaze from settling on Abby. The real reason for her slump. Her first terrible outing, her first game of strikeouts that she couldn't shake, followed Abby's letter. The one with the haunting postscript: *I don't know if I'd associate love with my summer relations.*

Kate contemplated the line, felt ill over it, for the rest of the summer. What did relations mean? Was Abby dating someone? Was she sleeping with someone? But she couldn't bring herself to ask. Not in her letter back. Not when she saw her coasting on the river like she had wings, controlling the wind and waves. Not when her knees wobbled as she landed in her arms or when she glimpsed her bare stomach and the rise of her breasts that she usually turned from. She didn't know desire could be so exhilarating, excruciating, or embarrassing, but mostly humbling. No wonder she couldn't hit.

"I'm trying. I really am," Kate said.

"I know and I'm not trying to punish you. I want to help." Coach Whitley sighed. "Which is why this weekend, I'm going to have Palamino hit leadoff."

Kate snapped her head back to her. "W-what?"

"It's just for the weekend. I'm shifting you to the middle of the lineup. It's less pressure and it'll give you a fair go against these pitchers. Get your confidence up." She patted Kate's shoulder. "It's just for the last few games of fall. They're just practice games, really." Coach Whitley nodded at her. "You're still the captain of this team."

It was a new title, one unanimously given to her after tryouts. Even Mick, who was a strong contender as their catcher, stepped aside.

"I know there's a lot of pressure on you—on the field and off it. You're doing exceptional and if you need someone to talk to, I'm here."

Kate nodded at her, appreciative but certain she wouldn't take her up on the offer. "Thank you." She shifted back to the field to hide her trembling lower lip, and the unshakeable sense that no matter how hard she worked for it, the game she loved so much was destined to slip from her fingers. And the person she loved so much, the one unwittingly responsible for her recent failures, was destined to too.

"I'm moving her to third base," Coach Whitley said.

Kate's eyes bulged. "Who? What?"

"Cruz. Now that Seaborn's gone, a waste of that arm of hers at second," Coach Whitley said.

"Did you tell her?" Kate's heart sank lower than she thought possible. No more turning two with Abby. No more moving as one. No more of that perfect harmony, in which they'd found so much more than a game.

"She wanted me to tell you before I made it official." Coach Whitley pursed her lips. "Did you know she could've gone back up to Division I this year?"

Kate shook her head.

"Half a dozen programs offered to pick her up and she chose to stay here. Hard to believe after last year's rough start, huh?" Coach Whitley smiled as she put her hands in her pockets and backed away to leave. "I have no doubt that's thanks to you. You did a good thing, Hutchins."

Kate lingered, too stunned to reply. While it wasn't a solution to her slump, she found a sliver of hope in those words. Abby chose to stay. And while it was likely for the team, and for Isla, and to finish her degree, Kate also knew it was for her too.

THE SENIOR CAMPING TRIP

The clouds broke in November, casting weak light through the orange and burgundy leaves. Abby leaned against Jill's mud-splattered SUV, smoking a cigarette as she studied the sky. Not a single cloud. She grumbled. The perfect forecast squandered any chance of canceling the senior camping trip. While she didn't have anything against her teammates or Coach Whitley, sleeping outside wasn't her style.

"Make yourself useful." Jill chucked her a sleeping bag.

Abby caught it and groaned. Kate staggered out of the blue house garage behind her with additional gear. After dumping it at the car, she plucked the cigarette from Abby's mouth.

"Hey." Abby scowled. "That's my last one in civilization. Maybe ever. Have you seen *The Blair Witch Project*?"

"No." Kate squashed it beneath her hiking boot. "Are you really afraid of camping?"

She shook her head. "I'm not afraid."

"You are, aren't you?" Kate grinned.

Abby smiled back, her cheeks reaching for the corners of her eyes. "I am not."

"Can you two stop flirting and help me?" Jill grunted as she maneuvered gear into her trunk.

Kate blushed and started loading sleeping bags. Abby frantically hefted up a cooler, thankful for the distraction of T.K.'s Mercedes swerving to a crooked park job along the curb.

"Please tell me we're not actually doing this." T.K. stomped over to join them.

"It's a tradition," Kate said.

"I don't need to sleep in the woods and squat piss to bond with you."

"It's one night, T.K., I don't want to either," Abby said.

"There better be cell service." T.K. tossed her designer bag to Kate before plopping into the passenger seat and slamming her door.

"Don't tell her," Jill muttered. "Okay, let's get going! Mick! Enough already!"

While everyone else packed the car, Mick lingered on the front steps, kissing Haley.

"I can't deal with this. It's not even cute anymore," Jill said. "You two get her. Sixty seconds and I'm leaving."

Abby and Kate chuckled. They observed the make-out session, leaning against the car as dried leaves clattered across the pavement.

"Have you ever liked someone that much?" Kate asked.

Abby's mouth quirked. "Not yet." She glanced at Kate. "You?"

"No." Kate shook her head but smiled.

Abby nudged her shoulder. "I'll get her."

Jill blasted her horn. "Sadie Louise McMechan, I swear to God if you don't stop sucking face, I'm going to leave you here!"

"Who the fuck is Sadie? Can I stay behind too?" T.K. asked. "I'll suck someone's face."

"I'm afraid that's not all you'd suck."

Abby bounded up the steps and grabbed Mick, who uttered a few final sweet nothings to Haley as if leaving for war and not twenty-four hours in the woods.

They rolled down the windows and blasted music on the drive to Lost Lake. The road winded up toward Mount Hood, bordered on either side by trees, jade and gold rushing by as Abby let the air slice through her fingers. A near perfect morning. One that still didn't compare to Kate's thigh brushing hers, stripes of light painting her cheeks, putting sparkles in her irises and smile.

Coach Whitley and her right hand, Coach Ackers, met them at the campsite, a dirt clearing nestled in ferns and overgrown brush. Jill and Kate took charge of setting up while T.K. raised her phone to the legion of trees and paced for service. Abby cursed and fumbled over the tent poles, though she considered it well worth it every time Kate's hand swooped against hers.

The coaches led them on a hike around the lake and up the butte. Mountains surrounded them on all sides, their visages mirrored in the water. Abby hung back with Mick, eyeing Kate ahead. She wrestled with the usual, expected longing, but today it was enough. In this slice of wonder, simple nearness felt like transcendence. Plus, Kate's ass looked fantastic in those hiking shorts. Abby bit her lip as she stared and tripped over a root.

Mick laughed and caught her by the hood of her sweatshirt. "Nice view back here, huh?"

Abby jerked away. "Thanks."

Mick raised her eyebrows as they trudged along. "I'm onto you."

"What are you talking about?" she asked, swatting at a bug buzzing near her ear. "I'm getting eaten alive."

"I'm talking about Hutch," Mick whispered.

Abby watched the group ahead, slowing to keep her distance. "What about her?"

"How long have you been in love with her?"

She kicked at the dirt. "I'm not in love with her."

"At first, I thought you were just giving her shit, but then I realized you were flirting. You're always together, always looking at each other."

"Coach partnered us together."

"You even started doing those awful morning runs with her. There's no way your chain-smoking ass is doing that voluntarily. Even Haley notices."

"Oh, well, fuck, if she notices it, then it must be true." Abby swatted another bug. "You're just so blinded by love that you think everyone else around you is too."

"You two are obsessed with each other."

"Shut up." Abby hissed. "I'm going to shove you off when we get to the top."

"You okay back there?" Coach Whitley shouted.

"All good!" Abby waved. Kate glanced over her shoulder at them. Abby growled into Mick's ear. "Kate is with Blake. I'm not in love with her and she's not in love with me."

Mick chuckled. "Well, I think she has a huge crush on you."

Suddenly a figure launched out of the woods, roared violently, and clenched Abby's shoulders. She jumped back and screamed, Mick cowering next to her. Abby raised a fist to strike when Jill's obnoxious laughter erupted, arms shielding her face.

"It's just me! It's me!" Jill cackled.

"Fuck!" Abby lowered her fist.

Jill doubled over, tears in her eyes as she hooted. T.K., Kate, and the coaches snickered too. Abby yanked Mick off the ground where she'd dropped to the fetal position.

"You suck," Mick said to Jill.

"I'm sorry." Jill wheezed. "Hutch told me that Cruz is afraid of the woods, and I couldn't help it."

Abby's mouth dropped. "I'm not afraid."

"You seemed pretty scared." Kate smiled.

"You almost punched me in the face," Jill said.

"I did warn you she'd do that."

"Okay, ladies, let's go!" Coach Whitley ordered.

Abby shoved Jill before bounding to catch up with Kate. Undeterred by her conversation with Mick, Abby prodded her sides, rousing a yelp. She tickled fingers up her back and arms as Kate squirmed, the sliver of contact, the sweep of fingers, a nibble for her larger hunger.

"Did you tell her to do that?" Abby chuckled.

"No, no." Kate laughed. "I swear."

"You're proving my point!" Mick yelled.

"What point?" Kate asked breathlessly.

Abby stopped tickling, glared at Mick, and mouthed a clear expletive. Kate didn't notice, or at least pretended she didn't as she hiked ahead. Abby stared after her, wondering how long she could keep up the charade everyone seemed to see through.

They stoked a fire and assembled s'mores when the moon and stars emerged. After hours of team building and setting goals, the conversation swerved from talk of softball to talk of summer. Coach Whitley, usually uninterested in their personal lives, asked about Mick's new girlfriend at T.K.'s behest. Jill shared her enduring relationship with Dylan Farrelly, a cross-country-running accounting major who was as goofy and redheaded as she was. Jokes about their future ginger children piled on. When it got to Kate and Blake, Abby's back tightened. She glared into the fire, didn't partake as T.K. and Jill screeched about the prospect of a wedding, and shoved a s'more into her mouth.

"What about you, Cruz?" T.K. asked.

Abby shook her head, cheeks stuffed with an aggrieved mouthful. "Not much to tell."

Mick snickered. "More like too much to tell."

T.K.'s mouth dropped. "Oh, now I have to know."

"There's nothing to know," Abby said, gaze darting to Kate, who stared at her through the fire.

"Let's just say people weren't only interested in her windsurfing lessons," Mick said. Abby smacked Mick's roasting stick, sending her golden marshmallow into the flames. "That one was perfect, dick!"

"I didn't know you were giving lessons." Kate frowned.

"She wasn't certified to, but don't tell the tourists that," Jill said. "Not that I think they cared, or that they were actually going to her for lessons."

"Honestly, I'm impressed with your ingenuity, Cruz," T.K. said.

"I'm impressed you know how to use ingenuity in a sentence, T.K.," Abby said, desperate to change the subject and hide her escapades from the one person they might hurt. "Tell us about Spain."

"Oh, where to begin?" T.K. threw her head back. "It started with Andres in Barcelona. I thought he was the most beautiful man I'd ever seen in my life. He walked right up to me and called me an angel. Best sex ever. I'm talking hours."

Coach Whitley stood. "Okay, it might be time for us to say good night."

"No, but Coach, there's more. He took me to a yacht party and introduced me to Valentina. A goddess. I kissed her all night, until her husband, Felipe, showed up. He's a professional polo player. He wasn't even mad. It was my first threesome."

"Okay, that's enough," Coach Whitley said as the girls shrieked with laughter. "We're going to bed. Don't stay up too late."

"Good night!" they called.

With the coaches gone, Jill sighed in relief and dug in her pocket. "Thank God. I thought they'd never leave. Good work, T.K."

"All of that was true. Valentina did this amazing thing with her hips where she rolled and put pressure on my—"

"Okay, enough." Jill revealed a brownie wrapped in cellophane. "You all down?"

"Hell yes." Abby smiled. "I'm not sleeping out here sober."

Jill unwrapped the edible and passed out a few pieces, pausing when she reached Kate. "You want to, Hutch?"

Kate bit her lip. "It's uh, pot, right?"

Jill nodded.

"Have you ever gotten high?" T.K. asked.

"No." Kate shook her head. "We signed a contract to not."

"Oh, please. This shit is legal."

Abby leaned in and lowered her voice. "Don't make her do it if she doesn't want to."

Kate ignored her. "It won't make me feel crazy, right? It doesn't last too long?"

"You'll just feel relaxed. It's nice." T.K. broke off a fifth of the brownie. "Here."

"Give her a smaller piece," Abby said.

"I can handle it." Kate glared.

She narrowed her brow back. "Fine."

"Bon appétit." Jill grinned.

Abby gritted her teeth to resist stopping Kate. Her eyes still said as much to her. And Kate's eyes responded in defiance, brow raised as she took her bite. Abby grumbled under her breath, and while she couldn't stop Kate, she could stop herself. She nibbled a crumb of brownie, then covertly slid the larger remaining portion into her jacket.

They poked at the fire and fell into low conversation as they awaited the edible's effects.

T.K. groaned. "I don't think I took enough. Do you have more?"

"No, just be patient. You're lucky I thought to bring any," Jill said.

"Fine." T.K. huffed and peered up at the sky. The others followed suit. "Is that Orion's Belt?"

"No," Mick said.

"Is it the Big Dipper?"

"No."

"Is it a UFO?"

"Yes," Jill said.

"Really?" Kate asked.

Jill sat up. "I mean, fuck, there's so many out there." Her eyes expanded to saucers. "As far as we know, all the stars are UFOs. And maybe the UFOs are actually stars."

Abby scoffed. "What?"

"The government wants to hide aliens from us. Best way to do it is in plain sight." Jill tapped her temple.

Mick snorted. "They're just stars."

"But you don't know. Have you been up there?" Jill asked.

"I just know what I know."

"But why?"

"Because I do. Don't fuck with me right now."

"I love you guys," T.K. sighed, throwing her arms around Kate's and Mick's shoulders.

Abby chuckled and poked at the fire.

"I'm just saying, how do you really know that they're stars and not UFOs?" Jill pressed.

Mick huffed. "Because I went to school. Because that's what we learned."

"Brainwashing!" Jill shouted.

"Keep it down," Abby said, glancing over at the coaches' tent.

"It's just always been that way," Mick said.

"Since when?" Jill asked.

"Since always, I don't fucking know. Since the history of education, Shupe, you stoner, conspiracy theory idiot."

"Socrates," Kate said.

The four of them swiveled their heads to her.

"What?"

"The history of education. Socrates would've been one of the earliest teachers, right?" She paused, glassily watching the fire, shoving a marshmallow into her already full mouth. "Or I guess the Egyptians, maybe? They had scribes. The Babylonians had libraries . . ."

T.K. and Jill snorted. Abby grinned, smitten as always.

"God, you're a nerd, Hutch," Mick said. Abby raised her roasting stick to hit Mick's, but she slyly moved it out of the way. "Knew that would get you wound up."

"Shut up." Abby blushed.

"I don't feel anything. I don't think pot works on me." Kate ate another marshmallow, her cheeks as plump as a squirrel's.

T.K. grinned. "I think it's working."

"How do you know?" she asked around a mouthful.

"How many of those have you had?"

Kate looked down as she tore another marshmallow in half, prepared to stuff it in her mouth. She shrugged, and they hooted uncontrollably. Kate chuckled along until they reached the point of tears.

"Go to bed!" Coach Whitley yelled from her tent.

While the scolding intensified their wheezing laughter, Kate stiffened. Her eyes stretched wide. "Coach knows."

Jill looked around. "Knows what?"

"She knows I'm high." Kate covered her mouth. "What do I do?"

"You're fine." T.K. patted her shoulder.

"I think she's really mad at me," Kate whispered.

Abby stifled a laugh. "You're just paranoid. It's okay."

"I'm paranoid? I'm not paranoid. Why do you think I'm paranoid?"

Mick snorted and buried her face in her hands. The harder they tried not to, the more they cackled. Except for Kate, who bit her thumb and clutched the marshmallow bag.

"What do we do?" Kate walked around the firepit, stumbling over a log on her way to Abby, who steadied her. "Am I stoned? What do you feel like? Do you know how I feel? You always know."

"I think maybe we should go to bed," Abby said. "Everybody."

"I'm going to watch for UFOs," Jill said, staring at the treetops.

T.K. raised her eyebrows at Abby. "Cruz, let's ditch these losers and go skinny-dipping."

"Jesus, no." Abby grabbed Kate's hand. "Come on, you'll feel better if you sleep it off."

She used a flashlight to navigate to their small tent, Kate clumsily bumping behind her. It felt strange to not be the one completely plastered. Usually, it was Kate with her wits about, watching over Abby. She didn't mind the reversal.

"Okay, come on, get in your sleeping bag," Abby said once in the tent, but Kate just plopped on her sleeping mat.

"No. I'm good."

Abby shoved the sleeping bag at her. "You're going to freeze out here."

"No, it's like, tight, you know, like a . . . a . . . a . . . bug thing . . . What am I saying?"

"I don't know."

Kate flopped down on her pillow. "Do you still hate camping?"

"No."

"Are you still afraid?" Kate snorted. "I'll protect you."

"Shhhhhh." Abby put a finger to her lips.

Kate smiled against it. "No, you shhhhh."

"Hutch, shut up!" Mick yelled from outside.

"You shut up!" Kate shouted back.

"Hey, hey, stop." Abby covered her mouth with her hand, her lower gut waking at the brief contact, Kate's amusement, and their proximity.

"Okay, okay." Kate laughed softly. "Oh, you're mad."

Abby smirked. She hovered over Kate, inches away in the flashlight beam. "I'm not. Just keep it down."

"You're so mad at me," Kate whispered.

"Stop." Abby chuckled, pulsing in the worst places. Her throat, her stomach, her groin.

Kate's mouth dropped. "Oh my gosh, are you high? You're so high."

Abby laughed, unable to control herself. Kate giggled too, her breath warm on her neck, her body brushing into Abby's. It took astounding willpower to not press back into her.

The tent shook as a softball hit it. "Shut up!" Mick shouted.

They reined in their hysterics, simmered down to a hiss, and then finally panted for air. Abby struggled to breathe against the throbbing, her elbow propping her above Kate on the pillow next to hers.

"I feel funny," Kate said.

Abby stared at her lips. "You'll be okay."

"Do you ever?" Kate cupped her cheek, traced her thumb at the corner of her mouth. "Feel funny?"

"Yeah." Abby squeezed her eyes shut.

"Do you still love me?"

Abby sighed, a sob unexpectedly bubbling in her throat. She muffled it, turned her face beneath Kate's hand, and deposited a kiss on her palm.

Kate grasped Abby's other cheek so that she held her face. "I love you too," she whispered.

A kiss waited on the end of the confession, pleading like so many times before. Abby swallowed it with the rest of what she wouldn't allow herself, determined to protect Kate, to not take what wasn't hers, especially in a haze of drugs and dizzying closeness. "We should sleep."

Kate's chin crumpled but she nodded.

Abby unzipped their sleeping bags and draped them over their bodies. She clicked off the flashlight, inconsolably aroused. "Good night."

Kate grasped her hand and Abby froze. She eased into her until they were spooning, and Abby couldn't help but move like they'd always done it. She wrapped her arms around Kate's chest and nestled her nose into her neck. Her heart quickened, the curve of Kate's backside between her hips, pushing her to the edge of giving in. She trembled as she inhaled the spot behind Kate's ear, before placing a careful kiss there. Kate exhaled into the dark.

"Is this okay?" Abby whispered.

"Don't go." Kate clutched her hand and shivered. "I feel like I'm going to float away."

Abby held her tighter. "I got you. You're just high."

"No." Kate brushed her lips to Abby's fingers. A slight second of contact that her breath hitched at. "It's just you."

Abby didn't dare break their enmeshed bodies. She already dreaded the morning, aware that this might be the closest they'd ever get. A blessing and a curse. A miserable pleasure that she sank into as she closed her eyes.

Kate woke to a throb so powerful that a moan gushed out of her like steam from a boiling kettle. And she was boiling, her skin burning with fever. She assumed she must be dreaming, eyes still shut, as the tingle between her legs overpowered everything else. Its demand for release had her instinctually thrusting. When friction met the itch with a pleasant wave of calm, she sighed, only to realize that she wasn't dreaming. She flashed open her eyes, full consciousness hitting like a fire hose, as she discovered the warmth wasn't a fever, but Abby wrapped around her, and the euphoric friction came from Abby's thigh between her legs.

Kate stiffened and peered up at her. She'd slept nestled in Abby's neck, locked in her arms, legs knitted together. Abby didn't stir, lips slightly parted as she breathed. They'd slept next to each other before during road games, but never like this. Never close enough for Kate to detect the tinge of cardamom and salt from her skin or to relish its heat.

She scooted away, so close to climax that it hurt. But before she could completely detach, Abby's arms tightened around her.

"Stay," she murmured.

Her stomach somersaulted. She prayed it didn't mean Abby had been awakened by Kate humping her leg. She wished to disappear when fingers traced between her shoulder blades. Kate's lungs released enough for her to draw in the chilly mountain air. And Abby's caress, more sweet than sexual, inspired her to dissolve into her while she reflected on how they ended up in a tangle of limbs.

She remembered being high. She remembered getting high because Abby thought she wouldn't and shouldn't. But she wanted some sort of vengeance, a defense against the anguish of Abby spending the summer having sex with tourists. The crushing truth that Abby wasn't hers and she wasn't Abby's.

Abby muttered incoherently and rolled to her back. She kept hold of her as Kate rested her head on her chest and draped an arm across her stomach. Abby's heartbeat echoed in her ear. Her chest oscillated as if on a sprint, and Kate wondered if it meant Abby was as turned on as she was. Just the prospect of Abby's arousal rekindled Kate's, and she sighed against it.

"Did you sleep all right?" Abby asked.

"Yeah." Kate swallowed.

"You were funny last night." Abby put her cheek on Kate's forehead.

"Sorry," Kate whispered.

"You feel okay now?"

"Just a little lightheaded."

"Me too."

Abby's hand stopped stroking Kate's back and shifted lower, rested on her hip, just above her ass. Abby turned so they were flush. Her eyes dilated and aimed at her mouth. Her lips coasted nearer. Kate clenched a fistful of her sweatshirt. She didn't care about Blake or her family or God. Just those lips. She panted, prepared to jolt up to meet Abby, to end the ache, when the tent shook.

"Wake up!" T.K.'s shadow hovered outside. "I literally can't go another minute without hot water or service."

Kate jerked away from Abby, who groaned, "Fuck."

"You guys, come on!" T.K. kicked the tent before stalking away.

"Are you okay?" Abby asked her.

Kate threw on her coat and tripped out of the tent. She hurried from the campsite, dodging trees and other campers, gasping, and staggering until she reached the lake. Fog drifted over the motionless water. Tears welled in Kate's eyes. She berated herself for how far she let it go. For how close she came to betraying Blake and everything she'd been taught. Her stomach lurched. Kate leaned against a tree trunk and gagged. Nothing came up. Just panic and a few hiccups. She pressed her forehead to the bark.

"You okay?"

Kate whipped around to find Jill. "I'm fine," she said.

Jill frowned as she wandered closer. "What's going on?"

"Nothing. I'm fine."

"You don't seem fine."

"It's probably just from the weed." Kate didn't know if that was possible, but she didn't care, and was thankful that Jill simply went along with it.

"Yeah, probably," she whispered before embracing her.

Kate sniffled into her shoulder. The enormity of her fear shrank her even further among the trees. Jill rocked her for the brief minute it took to recollect herself.

"You want to talk about it?" she asked.

"No," Kate said.

Jill's eyes met her with sympathy, and maybe a semblance of understanding. Part of her wished she knew. Wished that maybe Jill had the answer. But she knew with unbearable weight in her heart that no one else could help her. She prayed on the walk back to the campsite, but stopped halfway through, no longer sure that God would answer.

WINTER BREAK

Kate seamlessly slipped back into farm life when she returned home for Christmas. She woke up to darkness, bundled in layers, tugged on her barn coat and boots, and clomped through the fog to the chicken coop. Since first grade, she'd tended to the family's flock. All the Hutchins children helped maintain the farm, her mother assigning every child a task when they came of age. Kate preferred the chickens over the family dairy business, though she'd milked her fair share of cows and helped deliver more than one calf.

As she gathered brown and speckled eggs, bidding good morning to her favorite chickens, she breathed in and out to the count of four, narrowly avoiding hyperventilating as she'd done every day since returning. On the bus ride north for winter break, a premonition seized her. Well, not exactly a premonition, but the unshakeable sense that something horrible awaited. Some might call it anxiety, but Kate, for reasons she couldn't explain, believed that danger lurked at home. The danger being that her mother and father would take one look at her and detect her impure thoughts, her lust, the tent, and Abby.

She longed for her in the frost, not much different from the coolness between them since the camping trip. Like so many times before, they never fully addressed the blurred boundaries of that night.

"I'm sorry about the tent," Abby said at the next practice.

"We don't have to talk about it." Kate shook her head and repeated the phrase she told herself whenever she thought she might spiral into panic. "I was disoriented from the night before."

Abby nodded. "Right. I was mostly asleep." She bit her lip. "We're good though?"

"Of course."

After that, the only time they allowed each other a glimpse away from practice or studying was at the blue house, with their friends between them. Abby didn't flirt, didn't wink, didn't make any pointed jokes that might rouse Kate's temper, and did everything else at a respectable distance. It left Kate wondering which was worse—this new, sterile, safe version of them or facing the consequences of what she wanted.

She white-knuckled her way through Christmas with the secret, the danger, lurking inside. And while she successfully hid it, she suffered just as deeply. She didn't dare say Abby's name, let alone call and risk someone eavesdropping on one of their conversations, finding her overly joyous, flirtatious, the pieces aligning to reveal the truth. She sent a few texts instead, then hid her phone away, surviving off rations.

A few days before New Year's, her father, Ray, drove them to the baseball field. The same field she'd spent her childhood longing to play on instead of watching from the stands while he coached. Kate still enjoyed the alone time with him—a rarity as the middle of seven. She credited him for always finding small ways to make her feel seen.

"It's a blessed day to play God's game." Ray smiled at her, the same way he did his players. He said the phrase so often that after twenty years Eastern Washington Bible College painted it on the home dugout.

He lugged out a few buckets of balls, set up behind a net at the pitcher's mound, and tossed Kate batting practice. She swung with abandon. She didn't care about form. She simply unleashed. The last months of her hitting slump lingered, in fact, only seemed to worsen with her guilt, but away from Insley, she let herself go.

"Watch that back shoulder, Katie. Good." Ray's mild, patient instruction didn't distract her. She nodded along, adjusted, and roped another ball. "Don't forget the hips. Perfect."

She crushed at least fifty softballs, sending the neon spheres to the frozen outfield. When they ran out, Ray pitched her baseballs, and Kate chopped at those too. By the end of the session, she shivered under a sheen of cold sweat.

"So much for a slump." Ray threw an arm around her on the walk back to his truck.

"It's easier out here." Kate sighed.

"It's the same everywhere," Ray said as he tapped her forehead. "Remember, 'It's 90 percent mental. The other half is physical.'"

He chuckled at the Yogi Berra wisdom he'd quoted hundreds of times, and Kate laughed too. But on the ride home, the respite receded. The secret knotted her throat so tight she nearly choked.

"What's on your mind, Katie?" Ray asked.

She met his eyes, duplicates of her own. "What do you mean?"

He shrugged. "We haven't had much time to talk."

Kate assured herself he wasn't referring to her secret, even though she almost wished he would. Here, alone in his truck where they'd had countless talks about God and softball and life, she decided to untangle the cord if only to breathe. "I've been a little confused lately."

"About what?

She wrung her hands as yellow farmland rolled by her window. "My friend Mick has a girlfriend." Kate hated the stereotypical "friend with a problem" angle, but it was at least truthful. "They're really happy together. I'm having a hard time understanding why it's wrong."

Ray nodded. He spoke with the solemn, methodical assuredness of a preacher. "Have you turned to scripture?"

"Yes."

"And what has that told you?"

Kate bit her lip. "That it's unnatural."

"It's sin."

"But so much of that is in the Old Testament. Some biblical scholars believe the interpretation from the original Greek in the New Testament doesn't completely line up—"

"It's God's word." Ray frowned. "This is why I worry about you and law school."

Kate's gaze widened. "What?"

"I worry you'll turn away from scripture, from the church, and seek answers outside of God. You're confused because you're doing that now."

"I thought it's okay to have questions. You've always said that."

"Well, this question has a clear answer."

"It's not a sin. It's part of her. It's who she loves." Kate's pulse filled her ears.

"Just because it makes someone happy doesn't make it okay in the eyes of the Church." Ray narrowed his brow. "Is there another reason this has you so worked up?"

Kate shook her head. "No."

He patted her shoulder. She nearly jerked away, crushed, despite predicting this response. Something in her naïvely hoped he wouldn't be the one to let her down.

"Pray on it," he said. "And pray for your friend."

The next day, as if doubling down, Ray chose a reading to emphasize his point at breakfast. " 'The Creator made them male and female and said for this reason a man will leave his father and mother and be united to his wife, and the two will become one flesh.' "

Kate's mother, Beth, beamed at her, but she wouldn't understand why until later. Instead, she fidgeted under Ray's gaze, convinced that he knew the truth.

That's why she dawdled in the chicken coop as snow flurried on New Year's Eve. When she finished tending to the chickens, she joined her brothers with the cows and horses. She filled troughs and distributed hay, avoiding the house as long as possible.

They finished their chores ahead of the incoming storm, hauling extra wood on their way back. Kate stomped chicken shit and mud from her boots before entering the kitchen, where a surprise awaited. A surprise of the most unwelcome sort.

"Morning, Katie." Blake grinned from where he sat with her parents at the table.

"Blake." Kate barely had enough sense to hug him back when he embraced her. "What are you doing here?"

"I thought we could ring in the New Year together." He pecked her slackened lips.

Ray and Beth, who rarely allowed suitors at the house, nodded happily. She ran a hand down Blake's broad chest, confirming reality. With her parents glowing behind him, she understood this was it. This was the danger lurking at home.

"I'm happy you're here." Kate didn't even sound like herself. She raked fingers through her tangled hair. "I should clean up. I smell like manure."

Blake smiled. "I'll wait out here."

She scrubbed viciously in the shower, contemplated her phone when she got out, willing a text or a call from Abby, pleading for a sign. But it didn't come. She spent the afternoon at Blake's side, cringing every time her mother or sisters flashed her a knowing smile, like she'd won the lottery.

At dinner, he held her hand beneath the table, the massive Hutchins clan in attendance. Kate's phone rang with a call from Abby, but she ignored it. After dessert, they watched the countdown to midnight. Despite the late hour, everyone stayed, hovering as if excited to mark the New Year, but that wasn't what they lingered for. When the ball dropped and fireworks popped, Blake got down on a knee with a ring.

"Katherine Ruth Hutchins, will you marry me?"

Kate's phone vibrated in her pocket. She knew it was Abby and as she stared at the diamond, she couldn't shake how desperately she wanted to answer. She confronted one of life's magic moments and only thought of one person. Not the one in front of her. The one that long ago dug a hole in her heart and nested there. She wasn't Abby's and Abby wasn't hers, but Kate already belonged to her. Too much to belong to another.

"Kate?" Blake whispered.

Her chin quivered. She just had to say yes. Say yes and claim her ticket out. Say yes and end the confusion. Accept being locked out, take her seat in the stands. A reasonable second choice. Say yes and make every person in the room happy. Every person except her.

"I need a minute." Kate staggered backward.

Blake followed her into the kitchen and grabbed her arm. "Kate, come on."

"I told you I don't want to get married." She hyperventilated. "I want to wait until . . ."

"After law school," he finished. "That's three years from now!"

Kate pulled away. "I'm sorry. This isn't what I want."

Her parents appeared behind him in the kitchen's entryway. Her mother covered her face, tears brimming in her eyes. Kate charged out the back door, into the snow, and Blake ran after her.

"What about what I want?" he asked. "Please, Katie. I want to marry you, but three years is too long to wait."

Kate turned and met him under a fluorescent floodlight, sneakers sinking into the snow. Delicate flakes of frost floated onto her lashes and melted on her sweater.

"Why? Why does it matter if we're together?" she asked. When he raised his eyebrows, her sympathy retreated. "I'm not getting married just so we can have sex."

"Don't say that. It's not why I'm proposing."

"Then what's the rush?"

"I mean, don't you want it? Don't you want me too? Don't you want to be my wife?" Blake stepped closer, his throat bobbing. "Come to Florida. You can go to law school there."

"And what if you get called up or traded? Then we're back to where we started."

"Well, then you can transfer, or we do long distance, but at least we'll be married!" Blake threw his head back. "It's like you continually find reasons to avoid it!"

"Because I can't!" Kate sucked in a ragged breath. The cold air cut her lungs, nipped her cheeks, but she soldiered on. "I can't. I'm sorry."

Blake's big brown eyes, ever obliging, guileless, overflowing with goodness, reached out from a rising flood. "No. No, we can make this work."

Kate's bottom lip wobbled. His tears threatened to reinforce the last thread between them. Kate didn't know if she had the strength to sever it, but it made her more aware of its flimsiness. Blake was a thread. Even if she stayed, it'd never patch the trench.

"I don't love you like I should. Not enough to get married," Kate whimpered. "Can't you see that? I should be ecstatic. Every other woman would be ecstatic. But I'm not. Because I don't want this. I'm so sorry, Blake."

"No. Please." His voice cracked. "I'll wait. I'll wait, okay?"

"You don't need to wait for me. You can't." Kate rubbed his shoulders, hated the sobs wrenching from his chest, hated the shame stalking her no matter what she did. "We'd be unhappy. You deserve more than that."

She hugged him, shut her eyes, and for the first time since the camping trip, willed herself to finish a full prayer. A prayer for Blake. A prayer for forgiveness. A prayer for it to be over.

Blake's proposal at her family home in the middle of nowhere uncomfortably backfired. They trudged inside, wet and tearful, passing through the living room of family members who gaped. Her brothers cleared out of their room to give Blake space and Kate wondered if she should comfort him, not that she was allowed to be alone with him under house rules. Instead, she plopped onto her twin bed in the room she shared with her younger sister, ignoring Leah's questions, nearly lashing out at the most pointed: "Why would you say no to him?"

She cried herself to sleep. While their relationship wasn't enough to sustain her, while she didn't want to marry Blake, it didn't mean that the years didn't matter or that she hadn't loved him. Breaking him split her in two, but the alarm bells ceased. She'd saved him. Now she faced the daunting task of how best to save herself.

The next morning, with her face swollen from crying, she got up for her chores as if nothing happened. But rather than make it to the chicken coop, she was stopped by her parents in the kitchen.

"Take a seat," Ray said.

Kate swallowed. "Where's Blake?"

"Matt just drove him to the airport."

The family Bible awaited ominously in the center of the table. Kate's spine stiffened. The setup, the seat between her parents, transformed her from a twenty-one-year-old woman to a ten-year-old girl. She instinctually scanned her mother's lap, searching for the infamous wooden spoon. She'd only met it a few times, and that's all it took. A spanking, a slap for disobeying, seared the lesson in skin: *Honor thy father and thy mother.*

The Hutchins believed spare the rod, spoil the child. Ray never touched the girls, leaving such liberties to Beth, who, while small and mild in appearance, swung a backhand with abandon. He did of course, oversee the aftermath, which included sitting at that same kitchen table, reading every line of Romans aloud while he held the offender's neck above the Bible like one might shove a puppy's nose in its mess.

"You shouldn't have done that to him, Katherine," Ray said.

"I had to be honest." She didn't meet his eyes. "I can't marry him."

"Why?"

"Because I don't want to," she whispered. When she said no to Blake, she knew her parents might not understand, but hadn't planned for this.

"He's a good Christian," Beth said. "God sends you a man like that and you turn away. For what? Explain that to me."

"I don't know why I have to say yes to marrying someone I don't completely love."

"You will take a husband." Ray narrowed his brow. "Do you understand me?"

Kate finally looked at him. "What does that mean?"

"You know what I'm saying," he said. "A husband and children are God's plan. Yet you work so hard to turn away from it. Maybe we've let you run too far. It's my fault."

"It's not anyone's fault. It's my choice. I wasn't born to just serve a husband."

"Does this have something to do with our talk in the truck?" Ray asked.

Kate shrank back. "No. No, of course not."

"Then why did you say no to him?"

"Because I don't want it! Doesn't that count for something? Are you going to force me into a marriage I don't want?"

"I will if I have to," Ray said. "Especially when you're not thinking clearly. When something's taken hold of your mind."

She scoffed. "What's taken hold? Independent thought?"

Beth slapped her so hard that her vision flashed white. Her eyes prickled as she clutched her cheek. Kate slowly rotated her head back to bear the cross of her mother's glare. Beth's thin lips stitched into a line, her jaw went taut, her gaze empty. A look like that almost convinced Kate of what she always suspected. Her mother truly didn't like her. Another slap. Same cheek. And Kate, while a woman, while stronger now, didn't think to move. She didn't bring her head up this time. Didn't dare give her a third chance to strike her.

"You will fix this with Blake," Ray said. "I'll call him myself. You'll tell him you made a mistake."

"No, I won't," she said. Standing up for herself wouldn't end well, but she wouldn't go back on her decision. Not even if it meant a thousand more backhands.

"Then you won't go back to school," Beth said. "No more softball. No law school."

"You can't keep me from there!" Kate shouted. "I have a scholarship. I have my own life. And it's mine to choose!"

"This is my house." Ray launched up, chair legs scraping the floorboards. He hovered with an indignation she'd never witnessed. Kate shuddered. Ray had never touched the girls, but she now feared he might make an exception. "We've called Pastor Nolan and the elders. They've agreed to meet with us tonight. We'll discuss it with them."

Kate bolted before they could stop her and charged for the back door.

"Where do you think you're going?" Beth asked.

"Taking care of the chickens." Kate breathed shallowly, shaking but standing, wounded but walking on her own accord. The door slammed shut behind her as she crossed the snowy field and plotted an escape.

Before winter break, Abby and Kate had hatched a plan to set up Isla and Luca. It'd been in the works for months. Kate brought up Isla every so often while she interned in Luca's office, relayed his reactions to Abby, who would come up with something for Kate to mention next. It was a childish game, but an innocent distraction from their own complicated relationship. After deciding that Luca's flicker whenever Kate mentioned Isla and his frequent inquiries about her indicated his interest, they put a final plan into action. Kate invited Luca to speak to the Pre-Law Society and asked Isla to do the same.

Abby couldn't resist showing up for the big reveal. When Isla asked why she was going to the meeting, Abby claimed she needed to get a book from Kate. A suspicious excuse, but it didn't matter. The minute Isla spotted Luca, her world stopped.

Luca grinned so big that Abby did too, even though it wasn't for her. While Isla scolded them later, she accepted Luca's embrace and held on for much longer than necessary. It reminded Abby of the hugs she shared with Kate. The ones after they returned to each other, clutching on like they'd been lost.

Despite having no affiliation with the Pre-Law Society, Abby stuck around. She observed from the back as Kate introduced the guest speakers, moderated the conversation, updated the club on logistics.

Every so often her gaze drifted to Abby, and she would adorably stutter, blush, and clear her throat before continuing.

"I can't believe you stayed." Kate joined her when it ended.

"I couldn't miss that." Abby nodded at Isla and Luca, who spoke closely, as if the students in the room didn't exist.

Kate nudged her shoulder. "Between these two, and Mick and Haley, I think we're officially matchmakers."

"Let's do me next." Abby chuckled.

Kate didn't smile. "I don't think I could stand that."

"What? Don't you want me to be happy?" Abby raised an eyebrow.

"Of course." Kate's gaze electrified her. "That's all I want for you."

The tiny crumb alluding to enduring desire revived Abby, who'd spent the last month on her best behavior. She curbed the flirtation, stares, and even the time she spent with Kate to safeguard their friendship. She hated the fear that flashed across her face during the camping trip, even more than she hated that they never shared that kiss. But that night, Abby's stomach swooped, and what she'd spent weeks denying resurfaced with greater power—she still wanted Kate.

She spent winter break much like the year before. Christmas with Isla. A couple days at the McMechan house. She texted Kate sporadically, disappointed by the terse responses. Perhaps she read it wrong again. Perhaps they really weren't going any further.

She drank to cope with agony on New Year's Eve, joining Mick for the same party as she had the year before. Jill drove in to join them. They lamented Kate's absence, but Abby secretly shattered. She tried to immerse herself in the party, promising a midnight kiss to more than one person, but when the clock struck twelve, she called Kate. Mick ripped the phone from her before she could leave a drunk message.

She considered another call the next morning, lounging in the McMechan basement while they nursed hangovers. Abby half-heartedly flicked her video game controller for *Mario Kart,* wincing whenever Jill and Mick shrieked.

"You guys are giving me a migraine." She grumbled, but when her phone buzzed, she sat up, cured by Kate's name flashing across the screen. "Hey, hi. Happy New Year."

Mick rolled her eyes, and Abby chucked a pillow at her.

"Happy New Year," Kate said through static.

"I'm with Mick and Shupe." Abby dodged an incoming pillow. "I'm sorry I called last night. I know you're with your family. I guess I just wanted you with us."

"It's all right."

"Oh, and guess what? When I was leaving Isla's yesterday, Luca pulled up. I think they spent New Year's Eve together. Can you believe it?"

"That's great."

Abby furrowed her brow at Kate's flat affect. "How are you? How's your family?"

"I need you to come get me," Kate said.

"What?"

"I need to leave. I can't be here anymore."

Abby stood. "What happened? Are you okay?"

"Abby, please."

The strain, the sniffle on the other line, set Abby's nerves aflame. It launched a flood of adrenaline that had her twitching to strike whoever made Kate whimper.

"I'll leave right now," Abby said. Kate hung up before she could ask for details, texted her the address and nothing else. "Shit."

"What's going on?" Mick asked.

"I don't know. Kate asked me to get her."

"From Deer Park?" Jill asked. "That's like a six-hour drive. Seven in this weather."

Mick wrung her hands together. "Is she okay?"

"I don't know." Abby zipped up her coat and grabbed her boots. "I'll tell you when I get there."

"Hey wait." Jill stopped her. "Have you driven in snow before?"

"No, but I'll be fine."

“Not in your piece of shit car.” Jill tossed her keys to Abby. “Take mine. I have four-wheel drive and snow tires. Just go slow.”

Abby squeezed Jill into a hug. Mick joined the embrace, the trio securing arms around each other’s shoulders.

“Take care of our girl,” Mick said.

“I will.” Abby nodded. She gave Jill the keys to her own inferior car, sprinted out of the McMechan house, and sped off.

Abby spent the journey spiraling at the possibilities. She thought maybe someone died, but knowing Kate, she’d stay with her family. Maybe she’d had a fight with her parents, but she wasn’t the type to run away from an argument. She wasn’t the type to run away at all. But since she was, it pointed to a possibility that terrified Abby. Kate had said something about her. The night in the tent, the constant near misses, the letters, caresses, forehead touches. With what little Abby knew about Kate’s parents, such confusion wouldn’t be met with understanding.

After a six-hour drive, in which she only stopped for gas and a shitty cup of coffee, determined to make sure Kate didn’t wait an extra second, the car rumbled up the dirt path to a modest home nestled in acreage. A floodlight flipped on as Abby parked. By the time she got out, Kate exited, bags in hand, the front door slamming behind her.

“Let’s go,” she said, throwing her belongings in the back.

“Hey wait. What’s going on?” Abby asked.

A group of men stepped onto the front porch, shadows with arms folded across their chests.

“Abby!” Kate hissed.

She fumbled into the car, cranked it into reverse, and flew back down the driveway. It wasn’t until they reached the main road that she could assess Kate in the dim light. Her shoulders hunched, cheeks tear streaked as she twisted around to peer through the back window.

“Are you okay?” Abby rested a hand on her arm.

“Yeah.” Kate shivered. “Thanks for getting me.”

"Who were those people?"

"They're from our church." Kate's voice sounded smaller than Abby had ever heard it.

"What's going on?"

Kate hugged her knees and rested her chin on them. "Blake asked me to marry him."

Abby throttled the wheel so tight that her arms trembled.

"He showed up yesterday to surprise me. He had a ring and everything. Got down on a knee at midnight," Kate whispered. "I said no."

Abby's mouth fell, and she quickly snapped it up. If she wasn't driving, if Kate wasn't shaking next to her, she might have grinned. But relief didn't come. Not in the wake of her despair.

"My parents don't understand why."

Abby gulped. "Did you tell them because of law school?"

Kate peered over, inconsistent patches of light streaming over her frown. "Yeah. Because of law school," she said flatly. "They think that I should marry him and since I won't, there must be something wrong with me. I've turned away from God, become selfish, forgotten my place."

"They can't force you to marry someone. If you don't want to, that's enough."

"Not for them. I think my dad—" Kate stopped and Abby thought she might cry. "I think my dad suspects something isn't right with me."

"What do you mean?"

"Abby." Kate's tears shone through the dark. "You know what I mean. It's not just law school," she said with a crack. "It's you."

Abby's heart sputtered. "Kate, I—" She wanted to say that it was Kate for her too. Wanted to say what she always felt, what sent her charging into the snow, a six-hour drive behind her and another six hours ahead. But Kate's revelation lacked love. It slapped like an accusation. Like Abby had done something wrong, just as she feared. "I'm sorry."

"They said if I left, I couldn't come back." Kate's breathing picked up.

"Hey, it's okay."

"No, it's not. I left, knowing they'd forsake me. Knowing God's forsaken me." She rubbed her throat and inhaled desperately.

"That's not true."

"I can't." Kate pulled at the locked door handle. "I can't breathe."

"Hold on."

"I can't breathe! Just let me out!"

"Wait!"

She yanked at the door and Abby swerved to the side of the road before Kate hurled herself out. Abby bounded after her, chasing her down the snowy shoulder.

"Kate! Just stop!" Abby caught her after fifty yards, seized her arm, and refused to let her trek further.

"Let go!"

"No!" Abby forced her to turn.

Kate released a feeble whimper and collapsed into her. Abby held her up in the snow, Jill's headlights and the stars the only twinkle in nothingness. She hushed Kate as she moaned into her chest. When her wailing subsided, she drew back. She didn't look like the Kate that Abby knew, staring off, damaged by something she couldn't protect her from.

"It's going to be okay," she whispered.

Kate shook her head. "No."

Abby leaned in to kiss her forehead, but Kate turned away. They were the only people on the road, but Abby swore a truck plowed into her at the subtle pivot. When they returned to the car, Kate curled up in the passenger seat, rested her head on the window, and sniveled.

Kate slept on the journey back to Insley, and while they were right next to each other, while Kate was safe, Abby had never felt further from her. She relentlessly considered her part in Kate's torment, which at least guarded against drowsiness on the drive. But as Abby passed hours and miles on the dark highway, she arrived at the same bitter conclusion each time. She should've left Kate alone. Should've never leaned on her in the first place.

They reached the blue house just before two in the morning. While exhausted, Abby watched Kate for a few stolen seconds. The same way she did during road games when she couldn't sleep and required an undisturbed look—an assurance that she existed in the world. Now though, the sight of Kate's swollen eyes, frowning even in slumber, shattered her.

Abby swept the hair off Kate's cheek. "Hey," she said.

She blinked awake and shifted to see where they were. "You drove all the way back?"

"Yeah."

"Thank you." Kate's gaze softened, less accusatory than before, but still wary.

"I wouldn't leave you."

"I know."

She helped Kate carry her bags in. The house was as frigid as outside after being empty for two weeks. Kate flipped on the small heater in her bedroom and rubbed her hands together.

"I'm going to try to sleep," she said. "You should too. I don't know how you're still standing."

Abby nodded. "You're good here?"

"Yeah. I think I just need some time by myself. But thank you. For everything."

She lingered in the doorway while her stomach twisted into itself. "Is this my fault?"

"No. I just—" Kate shook her head, the tears restarting. "I just can't. I hope you won't hate me for it."

"Of course not," Abby whispered. She resisted reaching out to touch her. Instead, they said a staid good night.

She descended the stairs, so tired that dark spots clouded her vision. Rather than risk crashing on the way home, Abby flopped to the couch and shut her eyes, sickened by the certainty that nothing would ever be the same.

ANOTHER LETTER

Mick and Jill piled onto Kate's bed the morning after she left Deer Park. Jill shoved coffee into her hands and Mick wrapped an arm around her as she sat up.

"You okay?"

Kate peered into her mug as it flooded back. Her parents disavowing her. The slap. The visit from the church, old men laying hands on her head and back, so harrowing that she hoped to one day block it out entirely. They prayed over her, then commanded Satan to release her. Instead, headlights cast into the living room like a godsend. Of course, it was Abby. Abby driving hours to save her.

She did her best not to cry while she recounted it, but the tears came anyway in the safe huddle of her friends' arms. "Why do I feel like a terrible person?"

"Because you've never done anything wrong. Like ever," Jill said.

"I hurt Blake."

Mick chuckled. "Don't worry, he'll marry the first born-again virgin who flashes him her tits."

Kate laughed along through snivels. While she shared almost everything with them, she didn't mention Abby. She didn't confess that it wasn't just law school that made her deny Blake's proposal and cast her out from home.

"Have you talked to her?" she asked.

"Abby? Passed her on the way in." Mick narrowed her gaze at Kate. "She slept on the couch and sent us up before she left."

"She ran out so fast yesterday, I was worried she might crash my car," Jill said. "That's got to be a record. To Deer Park and back in the snow in twelve hours?"

Mick rubbed Kate's back. "I wouldn't expect anything less from Cruz. Especially when it comes to you."

Kate dragged through the next weeks in a daze. She went on longer, desperate morning runs, and buried herself in school. She half expected her parents to call and apologize. When that didn't happen, she contemplated calling and apologizing to them instead. She floated the idea to Mick, who threatened to snap her phone in half.

Collegiate Athletes for Christ offered far less sympathy. It took less than forty-eight hours for news of her heartless treatment of Blake to reach the church group. Kate thought she might take refuge among them, might find healing, maybe even understanding if she shared her troubles, but instead she encountered disdain.

There weren't sides, but if there were—and there most certainly were—everyone was on Blake's. She'd always known if they broke up, it would be that way. Blake was a campus favorite, a near celebrity after the draft, and while no longer at Insley, he was still revered by friends and teammates. A few peers patted her shoulder, but even they seemed baffled by her choice. The others glared, murmured, sneered like she'd become less-than overnight. She skipped the next Bible study and ignored calls from her group leader when she missed the one after that too.

She still attended church on Sundays, but her neck burned at the sermons. She swore the pastor chose readings of damnation for her specifically. When she prayed, she didn't ask for anything, not even forgiveness; she just repeated, *I'm sorry.*

And then there was Abby. Or, more accurately, a lack of her. Kate couldn't pinpoint who started the avoidance, but just like the other times they ventured too close, a painful distance stretched between. Abby didn't stop by the house. No more study sessions either. Kate didn't text or call, unsure of how to move forward. She still loved Abby, but by no fault of her own, she represented the bomb that upturned Kate's life. Now, she didn't know if she was brave enough to build anew in the ruins, to pick up the coals and risk getting burned by what she burned down everything else for.

They only came together on the field, but then that changed too. With Abby playing third base instead of second, they no longer turned two. It was as if the game itself sensed their rift. Kate resigned herself to the changes until Abby started warming up with Jenna Crosby at practice.

"We're supposed to be partners," Kate said.

Abby shrugged as she whipped a ball to Jenna. "I don't think Whit cares anymore. We probably could've ended that a while ago."

"Right." Kate nodded. "Okay."

"Okay."

Her focus drifted to Abby at practice, just like in the early days, overcome by the fierceness with which she played, her passion and raw talent. Third base required one crash for bunts and slap hits, and Abby charged as if she always played there, never fearing that a batter might pull back and hit a line drive at her, risking an inch closer like she enjoyed the gamble. While Kate observed her from shortstop, she willed her to look. To glance over her shoulder. To give her a flash of those dimples. It never came.

"We should study," Kate said to her in the dugout afterward. "For midterms."

"I'm good." Abby zipped up her bat bag and peeled out.

Kate's mouth dropped. "Hey!" She followed her, ignoring Jill's and Mick's confused glances. "Hold on a minute."

Abby didn't stop, so Kate ran her down.

"You're giving me the cold shoulder now?" she asked.

"Just returning the favor."

"I haven't been giving you the cold shoulder." Kate frowned. "I've just needed some time after everything."

"I know." Abby's face slackened, her dark gaze lightening to a wave of amber.

"Can we talk?"

They sat in the bleachers and waited for the team to clear out. Wind rippled the tarp that covered the infield. The stadium lights hummed. These were the short days. Waking up and returning home in darkness. It didn't seem possible that they'd ever make it to spring.

"Is it because of what I said?" Kate asked. Abby didn't look at her. "Is it because I didn't jump at being with you? Because I'm still confused and—"

"No." Abby's head shot up. "I always knew that was a possibility. I knew that you and me probably weren't going to get there."

"You did?" Kate whispered.

"Yeah."

"Then why can't we be friends?" She wanted to ask more. Like why Abby even wanted her then. Why did she let it get so far, if it would never pan out? Of course, that turned the question back on her—why did Kate let it get so far? She settled for the consolation prize of friendship.

"You look at me differently now."

"No, I don't."

"Yes, you do." Abby's breath materialized in the chill, emphasizing her words. "I don't want you to look at me like I took something from you. Like I'm the reason you and your parents aren't talking. Like I'm the reason you stopped going to CAC."

Kate's eyes widened. "How do you know that?"

"Because I wait outside that church for you like it's my own fucked-up religion." Abby sighed and then laughed, and Kate couldn't help but chuckle too.

Her heart swelled and simultaneously opened with that desperate hollow. That space she couldn't get around. "Why do you care if I go? You call it a cult."

"Because it means something to you. You believe in it." She

shrugged. "I can't be the reason you stop. I can't be the reason that you're unhappy."

"You're not." Kate's eyes burned with tears. "I just . . . this isn't easy. And I can't . . . I can't lose you too."

"That's what I'm trying to avoid. We just need some time. Some space for this to pass. And it will." She stood and canted her head at the diamond. "Plus, we still have this."

Kate frowned. "Yeah, but no more turning two."

"I'll still be next to you." She lifted the faintest of smiles. "See you tomorrow."

Kate murmured goodbye as Abby clomped down the bleachers and left. Out of all the losses that brutal, chilling winter—Blake, her parents, confidence in her faith, confidence in herself—this left her raw. When she turned away from the rest, at least she still had Abby. Even if she wouldn't let herself have all of her, she felt like hers. It made the rest of the hardship pointless if she wasn't.

She sniffled and trudged home, spiritually broken, no longer sure what she believed or where to turn. And that's when it happened. That's when the clouds parted.

That's when she got into Berkeley.

Kate checked the mail daily, investing her remaining energy into law school. Her hands trembled when she pulled out the envelope with the school seal in the corner. She whispered a prayer and ripped it open in the driveway, devouring the first lines through tears.

The news couldn't have come at a better time. Her hope for the present had worn thin, but this restored her hope in the future. In a dream that was hers alone. She didn't need her parents' approval. She didn't need Blake. She didn't need everyone to understand.

But she needed Abby.

Kate dropped her bag in the driveway and bolted down the street, clutching the letter. She didn't know if Abby was at her apartment but would start there. She'd go to the field, the library, and check every bar in town if she had to. Because she needed to tell her first.

Before reaching Abby's complex, footsteps echoed down the road, charging toward her. She made out a shadow in the distance, growing larger with every step.

"Kate?" Abby shouted.

"Abby?"

She sprinted faster until they met in the middle of the street, panting under a single streetlight.

"What are you doing?" Kate breathed into the frost.

"I needed to see you." Abby coughed, hands on her knees to recover. She straightened up, still winded. "Are you okay? What's wrong?"

"Yeah. Yeah, I'm okay." Kate chuckled, even though tears rolled. She shoved the letter at Abby, barely able to say the rest. "It's Berkeley."

Abby's eyes stretched wide. "It's Berkeley?"

"I got in." Kate swallowed a sob. Saying it aloud for the first time raised the hair on the back of her neck.

"You got in?" Abby repeated.

"Yeah."

"Holy shit!"

"I know."

"You got in?"

"I got in!"

"She got in! She's going to Berkeley!" Abby screamed for the neighborhood before swooping her off her feet. She squeezed her tight, spun in a circle, chanted it over and over. "I knew it. I knew you would do it. I fucking knew it."

She laughed and cried. The glances, confessions, traces of skin, and whispers of the last year undoubtedly conveyed their attraction, but this shared joy radiated love. A love that Kate had never experienced. Unconditional. Abby celebrated not what she wanted, but what Kate wanted. Just as she had championed her when she took over at shortstop. Just like she didn't want her to stop believing in herself or in God or her dreams. No one loved Kate like this.

"I'm so proud of you," Abby whispered into her ear. "I'm so fucking proud of you."

When Abby let go, Kate didn't break away, but slid down her front. Their faces hovered near when her feet hit the ground and Kate didn't balk. She lost herself in that gaze, the one that was no longer unknowable.

"I wanted to tell you first." Kate cupped her cheek and brushed her thumb to the spot she longed to kiss.

Abby rested her forehead against hers and sighed. "I love you."

The hollow born of Abby's arrival, of her sorrow and smiles, capable of unbearable aching and nourishing warmth, deepened from her chest to her toes. And Kate finally understood it. She thought that it was a hole, something open and empty because of Abby. But that wasn't it at all. The cavity formed because she gained something new in her. A part of herself. Kate was one before Abby, and when she met her, she became two. The hollow simply opened to make room for that last piece.

"I love you too," Kate whispered.

Abby held her cheeks in cold but tender hands. Her eyes darkened, gravity eclipsing her playful sparkle. Kate didn't recognize such a look, not even on the field, but it didn't scare her. It too belonged in that wondrous trench.

Their noses brushed first, their heads tilted to the perfect fit, Abby's hands landed at Kate's waist, and finally their lips met. The velvet trace started delicately, then expanded to a wave. A glide. Arms locked around her. Kate closed her eyes as they melted together. She already longed for the next kiss, while wanting this one to last forever. Abby's plump lips cushioned like a home she already knew, the taste leaving her faint and full. She committed to longer and closer. To more. But she left herself here. Free. In Abby. In herself. In the perfect surrender.

TOGETHER

The ball never sounded as crisp as it did during Abby's senior year, and a deep-rooted instinct told her it wouldn't again. The same instinct that moved her cleats and mitt a split second before a batter drilled a shot to her at third base. The same instinct that told her she'd knock the next ball out of the park right before it left the pitcher's circle. After eight straight games of her cracking a home run, the same instinct confirmed to the rest of the Eagles that a special season was afoot.

For Abby, the home runs weren't particularly new. She remembered the excitement of hitting her first one over the fence in fifth grade while playing with the middle schoolers. She'd done it many times before then, but only during practice. Audie put a bat in her hand when she learned to walk and even after he left the picture, her mother had devotedly fostered her natural gifts. And while rounding the bases after a big one thrilled young Abby, it soon became commonplace. Expected even by the time she reached high school and top college programs around the country recruited her.

But this was different. Not because of the sheer number or streak, but the love behind it. That full, safe, tender place that grew from Kate.

It was easy to say she would've waited forever to kiss her once they finally had, but it far exceeded Abby's expectations. Kate's soft but certain lips, her touch shifting from bashful to basking as she released herself into Abby's hold, overwhelmed her in all the right places. That part didn't surprise her. Not her thumping heart or the suggestive warmth or how quickly she needed more. But Abby didn't expect it to feel so real. As if she didn't need time to adjust to the thrill. Just like hitting those home runs. Perhaps because she'd never kissed someone she already loved so much.

It came with a different kind of waiting. Waiting for a secret moment to hold hands or simply be near each other, their intimacy no longer a torturous thing they ignored. Waiting to sneak into the blue house, slipping through the door that Kate left unlocked.

Abby did it often that spring, tiptoeing through the kitchen, wincing with each creak of the old stairs, hissing as she tripped over backpacks and laundry baskets before slipping into Kate's bedroom. They wheezed and snickered as Abby hopped out of her shoes in the dark, nearly falling over in her haste to slip under the sheets.

"Shhhh," Kate whispered, but Abby was already kissing her.

She never made out with someone as much as she did with Kate. They lost hours to each other's mouths, to long tastes and careful bites, to the extra pecks along cheeks and chins and beneath ears that evoked as many flutters as the wet, sloppy, hungrier traces of tongue. Abby, of course, physically wanted more, but happily waited for that too, content with how Kate fit into her arms as easily as she did her heart.

"I missed you," Abby said, even though it'd only been a few hours since they parted ways at the field.

Kate buried her fingers in Abby's hair, held her head in a way that hurt and healed her in one breath. "I missed you too," she said. "Did Whit talk to you?"

"About what?" Abby kissed her neck.

"The scouts."

Abby trailed her lips down Kate's freckled skin, along the sharp lines of her collarbone and the delicate dip of her throat. She smiled when Kate sighed so heavily that her chest trembled.

"Abby," she said.

"Mmm."

"The scouts."

"How do you know they're for me?" Abby hugged Kate's waist and tugged her closer. "You've been playing pretty well yourself."

Kate's hitting slump had disappeared after they got together, as though being unleashed in her own want stripped her down to that same special place. The one where the game flowed to and from her. Her line drives into the gap stunned teams. She didn't just sprint, often stretching hits to doubles, but toyed with opponents. After swinging away during her first at bat, Kate tested them on her second. She'd run at the pitcher for a bunt or slap, faking two or three times, before showing her cards, freezing the infield, and chopping a hit or nudging a bunt out of reach.

"Thank you," Kate said, pulling Abby's head up. Frail starlight streamed through the window, putting a shimmer in her gaze. "But I think we both know it's for you. Plus, you're the one with an extra year of eligibility."

Abby pulled in a deep breath. She'd started noticing them in March, in their visors and windbreakers. She usually ducked out the side gate, so that they left their businesses cards and inquiries with Coach Whitley. Arizona, Florida, Alabama, Texas. Powerhouse Division I teams eager to capitalize on her comeback, thrusting shiny flyers for master's degree programs she had no interest in. A full scholarship in exchange for those home runs.

"Why won't you consider it?"

"Why would I?" Abby scoffed. "I don't need graduate school. I'm barely going to finish my undergrad this year."

"Then what about the national team? I saw Skip Zamborelli."

Of all the scouts that came to court her, Skip's appearance bothered her the most. Not because she disliked Team USA's head coach, though he approached with a certain arrogance as he chomped gum in her face, implying her talents were too large for Insley, and that his generous offer was a risk other coaches might not take. No, what bothered her most was the way Kate's eyes lit up when she spotted him. As if for a split second, she thought he came for her. It shattered Abby when Kate's face fell behind his shoulder, just as it left her bitter that schools offered her a free education that she was frankly unqualified for, while Kate would take out thousands of dollars' worth of loans for law school.

Abby trailed a finger down Kate's cheek. "Do we have to talk about it right now?"

"Why not?"

"Because I just want to be here," she whispered.

Kate nuzzled closer, enmeshing their bodies so that they shared the same breath on the same pillow. Abby didn't want to think about the future, never really cared about one beyond the next day, anyway. She didn't want to think about anything beyond their secret bubble, in the uncomplicated quiet. Kate kissed her as if reading her thoughts, filling her mouth with sweetness in place of her worry. And when they grew tired, Kate's lips resting longer and heavier on hers between kisses, eyelids adorably drooping, Abby folded her up against her chest and slept.

Morning always came too soon. Abby was never a morning person to begin with, but sneaking out before the rest of the blue house woke was a worthy sacrifice. Especially since it always followed the best sleep Abby ever had. Lead-limbed, snoring, sheet-imprints-across-your-cheeks slumber that ended with Kate's gentle caresses and smile.

Abby slipped out of the bedroom like a thief, pecking her lips goodbye, though she'd see her in the library a few hours later, then at practice, then for another late-night rendezvous. Part of her enjoyed the game of sneaking. Dodging around corners, nearly knocking over Jill's bike in the hallway, holding her breath under the shield of someone singing in the shower. She'd nearly managed another clean break out the back door when a throat cleared behind her.

"What are you doing here?" Mick asked. "Did you sleep here?"

Abby let go of the doorknob, firming her face before the lie. "No, just got here." She turned back into the kitchen. "Out of coffee. Door was open."

Mick groaned. "Fucking Shupe. I'm going to change the locks."

"Don't do that," T.K. said, strutting in her miniskirt from the night before. She flung open the refrigerator door, ignoring the Post-it notes that covered it: *NOT FOR T.K.* "Ugh. You're out of creamer."

Kate entered behind her, eyes stretching to saucers when she spotted Abby by the gurgling coffee maker.

"Hi," she said.

"Morning." Abby suppressed a smile as Kate sidled up next to her to grab a glass of water. "Out of coffee."

"Oh. Right." Kate bit her lower lip.

Mick's head broke between their shoulders. "I know you think you're doing a good job hiding it, but I know."

Abby's grip turned white on the chipped mug she'd been sniffing for mildew. Kate froze and stared straight ahead.

"Know what?" Abby asked.

"You quit smoking." Mick smacked her back.

Her shoulders unclenched, and out of the corner of her eye, she noticed Kate release a breath. "Trying," Abby said while she poured coffee. At least it wasn't a lie. Kate hated her smoking and its taste on her lips. Quitting became miraculously easy.

"Because you're doing it, right?" Mick grinned.

Kate turned away to hide her flushed face.

"Doing what?" Abby asked.

"Playing next year!" Mick grabbed the mug from her. "Can you imagine? Team USA? You could win a fucking gold medal someday!"

Abby waited for Mick to flop down at the kitchen table before exchanging a knowing smile with Kate. She huffed and shook her head.

"And don't worry—I've been doing my research," Mick said. "I think you should go to Oklahoma. Their shortstop is graduating this year, but you could probably beat out their third baseman if you wanted to."

"No thanks."

"Florida then. We could live on the beach," T.K. said.

Abby furrowed her brow. "Why would you be there?"

"How about Arizona State? They're young, but I think they're poised to make a run for a national title." Mick rubbed her hands. "Don't worry though, we'll figure this out."

Abby frowned, again off-put by her own future. Kate shifted closer and gently nudged her shoulder.

"Good morning, family." Jill entered with Dylan behind her, the two of them in a mismatch of INSLEY ATHLETICS wear they seemed to have shared.

"Not good morning. You two left the door unlocked again," Mick said.

Dylan shook his head as he sat down at the table. "Wasn't us. I swear we locked it when we got back from the bar last night."

Jill plopped onto his lap, eating straight from a cereal box. "How do you know it's not Haley?" she asked through a mouthful. "Who I adore, by the way, but is getting a little too comfortable using all the hot water."

"I am not," Haley said, pausing on her way to the coffee maker to kiss Mick. "Plus, we shower together, so doesn't that count for something?"

"Ew." T.K. sneered. "There are too many people in this house."

"Yeah, starting with you," Mick said.

"Hey, I earned my squatting rights long before you all coupled up!"

"I think I should go," Abby whispered to Kate.

"Yeah." She nodded and followed, the two of them slipping out the back door where the argument echoed into the yard. Finally free, they broke into laughter. "I thought for sure Mick knew."

"Me too." Abby chuckled.

She glanced around, made sure no one saw them from the window, and laced her pinky through Kate's. Kate wrapped the rest of her fingers around her hand while they walked to the main road.

"Skip your run," Abby said, pulling her closer. "Come over to my place."

Kate shook her head. "No. You have to get ready for your midterm anyway."

Abby groaned as they stopped to face each other.

"I'm still your tutor, even if I'm your . . ." Kate trailed off, a blush blooming across her cheeks.

Abby smiled. They hadn't said it or shared it, but in every way that counted, even secretly joining the other couples in the blue house, they were together.

"Yeah," she said gently. "You're that too."

She scanned the neighborhood for witnesses, and when she found none, kissed her. A quick, too-short thing, that skipped through her chest all the same.

"I'll see you later?" Kate asked.

Abby nodded. "Yeah."

She waited to leave until Kate jogged away, aching at what they couldn't avoid. She didn't want it to end. Not the season. Not the school year. Most of all, not them.

"We're moving back to San Diego."

Abby grabbed Kate's hand beneath the table. Squeezed it like she might float away as Isla and Luca smiled across from them.

"The princess of Coronado returns." Abby pushed out an empty laugh. "Your mom must be thrilled."

"I'm not going for her. I'm going for me." Isla nodded at Luca. "For us. I think maybe I hid out here long enough."

Abby's stomach tightened. She didn't expect Isla to stick around forever, didn't know if she would either, but her departure signaled another end she didn't want. Like everyone around her was moving and changing and Abby wasn't sure how to join them.

"Have you decided what you want to do after you graduate?" Luca asked as he poured more wine. Abby liked him well enough, found him easygoing in a way that balanced Isla's prim and proper—even if they did look disgustingly attractive together, like they belonged in a luxury car commercial. "Isla says you might play one more season?"

"Maybe." Abby shrugged.

"It's okay to not know." Isla nodded at her. "Lots of people don't know what they're going to do after graduation."

"Yeah." Abby slugged back the rest of her wine.

"You must be excited for Berkeley," Luca said, mercifully shifting the conversation to Kate.

"I already feel in over my head," she said with a smile.

"No, you'll be great. The first year is a bear but you're not expected to know everything. If you can, try to get in with Professor Donaldson. He was my old roommate at Yale . . ."

As Luca and Kate spiraled into a law school conversation that Abby had little interest in, Isla leaned toward her.

"Help me with dishes?" she asked.

Abby nodded, glad to clear the table, though her throat tightened when it was just her and Isla in her marble kitchen, where they'd shared more meals than she'd expected when she first arrived at Insley.

"There's one more thing," Isla said as they scrubbed dishes together.

She diverted her eyes from the sliding glass doors where she'd been watching Kate on the deck.

"You're pregnant?" Abby asked.

Isla scoffed. "No." She handed her a pot to dry. "It's Dad."

Abby's hand instinctually became a fist. "Who is this dad you speak of?"

"Audie wants to see you play." Isla leaned against the counter. "He saw how good you're doing and thought he might come to a game."

"Am I supposed to be excited by that?"

"No. I just wanted to talk to you about it first."

Abby folded her arms. "That's the thing about him—he always comes around when things are good, just so he can make them bad again. He's never there when the shit is hard."

It took her back to his sporadic appearances during her childhood, disrupting whatever peace she and her mother managed. It took her back to two years ago, when Abby was drowning in grief. Now that the floods had receded, now that she was playing the best softball of her life, of course he wanted back in.

"I told him it probably wasn't a good idea anyway," Isla said. "It's just . . ."

Abby narrowed her brow at the way her voice wavered. "What?"

Isla stared at her for a beat and Abby knew whatever she said next wouldn't be the full truth. "He looks out for you in his own way," she finally said.

"Fuck, Isla—"

"That's it." She threw her hands up. "I'm not saying he's a good guy or you need to forgive him or that you even need to see him. Okay?"

Abby clenched her jaw. She dried a skillet like she might rub it to pieces until Isla touched her shoulder. A timid, uncertain hand that she left there.

"I'm going to miss you, you know?" she said.

Abby gulped and stopped drying. "I'm going to miss you too."

"But we'll see each other. You can both come visit." Isla smiled when Abby shifted to meet her gaze. "You and Kate."

Abby's eyes widened. "What?"

"I mean, well. You two. Are you . . ." Isla raised her eyebrows.

Abby blushed. "Yes." For all the secrecy and sneaking, it felt good to tell someone. And this, despite their parting ways, felt like a chance at something closer. Something like sisters. Like family. "Just, you know, don't make a big deal out of it."

Isla grinned so wide that her eyes nearly shut. "Okay."

"Stop smiling like that."

"I'm not." Isla handed her another dish.

Abby groaned. "You're still doing it."

"Sorry, you've just liked her for so long."

"I have not." Abby's mouth fell open, uncertain whether she'd always been that obvious or if Isla just knew her better than she thought.

"Don't mess it up."

"Wow."

"Kate's just . . . you know, she's special. Sweet. Really smart."

Abby's gaze drifted out the sliding glass door. Kate's hair tangled in the wind, her dress fluttering while she nodded and smiled. Abby sighed. "I know that."

Isla smacked her with a dish towel. "Sister to sister, she's out of your league."

"Out of my league?" Abby smacked her back with her own towel.

"Oh yeah." Isla laughed before hugging her. "I'm happy for you."

Abby closed her eyes as she held on. "Thanks."

She savored the chiding and Isla calling her sister. She savored what felt like the last breaths before a plunge. Everything was moving too fast and she wasn't ready. Not even close.

Kate knew she'd lose her virginity to Abby. She just didn't expect it to be after dinner at Isla's, though maybe she should have. It lived in the glances, in Abby squeezing her hand, in the talk of the future that lately felt equally terrifying and thrilling, in the way Isla grinned at her when she and Abby returned from doing the dishes. In the way Abby pecked Kate's cheek, uncaring of their audience. She'd fluttered with surprise, but it also grounded her. Like it solidified everything they'd always been.

"I'm sorry about my sister," Abby said as they walked to the blue house. "She just kind of figured it out."

"That's okay." Kate smiled. "You know you've never said that before?"

"Said what?"

"Called Isla your sister."

Abby's throat bobbed with a swallow and Kate wanted nothing

more than to hold her just like when she noticed her hiding a wince at the news during dinner. "I know it's dumb, but for some reason I just expected her to stay. Like I'd always get to come back because she'd be here. It's not home, but it's something."

"You can still come back," Kate said.

But she knew what she meant. As they walked through the neighborhoods of college houses with their overgrown lawns, surrounded by fragrant Douglas firs, the sky pastel pink before the moon arrived, it felt more like a picture than a place. Something they'd look back on but never fully return to. Perhaps that's why instead of stopping at the blue house, Kate said, "Let's go to your place."

Abby's cheeks twitched with a hesitant smile. "Okay."

They'd spent time at Abby's one-bedroom before, but never the night. Abby insisted on being the one to sneak in and out, and Kate secretly appreciated her roommates as an extra guard against temptation. Not that Abby ever pressured her to have sex, though it bubbled beneath the surface, the two of them often stopping just short with thundering heartbeats and moans caught in their throats.

The ceiling fan was working overtime in Abby's apartment when they entered, and she scrambled to crack open a window. Kate found it transient, like most college housing, easily picking out the furniture and décor that came secondhand from Isla. But she admired the pieces that were clearly Abby—the surfboard she'd brought from California, the concert posters, the trophies hidden in a closet, and the photographs.

Kate lingered on the snapshots of Abby's mother. Perhaps because they had the same smile and sparkle behind their eyes, and while Abby had come far, she looked happy in the photos in a way that Kate had never witnessed. There was another photo too, one she always considered asking about but never did. One of Audie on the Padres infield, Abby a toddler at his feet, wearing a matching uniform.

"You okay?" she asked when Abby flopped onto the couch next to her.

"Yeah."

Abby wrapped an arm around her and rested her head on Kate's shoulder. She knew it wasn't just Isla's news that unsettled her, but the rest. The future they kept avoiding.

They acted like Abby hadn't failed to make plans, and like Kate wasn't firmly set on her own separate path. Like they weren't a secret, like they wouldn't remain a secret, at least to her family so long as Kate stayed in the closet, which she didn't dare leave. Like moving to a different city together didn't seem recklessly fast and desperate, but like long distance didn't leave them just as doomed.

"How about you?" Abby asked.

Kate rested her head atop Abby's and laced their fingers together. "I'm not sure if talking to Luca made me feel better or worse about Berkeley. I thought getting in would be the hard part. It sounds like everyone's so cutthroat and competitive."

"So, you'll fit right in."

Kate's mouth dropped open as she shifted to face her. "I will not."

Abby grinned and Kate couldn't help but mirror it. "Please— under that sweet, calm exterior, you are super competitive." She tickled a few fingers up Kate's side and she laughed while she swatted them away. "Need I remind you about our little clash over short-stop?"

"That wasn't my fault! You weren't supposed to show up." Kate chuckled with Abby's hands twisted into hers. She tilted her head, swooning for those big eyes and tempting lips. "Though now I'm glad you did."

"Me too." Abby drew her closer. "I love you so much."

"I love you too."

They kissed slowly but deep, unfurling into each other across the couch. Kate always craved Abby's weight on top of her and the pressure of her rough but careful hands, holding her down. It counteracted the lightheaded sensation that accompanied Abby's lips skating along her neck.

Unlike the rest of their peers, Abby never treated her like a fragile virgin, incapable of lust. She eased her closer to it, awakened more in her, bringing her to a place unfamiliar but safe. Even without fully stripping each other down, Kate grew to know the nature of Abby's desire too. Her hitched breaths and tight limbs. The way her hips bucked when Kate's thigh slid between them. She knew a kiss beneath her jaw conjured a long sigh. Most of all she knew Abby would stop herself before ever making Kate uncomfortable.

And that night, as they lost themselves in lips, their skin balmy in the warm apartment, a sensual pulse overtaking her lower stomach, Kate knew something else. She wanted all of Abby. She wanted to have her always.

"Come with me." Kate pulled back as the idea struck her. It might've been a nonsensical byproduct of arousal but had also been budding for weeks. "Come to Berkeley."

Abby's gaze flickered. "What?"

"Play your last season at Cal." Kate nodded, cupped her cheeks, growing more certain as the plan grew roots. "I can even tutor you through grad school."

Abby gulped, her face falling with what Kate hoped was relief and not despair.

"You won't have time for that," she said.

Kate smirked. "No. I won't."

"Berkeley isn't interested," Abby said, though she grinned now.

"They will be if they know you are. Plus, Skip will put in a good word. He'd help you play for the Yankees if it means you'll help him win gold."

Abby brushed back Kate's hair, eyes turning glassy. "You're serious? You really want me to come?"

"I want all of you," she whispered before pulling her back down.

Even after consent, Abby moved with caution. She carefully suckled Kate's throat, drawing out moans, but it was Kate who dipped her hands beneath her shirt first. And Abby, ever accommodating, removed it. Kate shivered. She'd filched glances before, on the road and in the locker room, but never like this. Never did she permit herself to ogle, let alone trace her breasts and the ripples along her stomach.

When it was Abby's turn, her hands at the clasp of Kate's bra, she pulled back for the question she would ask over and over that night. "Is this okay?"

Kate nodded. "Yes."

Her bra disappeared in a flash. Kate resisted rolling her eyes at how easily Abby did it with a snap of her fingers because, in another flash, a light graze moved across her nipple. She held her breath, stiffened, then thawed under the touch. Abby massaged her breasts, tender enough for trust, but bold enough to build her up to more. To harder kisses and heaviness, as if to match the hammer in her heart. When she adjusted to the thrill, leaving her certain of the next step, she drew back for two important words.

"The bedroom," she whispered.

They kissed on the bed, and then it was time for Abby's bra. Kate fumbled on the first try, a little shaky, but Abby never stopped kissing her. She simply reached back to help. Kate shivered at the first trace of her breasts. At Abby opening Kate's hand to grab more. At their chests pressing together and heaving as one. And between the shallow breaths, Kate knew she needed the rest. All of Abby's skin on her skin.

Their legs linked, so that a light, equal pressure hit the perfect spot, and when Abby's hand paused at the hem of Kate's dress, she nodded.

"Don't stop," Kate whispered.

But Abby paused anyway. "Are you sure?"

Kate grabbed her cheeks and pulled her face back down, bringing their foreheads together. "I want you."

Abby's chin wobbled before the corners of her mouth twisted upward. "Okay," she whispered. "But we can stop whenever you want."

"Abby." She caught her breath and smiled. "I don't want you to stop."

In response, she groaned a rough, sex-charged rumble that lit fire in Kate's stomach.

Abby's hand made a slow journey beneath her dress, settling at her hip, fingering the edge of her underwear. Kate wished she hadn't worn something so chaste, cotton and sexless, just as she also wished that she'd shaved, but she hadn't planned for this. In fact, she was certain that if she had planned for it, set a date and discussed it, she might've backed out. Plunging in, playing the game without that mechanical form, was exactly what she required.

More questions, more yeses gasped into Abby's mouth, and soon her underwear slipped away. Her clothes vanished. She was naked for the first time with someone else. The first hint of fear hit her. But Abby met her in the same place. Removed her clothes and lay beside her.

"You're beautiful." Abby traced her cheek, eyes ablaze and a little watery.

Kate swallowed through tightness in her throat. "So are you."

They stayed there a beat, facing each other on their sides. If Kate ever doubted her sexuality, for all the times she told herself it was just infatuation and curiosity, this confirmed otherwise. The curves, lines, joints, the plush and taut that could only be of a woman, left her ravenous. She craved it, dripped for it, nearly balked at its beauty.

Kate gasped when all of them aligned and touched. Abby kissed her forehead, confirmed she was okay as Kate caught her breath in her neck. They stayed there, arms around each other, as if adjusting to new waters in the light sweat and shaking. When her body leveled out, she cupped Abby's cheeks and nodded.

Then Abby touched her. Two, maybe three fingers, she wasn't sure. They skated across in a precise, slick stroke and Kate moaned from somewhere deep and unknown. She clutched Abby's back and buried her face in her. Abby asked again, and Kate could hardly choke out, "Yes." Her hips choked it out too, pushing, searching for those fingers. And when they returned, her ever-active brain short-circuited, bringing it to the most beautiful of silences, allowing the rest of her to simply feel.

Her hips widened to welcome the pressure, the careful circles, and the dance that her body somehow knew the rhythm of. And just as she fully freed herself, eyes sealed, her mouth parted for an unavoidable hum, Abby brought herself lower. A gentle suck on her breasts, then a trail of kisses down her stomach, and lower, until another move would bring her to the very spot.

Fingers didn't make her feel as inexperienced as Abby's face inches from her. "You trust me?" She fluttered a kiss to the inside of her knee.

Kate gulped and nodded.

"You're perfect." Abby uttered it like a melody and followed it with a husky coax, the same one from the field. "Relax for me."

Abby's tongue drifted across her. She whimpered first. Then her hips released around Abby's dark head. She lapped her gradually, up to her center, then down to her opening, and back again. Kate clawed at the comforter, moaning between gasps. She thought Abby's tongue satisfied when they kissed, but this melted her.

And then it happened. The last groan as she held on to whatever part of Abby she could reach. Her entire body tensed against all that bliss, holding it for one breathless earthquake, before dropping into weightlessness. All that was hard turned soft. All that was loud turned quiet. A second of nothing that became her everything.

When she returned, Abby held her. Kissed her temple and murmured into her hair. "I love you."

"I love you too." Kate's chest no longer rattled but stung with pining as if she'd discovered a love too full. One not yet gone, but that she already yearned for.

"Are you okay?"

Kate shifted from the safe pillow of Abby's chest and kissed her answer. Her stomach flipped at tasting herself on her lips. Abby moaned, and her need evolved, no longer for herself, but for Abby. A longing to give her equal pleasure.

She timidly reached, met raw heat and slickness. Abby released an uneven sigh, a smirk lacing her rasp at the shell of Kate's ear. "See what you do to me?"

Kate worked in careful circles, assessing Abby's every twitch. The way her hips adjusted to what she liked, a light squeeze of Kate's breast, eyes and jaw clenched.

"Is this okay?"

"Yes." Abby breathed.

"Really?"

"Don't stop."

Kate would later be embarrassed at how she smiled, pleased with herself. And when Abby gave a final shudder, vibrating into her, grunting, "Kate," relief washed over her. Relief at not failing at sex. Relief at not just being Abby's but making Abby hers too.

They threaded together and Kate held tight, kissed Abby's throat. She knew in the dim light, aroused but content, secure but free, that this was it. She knew Abby felt it too, detected it in her gaze and whisper. "It's always been you, hasn't it?"

Kate's brow pinched with a sob. "And you for me too."

While the end of Insley and a decision about the future awaited them, this was their new beginning. The start of what would always be theirs.

When Abby broke the college softball home run record, the Eagles celebrated the best way they knew how. An uproarious night at Sunny's. And while the endless free drinks, praise, and an excuse to party would've normally satisfied Abby, she only wanted Kate. Just like when she rounded the bases earlier that evening, cracking a rare grin at the feat, she reached for her in the team's congratulatory dogpile. They hugged tight when she finally broke free, stopping just short of the kiss they both wanted to give.

At the bar she never lost sight of her. Abby enjoyed many toasts in her honor, accepted more high fives and shoulder slaps from fellow students she'd never met before, but always found her way back for a smile, for a sly glance at her across the crowd. She smirked at Kate's tipsiness and hiccups as she leaned into her.

"Want to get out of here?" Abby whispered.

Kate grinned back. "I thought you'd never ask."

The celebration continued when they reached the blue house.

"Anyone here?" Kate called into the dark hallway.

Abby snorted through the quiet.

With the coast clear they stumbled upstairs, giggling as they helped each other to the bedroom. Kate wasted no time tugging the letterman's jacket off Abby's shoulders, the two of them bumping into the wall while they kissed.

"Had to take you home before someone else tried to." Kate sucked on Abby's lower lip.

"Oh, please, no one cares that I can hit a stupid ball with a bat." Abby threw her head back as Kate kissed the spot beneath her chin that made her instantly wet.

"Yes, they do," she whispered into her ear. "It's sexy."

"You're sexy."

Kate tugged her to the bed where they wrestled off shoes and clothes, twisting into sloppy, beer-laced kisses. Abby grinded against Kate but then darted back and gasped when her hand hit a tender spot along her thigh.

"I'm sorry." Kate winced in sympathy.

"It's okay." Abby grunted.

While she'd broken the record for home runs, she'd also broken the record for most games hit by a pitch. It meant constant purple knots and bruises on her shoulders, back, and thighs. Of course, she didn't help her own case. Whenever an opposing team's catcher stood from their crouch, gesturing outside the strike zone to set four slow, unhittable pitches in motion, Abby tormented the pitcher. She'd harass them with a "Seriously?" or "Come on, give me one," or Mick's favorite, "Don't be scared, [insert pitcher name here]." Rather than passively walk her, the pitchers responded by taking aim.

"I'll get you some ice," Kate said.

Abby pulled her back down. "No, no don't go."

"That's what you get for goading them into hitting you."

"I know. I've learned my lesson," Abby said before kissing her.

"No, you haven't." Kate laughed, but plunged her tongue in her mouth anyway, sank into her and moaned. She pushed Abby's chest down and pulled back from her mouth to bring hers lower.

"Kate . . ." Abby sighed when she trailed her tongue between her thighs. It'd become her favorite thing to say. *Kate. Kate. Kate.* As if she needed to confirm over and over that she was the one responsible for every aching rise and pleasant fall.

Kate had blossomed far beyond a timid virgin. Not that Abby wanted her any less during those first uncertain times together. She should've known it wouldn't last long. As with everything else, Kate was a fast student in bed. It was as if she studied Abby, read how to make her come, practiced like she might take a hundred grounders or run a hundred miles, until she made it perfect. That first time she set her mouth on Abby, tongue roving, she thought her heart might explode. And Kate, whose appetites were much more insatiable than expected, never shied from new ways of being touched, unafraid of being pinned down or initiating, of connecting deeper. There was no more endless wanting. They simply went together.

By the time they retired beneath the sheets, Abby already wanted her again, nearly buckled at her wide pupils and skewed hair. She always thought Kate beautiful, but never imagined she could be this sexy. A version that belonged just to her. Kate rubbed into her, still wet on her thigh, when she heaved the word that nearly rolled Abby's eyes back into her head. "Again?"

She nodded and shifted on top of her when a gasp rippled behind them.

"Oh my God." Jill peered through the cracked door. Kate and Abby scrambled off each other. "Mick!"

"Shupe, get out of here!" Abby shouted. "Now!"

A buzz of static cut through the shouting and Jill pulled a walkie-talkie from her waistband. "Operation Cruzin' for Hutch complete. The Eagles have landed. On each other. I repeat, the Eagles have landed in bed. Requesting backup."

The walkie-talkie beeped back. "Copy, over."

"Is that T.K.?" Abby asked.

Jill grinned. "Yeah. She has eyes on the back door in case you try to escape."

Kate peeped out of the sheets. "How long have you been planning this?"

"Weeks." Mick appeared behind Jill and folded her arms. "Family meeting. Now."

"No!" Abby flopped back on the pillows.

Kate ducked under the covers. "Mick, please."

"Family meeting! We can wait downstairs all night, but you'll have to come down eventually." Mick smacked the doorframe before departing with Jill.

Abby groaned and joined Kate under the sheets, a useless hiding place for their lewd acts. She thought they'd successfully skirted their seemingly inebriated teammates at the bar, but it'd been their own reckless mix of alcohol and celebration that had them throwing caution to the wind.

"How long do you think we can stay up here?"

Kate sighed. "I think we're going to have to face this one."

They pulled on clothes in defeat. When Kate swiped Abby's UCLA sweatshirt, she raised an eyebrow, but Kate shrugged and slipped it over her head as if she was doubling down on getting caught. Abby secretly beamed with the adolescent thrill of announcing their relationship. Something she pretended didn't matter to her, but that night she realized how deeply it did. How much it meant to step outside their bubble to see if they could still float.

The living room had transformed into a makeshift courtroom when they arrived. Mick, Jill, and T.K. positioned chairs directly across from the sofa so that when Kate and Abby sat, they confronted them like a judge and jury. Mick leaned forward. "What are your intentions with Hutch?"

Abby's mouth fell. "Why do I automatically get the third degree?" She glanced at Kate, whose hand rested on her bruised thigh. "What about her? She might just be using me for sex."

Kate gasped. "I am not."

T.K. threw her head back and cawed. "I can't believe you two are having sex."

"You should've seen them going at it upstairs," Jill said.

Kate gritted her teeth. "We weren't going at it."

"I should've known. Hutch has had that post-sex glow for weeks now." T.K. grinned.

"Playing way better too. Took the hitting slump right out of you," Jill said.

"That's the power of good sex. I do it for maintenance."

"Oh, is that what you call it?" Abby scoffed. "How much maintenance does one person require?"

"I don't know. How much, Hutch?" T.K. asked.

"That's it. We're leaving." Abby grabbed a dumbstruck Kate's hand and stood.

"Okay, everyone cut the shit. Let's be adults about this," Mick said, nudging Abby back to the sofa.

"I think it's too late for that," Kate murmured.

Mick theatrically paced in front of them, repeatedly sighed, and didn't speak for almost a full minute. Abby and Kate exchanged glances before she finally broke into a soliloquy.

"Listen, you two are our best friends and we want you to be happy. You're cute together, in a weird opposites-attract way. I mean, I kind of wanted this to happen. It was obvious to everyone. Except you two. You're a genius, Hutch, but also an idiot. And Cruz, my God, I won't start on you." Mick shrugged when Abby flipped her off. "Anyway, it's great you two figured it out. I'm happy if you're both happy. I—we—just don't want to see you crash and burn."

"Wow, thanks," Abby said.

"No, I mean, we're always going to be there for you guys. Granted, this has irrevocably altered the group dynamic." Mick shook her head. "But it's not just about me or our weird family. It's about the season."

"I know." Kate nodded. "We were planning to keep this between us. At least until the summer. I don't need the entire team knowing . . ."

"That their captain is screwing the third baseman in the middle of a run for a title?"

"We won't be a distraction, and we won't let it impact the team," Abby said.

Kate squeezed Abby's hand. "It hasn't so far."

Their three teammates, lined up on their chairs, goofy and warm as ever, shined with laughter that didn't come.

Abby furrowed her brow at them. "What?"

"Nothing," Mick said.

"This just seems right." Jill grinned. "You two."

Mick dabbed fake tears. "They grow up so fast."

Before Abby could snark back, a pile on of hugs swept over her and Kate, arms and elbows flinging, pinched cheeks, ruffled hair, groans, a yelp at a knee meeting her bruise, but mostly smiles, laughter, and the closeness of kin formed in bond instead of blood.

"Be good to each other," Mick said, one arm around each of them.

"We will," Abby said, her eyes meeting Kate's through the group huddle. In her gaze and grin, she felt it. Berkeley and the rest. A future, a plan, that she might reach out and grab. She smiled back. They were going to make it.

SENIOR DAY

She thought she beat it like any other game she willed herself to win. And this matter of the heart certainly seemed worthy of victory—that victory being the absence of guilt for loving Abby entirely. It was easy to do in her arms, easy in the shield of night, and easy when they existed in their carefully crafted bubble. A place where they couldn't be wrong.

Until life squeezed in. Until the church bells rang distantly on Sunday mornings while she slept on Abby's chest. Until she opened her bedside drawer and skimmed her untouched Bible. Until Pastor Derek stopped her on the quad.

"Kate Hutchins!" he said with arms raised, as he approached from the opposite direction, so that she couldn't possibly ignore him. "We've missed you!"

She wanted to flee, and when she couldn't, she wanted to be sick. She held her books tighter to her chest. "I know. This season's just been so hectic."

"Yes. The team's the talk of the town."

Kate swore his plastic grin and accompanying squint weren't for the team's unprecedented success, but her secret. Like she was steeped in sin so strong that he smelled it on her. If that wasn't already the case, sweat sprang up along her back as she failed to come up with anything to say, standing dumb and guilty for things she'd yet to be accused of.

"Well, I know it's been a busy and, at times, challenging year for you." He paused. "I still keep in touch with Blake."

Kate nodded, wondering how it could get much worse, how to make her voice work, and if she did, what excuse she might make to slip away.

"Sometimes when we face pressure and change, it's the best time to lean on God and your church community," Derek said. Stiff spikes of hair poked out from his fedora, his wooden crucifix hung on a beaded cord necklace, and his arms tattooed in Bible verses bulged out of a too-tight T-shirt. Every stylistic choice landed like a desperate attempt at hip for the youth he led. "If you can't make CAC or Sunday worship, you can come see me instead. My door is always open if there's anything you want to talk about. Softball, school, boys. Trust me, I've heard it all."

She finally fished a few words out. "Right. I'll remember that. Thank you."

"I'll pray for you. For your season and that we see you soon." Derek smiled as he departed. "Don't be a stranger!"

Kate scurried off, just short of a sprint, not stopping until she rounded the corner of the nearest building. She threw her back against the bricks and gasped as the dreaded morning at the farm came back in vivid color.

It wasn't supposed to happen here. For months, it'd been enough that damnation never came, God never struck her down, and truthfully, she didn't regret reneging on her purity. By her own conviction, their love's profound reach couldn't possibly be wrong. But when the church bells rang, when the pastor called her back to the congregation, she wondered why a love so good could leave her so far from God.

Insley's student body rallied for Senior Day, the last home game before regionals. Athletic triumph wasn't the institution's norm, but on that bright May evening, the warmest day of spring thus far, fans packed the bleachers, spilled over to standing room only, and lined up along the foul lines. The baseball team led the crowd in cheers and chants. A handful of guys painted their beer-bloated stomachs maroon, spelling out EAGLES in a sloppy row.

Kate knew the rise in support wasn't solely due to the team's win streak, but also to Abby's record-breaking performance. A few newspapers and local stations picked up the story, initially running a blurb on her setting the new home run record, before someone realized her connection to Audie Cruz. That's when it spread to larger networks and sports shows, which aired footage of Abby alongside her famous father. Kate held her breath as Abby turned off the TV and chucked the remote. She glowered just as bitterly as they stepped onto the diamond for warm-ups that day and spotted signs in the stands: *Adios, Abby Cruz! It's outta here!*

"They're going to be disappointed if they think he's coming," Abby said to Kate as they waited between grounders.

"It doesn't matter as long as you're not."

"What about you?" Abby frowned. "Are you okay?"

Kate was grateful that Coach Whitley drilled a ball to her at shortstop, so she didn't have to answer. Per Senior Day tradition, the senior class's parents joined them on the field for a pregame ceremony. While Mick's, T.K.'s, and Jill's parents arrived, and Isla stepped in for Abby's late mother, Kate had no one. She considered calling her parents, but it'd been months since they'd spoken. While they rarely attended her games, she always imagined they'd be there.

"Kate?"

"I'm fine," she said.

The crowd's intensity left little time to dwell. Her fingers jittered through warm-ups, Mick struggled to bark over the noise, and Jill bobbled a few easy throws at first. It wasn't just the fans either.

"Check it out." Abby nodded at the seats along the home dugout. "Cal is here."

A chance at Berkeley. A chance at their future. One that made Kate's knees wobble. When she suggested Abby join her, she'd meant it. But that was before the church bells stole her sleep, before Pastor Derek, and before her heart and faith declared war on each other.

"I'm actually a little nervous," Abby said.

Kate didn't respond. Her eyes drifted to the rows below the Berkeley scout. Her mouth fell. "Oh my God."

"What?"

She staggered toward an out-of-place couple amid the students. As she drew closer, her heart sputtered. It was her parents, grinning as she opened the gate to meet them. "What are you doing here?"

"We couldn't miss this." Ray embraced her and her mother fell into the hug with him.

"You didn't call." She gulped. "After I left, I thought you wanted nothing to do with me."

"We owe you an apology," Ray said, and Beth nodded along. He frowned, lines deepening in his forehead as he rested a hand on Kate's shoulder. "God works in mysterious ways. If your heart wasn't with Blake, then it wasn't right to marry him. We have to trust you to make your own decisions and walk a righteous path. You've done it so far. You've made us very proud."

Kate's throat tightened. The tears rolled instantly. She cried because all along she'd wanted this, her parents, and now she understood how badly. She also cried because they believed her righteous and good, when she'd fallen so far from their expectations.

Ray hugged her again. "Hey, none of that." He chuckled in his papa bear growl, the one that assuaged Kate on her lowest days. " 'There's no crying in baseball,' remember?"

Kate hastily dried her cheeks. Out of the corner of her eye, she spotted Abby walking to the dugout. She stopped to meet Kate's gaze. Her amber eyes darkened, her jaw clenched, and she knew in the wordless exchange, one that put a pit in her gut, that everything was about to change.

The fivesome waited with their families ahead of the ceremony, in which the announcer would call them one by one before they accepted applause and flowers for their accomplishments. Mick's bubbly mom and dad babbled. T.K.'s divorced parents wouldn't speak to each other, her mother scowling at her father, who plugged one ear with his finger while he screamed into his phone. Jill's parents wore matching tie-dye shirts with her face printed on them. Isla talked lowly with Abby, who gazed off as if bereaved.

Kate introduced her parents to the strange mix of her friends and their families, balking when she came to Abby. "This is Abby Cruz, my—" Kate stopped. "The third baseman."

Mick, Jill, T.K., and Isla stiffened, or perhaps Kate imagined it. Either way, Abby certainly did. She didn't speak, just nodded at Ray and Beth as she shook their hands.

"Nice to meet you," Ray said. "You're Audie Cruz's daughter, aren't you?"

"I'm Isla, Abby's sister," Isla cut in, and Kate bit back a thank-you. "I'm a professor here, and Kate's my best student. You must be so proud."

"Isla helped me get into Berkeley," Kate said.

Beth's eyes stretched wide. "You got in?"

Abby glared. "You didn't know?"

"So where is Audie?" Ray asked. Kate didn't know what enraged her more—her father asking about Audie or that he ignored her news about law school.

"Your guess is as good as mine," Abby said. "But, since we're asking unpleasant questions, why'd you decide to come after you turned your back on Kate this winter?"

"Okay, let's not do this," Kate said through her teeth.

Ray furrowed his brow at Abby. "You're the one who picked her up, aren't you?"

"Dad, tell everyone who you voted for last election." Mick smacked her father's mammoth shoulder, and he hissed. "Or T.K., where'd your mom get her tits done?"

"Sadie!" Mick's mother pinched her ear.

"What? They're nice," Mick muttered, before T.K. squeezed her other ear. "Ow!"

"My surgeon's in Miami, sweetie. I can refer you," T.K.'s mother said as she finished reapplying lipstick and snapped her compact closed.

Kate glared at Abby, and she spitefully returned it. She thought enduring their last home game without her parents would be unbearable, but this was worse.

The PA announcer boomed above, kicking off the ceremony. Mick went first, then T.K., and Jill. The crowd roared for Abby, her lengthy list of hitting records, and her imminent title of conference Player of the Year. The announcer called Kate last, the captain, the Rich Aldren trophy winner, most stolen bases in school history, a contender for Defensive Player of the Year. When they stood next to each other for photos, first with their families and then the formidable fivesome, Kate's smile was made of plastic.

She struggled to steady herself. Their supporters chanting and stomping on the bleachers left her twitchy and nauseous. Fortunately, T.K. and Mick thrived. The first batter went down on a called third strike, the second popped out, and the third batter only took four pitches to send back to the dugout. The crowd rumbled as T.K. and Mick bumped fists and the rest of the team jogged off to bat.

As always, it was up to Kate to get them started. She tried to steady her breathing as she chopped a few practice swings on deck.

"Leading off for the Eagles, team captain and shortstop, number three, Kate Hutchins!"

Cheers followed. Kate settled into her left-handed stance, exhaled, completed her ritual three pendulum swings with the bat before flexing her fingers on the handle and resting her hands near her ear. The first pitch blew by.

"Strike one!" the umpire shouted with extra pizzazz as if also fired up by the fans.

Kate nodded. She always took the first strike. That was simply what a leadoff hitter did. She stepped out of the box and Coach Whitley gave her a flurry of signals—a tap to her nose, tug of her ear, hand to her stomach, her chin, then two taps to her left shoulder. Fake slap. Kate touched her helmet in confirmation.

The next pitch finished high, but she swung instead of faked and missed beneath it at a run. The crowd sighed with her. "Strike two!"

She could handle two strikes. She usually worked the count to two strikes. But that was on her own terms. Now her heart thundered. She glanced at the stands to her father, still making out his voice above the noise. "Come on, Katie! Eye on the ball!"

Kate firmed her grip. Skipped her pendulum. Held her breath. The ball veered low and outside, but she swung for the fences. "Strike three!"

She grimaced. She couldn't recall the last time she struck out on three straight pitches. Perhaps not even that entire spring. Certainly not since Abby. She refused to look at her in the dugout as their teammates slapped her shoulder in encouragement. Kate ripped off her batting gloves and nodded along. She'd struck out before. She could come back. It wasn't the start of a slump. She shouldn't even think of the dreaded word.

Izzy Palamino sliced a ball to third base, made it safe by a hair. Mick drew on the swell of the crowd, got up with a glint in her eye, the one before a bomb. She hit a double to left field and hustled her weathered knees to second, as the outfielder heroically launched a throw to stop Izzy from scoring.

The fans who weren't already on their feet stood for Abby. She sauntered to the box, cracked her neck side to side, licked her lips. One out, two runners on. This was where she thrived. Typically, Kate would've cheered, but this wasn't a typical game. Not anymore.

Abby took the first pitch as if she expected it. She stood in a half stance, drooped her chin as the umpire called ball, and chuckled. It was no wonder most pitchers in the league hated her. Why they'd rather hit her instead of force an intentional walk late in the game. It was a little too Audie Cruz of her, though Kate wouldn't dare say it even as she helped her ice bruises.

The next pitch came inside. Abby connected on a straight line, launched the ball to center field. Kate didn't know if the cheers or the home run came first, but their measly field vibrated.

"Adios, Abby Cruz! It's outta here! Three–nothing, Eagles!" the announcer boomed.

Abby carelessly chucked her bat, dawdled around the bases, nodded at the pitcher, but didn't crack a smile as she high-fived her teammates. Kate lingered in the background.

She didn't get on base that game, while Abby trotted around the diamond, racking up runs and applause. Every pitch mocked Kate. She swung desperately, whiffed with gritted teeth, sighed each time the infielders tossed to first for an easy out. By her last at bat, their opponents simply waited for her to do herself in.

The game was no longer meditation, no longer sprang to or from her. It thickened inside like tar, clogging the jet streams in which its magic traveled. Her parents' cheers and teammates' encouragement became an insult. Abby returned to a rival.

A low growl emanated from Kate's throat when the crowd chanted her name. She hated the signs and Abby's face on the program, even though Kate was the captain, the leader, the one who made sacrifices. Abby simply showed up and praise poured in.

When a grounder hopped her way at third base, Kate wished she might miss the throw to Jill. She just as quickly hated herself for such a thought, crumpled with more shame than she did at posting her worst outing of the year. The same shame that radiated in her chest when she shrank around her parents and denied who Abby was to her. No, she didn't despise Abby. She despised herself.

"Good game," Abby said after they shook hands with the other team and broke from Coach Whitley's post-game talk.

"You don't have to say that." Kate sighed.

They silently packed up their gear, Kate avoiding Abby's gaze as if it might reveal her cowardice. That morning, they'd woken up together and kissed before their home field curtain call. Now it resembled a dream. It couldn't exist with Ray and Beth waiting outside the dugout, with her hitless game, and with Abby a hero to the stands but a threat to her peace.

"So, I'm just the third baseman now, huh?" Abby hoisted her bat bag on her shoulder.

Kate glanced around to ensure everyone else had cleared out. "I'm sorry. I panicked."

"And you're okay with them being here?"

"What do you mean?"

Abby's gaze hardened. "Seriously? They excommunicated you for rejecting a proposal. Your mom slapped the shit out of you."

"It wasn't that bad," she said, but invisible flames ignited her cheek at the reminder. "I wish you hadn't said what you did."

Abby lowered her head. "I'm sorry. I just hate what they did." She furrowed her brow. "I don't know how you don't."

"What do you want me to do? They came here to apologize. I'm not going to turn my back."

"And what about us?"

Kate's throat went dry. *Us* echoed catastrophic. The phantom flames burned hotter. She imagined herself back in the cold kitchen, the family Bible on the table, the road split in two, of what she wanted and what her parents demanded. It'd been an easy, albeit painful, choice that winter. This should be easier. Picking Abby should be easier. Only it wasn't.

"They're only here for the night," Kate said. "I don't think now is the time to share."

Abby's lips wilted, but she nodded. "Okay."

She started to leave, and Kate sank. She threw her arms around her. "Hey wait," Kate whispered into her chest. "I'm sorry. I'm sorry, okay?"

Abby squeezed her tight. "It's okay. I love you." She murmured into her so quietly that the message arrived through vibration rather than sound.

Kate rubbed her back. "I love you too." But when they released, Abby inched too close for comfort, her mouth on a habitual route. Kate nearly flew out of her arms. "Not now."

Abby exhaled. "Right. Have a good time tonight."

Kate nodded. "I'll see you tomorrow."

But as she pivoted to leave, as she hugged her parents, as Abby snuck off from the rest of the seniors and their families, she knew it wasn't okay. Worse than that, a familiar fear warned that it might never be again.

THE NATIONAL TOURNAMENT: ROUND ONE

On the flight to Colorado, she noticed a man wearing her father's jersey. The unmistakable twelve stitched in gold with four letters above—CRUZ. Only it wasn't just her father's name or number but hers too.

Abby considered changing her name many times and taking her mother's, Sorrentino, instead, but blamed superstition. She'd played her first little league game with it, chosen the number with purpose in hopes she'd play like the hero who wore it—not the one who missed his court-approved visits, but the one she watched on TV. Her mother never changed the channel either, as if refusing to take that version of him away from her.

Usually, Abby ignored Audie admirers or tributes, but that day it sank invisible claws into her back. Then the plane dipped as if the sky felt it too.

Kate's hand fluttered onto hers from the middle seat, a rarity in the last few weeks. At least since Senior Day. Still, Abby squeezed it and didn't refuse her gaze. "It's okay," she said.

Kate's chin trembled and Abby knew she'd unintentionally addressed more than just the turbulence. She'd spoken to the strain and avoidance. They were still together but suddenly too busy. Too busy for late nights or sleepovers or sex. Busier than Kate had ever been despite classes ending and law school secured. Even kisses landed quick and flat, like an obligation.

"Are you mad at me?" Kate asked.

Abby gulped and shook her head. The last rift happened as they'd left for nationals that morning. Kate mentioned she'd found a possible place in Berkeley and that Abby should start looking too. Berkeley wasn't yet a done deal for her, but they'd offered a partial scholarship and grad school admission as long as she bumped up her GPA with summer classes.

"Or we could save money on rent and share a place," Abby said with a slight smile, but Kate's face fell. "I'm kidding. Kind of . . ."

"No, it's just . . ." Kate trailed off and her eyes shifted away like they always seemed to lately. "It's just living together before marriage."

"But sex is allowed?"

Abby didn't mean to push, wasn't necessarily ready to move in together either, but she hated the way Kate iced her out. Hated that Berkeley loomed like a separate journey rather than something they'd planned to do together. Like Kate wasn't the only reason Abby was going.

Kate cleared her throat. "I'm going to be elbows-deep in school and you'll have softball and if my parents visit—"

"Right." Abby clenched her teeth at the mention of them. "Harder to hide me."

"I'm just not ready," Kate said before slinging her bag over her shoulder and heading downstairs.

Ready for moving in together or living in truth, Abby didn't know. They'd hardly looked at each other on the bus or at the airport even though it hadn't really been a fight. Even though Abby wasn't mad about not moving in together. She was mad at how everything changed after Kate's parents showed up. That their presence haunted them, not much different than that jersey Abby spotted on the plane.

"I'm not mad," she said.

"Good." Kate laced their fingers together and rested her head on her shoulder. "I really want to win this one."

Abby pressed her cheek to the top of Kate's head. "Me too."

"Let's go Abby! Vamos!"

It'd been a decade since she'd heard his voice, but Abby recognized it in her soul, permanently imprinted by a childhood she rarely recalled. The jersey on the plane no longer seemed a coincidence but a warning she ignored.

The stands rumbled with it first. She swore she heard a whisper of his name but then decided it must just be her own. Her mother named her that because they sounded alike after all—a knockoff brand of the male namesake he wanted. But then his deep voice, with that lively accent, reached her ears while she dug in at third base.

"Let's go Abby! Vamos!"

Abby whipped around. Her skin buzzed as if lightning brewed, and then when she found him, it struck. Audie along the left field fence, raven hair slicked, linen suit and leather loafers immaculate, gold rings sparkling on his fingers. Bystanders and fans swarmed him.

"Abby." Kate brought her back.

She barely turned around in time for the pitch or to register that it hit Mick's glove for the third out before she was jogging off the field, her stare locked on Audie as the inning ended. He waved, his thick mustache rising in a smile, before he signed an autograph.

"Are you okay?" Kate asked.

"He's here," Abby said, though she imagined Kate knew too. Everyone knew as the murmurs picked up in the dugout. The dreaded word, *dad,* circulated around her.

Kate rubbed her back. "Just focus. It'll be okay."

Abby nodded and grabbed her bat. The Eagles led but were still the undisputed underdogs against West Georgia State. Of the whole national tournament really. A single error, a shift in the momentum, might make the game's gods turn on them. Though Abby was certain they'd already turned on her.

"Come on, Abby!" Audie shouted as she went up to bat. "Aye! *Aplasta la pelota!*"

She hated his power over her. Hated that he echoed with a frequency she never forgot. She recalled his visits. Birthdays, a drunk Thanksgiving, a few Christmases standing on the porch while her parents argued and the neighbors threatened to call the cops. It always ended in screaming and her mother clutching a liquor bottle.

"Vamos, Abby!"

She came to as she chopped under a rise ball and flew out to left field. "Fuck."

Abby trudged through the remaining innings and outs, consumed by the very person who made the game part of her. The only one with the power to take it away.

When it ended and the victorious Eagles sent West Georgia State to the loser's bracket, Abby hurried from the field. Kate didn't say a word. She simply didn't leave, trailing behind her toward the team bus.

"Abby! You're really not going to talk to me?" Audie shouted, but Abby walked on. "I came here to see you. I deserve to talk to my daughter!"

She halted at the last words. *My daughter.* Abby turned with her jaw locked into stone. Her nose reacquainted itself with him first. Cigars and cologne masking the tang of liquor in his sweat. Then she scanned the rest. A collage of her features. Iridescent amber irises, a wide nose with a slight crook from multiple breaks sustained on the field and in bars, thick lips raised in a half smile. Audie was nearing sixty, but for all his vice and hard living, it barely showed.

"It's wonderful to see you, mija." He opened his arms, but Abby stepped back.

"Don't," she said.

"Just like when you were a little girl." Audie chuckled. "Our little storm."

"I don't want you to come to any more games," Abby said. She miraculously stayed level enough to make the demand without shouting, mostly thanks to Kate hovering behind her.

"Why are you not playing shortstop?"

"We already have a shortstop. The team needs me at third."

Abby pivoted for the bus, but Audie grabbed her shoulder. She jerked away as big, angry buttons sprang along her spine and bubbled beneath her skin, waiting to be pressed. It would just take one careless bump, and she'd lose it. And Audie was plenty careless.

"Why is the head of Team USA calling me? Skip says you've ignored multiple invitations to try out—"

"Why do you care? Why are you even here?"

Abby's neck smoldered. More of her teammates took notice. Mick and Jill circled closer, lingering behind her and Kate like guard dogs.

Audie shook his head, switching to Spanish in his frustration. "I've seen you play. You're wasting your potential. You should be preparing for gold. If you don't want to play for Skip, you can play for Puerto Rico. You should be competing for a D1 championship instead of slumming it here!"

This hit the biggest button straight on. "Who are you to talk about my potential? About *my* team!" she roared back in English. "We haven't talked for years, and you show up to lecture me about fucking softball? You decide to care now because I can hit a ball like you?"

"¡Soy tu padre! Of course I care." Audie snarled, threw his arms out at his sides. "You think I haven't been around? Who do you think pays for you to come here?"

Abby scoffed at his blatant, desperate lie. "No, you don't. It's covered because Isla works for the university."

"After what you did? No." Audie tsked. "Whose idea do you think it was for you to transfer? Huh? Do you think any team wanted you?"

Abby's knees wobbled, and she might've fallen if it wasn't for Kate subtly bracing her back. She shook her head. "No. You didn't. You never had any money."

"There's a trust, mija. I made your sister the executor. You'll get it when you graduate."

"Oh, you're paying me off now?"

"It's always been there!" Audie shouted. "Your mother wouldn't let you have it! She kept it from you to punish me. She didn't care if it punished you too."

"You're a liar!"

The fans, parents, and players around them lowered their conversations.

Kate's mouth met her ear. "Let's just walk away."

Abby heaved for air. That dreaded squeal arrived, ringing like the phone when the police called that night with the news, the same warning squelch that her world was cracking, and she'd never be whole.

"It's not true. And even if it is, even if you throw money at me, it doesn't make you my father. You haven't been a father for twenty years!"

"That's just the story you tell yourself! The story your mother brainwashed you with!"

The ring hit its crescendo. Burst in her. The calm sliver she clung to, more for Kate and her friends than for herself, snapped. The tendons in her neck corded and her lips stretched back from her teeth. "You don't know! You never had to be there!"

"No, you don't know!" Audie screamed through spittle. "I wanted to see you! But she kept me away. Poisoned you against me so that when you got older, you didn't want me around even when I tried!"

"Because you made her fucking crazy!" Abby's heart thundered. Her vision flashed red, then black, so that later she wouldn't remember the rest. "Every time you showed up, she cried and drank for days until the next time! She's fucking dead because of you!"

"Don't say that! I loved her, but she was a sick woman!"

"Like you're any better? I can smell it on you!"

Abby didn't think. She just shoved him. And like any mirror would, Audie launched back, as if her explosion lit his nearby fuse. He reached, clutched her cheeks in a single hand, and squeezed.

"No!"

A blur of color and bodies and yelling. Kate ripped Audie's arm away. Jill and Mick jumped in too, dragging them back as Abby tried to swipe at him. Bystanders swooped between the Cruzes, who shouted nonsense, lunged, and pointed at each other.

"Everyone on the bus! Now!" Coach Whitley herded them away.

Abby didn't remember getting on the bus, or Kate's murmurs and arms, or covering her ears and rocking in her seat. But she remembered the words that left her mouth as if echoing from a tunnel, ahead or behind her, she wasn't sure.

"I can't do this," she whispered.

Kate squeezed her hand. "Can't do what?"

"Any of it." She rested her head against the cool window, farmland and fence posts rushing past. For once, she was grateful that Kate had nothing to say, as if admitting defeat. As if accepting that she couldn't outrun the curse.

Crickets chirped and the hotel pool glowed fluorescent blue. Abby lounged on the edge, a trail of smoke twisting up from her fingers. Kate paused at the metal gate and sighed in relief. She half expected her to disappear after Audie. Perhaps because the last time Kate saw her so distraught and inaccessible, unharmed but not quite safe, was when she wandered away in Phoenix.

"I thought you kicked those for good."

"Sorry." Abby blew smoke over her shoulder.

"It's okay." Kate sat beside her. "I think today warrants a free pass."

"Are you all right?"

"Me?" Kate tucked a piece of Abby's hair, still damp from the shower, behind her ear.

Her throat bobbed as she tapped ash from her cigarette. "You pushed him away."

"I'd never let anything happen to you." Kate's mouth turned up at the corners in a weak smile. She wasn't one to fight, but had quickly discovered the exception, unsurprised that as usual, it was Abby. "Had he ever been physical like that before?"

"No. Never." Abby's eyes turned glassy while she stared into the pool. "My mom threw a plate at him once and he had to get stitches, but even then, he never laid a hand on her or me."

Abby's phone vibrated between them and flashed with Isla's name. She didn't move to answer it.

"Have you talked to her?" Kate asked.

"No. She should have told me about the money."

"Isla loves you. I'm sure she had her reasons."

Abby lay back on the concrete and sighed. The pool filter whirred into the quiet. Kate grabbed her hand as if she might keep her from drifting away like they had been for weeks. A drift she'd done nothing to help, that weighed on her with every excuse she made to passively pump the brakes while she figured out what she wanted. A drift that would inevitably widen as she contemplated the news she'd delayed for several days and now ripped off like a Band-Aid.

"My parents will be at tomorrow's game."

She held her breath in the lull. Abby chuckled, more like a growl than a laugh. "Of course they will."

"It doesn't have to be a negative thing. I was thinking we could all get dinner together after the game," Kate said, like she'd rehearsed in her head, but it landed shrill and desperate.

Abby raised a brow. "As the third baseman or your girlfriend?"

"I know it's not ideal, but it's a step in the right direction." Kate frowned. "Maybe they can get to know you and you can know them. They'll love you as much as I do."

"I'm not going to be a lie, Kate." Abby sat up, an edge working up her shoulders. "And I definitely won't stand by while you make yourself smaller for them."

"It's not that simple."

"They tossed you aside when they couldn't control you. How can you not see that?"

"You don't think I've thought about it? It tears me up." Kate gulped, wounded, but also relieved to finally have an honest conversation. "I can't just turn my back on them. I don't care if it makes me naïve or weak-willed. I want them in my life."

"Even if it means sacrificing who you are?"

"You know it's hard for me. The way I was raised and what I was taught to believe." She stopped, barely able to say the rest. "A love like ours is sinful."

Abby's gaze narrowed. "Don't tell me you really believe that."

"That's the problem. I don't know what I believe." Kate's stomach churned the same way it did every churchless Sunday and prayerless night. "I've lost my faith, and that terrifies me."

Abby's face crumpled. "I can't compete with God, Kate."

"You're not supposed to." She sank at knowing the people she loved most couldn't coexist. That they'd never understand each other, leaving her stranded in the middle, alone, permanently unsatisfied as she gave up one to have the other. "Part of me hopes, believes that maybe they'll change. Maybe there's a reality where they can accept me for who I am. That God can too."

Abby scrubbed a hand down her face, but she didn't seem angry anymore. "I know what it's like, waiting for someone to change. Wanting them to but not being able to cut them off when they don't." She lowered to a whisper. "But that's the thing, Kate. They don't change. They show you exactly who they are."

Kate rested her hand on Abby's arm to soothe what bubbled beneath. The years, the crash, the phone call, her mother and father, so clearly haunting her even when she pretended they didn't. "Abby, I—"

She cleared her throat in dismissal. As if to say they'd had enough for today. Abby's gaze returned to that unrecognizable landscape Kate thought she'd long ago figured out, etched with the missing pieces she'd never understand, no matter how well she knew her heart.

"We should get some rest." Abby caressed Kate's chin. "Big game tomorrow."

It was kind, but distant. Something felt wrong. Cold between them. She shuddered on a breath as Abby helped her to stand. Kate's place in the middle expanded, leaving her emptier, lonelier, further from everyone she loved and felt destined to lose.

THE NATIONAL TOURNAMENT: QUARTERFINALS

They didn't sleep the night before the game. They just tossed and turned. No one offered a hand or graze beneath the covers to soothe, and at breakfast they didn't speak.

Kate didn't know if Abby was angry with her or simply tied up in her own thoughts about Audie and the fallout. But when they arrived at the field, her parents hugging her the second she stepped off the bus, Kate knew it was anger that sent Abby stomping off. Knew it in her glare across the locker room. It made Kate ill enough that she barreled into the bathroom and splashed cold water on her face.

Mick's cleats clicked in behind her. "You okay?"

Kate nodded and caught her breath. "Just nerves."

"You're okay." Mick patted her back. "We got this."

Every game could be their last. Every grounder. Every at bat. Unlike Abby, whose future in the game seemed endless, her talent boundless, Kate's career would end even if they won the trophy. And that's what made her sickest—everything around her was coming to an end or at least on a collision course in which only one might survive—her relationship with Abby or her parents. Her relationship with God or her heart's true desire.

"Strike three!" the umpire would echo in her ear twice that night. She never reached first base during her other two at bats, nauseous as her parents cheered for her, nauseous as the Eagles fought to stay alive, nauseous as Abby took to the field like war.

She charged relentlessly at third base, as if she wanted to get smacked in the jaw or nose. On her opening at bat Abby drilled a shot right at the pitcher's head, then made eye contact with her like she'd done it on purpose. So, it was no wonder, the next time Abby sauntered to the batter's box, a chill touched Kate's spine.

"Come on, Cruz!" Mick yelled from the on-deck circle as Abby sliced a practice swing.

The opposing pitcher glared as Abby crowded the plate. The same cocky invitation, a dare really, she'd extended all season. The pitcher brushed her back with a ball that nearly skimmed Abby's thighs.

"Ball, inside!" the umpire shouted.

Abby spit and opened her arms at the pitcher. "What was that?"

Kate clung to the dugout fence so hard it indented her palms. The feeling swept over her. Something wasn't right.

The pitcher grunted and sent another ball zooming higher, this time a sliver from Abby's chest.

"Jesus!" Jill widened her eyes at Kate. "Did you see that?"

"She's doing it on purpose," Kate said, but she didn't mean the pitcher.

"Do it again!" Abby pointed her bat at the circle. She and the pitcher stared each other down, and the field fell silent except for the droning stadium lights. "Do it again, I dare you!"

"Come on, batter!" the umpire shouted.

"Do it!" Abby smacked her helmet twice and settled into the box.

Kate covered her mouth ahead of the windup, swore she saw it before the pitch. She wanted to close her eyes, but held on. The ball veered exactly as expected. Higher, tighter, faster. It collided with Abby's helmet, cracked the plastic, spurring squeals in the stands and dugouts, as the formidable Eagle became a heap on the dirt.

She'd hit the median. The crunch, the force throwing her head back, and the ring in her ears convinced her for a few glorious seconds that it was over. Then she opened her eyes, home plate beneath her like heaven sent her back.

Abby blinked away the black spots in her vision. The umpire stood above, but she couldn't understand him. She staggered to her feet and assessed her hands. She wasn't injured. Nothing hurt except her ears from the incessant whistling tone.

"You okay?" Mick came through garbled. "Abby? You with me?"

She swayed, but nodded. The helmet did its job. If anything, the impact of the pitch just shocked her. Put distant images in her sight. Her mother's car crushed into metal scraps. Her casket beneath a pile of lilies.

"Cruz, you all right?" Coach Whitley eased toward her.

Abby removed her helmet. A gnarly crack ran down the ear hole. The face mask hung on its hinge. The pitch could've killed her. She didn't know if she was angrier that it almost did or that it didn't finish the job. Abby gritted her teeth at the pitcher. But it wasn't the pitcher she imagined. It was Audie. It was her mother. It was Kate's parents.

"Why don't you come at me for real!" She chucked her helmet at her. It didn't reach the circle, didn't come close, and she hadn't intended it to. If she wanted to hit the pitcher, she would've. But it still triggered what she needed.

The pitcher stalked toward her as someone jerked Abby back. She thought it might be Mick or the umpire, but it was the opposing catcher, riled up in her ear. "What the fuck is wrong with you."

Abby welcomed it. Fed on it. She turned to push the catcher, but Mick was already yanking at the woman's arm. The pitcher reached Abby just as the umpire stepped in, not allowing for anything more than a push.

"Fuck you!" Abby turned on him. "She did that on purpose! You saw it!"

"One more word and you're out of here!"

Abby opened her mouth to say it, even if it meant getting thrown out. Especially if it meant getting thrown out. Instead, Coach Whitley stepped in front of her and pointed a finger at the umpire's chest. "Are you out of your mind, fuckwit? She could've been killed!"

"That's a warning!"

Mick and Jill dragged a flailing Abby to the dugout. The ringing persisted until Kate. The only person strong enough to cut through the chaos. She asked if Abby was okay, then whispered the rest like she'd done something unforgivable. "Why did you do it? Why did you have to do it?"

"That's it! You're out of here!" the umpire screamed.

"Fucking wombat wanker arsehole!" Coach Whitley kicked dirt at the ump's feet, unleashing the most artful combination of insults Abby had ever heard. Full fucking kangaroo.

Coach Ackers dragged her away to boos and clapping. The stands rattled, both teams screamed at each other, adrenaline oozed, a perfect mirror to Abby's turmoil. It satisfyingly scratched the scab over every grizzly wound.

Abby slipped on a new helmet. She ignored the dejected slump of her teammates at Coach Whitley's suspension and the jeering as she took first base. She searched the stands for Audie, then searched them for her mother. While she didn't find them, she felt them. The field rippled under their influence. While she'd survived the crash, Abby sensed the end. As she met Kate's gaze across the diamond, she knew she sensed it too.

Insley beat Colwood College to advance to the semi-finals, but a decade later, no one would remember the score. They'd remember Abby getting hit and Coach Whitley getting ejected. They'd remember Mick and T.K. going out for revenge the next inning—Mick giving the signal, a prominent middle finger, to T.K., who blatantly drilled the next Colwood batter in the thigh. They'd remember how Colwood's bench cleared and that the haggard umpire issued a final warning to both teams, narrowly preventing a full-blown brawl.

And while Insley won, it didn't feel right. Not to Kate. Not when the game cracked open under the pressure, spewing with the anxiety and rage that she and Abby skirted around, but never talked about. Now that it threatened them on the outside, risking the game, Kate knew they'd hit more than an impasse.

That's why Abby, with her bag packed, didn't surprise her when she entered their hotel room. That was the final score Kate would remember that day. It might as well have flashed on the board hours ago.

"Thank God," Mick said when the door shut behind Kate. "Tell her she can't leave."

Jill, T.K., and Mick stood helplessly, with the same worry everyone brought to Kate. The plea to keep Abby in check. She didn't know how much longer she could keep answering the call.

"Don't go," she said.

"I'm sorry." Abby adjusted the duffel bag on her shoulder and started for the door.

Kate blocked her path. "Why'd you do it?"

"It doesn't matter." Abby glared. "I'm the one that got hit."

"It does matter. You don't get to leave like this," she said. Abby tried to brush past, but Kate put a hand on her chest. "Haven't you risked our chances enough? We already have to play the semi-final without Coach."

"Jesus, it's just a game!"

Jill slid between them. "Guys, come on. Let's not blame each other."

"It's a team! It's not only about you!" Kate yelled.

"Then win without me." Abby raised a brow at Kate, then glanced at their teammates. "That's what I thought. You just want me here so I can help us win."

"That's not true."

"Then why am I still a secret? You only want me so long as you don't have to risk anything to have me."

"And what have you risked? What happened tonight was all about you. You didn't care about what it meant for anyone else."

"Fine." Abby dropped her bag. "You really want to have it out?"

Kate bit her lip to conceal that the prospect terrified her. She turned to their friends. "Can you give us some privacy?"

Mick's eyes widened. "You sure?"

"Go, Mick." Abby grunted.

Kate sat at the end of their bed as the door rattled shut. She didn't want to scream. She didn't really want to fight. As Abby stood across from her, unreachable, Kate still recognized the person she loved. The person she gave everything to.

"Don't go like this," she said. "It doesn't have to be this way."

Abby's brow pinched. Her lower lip quivered just once before she shifted her gaze to the baggage at her feet. "I can't do it. I can't stand by while you slip away from me."

"I'm not." Kate couldn't bring herself to lie. Not even in the heat of an argument. Not to Abby. "I'm not trying to. I'm sorry." She drew in an uneasy breath, gathering whatever flimsy strength she had left after weeks of anxiety. "I know it's not fair, but I spent over twenty years fearing God and imperfection. That doesn't just disappear. Not when I see my parents." A knot filled her throat. "Not when I feel like I have to choose between them and you. It makes me wonder if I feel this doubt and uncertainty because it *is* wrong."

She'd hoped to find a hint of comfort in Abby's gaze, but she received her so empty that it punched her in the chest instead.

"You mean *we're* wrong?" Abby crossed her arms like it was disgraceful. "It's love, Kate. How can that not be good?"

"Then why doesn't it feel good right now?" Kate's chin wobbled.

"Because you're fighting it. Because you're afraid. Because you're letting your parents win."

"And you're not?" She shook her head, regaining momentum, building a case that she never considered unleashing before. But this wasn't her Abby. Not this angry, spiteful, version. So, she didn't need to be her Kate. "You don't talk about your past, but it's here, looming, all the time. Not just Audie, but your mom—"

"Don't." Abby shifted, her muscles coiled like she might pounce, and Kate nearly shuddered. She knew Abby would never hurt her, but she recognized the same darkness that exploded at the game. "Don't talk about her."

"Sorry," Kate whispered, even though she wasn't sure she should be. "Why can't you see how much everyone cares about you? How much everyone wants to help you and see you succeed? Not just me but Isla, Mick, Jill, T.K., Coach, the whole team!"

"Well, maybe I don't!" Abby paced, scrubbed her hands down the back of her neck. "Maybe I don't care as much as everyone wants me to!"

"Why not?"

"Because I'm not whole!"

Kate didn't realize they'd both been panting and screaming until that moment. Didn't realize they hadn't met eyes until then either. Didn't realize that they both had tears rolling down their red cheeks.

"I can't fix that for you," she said with a sniffle.

Abby rubbed her eyes with a fist and snatched up her bag. "I know."

"How can you leave like this? How can you give up?"

"What am I giving up, Kate? Huh? Berkeley?" Abby sighed. Her body let go with it, losing inches in height. "We both know I don't belong there. And this fucking game." Her mouth drooped forlornly, and Kate nearly gave into it. "I only came back to it because of you. I only felt it again because of you. And now . . . I don't want to feel like I'm on the outside. Like you might toss me aside whenever you fear coming out."

"But I can't be everything for you either," Kate said. "I can't be the only reason you keep playing or go to Berkeley. I can't stand by while you shut down until you blow up. I can't be the one to pick up the pieces. Not when I'm struggling too." She dabbed at her tears, stunned that this was where they'd ended up, but she couldn't imagine another way through. "You're not the only one, Abby. It's like you can't see beyond yourself. You're always supposed to see me, but right now I don't think you can at all."

Abby frowned. "And what should I see?"

"That I'm suffocating beneath you," she whispered.

It was gentle but cutting. She almost regretted saying it, but it'd come out naturally, like it was the only answer she had in the mess.

"Well, allow me to help." Abby brushed past her for the door.

"If you love me so much, why are you doing this?" Kate turned to face her. "Why can't you figure this out with me?"

"Because I don't need to figure it out. I know where I stand here." She placed a hand over her heart. "I know exactly how much I love you. No one, not even God, can change that for me. Can you say the same for your parents? Can you even say the same for yourself?"

Kate couldn't answer. The tears kept streaking, and her arms stayed tight across her chest because she'd never felt so cold or small or lost in Abby's eyes. She loved her, but she didn't know how to keep her. Not like this.

"I didn't think so," Abby said. Whatever sympathy, whatever hope, whatever love she spoke of just seconds ago, vanished. A glare overtook her bloodshot gaze. "You always played the game like a coward. You love like a coward. I have no doubt you'll keep living like one too."

Abby slammed the door, and while Kate shed plenty of tears through their fight, she let herself cry. Really cry. Into her hands, hunched over, covering her mouth to restrain a wail. She let go of it all but gained no clarity. The worst kind of surrender.

THE NATIONAL TOURNAMENT:

SEMI-FINALS

She made it as far as the hotel lobby, but when she confronted the glass doors, her damp, empty face an unfamiliar reflection, Abby couldn't do it. For one, she had nowhere to go. More importantly, she wasn't ready to lose Kate completely. She knew if she abandoned the game, there'd be no return. It still bound them together, their start and now, maybe their end. She resolved to see it through.

She made Izzy Palamino switch rooms with her, then spent a restless night before the semi-finals replaying the words she wished she hadn't said and the ones she wished Kate hadn't said too. She wished Kate didn't consider her a burden, wished that she said she loved her unconditionally. She wished she hadn't called her a coward. She even wished she didn't blow up the game, didn't self-destruct, didn't feed into the curse.

In the morning, through team breakfast and the bus ride to the fields, they kept their distance, not daring to look at each other. They didn't need to. The rawness, the hurt, radiated between. The rest of the Eagles entered the game on equally shaky ground. Coach Whitley's one-game suspension deflated everyone's spirits, and despite Kate's and Abby's best attempts at hiding it, the team picked up on their despair.

"We can do this," Kate assured in the huddle after morose pregame warm-ups. Her eyes were bloodshot and swollen, but she forced a smile. Abby ached with regret and admiration at how she never gave up. She never let anyone down, no matter how badly she hurt. Abby couldn't say the same. "I know we're tired. I know we're hurting, and I know we wish Whit was here, but we can do this. We're so close. Just push a little longer."

When they jogged out to their positions, Abby extended an olive branch. "Hey, you okay?" she asked.

But Kate didn't say a word.

Meanwhile, Southern Colorado strutted onto the diamond. They enjoyed a home-state advantage and a lineup twice as deep. When they scored first, their fans chanted and rang cowbells while the players' shirtless boyfriends bumped chests in the stands.

The Eagles hardly put up a fight. No one could hit. When Abby got on base, no one cheered. Not that she deserved it. Mick grimaced each time she squatted behind the plate. The other team clobbered T.K.'s pitching. And then Kate, of all people, made the game's biggest blunder.

A batter launched a shot to shortstop with one out and runners on first and second—a routine double play. All Kate had to do was lob it to second base. Abby had seen her do it a thousand times. But not today. It happened in slow motion. Kate fielding the ball, and then, out of nowhere, freezing. Terror streaking across her face. Double clutching but not letting go.

"Throw it!" Abby shouted.

By then, it was too late. The runners neared their bases. Instead of killing the play and stopping the bleeding, Kate winged the ball to Jill at first. It flew high and wide, far off course, a complete miss. Jill reached to stop it, but it soared out of play. One runner scored. Then another. 3–0.

"Fuck," Abby muttered under her breath as Southern Colorado's fans erupted.

Kate covered her face. She never missed a throw and rarely made an error. This wasn't just a mistake. This was no different from her hitting slump. A result of the heart. Abby sank at her part in it.

"It's okay," Abby said to her. She wanted to do more. To say more, but the stadium vibrated with noise. "Shake it off. You got the next one."

Kate expelled a ragged sigh and settled into position.

"One out! Look 'em back, hit one!" Mick barked behind the plate. "Outfielders cut four!"

The next hitter fired a ball to Abby. She backhanded it, stared down the runner at third base, froze her in her spot, and threw to Jill for the out. Still 3–0.

"Two down!" Abby punched her glove and nodded at Kate. "Come on, we got this!"

"Two outs!" Kate shouted shakily.

The shaking revealed that she wasn't ready, and on the diamond, ready didn't matter. The less you wanted the ball, the more often it found you. Abby equated it to her experience hiding in the back of class when she hadn't done the reading, and the professor went rogue with the Socratic method. *Not me. Dear God, not me.*

Kate stopped the next grounder clean when it reached her but hesitated to throw. Abby wanted to close her eyes or turn away from the crash. After the prolonged pause, worry passing across her features, Kate rushed the throw to first base, chucking it high once more. Jill jumped to snag the ball and brought it down to the bag for a photo finish. The runner collided with her. They tangled, tripped, and tumbled.

"Out!" the umpire called.

Jill clutched her ankle in the dirt. The Southern Colorado runner groaned and called for help.

"Fuck." Abby cut across the field to Jill and kneeled to meet her. "You okay?"

"Son of a bitch." Jill clenched her teeth. Red splotches stained her sock where the runner's metal cleat took a bite of her.

"Can you stand?" Abby asked.

Jill nodded and accepted Abby's hand to haul her up. She whimpered when she put weight on her ankle. "Shit."

"I'm so sorry, Shupe." Kate joined them, completely ashen.

"Don't be." Jill draped her other arm over Kate's shoulder. "I'm fine."

Abby and Kate exchanged glances as they helped Jill to the dugout. Kate's lower lip trembled before she broke away from Abby's eyes. "This is my fault."

"It's not," Abby said. "Don't do that now."

In the dugout, the team trainer removed Jill's cleat and sock, revealing a jagged imprint from the spikes. Her ankle was already swollen and purple. The other team's runner still lay holding her knee at first base, pausing the action.

"How is it?" Coach Ackers asked the trainer.

"I can play," Jill said, but the trainer shook his head.

"We can't risk it, Shupe. I'm sorry." Coach Ackers glanced down the bench. "Quong, take over at first."

"Wait, Coach," Mick said. "T.K. is done."

T.K. shook her head, sweat running down her temple, the maroon bow in her bleached hair falling limp. "I can go another."

"They're crushing your curve, your rise is gone to piss, and you're missing your spots because you're tired," Mick said.

"My rise isn't piss."

"All you have is off speed and the top half of their lineup is about to get a third look at you." Mick pivoted to Coach Ackers. "She's done."

Coach Ackers gulped. While a decent pitching director, she wasn't exactly up for leading the team in the World Series semi-finals. She wrung her hands together. "Okay, Quong, go warm up. Ogden to first."

The freshman, Chloe Ogden, knocked over a row of bats at the news. "Me? Now?"

"Yes." Coach Ackers clapped her hands half-heartedly. "Come on. Let's rally."

Coach Ackers departed for third base, leaving them in miserable quiet while a stretcher arrived for the injured base runner. Abby stared at their blank column on the scoreboard. If they continued down this path, their season would end in three innings.

"You heard her. Let's go." Abby turned to the dejected squad. "It just takes one. One pitch. One hit. One run." She glanced around when no one responded. "Come on! Are you going to quit? We might as well pack it up and walk away."

Abby cringed at her own charge, especially when she caught Mick's raised brow. She stared down at the dusty dugout floor, littered with sunflower seeds and paper cups.

"I get it. I know we're in the gutter. And I know it's my fault."

She wasn't one to lead or give speeches, but something in her gnawed. Not just the end but the beginning. Her first tournament with Insley. The first time she felt the game again when she thought she never would. She owed them the same.

"I'm sorry for the fight. I'm sorry Coach Whit can't be here because she had to defend me." She sighed. Some of her teammates uncrossed their arms. "I'm sorry I almost walked away. But you know why I didn't? Because of you idiots. Because this team means everything to me. You've never given up on each other or me. In fact, two years ago, this team saved my life."

She assessed her friends. Jill's bloody leg propped beneath a bag of ice. Mick beet red with eye black smeared down her cheeks. T.K. sagging into the bench. And Kate, their heart and soul, cast off, head buried in her hands. This wasn't the send-off they deserved.

"This is it. Do it for yourself. Do it for each other." Abby settled on Kate, gazing a million miles away. "And if you can't do it for yourself or this team, then do it for Kate. How many times has she picked you up? How many times has she put us on her back? We wouldn't be here without her."

"For Hutch," Jill said, raising a fist.

"For all of us." Mick nodded, wincing to stand. T.K. helped her up from the bench. "Now or never, assholes."

The team clapped, started a chorus of "Let's go, right now, rally, rally, rally."

"Let's fucking do this," Abby demanded in the huddle. They stomped their feet, cried "Eagles!," whooped, screeched, and spiraled into nonsense. Southern Colorado glared as the gurney with their fallen teammate rolled away to apathetic clapping. The Eagles didn't care. The Eagles might be classless underdogs, might have already fucked themselves, but they would fight. They shoved each other, slapped hands, hit helmets, stomped on the steps, yanked at the fence, and taunted the opposing pitcher. A small riot. When Izzy Palamino, their first batter up, smacked a double, they roared.

Kate didn't move. She stayed hunched over, supporting her head in her hands. A few players patted her shoulder, chatted her up, but she didn't bounce back. Abby ambled over.

"Hey," she whispered.

Kate's misty blue eyes shifted, the clouds clearing when they landed on Abby. She didn't think Kate overdramatic. Anyone who cared about the game, who wanted it as much as Kate, would hate themselves for the error. Not just an error, but a game-losing, season-ending, haunting fuckup. The kind of error that was so horrendous, you weren't mad, simply happy you weren't the person to do it.

"Come on. We need you." Abby squatted in front of her and rested a hand on her knee.

"I ruined everything." She placed her trembling hand on top of Abby's. "I'm sorry."

"You didn't ruin anything. There's still time left."

"I don't know if I can."

"You can." Abby helped her to stand. A year ago, Kate had helped her return to the field. Now it was Abby's turn. "The team needs you. I need you."

Another hit and a crescendo of cheers filled the ballpark, but Kate melted into her arms. Abby hugged her back.

"Cruz! You're up!" Jill shouted.

Abby released Kate and put on her new helmet that didn't quite fit, snagged the wrong bat, and forgot her batting gloves. She didn't bother with a practice swing. She unloaded on the first pitch to knock in a run. 3–1. They were going to do it. They were going to win. They were going to hang on to each other for one game longer.

The Eagles scrapped back 3–2. Madison Quong pitched her heart out. Chloe Ogden trembled but never missed a ball. When another grounder came to Kate, Abby held her breath. Kate charged it on a bounce, threw it to Chloe on the run for the out, and sighed in relief.

In a stroke of poetry that only offered itself on the wings of competition, Kate got her redemption. The entire field went still in the last inning as she approached the plate. Abby and so many others already knew what was coming. It's like the entire stadium knew.

Jenna Crosby on third base. One out. Coach Ackers clapped and pointed through a flurry of signs, calling for the ultimate sacrifice. A squeeze bunt. There was no one else more primed, more prepared, more destined for it. It wasn't the glory of the home runs that Abby muscled out of the park, but the finesse, the willingness to surrender that made it work.

The players clutched each other's hands. Abby, who never prayed, willed the softball gods to smile down on them. The pitch came and Kate squared for the bunt, Crosby already at a dead sprint for the plate. If Kate hit it wrong, it was over. It required a gentle touch. A focus through the cheering and heat.

Kate tapped the ball just right, slotting it between the pitcher and first baseman. They crashed on it, but the ball veered out of reach, enough for Crosby to slide beneath the rushed toss to the catcher. Her fingers brushed the plate as Kate sprinted to second base. 3–3.

Erica Hightower struck out. Two outs.

Mick limped up to bat next, the game-winner on the line. She launched a shot to the fence, sending Kate on a sprint from second, arms pumping, legs propelling her to cut around third. The throw came in to the catcher, but Kate had the jump. They faced off as the ball flew in, and despite the tie, Abby knew it was over as Kate lowered her shoulder. She plowed into the catcher and skimmed the plate. Another lull over the field. Another pause that dragged on forever.

"Safe!" the umpire cried.

4–3.

The team rushed Kate, but Abby stayed behind. Grinning, yet determined not to ruin it. Plus, they still had to get through Southern Colorado's final at bats. She wouldn't let herself feel it until Madison Quong struck out the last batter, until Mick collapsed in celebration and exhaustion, until Jill and T.K. hobbled out of the dugout to join the victorious Eagles, and Kate launched herself into Abby's arms.

She cried into her chest. "We did it."

Abby squeezed her back and shut her eyes. "You did it."

Kate pulled back, gazing at her through tears that Abby couldn't discern as happy or sad, leftovers from their fight or a signal that all was forgiven. But at least they had this. This moment on the field when everything felt right again.

"Thank you," Kate whispered.

Abby swallowed a pit of tears, reached for her, but the rest of the team piled around them in celebration. She withdrew in the laughter, taking in Kate's joy, one she broke from more than once to glance at Abby, as if making sure she was still there, in the precious breath before their final game, without the pressure of what came after.

THE NATIONAL CHAMPIONSHIP

She suited up like it was a funeral. She, of course, had suited up for one not long ago, but had blacked most of it out. On the afternoon of the national championship, however, Abby would never forget dressing for the end. She deliberately tugged on her socks and stirrups, tucked in her maroon jersey after running a hand across her last name and number, and tightened the belt around her pinstripe pants.

Most of her teammates had a pregame ritual or superstition they followed, part of the Church of Softball, but not Abby. For all her belief in the game, she didn't subscribe to its superstitions. But suiting up for the last time as an Eagle resonated like worship. She let it wash over her as she sat on the wooden bench in the locker room, hands clasped, mitt beside her, aware that her future in the game didn't have to end today, but no matter what she chose, a part of it would be lost forever.

"Come here, Cruzer," Mick said behind her.

Abby turned around and smirked. She let Mick apply lines of eye black on her cheeks, once again falling into reverence, this time for the quiet friendship they had formed two years ago. Even while caught in the middle of Kate and Abby's fight, Mick didn't abandon her. She didn't say anything about it, just reminded Abby to eat, smacked her on the back too hard like she always did, joked and called her names. Their own love language. They spoke it there in the musty locker room, sunlight highlighting the floating dust as Mick applied the oily lines that Abby usually resisted.

"The knees going to make it today?" Abby asked.

"Seven innings and they're going into well-deserved retirement." Mick hit her with a knowing smirk. "I'm more worried about Hutch's shoulder."

Abby peered past her, through the small window of the trainer's room where Kate sat on the table. Mick patted her back as she departed, encouraging Abby to go to her. Not that Abby needed any prodding. Her metal cleats tapped across the concrete, taking her to Kate's side as the trainer taped her shoulder.

"How is it?" Abby asked.

Kate's gaze brightened, despite the wince that hadn't unhitched from her face since the semi-final collision. The trainer diagnosed it as AC joint separation, a gruesome strain of the ligaments between her collarbone and shoulder. Kate could barely raise her arm, let alone throw, and while there wasn't enough ice or rest to help her before the finals, everyone knew she'd push through.

"I'll be all right," Kate said. "At least the throw from second is shorter."

With the team's onslaught of injuries, Coach Whitley returned from her suspension in time to make creative adjustments to the lineup. Jenna Crosby had broken two fingers in the semi-finals and since Kate couldn't make the throw from shortstop anyway, she moved her to second. It set up Abby to shift from third base to the place she always seemed destined for—shortstop.

"I guess we'll get to turn two one more time," Abby said.

"Yeah." Kate smiled.

She sat with her jersey unbuttoned and pulled down around her right arm. Abby studied the familiar curve of it, the freckles she'd kissed, the healing that came from its embrace. When the trainer finished taping her, Abby nodded at him. "Can you give us a minute?"

He nodded and left. Kate grimaced as she attempted to pull her jersey back on, but Abby stepped in, gingerly slipping it back into place. She buttoned it, eyes trained on the jersey's stitches, on the rattle of Kate's breathing. "Thank you."

"You're welcome." Abby met her eyes. "I'm sorry. For everything."

"I'm sorry too."

"No. You were right about me. About us."

Kate shook her head and grabbed Abby's hand with her strong one. "I looked for you last night." Her throat bobbed. "I wanted to tell you I don't want this to be it. This can't be it."

"It's not. We have a whole game to play. A trophy to win."

"I mean after," she said.

Abby stared at their interlaced fingers. They wove into her like a lifeline, pulling her toward that future they once fantasized of. Kate in law school, Abby back on the field. A dream scenario she could talk about but failed to see.

"I never wanted to fight with you. I never wanted to lose you," Kate said. "You have to know that I didn't mean what I said."

"I never wanted those things either." She squeezed her hand. "Let's get through this game first, okay? Together."

Kate squinted at her and Abby nearly glanced away, scared of what she might detect. That this game wasn't a new beginning for them. This game was the end.

"Okay," Kate finally said.

Abby helped her down from the table, and Kate hugged her. "I'm going to miss this," she whispered into her neck.

Abby closed her eyes and sighed. "Me too."

For the first time all tournament, the Eagles played in front of a full ballpark. Cameras rolled to broadcast the game for a predictably small audience on a subscription network. The sun beat down on the freshly raked dirt with a touch of humidity in the air, hinting of summer.

The team gathered as Coach Whitley read the lineup one last time, and when the huddle shifted to Kate for the last speech, Abby's throat swelled. She shivered as the captain surveyed each player, her blue eyes a scepter of power. Abby notched it in her memory, and years later, would have more images of Kate in her head that day than of any score or play.

After a prolonged pause that infused hair-raising static, Kate nodded. She delivered her short sermon with chilling conviction. "Let's fucking do this."

The Eagles received Kate's brief direction and unprecedented f-bomb in a frenzy. They cheered, jostled each other, and shrieked away nerves. Abby's cheeks ached from smiling and her heart melted from pride and pining when Kate's gaze latched onto hers.

Abby admired her all game. Her dives across the dirt, her pained throws for the out, her confidence at bat as she knocked in runs, faked a bunt, and hit a hole. Her laughter, her cheering, her celebrations, a light graze to Abby's back as they jogged off the field together, all conspired to keep her. And when they turned two to end the game, Abby thought the world intended to force her hand.

Abby slid on her knee to stop the grounder on her weak side, threw it without looking, knowing Kate would arrive. And she did. She stomped the bag for the first out, narrowly avoided the sliding runner, and hurled a laser to Jill. Pain and hope creased her features at the movement of her battered muscles. They froze as the ball traveled for the win. Jill stretched on her good leg for the catch.

And just like that, it was over.

They'd won a national championship.

Mick chucked off her mask and lifted T.K. off her feet. Jill threw the ball high in the air before limping to join them, her sock stained red with blood. Abby and Kate clung to each other, holding on through tears. In the waves of bouncing bodies, Kate seized her cheeks, didn't seem to care about the possibility of being seen by her parents or anyone else, and kissed her. The raucous team served as a shield against unwanted attention. Their eyes met at release, Kate's radiating the future, Abby's the end.

"Come with me," Kate said.

Abby's lips parted to speak, when someone poured a water cooler above, soaking them from head to toe. The dogpile overcame them. Abby chuckled at Kate lying beneath her, their noses hovering close, their teammates' arms and legs a jungle around them. She brushed wet hair off Kate's forehead. Nearly stole another kiss. She whispered "I love you" instead. Kate whispered the same with her mouth against her ear.

They'd lift the trophy together. They'd spray the champagne she and Mick snuck into their hotel room. They'd kiss and hold hands and fall asleep as one. But before dawn, while everyone snored in drunk exhaustion, Abby gathered her things. She watched Kate nestled in the covers with a stone in her chest. Uncertain of what it would mean for them five years later, she left her a letter and slipped out the door.

THE END OF SENIOR YEAR

Dear Kate,

Two years ago, when I came to Insley, I never imagined that the end would be this hard. I planned on dropping out after a few months, but then there was you. Pulling me out of the darkness, whether I wanted you to or not.

I didn't mean to fall in love with you, and I know you definitely didn't mean to fall in love with me. I know it scared you, and you're braver than I ever gave you credit for going there with me anyway. You've never been a coward. Not once.

I don't think I've ever been honest and told you it scares me too, because I don't know how to have a love like this. A love that's patient and slow. Life has always been hard and fast for me. Uncertain. Maybe it's the way I grew up. Maybe it's just something inside I can't quite shake.

Whatever it is, it's keeping me from you and the future you envision for us. I can't quite see it. I can't make the type of promises that you deserve. The main promise being to not sabotage this.

Even if I could, I think there's more out there for you without me. You're brilliant and you're going to be an amazing lawyer.

You're going to meet so many more people. Better people. You don't need me to hold you back from that. You don't need to worry about me, like I know you've had to do for so long.

I'll always love you, Kate. You've made me a better version of myself, and I'm sorry I still can't get out of my own way. I know this is going to hurt for a while, but I think it'll be the best thing for you, even if you don't understand. I don't completely understand. But we're not entitled to understanding. I only know that I have to go and I can't pull you down with me this time. Even if it means leaving a piece of me behind.

Don't try to be so perfect, okay?

Love,
Abby

• • •

Dear Abby,

I can't tell you how many versions of this letter I've written. I suppose no matter how mad I am that you left, by the end of this I want you to know I still love you. I still hope that you'll come back.

After that morning, I lived in denial. I was convinced we'd get back to Insley, and you'd be there. I planned on being furious at you, but I never got the chance. You really were gone.

Isla said she didn't know where you went, but I didn't fully believe her. I tried your phone, we all did. I went to your apartment to find it empty. It made me ill for days. I couldn't get out of bed. Mick and Jill had to pick up my cap and gown for me. I thought, hoped, you might turn up at graduation, which motivated me to go, but when you weren't there, it was like you'd left all over again. Only this time I couldn't deny it. This time, I couldn't wallow and wait.

We packed up the blue house for the last time. I spent the summer at the farm, which stings knowing you'd disapprove. I worked as a paralegal and on the shuttle back and forth between civilization in my brother's truck, I called our friends asking daily if they'd heard from you. Always nothing. Everyone promised you were okay even though I know they worried too. I just think they hear it in my voice—how close I am to breaking without you.

Mourning, worrying, aching for you in secret has been the most painful thing I've ever done. I suppose I could've shared my heartbreak with my parents, but to what end? To lose them too?

There were many days I thought I might not get through. I wasted countless wide-awake hours wondering where you were and what I could've done. That pain made me think of you too. It must be a small fraction of what you felt when you lost your mother. Because while you're alive, this is grief too. A sort of brutal half grief, like escaping severely injured. Alive but hurt and changed, fearfully aware that nothing will be the same again. I should be grateful you're okay, but it's almost an uglier wound, to know you're lost to me anyway.

By the time I left for Berkeley, I'd given up on you. I tried to accept you were never coming back, tried to let the summer become a scar. School promised to be a fresh start that I desperately needed.

So, imagine my shock when the registrar called me to their office to inform me that an anonymous benefactor had covered my full tuition. Not just the first year, but all of it. Certainly no one in my life has that kind of money. While I've received scholarships, I don't think I won enough favor for anyone to fully sponsor my law education. Which just leaves you.

I called Isla right away. She stonewalled me, so don't blame her. When she didn't break, like your location was the nuclear codes, I told her I would drop out of law school and dedicate my time to finding you. A little melodramatic, but it did the job.

She claims you don't have a phone, which is just reckless enough of you that I believe it. I worry that you're traveling around Europe without a way for someone to reach you or you them. What if something happens? But I suppose that's the point. It's not my concern anymore and you've made sure of it. All I'm left with is a postal box in Amsterdam that I'm not even sure you'll check.

In your letter, you said there's more for me without you, but it's my choice to make. That's what I hate most about you running away. You didn't give me a chance to fight. You say that you'll hold me back, but the person I love and know never did. If anything, you championed me. I can't understand what changed. I spend hours every day trying to figure you out. If you feel like you're not enough, think how I must feel. I gave you everything, and you still walked.

As for what I need to figure out, I already have. It was always you. It's always going to be you. So, I'm asking, pathetically, wholeheartedly, and unafraid of humiliation, that you come back. Come back home, Abby.

I promise I won't be mad. We can get a little place in Berkeley. You don't have to go to grad school or play softball. You can surf. You can do whatever you like. And I'll tell my parents. I'll tell them I found the love of my life, that there won't be another. It'll be okay so long as I have you. I'm not afraid of that anymore. Not after this.

We can figure it out. I want to figure it out. I just want you with everything in me.

Love,
Kate

P.S. Thank you for paying for my tuition. I'm not in a position to refuse it, but one day I'll repay it.

FOUR YEARS POST-GRADUATION

She'd just finished the bar exam when she got the call. Her back spasmed and her shoulder, a stubborn vexation from an old injury, had locked up after two six-hour days of test taking. She answered outside beneath the July sun, trollies rolling by while she worked the kinks out of her neck.

"She said yes!" Mick shouted through the phone.

Kate's mouth fell. She'd known the proposal was approaching, but forgot the exact date in the swirl of graduation and studying for the bar. Knowing Mick, she hadn't mentioned it for that very reason.

"Congratulations! I'm so happy for you, Mick," Kate said. "I can't believe one of us is getting married."

"Well, one of us technically already has. I'll just be the first to have a big, gay wedding."

Not long after graduation, Jill got pregnant with the surprise she deemed her national championship baby, conceived the night after they raised the trophy. Rather than wait, she and Dylan legalized their union at the courthouse, wearing flower crowns in front of two random witnesses. They welcomed the newest member of the ferocious fivesome seven months later. A fire-haired Juniper Faye Farrelly.

"So, what's next? What do you need me to do?" Kate asked.

"Well, I think Haley already has half of it planned. We'll probably set the date for next spring. But I'm getting the band back together for this one." Mick laughed nervously, and Kate stiffened. "I need all of you up there with me. You, my sister, Shupe, T.K. . . . and uh, Cruz."

"Right." Kate squeezed her eyes shut at the name. "Of course. Just let me know what you need. We're here for you, Mick, and I'm so honored."

"Oh, don't be honored. I just need you to make sure that the bachelorette is a full-blown, near-death experience."

"I'll talk to T.K."

"This is why I love you," Mick said.

"Love you too."

"Okay, I got to go. Cruz is calling me back."

Kate hissed as the line went dead. She couldn't blame Mick for wanting Abby in her wedding. They were friends. Of course, that's what stung. While Kate hadn't heard from Abby, everyone else had.

Four years ago, when her letter didn't prompt a reply, Kate considered sending another or asking Isla for a new address. She pathetically believed Abby wasn't responding because she hadn't received it. But then a few months later, Mick let it slip that she'd heard from her over Christmas. She provided sparse details, like Kate might snap or jump on the next plane if she revealed too much.

Kate feigned indifference, but the small updates hurt. Abby called and visited Mick regularly, flew in for Juniper's first birthday when Kate couldn't, and partied with T.K. in Los Angeles. It infuriated her. Abby only appeared whenever Kate was too busy, ensuring they never crossed paths.

For that first year, as Abby returned to everyone except her, Kate held out hope. Maybe she hadn't gotten the letter. Maybe she thought Kate wanted nothing to do with her. She didn't follow her on social media and didn't get her new phone number from Mick or Jill. But she also didn't let herself move on.

She didn't date her first two years at Berkeley. She buried herself in school, determined to join the law review, to get the best internships, using every test and assignment to block Abby out.

Until she met Ryan.

She'd never noticed him in their class of three hundred, not that she truly noticed anyone. A few cute girls maybe, a desire she was too scared to pursue again, but no one of the opposite sex. She laughably decided if being an attorney didn't work out, she'd join a nunnery.

They met at the law school welcome-back BBQ to start their third year. The gathering was one of Kate's favorites since it included an annual slow pitch softball tournament. After her performance the first year and word spreading of her national championship ring, teams fought over her. The Bad News Barristers drafted her first, while Ryan got picked last by the Master Debaters.

Kate noticed him because he wore a glove that must have been twenty years old, fidgeted uneasily at second base, and had a weak arm during warm-ups. So, on the first pitch, she drilled a shot at him on purpose. It hit him square in the face and he dropped like a sack of bricks.

She didn't bother to run to first, and instead sprinted straight for him, as everyone gasped in horror. Ryan held his nose while Kate hovered above. "I'm so sorry," she said.

"They put me at second base because no one was supposed to hit it that hard at me." His blood-stained hand stifled a chuckle.

"Sorry. You were an easy target."

"And I thought you were brutal in mock court, Kate Hutchins." He accepted her hand, and she helped him up. Kate cringed at not knowing his name. His hazel eyes sparkled with amusement despite his likely broken nose. "This will be a funny story to tell our kids at least."

Kate laughed. "Wow, this is when you decide to make your move?"

"You're right. I'm definitely concussed." He grinned and Kate smiled back. "I'm Ryan Eckhardt. We're in like every class together."

"Yeah, right, I know you."

Ryan grinned again, unbothered despite the blood on his lips, inspiring a lightness that Kate missed. While he left the field, their classmates fussing over him, Kate returned to playing. He cheered for her from the stands, an ice pack held to his face, and when the game ended, she brought him a beer.

"A peace offering?" Ryan asked.

"I just don't want you to sue me," Kate said. "Not that you'd have much of a case with assumption of risk."

"Ah, but I think this might fall under intentional acts," Ryan said. "What with you going after the weak kid and all."

"Right, the jury's definitely going to believe a six-foot-two giant is an easy athletic target."

"I'll see you in court." Ryan winked.

After that, Kate couldn't help but notice him. They talked before and after class. Ryan's background eerily mirrored hers. He'd grown up in a large Mormon family on a farm in Idaho. When he got into Dartmouth, rather than being proud, his parents condemned him for not completing his mission trip to Brazil. He compounded their disappointment when a few terms in New England made him a liberal sympathizer and led him to Berkeley.

Kate admired that he hadn't turned on religion afterward, but rediscovered it. He'd had his heart broken too, lost his virginity, and battled the same demons as Kate. He was the first person she felt she could talk about it with.

"I've spent the last year convinced the pain was a punishment from God for my transgressions," she said on one of their walks along the beach. Seagulls scampered about their feet and the waves washed away their footsteps.

"God's not vengeful, and the pain is just part of it. It means you really loved someone. There's nothing wrong with that," he said.

"You can't be sure though."

"No, I am." Ryan grinned sheepishly as he shoved his hands in his pockets. "Even the bad parts are within His plan."

Ryan took her to church. Not the church of her youth or his, with its stiff pews and pulpit. Hundreds of people attended on Sunday, met by jovial greeters and free lattes in the coffee shop. The sanctuary resembled an amphitheater with its massive stage, jumbotrons, and speakers. Kate found it more concert than liturgy, with a band that dressed like discount folk artists, pounding drums and riffing guitars. The congregation raised hands, sang along with the lyrics on the screens, and swayed for their catchy ballads about Jesus with the fervor one might find at a music festival.

She couldn't help but snort during the first song.

"What?" Ryan asked.

Kate shook her head. "Nothing."

It took her a while to accept it as church. Probably because it felt easier than what she knew before. No end of days, no guilt, no God glaring down at her. With its flashy colors, its simple, feel-good sermons, and the smiling faces, she lost herself in the crowd and felt lighter when she left, like she'd done her job. She was still a Christian. She was still faithful. Even if she chose the trendier, more palatable option. Even if she didn't feel it in her chest. This was right. And Ryan was right along with it. He believed, raised his hands in praise, helped her not dread Sundays, and like her, made a pact with God—despite reneging on his purity, he committed to waiting for marriage until the next time as a born-again virgin.

Church became a regular occurrence, followed by studying together, coffee and lunches, beach walks, and football games. They became friends. Kate emphasized only friendship, and Ryan respected her boundaries. Until finally, she didn't want him to.

She confided in Mick, who encouraged her to go for it. In fact, Mick relentlessly insisted she get back out there, which unsettled her. She assumed it meant Abby was doing just that. But she couldn't. Not until she knew for sure.

She met Mick in Portland over winter break, where she was teaching history and coaching softball at her old high school. They grabbed drinks at a sports bar downtown, Kate strategically ordering more rounds, until she had Mick exactly where she wanted her.

"I need you to tell me the truth," she said.

Mick gulped and slammed down her beer. "Oh God, about what?"

"Did she get the letter or not?"

Mick groaned. "You promised you wouldn't put me in the middle."

"And I haven't, but I need this. I can't move on until I know." Kate frowned. "It's like I'm standing still, waiting. I mean, isn't that pathetic? I'm still waiting for her."

"She got it." Mick buried her head in her hands. "Why do you guys make me do this?"

Her entire body went rigid. "She got it?"

"Yeah."

"What did she say about it?"

"Nothing. She said you sent her a letter in Amsterdam and that she still feels awful—"

"Oh, she feels awful?" Kate scoffed. She would've let tears loose if her anger didn't lock them in, firming her trembling bottom lip into a locked jaw.

Mick grabbed her hand. "Kate, it's time to move on. You deserve to be happy, but I don't know if that's ever going to be with Abby."

Kate asked Ryan to dinner. When they kissed, she nearly flinched at the taste and rough trace of his cheeks. It wasn't bad, but it was different. Different from the gentle warmth of Abby. Different too, because with Ryan, there was calm. There was slowness. No pressure about right or wrong, no avoiding God. Ryan fit seamlessly into her present and her future. He wasn't Abby, but he was almost perfect.

When Mick proposed to Haley, Kate believed she'd moved on. She was at the precipice of her dream career, in a stable relationship with a man she loved. But on the sidewalk, after the call, she plummeted.

"You always finish tests before me," Ryan said as he joined her.

Kate raised a brow and said what she always had to: "It's not a competition."

Of course, despite their best efforts, it always ended up a competition. And Kate, for lack of a better word, and by no means keeping score, always won. It was fun at first. Debating in mock court and comparing test scores. Getting the most questions right during their lectures and study groups, fighting for and securing senior editor positions on the *California Law Review.* They went to trivia, played chess, hiked, and ran together, but Kate swore she caught his gritted teeth when he couldn't figure out how to beat her, and while he was faster than her, she worried that even if she could finish the San Francisco Marathon first that it was better she didn't.

The tiffs and teasing seemed minor, acceptable by-products of their personalities, until Kate's clerkship. They both applied to positions with the Supreme Court of California, coveted spots with hundreds of applicants. They smiled and joked while they gathered letters of recommendation, proofread each other's writing samples, and even celebrated together when they both made it to the interview round.

She never considered it might implode when Justice Levitsky offered her a clerkship and Ryan received none. He stared off in shock while he digested the news, and Kate, who wanted to celebrate, didn't dare smile. She rubbed his arm while they sat beneath the bell tower after class, watching people cycle through the quad.

"It's going to be okay."

Ryan shrugged her off. "No." He shook his head. "Not now. I just need a minute, okay?"

Kate withdrew and frowned. "I thought you could at least be happy for me."

"Happy for you? I wanted this too." Ryan snatched his jacket from the brick steps and stood. "You just always have to win, don't you?"

"It's not a competition. It's my career."

"And what about mine?"

He stomped away before she could stop him, and truthfully, she didn't want to. Her thoughts drifted to where she tried so hard to not let them. Abby. Not that long ago, they had competed for the same position, but it never ended in bitterness. Sure, Abby was better, but Kate hadn't held it against her. And Abby, for her part, had supported Kate, shared tips, and when Kate took over at shortstop, she didn't scowl or pout. She had always been genuinely happy for her, whether it was softball or the rest, and when Berkeley accepted her, Abby didn't once complain about what it might mean for her. In fact, she footed the bill.

Kate scolded herself for the comparison, the game she always fell into with poor Ryan, who wasn't just competing with Kate but unwittingly with Abby. For that, she gave him slack. She forgave him the second he turned up at her door that night, tail between his legs, and a flower arrangement in hand.

They finished law school, agreeing to not share where they landed in class ranking. A new chapter. A clean start. It felt worth it when Kate introduced him to her parents at graduation. But when she looked at the pictures that showed her with a hollow smile that didn't reach her eyes, she wondered if it meant anything at all. It was supposed to be different than when she graduated from Insley, and it was in every way but the most important. Abby still wasn't there.

"So, are you going to be okay at the bachelorette?" Jill asked her during their weekly group call.

"What do you mean?"

She was inching toward the end of her clerkship, had passed the bar on the first try—another feat she dreaded sharing with Ryan—and set her sights on landing at a firm that was as prestigious as it was altruistic. It was more than enough to distract her from the upcoming reunion.

"I'm talking about Cruz!" Jill yelled over Juniper banging pots in the background.

"Yeah, I'll be fine." Kate glanced over her shoulder to ensure Ryan was still crouched over his work at the dining room table. "I'm surprised she's even coming. She avoids me like the plague."

Mick snickered. "I have the power to bring feuding nations to peace. It's like witnessing the fall of the Berlin Wall."

"I wouldn't speak so soon," Jill said. "The Cold War is going strong."

"We're adults," Kate said, as she rubbed her burning neck. "Abby and I are a nonfactor. Feelings haven't been there for a long time. We've both made ourselves crystal clear."

Clear, except that Kate still eyed the one number in the wedding group chat that wasn't in her phone. Abby's new number. She didn't save it, certainly didn't text or call, but stared at her few responses like a coded ransom note—one that held the key to cutting ties for good.

"Who's Abby?" Ryan asked when she hung up.

Kate shook her head. "Just an old teammate."

She frowned when she turned away, because it wasn't even a lie. After four years, despite everything they'd been through together, that's all Abby was to her now. All she let herself be.

She'd just stepped off the plane from Tokyo when she got the call. Abby hobbled on crutches as she searched for her ride outside LAX, ACL torn to shreds, her softball career finished for good. So, in true ethereal fashion, the game beckoned her back. Not to the field, but to the family she found on it.

"What are you doing?" Mick answered on the first ring when she dialed her back.

Abby grumbled. "Going to see an orthopedic surgeon. Sorry I missed your call, I just got back from Tokyo. Total fucking shit show."

"Okay, okay, enough about you. I'm getting married."

"Oh, shit."

"Yeah shit."

Abby grinned. "Damn, congrats, Mickey. And to Haley too. She's a saint."

"I'm not calling for your well-wishes. I need you for this one. I'm cashing in on my favor," Mick said. "You, Shupe, T.K., Hutch. It's time for us to come back together."

Abby sighed and patted her pockets for a cigarette. "I appreciate it, Mick, and I love you, but I don't know if that's a good idea. You and Kate are closer anyway. I'll still come to the wedding."

"Nope. This is what I want. This is what I get."

"Fucking bridezilla." Abby chuckled.

"You're damn right. Plus, I want to tear up Vegas for the bachelorette."

"Okay, fine, I'll come."

"Bye, idiot."

"Bye."

Abby groaned. She didn't think her luck could get any worse lately, but she should have known somewhere lower always waited in the wings. And this day, when the call home finally came, had taunted her across the globe.

In the aftermath of the national championship, she had scrambled to put as much space as possible between her and Kate, gathering her shit and driving south before the team returned to campus. That's when she broke her silence with Isla, cashing in on a place to crash. She spent the next week on her couch at her new home in San Diego, helping her and Luca unpack, drinking on the beach every night, the Pacific cooing in the backyard.

"Maybe I can just stay here," Abby said while she watched the waves with a bottle of champagne on what would be graduation day.

Isla flopped down on the sand next to her. "You're welcome to, but I think you should settle a few things first."

"I'm not talking about Kate with you. You promised." Abby slugged more champagne. "I'm still recovering from you getting between me and Audie and the trust fund business."

Despite Abby's protests, the money hit her bank account after Isla confirmed she had just barely passed her last classes. It was more than she knew what to do with. Money she also refused to touch. At least for now.

"I've apologized for that, hence your open invitation to hide in my pool house." Isla shook her head and frowned. "I'm not talking about Kate. I'm talking about your extra year of eligibility and grad school. You should still go."

"I'm not going to Berkeley."

"Then somewhere else."

Somewhere else being Alabama or Florida. Somewhere she wouldn't have to see Kate and might get over the heartbreak. But she couldn't picture herself there, back in the classroom, playing alongside new teammates. She also couldn't imagine lasting more than a month before dropping out. Abby shook her head.

"Okay, well, what about Team USA?" Isla asked.

"It won't be far enough," she whispered.

She needed more than state lines between them. She needed countries.

That's when it whispered between the waves. Puerto Rico. A call from roots she didn't know, or maybe the game itself. She didn't have a real explanation, except that she needed two things, and it offered both—softball and an escape.

In the morning, she contacted the national team's coach, and he offered her a tryout. She bought a one-way ticket and packed a single bag.

"I don't like this. You have no one there," Isla said when she drove her to the airport. "Is this about Dad?"

Abby glared. "No."

"You're literally returning to where he grew up. You don't think that's like some Freudian thing?"

"It's the only other place I can play that's not here. I'm not going to explain it." Abby's knee bounced while she checked her passport. "Can you just do what I asked?"

Isla drew in an exasperated breath. "You told me not to get in the middle. Paying Kate's tuition is doing exactly that."

"She won't know it's us."

"I have a better idea. How about instead of anonymously giving her two hundred grand, you call her like a normal person? Apologize? Make up?"

"This is all I can give her right now," Abby said.

Isla's face drooped. "Fine."

They hugged at the airport as planes squealed overhead.

"You're a better sister than I deserve," Abby said.

"I know." Isla pecked her cheek when they released. "Be safe."

She made the national team the next day, jet-legged, but buzzing with the adrenaline of having nowhere and no one in this next venture. The feeling only lasted a few hours. The coach added her to the starting lineup six pitches into batting practice, four of which she knocked over the fence.

Abby spent the summer sharing a flat with a few teammates in San Juan while they trained for the World Cup. She improved her Spanish and lived out of a suitcase. Between practices and games, she pined for Kate, but it was easier without her phone number, without her address, as if the world was too big to find her again. Maybe even too big to find herself.

Despite telling Isla her decision had nothing to do with Audie, and wholeheartedly believing it, Abby couldn't resist retracing his footsteps. Her teammates warned her not to go to La Perla, but it called to her. She walked through the maze of crumbling sidewalks, passed the homes with peeled paint and tarp roofs, aching each time a child thrust an empty palm at her. She watched the ocean hit the rocks and tasted salt in the breeze, marveling at the views people would pay millions for, yet the neighborhood stood here, destitute, isolated, alone.

In interviews, Audie always claimed he was glad to have left his home behind, but Abby felt him there. His hardship and his anger. When the hair rose on the back of her neck at nightfall, danger lurking in dark cars and corners as she hurried from the slums, she felt it lurk in her too.

It wasn't all bad. She spotted his posters and memorabilia in sports bars. He was the hometown hero. Kids still wore his jersey while they played ball in the streets. She never told the locals of their connection, but sometimes they looked twice and bought her a drink. Most days, she didn't know if it brought her closer or further from him.

Despite Abby's contributions, Puerto Rico lost the Women's Softball World Cup in the Netherlands. Team USA dominated as expected, but Abby didn't care, not even as Skip Zamborelli spurned her for not joining his roster. "You could've won a championship," he said.

Abby shrugged. "I've already won a championship."

The only one that mattered. The one with her friends and Kate for the one place she considered home. While she'd done a decent job distracting herself, the sting found her chest. The next Women's Softball World Cup was two years away. Puerto Rico wouldn't start training again for several months and Abby didn't know what would fill her time until then.

So, she rented a room in Amsterdam, dipping into the plump trust fund she wanted to resist, but she had no self-restraint. Not when the drinks or drugs flowed. Not when she roamed through Berlin and Brussels, Paris and London. She ate and drank and danced and fucked her way through a few months, jumping on the next train when she worried about the future. It almost worked. Until she received a letter with a Berkeley address in the corner.

She tore it open, devoured the lines in tears, and hated herself all over again. She convinced herself she'd saved them both by leaving. Instead, she'd left Kate in a despair she knew well. Another thing she wouldn't forgive herself for.

Traversing Europe quickly lost its sparkle, no longer enough to distract her from loneliness or lack of direction. She defeatedly returned to the pool house, in a deeper depression than before. Whenever Isla tried to broach the subject of Kate or what came next, Abby stonewalled her. So, she employed other methods.

After a week of sleeping the day away and drinking poolside, Abby woke to a bucket of water. She bolted up in bed, gasping and drenched.

"Morning, sunshine," Mick said as she chucked the empty bucket aside.

"What the fuck!" Abby wiped soggy hair out of her eyes. "How'd you find me?"

"Your sister," Jill said.

Abby's mouth dropped. It'd been five months since nationals.

Since she resigned herself to never seeing them again. If anything, Kate deserved their friends after the split, and with Abby's unceremonious departure, she didn't expect they'd want anything to do with her. Their arrival threatened tears she couldn't handle. Rather than let them spill, she deflected to the less pressing but equally unavoidable questions.

"What the fuck, Shupe? Are you pregnant?" Abby asked.

"You're not supposed to ask people that," Jill said.

"Yes, she's pregnant." Mick folded her arms. "You would know, if you didn't ditch us."

Abby couldn't resist a smirk. "Are you the father?"

"Still waiting on the paternity test." Mick winked. "Heard you won't shower; thought we'd help you get a jump start."

"Mission successful." Abby peeled the wet sheet back and wrung out her T-shirt. She reluctantly met Mick's and Jill's faces, and her throat caught on a whimper. "Why are you here?"

"Trying to figure out what the hell you were thinking." Mick sat on the edge of the bed. "Dipping out the side door? Leaving Hutch a fucking cop-out letter?"

"I'm not enough for her, Mick. You both know that." Abby looked away at Jill's mournful sigh. "I almost ruined everything at nationals. I'm not about to ruin her."

"You think she deserves this though? You think we deserve it?"

Abby buried her head in her hands and sniffled. "How is she?"

"She's Kate. She's strong," Jill said. "But she's really hurt. This crushed her, Abby."

More tears streamed. "She sent a letter." Her voice cracked, and then the rest of her did too. "I don't know what to do."

Mick gripped her shoulder hard, but it was a comfort as Abby wept. Jill took her other side, with another arm to strap her in. They held her heaving body between them, fixed and wordless. It brought Abby's fit to a simmer, and when she could breathe again, Mick spoke solemnly.

"You either get yourself together and go after her with everything you have." She paused and exhaled, like it pained her to say the rest. "Or you don't respond. Leave her be and try to find a new normal. But nothing in between."

Abby scrubbed her cheeks. She had a last chance to decide. Only there wasn't a decision. She wasn't ready, didn't have anything to give Kate, and nothing to give herself.

"Either way, you're not getting rid of us so easily," Jill said.

Abby lifted her head. "But what about . . ."

"You're stuck with us," Mick said. "I know whatever is happening with Hutch is complicated, but we're not going to choose between you guys."

"Plus, who else is going to be this baby's hitting coach?"

Abby smiled through tears. She'd never understand why Mick, Jill, and T.K. kept her in their orbit, when they didn't need to. Their calls, their video messages, their visits and hers, holiday plans, and baby Juniper would keep her afloat for years to come.

After their visit, she jumped back into the game. There were rumblings of a league starting in the U.S., but Abby flew to Italy. Several of her teammates from Puerto Rico played there, and while it was hardly a living wage, it kept her on the field.

She spent two seasons in Milan, playing shortstop for Bollate, knocking home runs across Europe. The Italians called her *Sprezzatura* for her fearless play and countless flings, and while she settled into her team and a routine, the temporary apartments and hotels left her adrift, unsettled, as much in life as at heart.

When Canada's fledgling professional league recruited her, Abby moved to Toronto. She reasoned that it was a closer flight to Isla and Mick and Jill, even though in its meager two seasons the league only had four teams and scarce sponsorship deals. She made less money than she did in Italy. Few fans filled the stands and despite the league's promise of publicity and new investors, bringing in players like Abby to drum up interest, none of it came to fruition.

When the season ended, she experienced the same story she'd heard from countless softball players in America and around the world. The league folded without a warning or press conference. The front office just sent an email, asking the players to gather their things after the last game. There wasn't enough funding, not enough fans, and no way forward. For Abby, it wasn't the end of the road, but for many of her teammates, it was a sudden, cruel end. While they passed a few bottles of liquor back and forth in the stands, watching the sunset over the field, she wondered if this was all there was.

Isla and Luca's wedding a month later reinforced her growing restlessness. As Abby admired her sister, dancing in the arms of her new husband, she tried to imagine it for herself but stopped short. Worse than that, as she slammed drinks, she couldn't stop thinking about the one person who deserved to be there.

"They make quite the pair," Audie said to her as Isla and Luca cut the cake.

Abby avoided him during the wedding. He didn't walk Isla down the aisle, but they were cordial, shared conversation, laughter, a hug, and a dance. Abby didn't know if she thought less of her sister or envied it.

"May I join you?" Audie nodded to a chair at the otherwise empty table.

"I guess."

He'd aged since their last run-in. White had set in at the temples of his jet-black hair and new folds creased his cheeks. "The game strikes again," he said, while he puffed on a cigar.

Abby furrowed her brow. "What?"

"Your sister says you and your teammate got her and Luca together, yes? The girl with the pretty eyes?" Audie asked. Abby swallowed a knot in her throat at the mention of Kate. "You don't play softball, you don't go to Insley, you don't meet the girl who goes to law school, who Isla and Luca end up helping. The game. See?"

Abby swirled her scotch. "Sure."

"You look beautiful." Audie's eyes, so much like her own, glinted gentler than she remembered.

"Yeah, well, Isla chose the dress."

"I hear you are playing."

"You heard right." Abby grabbed the cigar from his mouth, took a long drag, and exhaled into his face.

"Good." Audie grabbed another cigar from the inner pocket of his tuxedo jacket. "You are doing well?"

"What do you care?"

Audie winced. "I suppose I should apologize for our last meeting. I shouldn't have put hands on you. Or said the things I did." He contemplated his cigar. "I suppose you know how to push my buttons better than anyone. But it helped me to make some changes."

"Yeah, like what?" Abby narrowed her eyes. She'd heard the same song and dance before. "Isla told me you moved back here to work for the Padres, but that's for you. Everything you ever do is for you."

"I've stopped drinking. I should've done that a long time ago. To be there for you and your sister."

"Well, we'll see how long that lasts."

Abby blew a delicate ring of smoke to hide that the revelation surprised her, and that it gave her a rare smidge of hope. It was too late to talk to her mother, too late to sort through her complicated childhood, but, just maybe, Audie wasn't entirely bad. Just as she wasn't. Because whether she admitted it or not, they were more alike than different.

"I saw where you grew up when I was training in Puerto Rico."

Audie chortled bitterly. "I do everything in my power to get away. A generation later, you choose to go back."

"Have you?" she asked. "Gone back home?"

"No. Have you?"

"Where's home?"

Audie frowned. "Well, I won't keep you."

"I'm sorry too." Abby closed her eyes and sighed. "For my part in our fight."

Audie's mustache quirked with a half smile. "Do you want to dance?"

"Seriously?"

They watched the wedding guests twist and sway to music.

"Do you have someone special?"

Abby shook her head. "No."

"But someone you wish was here."

She bit her lip and allowed him a full glimpse of her face.

"I let her go," Abby whispered.

Audie canted his head, and it reminded her of Isla. That tender curiosity. "Why?"

"Because I didn't know how to hold on to her." Abby threw back the rest of her drink. "I wonder where I get that from."

Audie shrugged, a teasing sparkle in his gaze. "Beats me, mija."

"This was great." She strapped her heels back on and patted his shoulder. "Let's do it again in three years."

Abby moved to Japan next. The league offered an actual paycheck, something she didn't need her trust fund to supplement. Its fan base grew every year, sponsorships, even television deals. It was the closest she ever felt to a true professional career.

Tokyo was also like nothing she'd experienced. The neon signs stacked atop each other, the honking traffic, motorcycles gunning by, smoke and smog, all reflected in the stretch of skyscrapers that spanned as far as she could see. And people everywhere, at every hour, a constant tide that she failed to swim in. Abby always considered herself rudderless, but never had she been this impossibly lost.

She struggled to communicate with her teammates, with anyone really, mostly just nodding along in the locker room until they took the field. Fortunately, that was the same in every language. Fielding, hitting, listening to the ball. She was fluent in it across the globe.

The bottle remained a dependable ally in the foreign landscape. That year, Kate graduated from law school, and while Abby resisted reaching out or asking their friends about her, she broke her rule and looked her up. She beamed at the accomplishments listed during commencement: top of her class, *California Law Review,* a clerkship with the Supreme Court of California.

Abby lost herself for days after, drinking with teammates, and when they tired, anyone who might partake or invite her to join their *nomikai.* She developed a taste for sake, never declined a second party or third, stumbling through karaoke and *izakayas,* falling asleep on the sidewalk alongside the businessmen snoring in their neckties.

In that same depressed, hungover stupor, she agreed to what launched one of the strangest chapters of her career. A battle of the sexes–themed game show enlisted her and a few of her teammates to participate in an episode, pitting them against men from Japan's professional baseball league. Abby barely understood the rules when a producer explained them backstage.

They played on a regulation-sized field inside a large studio. Multicolor lights bore down on the artificial diamond. High-pitched video game music never ceased. The host screamed the premise in Japanese to a roaring crowd. Abby, who chugged several drinks backstage, likened it to an acid trip. In fact, she seriously contemplated whether someone slipped her something during a party the night before.

Despite the strangeness of the softball nightmare, she did the one thing she knew how. She plucked up a bat and stared down the pitcher as the announcer echoed from the speakers:

"San, ni, ichi, starto!"

The baseball flew in, smaller and zippier than the yellow softball she typically played with, but she picked up its trajectory, took advantage of its speed and size, and cracked a home run. She did it six more times while the cameras rolled, stunning the male pitcher, sending the audience and host into a frenzy. Horns rang, confetti rained, and strobe lights pulsed. The audience screamed and jumped. The announcers deemed her "*Hanmāgaru!*"

No longer frightened, Abby raised her bat to the crowd, and they chanted it at her: "*Hanmāgaru!*"

When the home run derby ended, she asked the host, "Did I win?" and she swore all of Tokyo laughed along with her.

Sponsorships followed. She starred in a commercial for Shiso-Plum potato chips. It took her two dozen takes to say the slogan correctly in Japanese and another dozen to not gag when she took a bite. Mick, Jill, and T.K. replayed the commercial during their phone calls, stitched in hysterics. Mick somehow bought half of the marketing materials with Abby's smile plastered across them and Abby sent them all the Shiso-Plum potato chips they could want. More endorsements and advertisements poured in. She made a return appearance on the game show and her bobblehead sold out at the stadium shop.

More people recognized her. She already stuck out with her height and tan skin, but now they knew her from television and billboards. Kids asked for autographs and photos and wore her jersey. In the streets, people pointed and yelled, "*Hanmāgaru*!" as she ducked into bars.

Whatever version of glory this was, Abby hated it. She was at the top of the league, playing for a living, but miserable. She was surrounded, in one of the most bustling cities in the world, but lonely. She'd successfully chased the game without a care for the consequences. But all she wanted, after all this time, was the same. She wondered, in between drinking and batting practice, if it was too late. If she might turn back the clock and choose Kate.

That's what flashed through her mind in the middle of her last game, dehydrated from the night before, despising the chants of her name and her stupid face on posters. She couldn't hear the ball. She couldn't feel it anymore. As she rounded the bases after crushing a triple, her ACL snapped. The game didn't whisper it, but shouted it while she lay in the dirt, the stands spinning above—her time was up. When Mick rang with news of her engagement twenty-four hours later, she knew she couldn't outrun it much longer.

LAS VEGAS

A drink on the plane failed to subdue her nerves, perhaps because even the turbulence reminded Kate of Abby. She'd spent weeks bracing herself to see her, had nearly backed out of the bachelorette and told Mick she was sick more than once. Of course, sickness didn't seem that far-fetched when she arrived at the Bellagio, trembling and queasy in anticipation of their reunion.

But Abby wasn't there.

Their large group, which included Mick's cousins, sister, high school and work friends, and their senior softball class, gathered in conjoining rooms, a mess of hair straighteners, curling irons, makeup, and bottles of booze as they prepared for a night out.

"This is the first time in four years that I have no baby and no husband. I need clubs, I need shirtless men, I need to have a wardrobe malfunction, and I need to drink my weight in liquor," Jill said as they poured shots in the bathroom. "I don't think that's too much to ask."

"Yeah, because that's an average Wednesday night for most of us." T.K. curled her long, amber hair, diamonds adorning her wrists, neck, and most fingers. She'd gone into Los Angeles real estate after college and, when she wasn't selling houses, traveled with her Hollywood agent boyfriend.

"Speak for yourself." Kate eyed the door, waiting for it to open.

"I'm just saying I'm never getting off birth control. No offense, Shupe," T.K. said.

"But I love Junie." Jill frowned from her seat on the edge of the bathtub. "I miss her. I think I should call."

T.K. rolled her eyes as Jill slinked to the bedroom. The tight quarters, the gossip, the shrieking girls, were reminiscent of their college road trips. Kate could at least revel in being dumb kids for another weekend.

"So, are you excited to see Cruz?" T.K. asked.

Kate tightened her face against a reaction while she assessed herself in the mirror. "I wish everyone would stop saying that."

"I think she's excited to see you." T.K. wiggled her eyebrows. "Nervous probably."

Kate cleared her throat. "I assumed she ditched."

"Oh, she's coming. Trust me."

Kate smoothed out her dress, a too short, too tight, too revealing loan from an insistent T.K.

"You two hang out a lot?" she asked.

T.K. shrugged as she leaned closer to the mirror and applied lipstick. "Kind of. I mean, I helped her buy the condo in Malibu, but she's barely there. It's like a glorified storage unit. We meet up when she's in town though." T.K. flicked her eyes to Kate and leaned back from her reflection. "Honestly, when she's in the States, she's mostly with her sister. I can barely keep track of what country she's in. No one can."

Kate nodded and looked down at her feet while she endured another gut punch. The one that came from Abby being so close, but so far. That everyone else had heard from her, while Kate got nothing. Like she'd done something wrong. An unfair punishment that she couldn't perfect herself out of.

"Hey." T.K. lifted Kate's chin and smiled. "You look hot. Here." She brought red lipstick to Kate's mouth. She felt like a helpless college student again, secretly wishing to be cool and for Abby to notice her. "Cruz is going to die."

"I'm not trying to get anything out of Abby," Kate said.

"Oh, I know. But torturing her might be nice, don't you think? Remind her what she missed out on?" T.K. winked.

The confidence boost, the plot of revenge, and the booze bolstered Kate as they hit the bars. More than one head turned on their stroll through the casino. T.K., familiar with every spot on the strip, got them into Room X, a nightclub with caged dancers, a light show, shirtless bartenders, and a celebrity DJ who Kate didn't know but everyone else screamed over. She really was back in college, clueless and overstimulated.

"To Mick's last weekend of freedom! May she make her best mistakes now, before she makes the biggest one of all!" T.K. toasted.

"You're awful," Jill slurred.

"To Mick!"

It wasn't yet midnight, but they'd already gotten sauced at dinner and a show, sufficiently spiraling past tipsiness. T.K. paid for bottle service, so alcohol streamed steadily to their booth along with countless drinks sent courtesy of winking, sweaty men.

"Where the hell is Cruz?" Jill asked.

"Her plane landed a bit ago." Mick shrugged. "She'll be here."

Kate blanched as she scanned the crowd.

"Come on." T.K. handed her a shot. "Let's dance!"

"I don't know." Kate hiccupped.

"Dance! Dance! Dance!" Jill jumped up and chanted.

The three of them bumped their way to the floor. Kate swayed at T.K.'s and Jill's behest. She wasn't one for dancing, but the music, the energy, and her buzz inspired her to bop along. She jumped around with Jill and let herself forget about Abby. T.K. quickly found an admirer to dance against, and when a husky voice met Kate's ear, she startled.

"What's your name, beautiful?" the man asked.

Kate laughed. "Um, no thank you."

"No Thank You? Beautiful name. What is that, French?"

"Hey, back off." Jill draped an arm around Kate. "She will sue you, and you do not want to know her hourly rate."

Kate snorted as the guy became disinterested and tried his luck with a more available short dress. As she recovered from the fit of laughter, her gaze landed on what she'd longed for. Abby. They stood in swarms of strangers, but the red and purple–hued sea parted, and they found each other without trying. The bass dropped to a low note and Kate's stomach dove right along with it, static lighting up her skin and prickling her spine.

"Fuck," she whispered.

Abby raised her hand and nodded. She wore gold and black patterned trousers and a matching vest, something designer, arms toned and strong, hair dark and cropped short. Just as broad and beautiful as five years ago. Maybe more so.

"Cruz! Finally!" Jill shouted.

She skipped across the dance floor and flung her arms around Abby. T.K. followed, but Kate bolted. She weaved and ducked through the crowd, losing Abby and their friends as she posted up at the bar. She needed another drink. The bartender ignored her and while she'd get prompt service at their table, she wasn't about to watch Abby reunite with all the friends she kept except her. So, she took matters into her own hands and reached over the bar for a bottle of vodka.

"Hey!" The bartender caught her immediately. "Don't reach over the bar!"

"Okay, okay!" Kate darted back, startlingly aware that she was drunker than she thought. "Can I please have a vodka soda?"

He glared. "Yeah, just wait."

Kate dragged in a ragged breath. When the drink finally arrived, she hissed "Jerk" under her breath and the bartender scowled. She barely got a sip down before the source of her anguish descended the stairs. Abby ambled easily, Mick, Jill, and T.K. behind her. Kate clenched her drink.

She wasn't ready. It'd been five years without a word. Five years like she was nothing. Abby had gotten the letter and never wrote back. She'd broken Kate, and she knew it. Now she walked over like it was nothing.

"How's it going, Hutch?" Abby asked.

Kate lost it at the four simple words and Abby's beautiful face stopping across from her. During the brief lapse in which rage and intoxication paralyzed her judgment, Kate threw her drink in Abby's face.

While Abby expected some sort of consequence for her actions after the national championship, she never predicted it would be vodka dripping down her face at a Las Vegas club. Kate glared straight through her, clutching the empty glass. She shuddered on the receiving end of it. An unnatural haze over the person Abby spilled tears for and drank to forget.

"That's it!" the bartender shouted. "She's out of here!"

"I think it just slipped out of her hand." Jill patted the man's forearm.

He jerked away and snarled. "No, she's been causing problems all night!"

"Her?" Abby's eyes widened.

She knew Kate had changed. When she spotted her on the dance floor, batting off an admirer, she exuded more confidence and beauty than Abby remembered. She froze and gawked, thankful for Jill and T.K. knocking her back to reality with their hugs. But of all the changes, including Kate's new spite, Abby doubted her a troublemaker.

"I'm getting security," the bartender said.

"Don't bother." Kate scowled. "I'm leaving."

"No, no, we'll all leave then." Mick belligerently swayed between them, a hand on each of their shoulders. "Isn't this nice?"

"We're not leaving. I've already paid for bottle service." T.K. turned to Abby and lowered her voice. "And a stripper."

Abby sighed. "Mick, you can't leave your own bachelorette."

"What about Hutch?" Jill asked.

"I'm fine." Kate waved her off.

"You have thirty seconds to get out of here!" the bartender shouted.

"I'll make sure she gets back," Abby said.

Kate hit her with a stare that could cut ice. "I don't need your help."

"Well, I have to go back to the hotel and change thanks to you," Abby said as Jill dabbed her face with cocktail napkins.

"Fine." Kate bumped past her.

Abby gritted her teeth and debated staying behind. Her outfit would dry itself out, but she had waited five years for this. Five years for a few seconds and she was already gone. "Fuck," she whispered.

"You gonna get her or what?" Jill asked.

"I'll be right back."

"Go Cruz Missile!" Mick yelled.

Abby sprinted to catch up with Kate on the strip, ducking by feathered showgirls and an Elvis impersonator. The blurring lights, the noise, the cigarette smoke, and crowds reminded her of Tokyo. She eyed Kate's backside in that tight black dress and trailed it like a magnet.

"Can you slow down?" Abby shouted after her.

She didn't turn around or stop. "No!"

Abby huffed. Of course their reunion required a chase. One thing hadn't changed—Kate was still faster than her, even inebriated and traipsing on heels. She almost reached her, dodging handbillers pushing flyers for escort services, when a pair of men whistled at Kate.

One of them stumbled and reached. "Don't you know legs like that are a crime?"

"Fuck off," Abby said, cutting between them. "She's with me."

"Oh yeah, what happened to you, sweetheart?" he asked Abby.

"Fell in the fountain at Caesars."

Kate chuckled and Abby grinned as the unwanted attention staggered away. When their amusement faded, they stood across from each other, along the railing of the Bellagio's famed fountains. People cheered for the show as water shot into the air in time with the music and lights. Dean Martin crooned from the speakers, something about love being a kick in the head.

Abby's heart picked up its sprint even though she finally had a chance to catch her breath. "I'm sorry," she said.

Kate's clenched jaw unhitched. "That's it?"

"I know I owe you more than that."

"You left me! So, you don't get to be sorry!"

"I was doing what I thought was best!"

"Abandoning me?" Kate stalked away as water cannons spanned across the man-made lake. "After everything? I was ready to go all the way with you!"

"Well, I wasn't!"

Kate wiped chestnut tresses out of her face. Her hard edges gave way to a wobbling chin, and the gentle, blameless eyes that Abby always surrendered to.

"You got the letter," she whispered. "You couldn't even write me back?"

"I wanted to, but—"

"But what? I begged you like a pathetic idiot to come back to me." Kate shook her head as if trying to erase budding tears. "You knew exactly where I was for five years and nothing! Not even a rejection? Believe it or not, that would've been better. Do you know how much time I wasted waiting, praying, talking to God about you?"

Abby's throat tightened. She didn't think it possible to regret her choices more than she did, but this self-loathing sank into her bones, promising to never leave. "Kate, please. I'm sorry."

"I left the door wide open for years, cracked longer than I should have just in case, and for what? Five years of silence? Five years of you talking to everyone but me? You don't get to be a victim in this!"

"I couldn't write it because I was never over you! I know I'm not a victim. I'm the fuckup! I made the first mistake, the last mistake, the several in between, the worst of which was thinking life might be better for us without each other."

"Yeah, well, maybe it is!" Kate shouted as the first tears freed themselves.

"I always hoped it would be for you." Abby frowned. "I'm sorry, okay? And I deserve whatever—" She stopped as Kate turned on a heel and walked off, restarting Abby's chase. "Hold on. Don't walk away!"

"Oh, you mean like you did?" Kate shouted over her shoulder.

Abby dodged past more stumbling tourists. "I get it, but can't we just talk this out?"

"What's left to say? You're selfish! And you're a jerk! And—" Kate paused when Abby swiped her wrist and tugged her back, forcing her to turn. They nearly bumped into each other as her final grievance fell to a whisper. "And-and I gave you everything I had . . ."

Kate's cheeks flamed scarlet under the strip's erratic spotlights. She stared into Abby as if breaking ground on all her regret and misery. Then the probe drifted downward to her lips. Their chests galloped in identical rhythm, separated by inches that radiated heat, the shared air laced with her tingle-inducing scent, always fresh with a hint of sweetness. Something that was just her. Abby swore Kate's face eased closer, but maybe it was hers, coasting without permission, instinctually seeking what she once knew so well.

"No." Kate sighed. Abby knew that sigh. It left her burning. Kate pulled her hand from Abby's and pointed a finger in her face. "Don't."

Abby's mouth fell. "I didn't."

"I'm still mad at you." She huffed. "And whatever that was. No. No more."

She stomped to the hotel, and Abby trailed her, keeping pace a step behind. They hadn't done anything, but Abby knew why Kate recoiled. She knew what she felt. It electrified her, left her dazed, dumb, and bothered. Kate crossed her arms on the elevator to their rooms.

"I missed you," Abby whispered as the doors slid closed.

Kate stared at her for a beat, then cleared her throat. "I have a boyfriend."

The elevator dinged and Abby grumbled. "Of course you do."

They trudged down the hall and Abby shoved her hands in her damp pockets, unsurprised by the revelation, despite holding out hope. Of course, Kate had found someone. She was gorgeous and brilliant, worthy of groveling from the highest suitor. It didn't sting any less, popping the excited bubble in her chest.

"You going to be okay?" Abby asked when they reached Kate's room.

"Yeah," she said as she opened the door. Kate narrowed her brow. "You're not coming in?"

"I got my own room," Abby said. "I thought it might be for the best. We're not in college anymore, you know?"

"Right."

"Sleep well." She turned away quickly, like ripping off a bandage.

"Abby." Kate stopped her and sighed. "I missed you too."

Abby lifted a faint, toothless smile and Kate looked away.

"Let's just try to get through this. For Mick."

"For Mick." Abby nodded. She couldn't stop her gaze from flicking to Kate's mouth, from daring to drag lower. Kate sucked in a breath, stepped into the room, and slammed the door in her face.

Abby threw her head back and exhaled. She knew she should leave for her room, but rested her forehead on the door instead. She swore she heard a rustle on the other side. After a minute she retreated, still closer to home than she'd been in five years.

Kate woke to a hammer splitting nails between her eyes and Jill's unbearable, saccharine babbling.

"Here, say hi to Aunt Kate." Jill, reeking of garbage and glowing three shades of green, extended the phone to her.

Kate hissed no, but exuded the closest to chipper she could muster when the receiver hit her ear. "Hi, Junie," she said, while Jill scampered to the bathroom and gagged.

"Tell the kid to take a nap," T.K. groaned.

Kate pinched the bridge of her nose as Juniper prattled on, the night's memories worsening her nausea. She couldn't recount the finer details, but the fury still tickled her skin as if it branded her. She murmured along a few more minutes before she said goodbye to Juniper, nearly puked in a cold shower, and escaped their putrid room for an elixir of coffee, aspirin, and whatever resembled fresh air.

She ended up at the pool, which people swarmed as if everyone hadn't just been out hours ago, beach balls bouncing, a DJ scratching records and judging a dance contest. Kate wasn't looking for Abby, but of course she found her. They always found each other.

She reclined on a lounge chair, smoking a cigarette, coffee in hand while she chatted with two women in bikinis. Kate rolled her eyes. Abby wore a sports bra and tiny shorts, thighs chiseled like a Greek sculpture, biceps bulging larger than in college, her skin toasted as if accustomed to tropical climates. Kate considered retreating when Abby noticed her. Her dimples popped in the distance.

"Don't do it." Kate hissed at her feet, but they marched against her will.

Being hungover in front of her shirtless, unfairly-growing-more-attractive-with-age ex would've sufficiently mortified Kate, but the yellow-bikinied blonde and her red-bikinied friend, bubbly and large chested, nearly did her in. As if to double down on seductiveness, Abby and her new friends weren't speaking English.

Kate plopped onto the open lounge chair beside her. She didn't bother to say hello as the girls giggled and left Abby with a few last unknowable words.

Abby swiveled to Kate the second they turned their backs. "Good morning."

Kate rubbed her temple. "Am I that hungover, or were you speaking Italian?"

"*Sì. Solo per te, il mio cuore.*" Abby smirked. "I played a few seasons in Milan."

"You're infuriating." Kate drank her coffee, while her shifting gaze conveniently hid behind sunglasses. She scanned Abby's stomach, the skin she used to kiss, then lower, and cleared her throat. "You should stop smoking. I hate that you still do it."

"I know." Abby squashed the cigarette in an ashtray. Music thundered across the pool while people splashed. Kate didn't understand how no one else had a hangover. "How'd you sleep?"

"Not great."

"Does Shupe still do that kicking thing when she gets drunk?"

"Yes." Kate rubbed at the ache in her shoulder that hadn't stopped in five years.

Abby frowned. "Thought you would've had surgery by now."

"Unfortunately, no. It wasn't a full tear, so I'm stuck in the middle. Bad enough to hurt, but not enough to fix."

The ensuing quiet became sludge between them, too daunting to wade through, and though the dry desert heat boiled the illness in Kate's gut, she didn't leave. Their last conversation left much to be desired. Now was their chance. Abby seemed to know it too as she removed her sunglasses.

"Are you okay after last night?" she asked.

Kate looked away. "It's a little blurry."

"Well, I knew you might despise me, but the drink in my face was a nice touch."

Kate grimaced. "That might've been a step too far."

Abby chuckled and shrugged. "I probably deserve it."

"No, you don't." She sighed. "I swear, you're just the only person who can make me mad like that."

Abby frowned with half her face squinted against the sun, childlike in a way that threatened to diffuse Kate's resentment to nothing. It wasn't fair how easy it was to be with Abby despite their problems, nor fair how much she already wanted more of her. Maybe Abby had been onto something with their breakup. They couldn't afford to be in each other's lives if they wanted to move on.

"There was just so much, still so much, that hurts." Kate had had years to think about what she might say to Abby. In her fantasies, the ones that kept her up at night, she grilled her like they were in a courtroom, complete with opening and closing statements and a cross-examination, articulate and scathing until she confessed her faults. But now, Kate fell into that gentle place, where they humbly told each other everything. "I'm still angry and I don't know what to do with it."

"I know. I'm sorry for everything I put you through." Abby's throat bobbed. "I know it's too late and I know it doesn't make it better, but I kept the door open for you too. Even if I built my house where you couldn't find me."

"Why though?" Kate gathered her remaining strength to deliver the one question she couldn't shake. "You knew how much I loved you. You know how much it hurts to lose someone who's part of you." A cry built in her chest and her voice went shrill around it. "How could you do that to me? Did you not love me as much?"

"Of course I loved you as much." Abby's gaze bulged. "Kate. More." Her forehead crumpled before she spoke. "I don't expect you to understand or forgive me, but I couldn't hold on. Not for the future you saw for us. There were things for me to figure out."

"And have you figured them out?"

Abby just shrugged, sad and empty.

"I guess it doesn't matter. It's too late anyway," Kate said.

"I guess so." Abby put her sunglasses on and sniffled.

Kate's back unclenched. Twelve hours and Abby had scaled her walls. Of course she had. She knew them better than anyone. Just as Kate knew Abby's and always would. In five years, ten, twenty. It wouldn't change. At a pool party in Las Vegas, screaming at each other on the Strip, in a club of strangers, they were tethered to one another, not out of want, but because it's simply who they were.

"Thank you for the apology." Kate examined Abby in the silence, noting the subtle differences. The new tattoos, her stronger body, a trace of melancholy permeating her features. All evidence of the years gone by without her. She pointed at the grisly scar on her right knee, the unmistakable tread of stitches from surgery. "What happened there?"

"Last summer in Tokyo."

"What was the game telling you with that?"

Abby chuckled. "That I overstayed my welcome."

She had a million more questions. She wanted to know about Abby's career, her travels, every minute she missed. But another part of her didn't know if she could take it or, worse, risk falling back under Abby's spell. "We should meet everyone for brunch." She stood to leave.

"I don't want you to hate me," Abby said, and Kate turned back. "I know I made my bed, but I don't know if I can leave here without knowing."

Kate tilted her head. The desperation, that hopelessness she recognized from when they met and that she had always longed to erase, reopened the hollow spot in her chest. "I don't hate you," she said with the compulsive lilt she once used for love. "I could never hate you, Abby."

They hugged. She sighed into Abby's tight hold, her nose against her chest. Her lungs opened bigger for a breath that soothed her heart's tattered parts. She didn't know if either of them would let go if it weren't for the clapping behind them.

"Oh my God, someone take a picture!" Mick shouted.

"Are you guys going to kiss?" Jill asked.

They pulled away from each other. T.K. appeared to be taking a photo and Mick had her arms raised in victory.

"Jesus Christ," Abby grumbled.

Kate, completely knocked out of the brief reverie, hurried to scold them. Abby took up the rear at a distance, returning to hitched shoulders and a cigarette. It took all of Kate's fortitude to not look back.

They adopted cordiality for the bachelorette's next twelve hours. Kate played it safe after the hug. She didn't sit near her, didn't draw close, talked to everyone in their group except her. But in the calculated space, there were still eyes, partial smiles, a pause in their separate conversations, a glance across the precariously built space that revealed exactly who they still were.

Despite her best intentions, it wasn't as simple as shaking Abby off. She couldn't chalk up her faults and call it finished. No one could. Even in their large group, everyone near her laughed louder, spoke freer, subconsciously inched closer. Abby wasn't the center of attention. She was gravity. For all her self-deprecation about lacking ambition or book smarts, she knew the world, knew people, almost always knew what to say to instill ease or inspire a smile. She glided, a stream everyone wished to drink from, despite the occasional flood.

Among the thirsty herds, Abby sought Kate. From the very beginning, from that first run-in, first practice, Abby had chosen her as if unaware or unimpressed by what others jockeyed to offer. Kate, who had spent her childhood ignored and her young adulthood on a pedestal of naïve, virgin perfection, never understood passion before Abby. She didn't require such devotion, would've fallen for her without it like so many others, but Abby gave it anyway.

By dinner, they sat side by side, thighs brushing, shoulders hinting of warmth. Whispered jokes through the overpowering music. An inhale of perfume, of pheromones, of skin. Exactly who they still were.

"You want to play?" Abby asked at the blackjack table. The way she posed the question reminded Kate of the past. Abby never assumed she didn't want what the rest of them did.

"I don't know how," Kate said.

Abby grinned. "I'll show you."

She smiled under the guidance, at the cards in her hand, the chips that Abby piled in front of her, the casual instruction, a tickle of breath at her neck. Kate didn't care about winning or losing. She trembled under Abby's hand briefly on her shoulder and the murmurs in her ear.

When they crowded around the packed roulette table, Kate didn't shirk from Abby bumping in behind her. She leaned into the familiar curve of her chest. While their friends jeered and the wheel spun, as drinks magically refilled, poker machines jingling, Abby's arm discreetly coiled around her waist.

"What do you think?" Abby asked in a gravelly coax that Kate clenched at. "Time for lucky number three?"

"You believe in luck?" Kate raised an eyebrow.

Abby shrugged, pressing tighter into her backside, hand teasing her hip. "I believe in you," she said before betting a tall stack of chips on Kate's old jersey number.

She grabbed Abby's hand as the wheel spun, the ball clipping along as their friends hooted and screeched. Abby didn't watch the numbers, and when the ball hit the pin, Kate turned to find her eyes already set on her. Their boisterous group erupted, but Abby didn't flicker, as if she knew fate. Of course, she won. She always won.

Kate bit her lip, dropped her hand, and backed away. Her heart skipped. She knew as Abby gifted Mick her thousands of dollars' worth of chips that a decision awaited. But she also knew there was no decision at all.

Mick leaned on Abby's shoulder when they finally returned to the hotel, babbling incoherently. "This is how it should always be. All of us together."

"We're just glad you're happy." Abby grunted. "Come on, you got to help me out here, idiot. I've got half a knee."

Kate swooped in on Mick's other side and blushed at Abby's smile across from her.

"Are you two ever going to stop torturing each other?" Mick hiccupped.

"Probably not," Kate said. Abby's eyes shifted downward with her smile.

They dropped Mick onto her bed when they reached the room, Abby removing her shoes, Kate tucking her in while the rest of the party flopped into their beds.

"Night," Abby said to Kate and dipped out before she could say it back.

Kate furrowed her brow, the decision pulsing inside. She considered her suitcase, her pajamas, and the spot next to a snoring Jill that she should most definitely retire to. She scurried into the hall instead.

"Hey," Kate called after Abby as the door slammed behind her. "Where do you think you're going?"

Abby stopped and whipped around, her eyes dark and brooding in a tell that Kate shuddered at. She ventured a few steps toward her. Abby stalked too, slow but certain. "What do you want from me?"

It echoed from the field and their fights. The static hit her neck, buzzed up her chest. And when they came within reach, Kate kissed her. She knew Abby wouldn't do it first. Even as she devoured her with that gaze, she always retreated before overstepping. Kate knew if she didn't dive in impulsively, she wouldn't either. But she needed it. Those lips on hers, not to get Abby back, but to get herself back. The part still with her.

Abby seized her cheeks. Her tongue slipped in without an invitation, without needing one, as they bumped into the wall. It was desperate and long, more suck than sweetness, as if they intended to inhale each other to nothing. Kate moaned and clutched harder, dizzy from everything that was familiar, everything she'd forgotten, and everything that felt new too. She feasted on her mouth, the trace of liquor and cigarettes on her tongue something she hated in all other cases but accepted because her same Abby lived beneath. Her body woke up to it in an instant, never forgetting what this led to.

But then they required air, and in the brief break, Kate remembered Ryan. She stiffened, and when Abby obliviously moved to continue, she put her hands to her chest to hold her back.

"I'm sorry." Kate gasped. "I'm sorry."

"No, it's okay." Abby stepped away, ruddy and panting. Her eyes were dilated saucers, but she was otherwise astoundingly calm.

"I shouldn't have done that." Kate cycled toward the familiar anxiety that she'd narrowly avoided for nearly five years.

"It's okay."

Kate rested her hands on her knees. "Fuck."

"Hey, it's okay," Abby said. "Kate, stop. Breathe. It was just a drunk kiss. No harm done."

She lifted her head and met Abby's face. She willed herself to believe it was just one kiss. No harm. Ryan didn't even have to know. Because it meant nothing. It had to mean nothing now. "Okay."

"Okay." Abby nodded, the smallest frown flashing before she glanced around the hallway. "You want to get some food?"

Kate squinted, still gathering her bearings. "What?"

"Pizza maybe? Unless you want to go to bed."

"No. Yeah. Food."

Abby grinned. "No. Yeah. Food." She grabbed her hand, and Kate didn't dare let go.

No one would ever believe the night she spent with Abby in Las Vegas was entirely innocent, but after the hallway, they didn't share another kiss. Abby ordered pizza and a bottle of champagne to her room, and they flopped into bed like they were bunking for another road game.

"What's the champagne for?"

Abby popped the cork. "You."

"Me?" Kate furrowed her brow.

"The new job. Special counsel at Cortell & Griffin. You've got to be the youngest one. I saw the directory. It's like an AARP yearbook," Abby said as she handed her a glass.

Kate chuckled. "Mick told you?"

Abby blushed. "No. I looked you up." She raised her glass. "This is for the other times too. The law review, the clerkship, graduation. It felt weird to not celebrate with you or tell you I was proud."

Kate's heart split and the tears nearly bubbled again. All she could do was clink her glass to Abby's in return. "Thank you." She sipped and tried not to think of Ryan. Of how he had winced when she got the job and heard the salary. Of how badly she'd wanted this from him but shrank each time she accomplished something instead.

"And you like it? You're getting to do what you wanted?"

"I think I will eventually. I hope." Kate nodded slowly. "I know it might not make sense, going to a big corporate firm like Cortell & Griffin."

"It does. It's the best, right?" Abby said.

And unlike Ryan, Abby didn't say it like an accusation, but like she was seeing Kate fully. Like she always had.

"Yeah." She stared at her pizza. "I still want to pursue the hard cases. The ones that come down to fairness, to not letting anyone get walked all over, or cast aside. I think maybe I can do that there—have both. Enough power to make a difference. Maybe change something from the inside out."

Abby's gaze brightened when she finally met it. "You will."

Kate didn't let herself smile but nodded. "Plus, now that I have the job, I can start paying you back for my tuition. With interest, I insist."

"Nope," Abby said through a mouthful. "It was an investment in the future. My tiny contribution to the good of mankind. You can pay me in free legal advice."

"Please don't put yourself in a position to need it." Kate grabbed another slice of pizza. "You really shouldn't have done that with your money."

"What else am I going to do with it? I feel guilty every time I use it while my teammates scrape by on pennies. I don't deserve it."

Kate swallowed and dabbed her lips on a napkin. "We don't get to decide what we deserve."

Abby raised a brow. "What is that? Book of Job?"

"You read it?" Kate's eyes widened.

"No, I just remember you talking about it that day."

"I remember it too," she muttered as it returned to her. The day she knew she loved Abby. The day she knew she'd always be part of her. Their souls meeting in quiet understanding. Abby's gaze found her in that same place, as if she also felt it tug inside.

Kate cleared her throat and returned to her pizza. "You've really been everywhere, haven't you? I should toast you. Hitting home runs around the world."

"It's really not all it's cracked up to be."

"Mick says you're kind of famous in Japan. Here." Kate brought her napkin to the corner of Abby's mouth and wiped pizza sauce away before she could stop herself.

"No, I'm not."

"She says they call you something."

"Oh God." Abby groaned and flopped back on her pillow.

Kate laughed. "What is it?"

"*Hanmāgaru.*"

"*Hanmāgaru*?" She repeated it, and Abby smiled so big that Kate's cheeks smoldered. "What does it mean?"

"Hammer Girl."

"Hammer or hammered?"

"Depends on the hour."

"Do you really do commercials there?"

"Yeah."

"Do one." Kate grinned.

"No."

"Do it! Please!" She tugged at Abby's arm. "Please, please, please, do it. Just for me. Just once."

"Okay, okay." Abby sighed and sat up. "This was my first one for Shiso-Plum potato chips. And you can't laugh."

"I would never."

Abby huffed before holding an invisible potato chip by her face. "*Saikyō no pureiyā ni fusawashī, daitan na furēbā.* And then I take a bite." She mimed a bite before returning to her overzealous delivery. "*Hōmuran no aji*!"

She topped it off with a swing, hitting the invisible chip out of the park, and flashed a cheesy grin for the nonexistent camera. Kate laughed so hard she thought she might pop a rib.

"They taste awful too. I must've done a hundred takes."

Abby laughed with her until they wiped tears. Their hands grazed, Kate's finding Abby's shoulder, Abby's drifting across her knee. They stayed like that even after their giggles subsided. Kate ignored how much she wanted to kiss her again.

"What does it mean?" she asked when she caught her breath.

"Something about the taste of a home run." Abby chuckled. "I can't believe Mick never showed you. She found bootlegged copies to torture me with."

"I can't imagine you doing commercials. Do you like it?"

She scoffed. "No."

"Why do you do it then?"

"I don't know." She leaned back and stared at the ceiling. "I'm starting to wonder why I do half the shit I do. I used to say it was for the game, but I can't feel it again."

Kate lay next to her, on her side, and Abby shifted to face her. "Why not?"

"I don't know. Maybe I'm tired." She sighed. "Leagues always changing and failing, new teams. Tokyo was better I guess, but maybe I lost something after the game show and the commercials. I stopped hearing it or I stopped listening. It warped the field into this thing I didn't understand anymore. Shiny but spiritless."

Kate's heart thundered in recognition, in awe and admiration. The way Abby always cut through what she failed to. She couldn't help but think of the jumbotrons and church concerts. The go-through-the-motions faith she'd fallen into.

"What?"

"Nothing. I just missed hearing you talk like this."

Abby's gaze softened. "What about you? You still believe in the church thing?"

Kate smirked. "Yes, I still believe in the church thing."

"And the parents?"

"Yeah. They're around. We still talk."

"Good."

"Good?"

"I don't know." Abby shrugged. "They like the boyfriend?"

"Yeah. Ryan's great," she said, voice rising as she rambled, wishing to hurry through the subject. "He's a lawyer. We met at Berkeley actually. He helped me stop fearing church, and he's a born-again virgin too . . ."

"Oh."

Kate shut her eyes in mortification. "I don't know why I told you that."

"No, it's fine." Abby grunted and sat up. "Just feels like we're back at Insley again. Blake 2.0."

Kate scowled. "No, it's not."

"All right fine, it's not." Abby poured herself another drink at the minibar.

"It's not like you're much different either."

"I never said I was."

Kate frowned as Abby returned to the bed, ice clinking in her glass. "You're drinking too much."

"We're at a bachelorette in Las Vegas."

"Abby," Kate said, knowing full well she could stop her mid-breath, stop her from just about anything, by saying her name. "I can see it. The same as back then."

She'd noticed it in her sunken eyes and the weakness in her smile. While Abby was stronger in many ways, beautiful and magnetic, Kate knew it covered up a flimsy version of her Abby. She knew in her gut, an instinct, that something wasn't quite right.

"I'm okay," Abby said, though her hand shook as she set her drink on the nightstand.

Kate didn't follow up. It wasn't her place anymore. Abby was no longer hers to worry about. She lay back down on the starched sheets, hating the distance she felt as Abby settled beside her.

"What about you?" Kate asked. "Are you seeing anyone?"

Abby nodded, and her stomach hardened.

"Her name's Dani. She was one of the nurses when I had my ACL surgery. She'll be at the wedding."

Kate stretched one of the most painful smiles she could remember. "Good. I'm glad you have someone to take care of you."

"I don't need someone to take care of me."

"Oh yes, you do. You always have." Kate chuckled gently. "I always thought I'd be the one to take care of you."

"You still could be."

Kate's fake joy dwindled. "I think we ran out the clock on that one."

"Yeah," she whispered.

The clock glowed over Abby's shoulder. Two in the morning. The dim lamplight enveloping the sterile hotel room and the casinos flickering outside left her tired and sad. Empty. Shiny but spiritless. She wondered how they got this far away from each other. She could've cried.

"I should go."

"Don't." Abby's voice cracked, and she grabbed her hand. "Please."

"You know we can't—"

"I know. I don't want that. Just stay and talk. Or don't talk." She cupped her cheek. "Please."

Kate exhaled and closed her eyes. "Okay."

They talked for a little longer. Abby gave Kate a shirt and shorts to wear for bed. She melted into them like she did at Insley, the memory of Abby's body left in the fabric.

"I don't want to fall asleep," Kate said as they wrapped together.

Abby rubbed her back, chin resting atop her head. "Me neither."

But then the day caught up with her. The anger and the joy and the anxiety pressing down on her eyelids. Kate drifted with her face in Abby's neck, breathing her through the dawn. And it wasn't sex. But it was more.

When she woke up to Abby spooning her, she thought it might be a dream. And when it wasn't, the heaviness returned. The heaviness of leaving, and of Ryan, and of Abby. But she didn't move. She watched Abby sleep, aroused but older, wise enough to be wary even as her body hummed.

"We missed our flights," Kate whispered when Abby's eyes blinked open.

"Good," Abby croaked.

"Also, don't check your phone. The group blew mine up. I'm sure they've done the same to yours."

Abby pinched her forehead and sat up. "I can book you a new flight."

"No, I should get it."

"Right."

They hovered, pausing at the place where a good morning kiss once lived. Kate sighed into it and Abby raised a crooked half smile that nearly reeled her closer.

"Are you okay?"

Kate nodded. "Yeah. I just need some aspirin."

She retreated to the bathroom, hating herself for not outgrowing this, for still faltering in the face of Abby. And yet the person she saw in the mirror, tired, hair askew, Abby's baggy shirt hanging from her shoulder, didn't alarm or send her spinning. She looked like herself. An old version of herself with a glow she almost forgot.

It didn't last long. Not after she rifled through Abby's bag for aspirin and found an orange bottle instead. The instinct rang in her ears. She found three more buried with it. All prescription painkillers. All prescribed by different doctors.

She charged back into the bedroom and chucked a bottle at Abby. "What are these?"

"They're for my knee."

"Oh, really? All of those for your knee? Your surgery was almost a year ago."

"Yeah, and the doctor isn't sure that it took." Abby's brow hardened. "Why are you going through my things?"

"Are you hooked on that crap?"

"No!"

"Those are all from different doctors! I'm not an idiot!"

"Why do you care?" Abby shouted.

"Because I love you!"

Kate threw another bottle at her, and Abby narrowly dodged it. She reached for her, but Kate put her hands up to keep her at bay. The tears burst out of her. The cry of being together and apart all at once. Of Abby falling further from her grasp, somewhere she couldn't follow, no longer the one who could help her.

"Don't you break my heart twice, Abby," she whimpered. "Don't you do something stupid. Do you understand me?"

Abby nodded. She eased to Kate again and this time she let her, sniffling into her arms when they embraced.

"It's okay," Abby whispered. "I'm okay."

"No, it's not. You're not."

Abby squeezed tighter, her words wobbling. "I love you too. I promise I'll be good," she said. "You don't need to worry."

But she worried all the way to the airport. They shared a ride and held hands in the back seat. She gripped on, scared that when she let go, Abby would be lost to her. When they parted at security, she nearly wept again, but kept firm, returning to the person she didn't recognize in the mirror. The one who loved Ryan and didn't need Abby anymore.

"You still hate flying?" Abby asked her as they lingered across from each other, motionless in the bustle of travelers.

"You know I prefer my feet on the ground," Kate said. "I guess I'll see you at the wedding."

"Yeah. Looking forward to it." Abby strained with a painful smirk.

Kate laughed. "No, you're not."

"Yeah, I'm not." Abby chuckled and hugged her. "What happens in Vegas, right?"

"Right." Kate's throat tightened at their release.

Abby tilted her head. "Listen, I still—"

"Don't."

"Okay." Abby grabbed her hand and pecked the top of it. "Get home safe."

"You too."

They merged into their separate streams of people. Kate strode against her desire, glanced over her shoulder for a last glimpse of Abby, and frowned when she didn't spot her. She exhaled, weaving through newsstands and travelers, internally listing the many reasons to move forward.

"Kate!" Abby's footsteps pounded behind her.

"You're going to miss your flight—"

Abby folded her in her arms and stopped short of a kiss. Their foreheads met in another flood of memory. The car at the mouth of the driveway. Eyes closed, lips never touching.

"I should've never left or stayed away." Abby breathed against her and Kate swore she detected her heart in the brief skim of their skin, pounding the same as hers. "I'll see you next week."

As Abby backed away, nodding with one last glimmer of those amber eyes, something frightening roared in Kate. She knew, with a confusing mix of hope and dread, that Abby wasn't ready to let her go. But more than that, as her plane took off for San Francisco, she knew that something horrible awaited.

THE WEDDING

Abby washed the Percocet down with scotch in the bathroom. She held out through the ceremony, despite the agony of spending the day next to Kate. Getting ready, taking photos, standing side by side as Mick and Haley exchanged vows, as if nothing had happened between them. As if she hadn't spent every night sick, every day distracted, contemplating her phone, plotting how she might win her back. She never stopped loving or wanting Kate, but Las Vegas reawakened a monster in her. Abby finished her drink and charged back into the reception.

"There you are." Dani stopped her and pecked her lips. "I feel like I haven't seen you all day."

"Sorry. Bridesmaid duties." Abby kissed her again. She frowned at neglecting her during the wedding and brushing her aside since the bachelorette. Dani didn't deserve it. More accurately, Abby didn't deserve her. Of the many women she'd dated and slept with to get over Kate, Dani was the sweetest, the smartest, the most patient. She'd stuck around the longest and if it hadn't been for Las Vegas, Abby might have considered a future where they were close to happy.

Dani brushed her cheek. "Are you okay? You're sweaty."

Abby diverted her eyes. Dani had caught on to her opioid abuse a few months ago and made her flush the pills down the toilet. After a week of sweating out her mistakes on the couch, she thought she might've kicked them for good. But as Las Vegas crept closer, she sought relief. She told herself just one to help her sleep in the weeks leading up to it, and soon she was begging doctors for more, complaining of knee pain, back on the hook by the time Kate threw a drink in her face.

She'd tried to slow down since, hating the disappointment in Kate's eyes, surviving on half pills to avoid vomiting and the chills, but her teeth clenched for more, agitated and restless, an eye always on the clock. Today she couldn't take it.

"I'm good," Abby said. "I'm just regretting the suit."

"I think it's cute."

"Just cute?"

"Sexy." Dani tugged on her lapel. "Come dance with me."

Abby shook her head. "I don't know. The knee is killing me today." Her gaze drifted past Dani's shoulder, landing on Kate across the way, radiant in her burgundy dress with hair tumbling in waves. "I'm going to grab a drink. You want anything?"

"No, but hurry back and sit with me. Dylan's nice, but I'm going to go crazy if I have to listen to him talk about hedge funds any longer."

"I'll be there soon." Abby kissed her. "Thanks for being such a good sport."

"You owe me," Dani said as Abby slinked off to the bar.

She ordered another scotch and found T.K., Jill, and Juniper. "Is this where all the cool kids are hanging out?" she asked.

"Not anymore," T.K. said.

Abby clocked Jill's glass and narrowed her brow. "Water? Are you pregnant?"

"No, I just haven't recovered from the bachelorette. I've been puking all week . . ." Jill trailed, and her eyes widened. "Oh my God."

"Congrats?"

"Condolences," T.K. said before nudging Abby. "Dani's cute."

"Thanks." She searched for Kate and found her next to Ryan, his hand at her waist.

"So, I think it's an appropriate time to discuss Las Vegas . . ."

Abby didn't acknowledge her, busy staring daggers at Ryan, despising his dimpled chin and golden hair. "How does she always find the most attractive, successful jerks to date?"

T.K. swirled her drink. "Some girls have all the luck."

"He's not that great." Abby scowled and sipped her scotch. "He looks like he's campaigning for Congress."

"Well, Hutch is the all-American-girl type," Jill said.

"What does that make me?"

"The one mother dearest warned about." T.K. snorted and Jill cackled along.

"Wow, thanks guys." Abby glared. Juniper whirled between their legs and yanked at Abby's hand. She let her swing and play, a miniature Jill with her red curls. "What do you think, Junie?"

Juniper giggled. "I think you're funny."

"Well, at least someone has something nice to say."

Jill cleared her throat. "So, Vegas."

"What about it?" Abby twirled Juniper around to avoid their eyes.

"Did you and Hutch fuck?" T.K. asked.

"Jesus!"

"Earmuffs, Junie," Jill said, before smacking T.K.

Abby clapped her hands over Juniper's ears. "The kid is right here."

"She doesn't know what fucking is," T.K. said before dropping her mouth at Jill. "Does she?"

"No, but we just got her to stop talking about the Kinsey scale at preschool. Thanks for that, Cruz." Jill rolled her eyes.

Abby shrugged. "I think it's good she knows that sexuality is fluid."

"Okay, while earmuffs are in place, what the hell happened between you and Hutch?" T.K. asked.

"What are we talking about?" Kate slinked in beside them.

"Nothing," Jill said.

"Really? Because my ears are burning."

Abby blushed and looked away. Despite their night together, she didn't know how to pursue Kate. Not anymore. She'd made it clear where they stood and moved on. It was Abby who couldn't.

"I think Junie's ears are burning too." Abby chuckled and removed her hands from the flower girl's head. "What do you say we get some cake?"

"Yes!" Juniper threw her arms in the air.

"She's already had two pieces," Jill said. "I don't want her going crazy on sugar."

"Oh, lighten up, Shupe, it's a wedding." Abby winked and tossed Juniper over her shoulder.

"Who's Shupe?" Juniper giggled as Abby carried her off.

"It's what we called your mom when we played softball."

She shared a piece of cake with Juniper near the dessert table, lifting her to stand on a chair so that they could eat from the same plate. Mick and Haley made the rounds among their family and friends, grinning, laughing, stopping for photos. Abby had teared up at the ceremony. At the idea of having someone so completely. At believing in forever.

"Can we have more?" Juniper asked, licking frosting off her fingers.

"No, your mom will freak out," Abby said.

She spotted Dani waving her over to their table. Abby waved back, sighed, didn't want to return. Didn't want to be anywhere.

"Here." Juniper ungracefully shoved a forkful of white cake at her mouth.

Abby accepted it. "Thanks."

"Now, this is where the real party's at." Kate brushed beside her. "How's the cake, Junie?"

"Good," Juniper chirped.

"Do you have a minute to talk?"

Abby nodded. "Sure." She grunted as she set Juniper on the ground, high-fived her, and sent her skipping back to Dylan.

"It's crazy that I haven't seen you with Junie before." Kate smiled. "She adores you."

"She just likes that I let her do whatever she wants."

"You're cute with her."

Abby nodded, her lips drooping. She didn't know when she had become so pathetic, but simply being around Kate wore her down.

"What did you want to talk about?"

Kate's eyes darkened, no longer adoring Abby's bond with Juniper, but back to the apprehension from Las Vegas. In fact, Abby knew the question before Kate even said it. They never needed many words. "The pills—"

"Are gone."

She hated lying. She was a pro at deflecting, but she was mostly honest. And with Kate, there was no other way. Lying to her only reinforced that she was floating in dark waters, just like her thumb rubbing the pill in her pocket.

"You promise?" Kate searched her gaze, so close to the truth that Abby squirmed.

"I promise." She cleared her throat. "Shouldn't you be with Bryan?"

Kate tightened her jaw, resisting a laugh. "You know his name is Ryan."

Abby smirked. "I just assumed it was short for something."

They eyed the dance floor side by side. Typically, the right mix of pills and booze numbed the pain and blunted the rest. Except with Kate. Even drugs couldn't stop that flutter, the rapid banging in her chest, or the childish need to crawl into her.

"I've been feeling a little guilty."

"About the kiss?" Abby whipped her head to her in panic. "Did you tell him or—"

"No. And it's not the kiss," Kate said with a sigh. "Spending the night together."

"We didn't do anything."

"Yeah, but I think sex might've felt less intimate."

"Oh, now you tell me." Abby chuckled. She nudged Kate's shoulder. "Don't feel guilty."

Kate kept her stare trained on the dance floor. "I talked to Dani. She's sweet. Pretty. She seems good for you."

"Yeah, she is." Abby gulped more of her drink. "Ryan is nauseatingly perfect, huh?"

"Stop."

Kate's back clenched at that word. Perfect. Abby knew she might react that way, but didn't intend to ridicule her. Not during what could very well be their last time together. After this, it would just be weddings and babies, and perhaps not even that. Abby didn't know if she could bear to do it again. As she fingered the pill in her pocket, she didn't know if she'd even be around to do it again.

"I'm sorry," Abby whispered. "I'm just having a hard time knowing this is it."

"We can still be friends."

Abby shook her head. "You know that's not true."

"I know." Kate's chin crumpled.

When their eyes met, she considered begging, crying, grabbing her by the hand in one last effort to salvage them. But there was nothing to salvage. Maybe even less than five years ago.

"Dance with me?" Abby asked.

"What about—"

"It's our last time." Abby spilled her soul into her stare as she grabbed her hand. "Please."

Kate laced their fingers together and followed her to the floor as a slow ballad started. She eased into Abby, looped hands around her neck like a high school dance. Abby rested her hands at her waist, doing her best to enjoy it, to not crumple on the hardwood beneath the twinkling lights.

"I can't get used to seeing you like this," Abby said.

"At a wedding?"

"Just all of us. Grown up."

Kate's mouth quirked. "Am I everything you'd thought I'd be?"

"So much more," she whispered. A lump filled her throat and the rest spilled without her permission. "I want you back, Kate."

"Abby . . ."

"I'm still in love with you. I've always been in love with you. It's not going to change for me." Abby gulped at Kate's eyes glistening like shattered glass in the silence. "I'll beg. I'll wait. I'll change. Whatever it takes."

Kate unhooked her arms from her neck. "I wish you wouldn't say that."

"Kate."

"Thanks for the dance," she whispered, before charging out of the reception.

"Hey, hold on." Abby hustled after her through the sea of wedding guests, indifferent to Dani's scowl across the way. She followed Kate out of the ballroom and into the mahogany hallway. "Hey!"

"Abby, it's over!"

"Not for me!" She shook from her toes to her tongue, sweating pills and booze, gritting her teeth while she fought for them one last time. "I get that you don't want to be with me and I'm a mess, but what about you? Still the same scared girl from college, hiding in religion and chasing perfection! How could you go back to it after everything?"

Kate reared back, red and breathless, but all a doped-up Abby could think was at least she turned around. "Of course I went back! I was scared!" Her shout splintered. "You left me nothing! Nothing in my heart—no you, no faith, no God. Why would I lose that too? How is it any different than you making a career out of running away?"

"Because I don't think you lost your faith!" Abby shook her head. "I think you couldn't understand it anymore, and that terrified you. You're terrified when things aren't black and white or good and bad."

"And how would you know? You don't even know yourself. You're so far gone, I barely recognize you!" Kate sniffled, but didn't cry. In fact, the way she reduced her volume and squared up to Abby was somehow worse. "And it kills me too. It kills me that you won't save yourself."

Abby didn't know how she withstood such a direct hit, but she was desperate. The most desperate she'd ever been. She grabbed Kate's hands. "Please, don't do it. You don't have to choose me, but don't choose this. Please, Kate."

"Everything okay out here?" Ryan asked behind them.

Kate tugged her hands out of Abby's and nodded. "Yeah."

His brow knitted together as he drew closer. Abby had met him at the rehearsal dinner, found him affable but boring, just as she expected. She considered whether she might pick a fight with him next, when Dani barreled into the hallway.

"Hey," Abby said to her, but she didn't stop.

"I'm leaving."

"Fuck."

Abby half-heartedly trailed behind her. By the time she reached the winery's circular driveway, Dani was climbing into a car. Abby could have followed, had enough time to stop or chase her, but let her pull away.

She flopped onto a bench outside, hand wavering as she lit a cigarette. It took her a dozen tries with the lighter. Another dozen to get the cap off her flask. She wasn't about to go back into the reception with another fuckup under her belt. Instead, she listened to the band's muffled drums and saxophone from outside, eyes cast on the empty vineyard long enough for the sky to turn from orange to dark purple.

"Hey."

Abby swiveled her head to Ryan. He stalked toward her, shoes crunching the gravel above the chirping crickets.

"Can I help you?" she asked as she stretched onto unsteady legs.

"Stay away from her," he said. It was firm and simple. He loomed in his tux, veins in his neck straining. She longed to lure him into taking a swing. She wasn't sure what it would solve, but knew choosing her own hurt would temporarily make her feel better.

"I'm out here, aren't I?"

Before either of them could say more, the door squealed open and

Kate peeled out, just as dashing as before, like their fight hardly touched her. When she reached Ryan, he put a protective arm around her, and Abby miraculously resisted snarling.

"We're going to head out," Kate said. Her gaze fell into Abby's, but not too deeply, as if restrained by that arm around her. As if it made her someone else entirely. "Take care of yourself."

Abby nodded, her throat bobbing because she wouldn't see her again. Her bones ached with it, her heart squeezed, and her ears rang, everything in her urging her to double down, but she was too tired to fight. She'd already lost.

"You too," she whispered.

She popped another half pill, stalked back into the reception, and didn't look back. She posted up at the bar and drank until she slurred. T.K. and Jill tried to console her, but Abby shirked them and blacked out before the bartender cut her off. In the muddled, painful recap, she apparently knocked over a waiter, resulting in a shattered stack of plates. She advised the startled guests to fucking relax, among other pearls of wisdom, until Mick finally stopped her. Dylan and Mick's brother dragged her out of the reception with T.K. and Mick following behind.

"I'm never going to get her back," Abby said as they shoved her in a car.

"Got to let her go, Cruz." Mick squeezed her shoulder, bow tie drooping like a mirror to her frown. "And you've got to take care of yourself. Okay?"

Abby nodded, threw her head back on the seat, spinning and sick, alone on the road of her own inevitable crash.

ROCK BOTTOM

A week after the wedding, after Dani broke up with her, after she apologized to Mick and paid the catering company for the damages, Abby decided she was going to win a gold medal. She was twenty-seven, still in her prime, minus the injury and the addiction she was in denial of. But she needed the game. She needed it in a new, bigger way, and the Olympics promised just that.

She had two years to get herself right, to rehab her knee, to make the team as starting shortstop. She wouldn't play for Puerto Rico. While she adored the team and island, they weren't as competitive, might not even make the cut for Stockholm, so she set her sights on Team USA.

As if in answer to her ambitions, a new league started in America. Six teams on the West Coast. Abby conveniently landed in Los Angeles, but inconveniently, with the league in its infancy, teams relied on local college fields and facilities. It brought her back to UCLA. The same school that kicked her out for partying months after her mother's death.

She swore she heard her whispers in the stands, swore she saw her in the corner of her vision at practice. Of course, that might've been the pills. In between physical therapy, strength training, and traveling for games, Abby subsisted on vice, barely ate, only slept if induced by drugs and booze.

Every week she told herself she'd stop, but then the pain came. The pain with every twist of her knee in the batter's box. The pain in her chest too, since losing Kate. It didn't help her game. She was slower to the ball, got caught on her heels, couldn't keep up with the younger players. She started striking out. The worst batting average of her career, when she needed it most. She couldn't remember the last time she knocked one out of the park. She slowly plummeted in the lineup, from fourth to sixth to ninth. Every time the umpire called strike three, she gritted her teeth, smacked her bat in the dirt, chucked her helmet into the wall. In the field, she tripped, strained her knee further, reacted instead of surrendering.

When Mick called a few months later, she considered letting it go to voicemail, but after the wedding, she owed her.

"Hey," she answered from her couch, a bag of ice on her knee, sweat rolling down her temple. She'd gone almost an entire day without a pain pill, but her skin crawled. "Is it the catering company? I've paid them twice now. I think they're scamming me."

"She's getting married," Mick said.

Abby sat up as her heart launched into her throat. "Who?"

"Who do you think?"

"Why are you telling me this?"

"I'm telling you so you can do something."

"Do something?" She thought her chest might explode. Thought her head might explode too. Her ears whooshed with that awful ring. The ring of losing. The ring of everything falling apart. "She clearly made her choice."

"You know it's bullshit!"

"Of course it is!" Abby shouted. "But who are you to tell me what to do about it?"

"I'm your friend. I'm your family. Someone has to tell you that you're being a coward. That it's time for you to get your shit together and go after her or you're going to lose her forever!"

"Fuck you!" She launched up from the couch. "Stay out of my life! Stay out of my business!"

"I'm trying to help!"

"Help? Why would I ever turn to you for help? I should've never listened to you five years ago! I should've gone after her then, before everything turned to shit!"

"Abby—"

"I don't need your help, Mick! You're not my family, okay? So, fuck off and stay fucked. I don't want to hear about Kate, and I don't want to hear from you!"

She hung up and hurled the phone into the couch cushions. The room spun. Sweat soaked her clothes, and her heart thundered so hard she thought she might have to call an ambulance.

She stumbled into the bathroom, snatched the last pill bottle from the medicine cabinet, and poured its contents into her palm. For a terrifying flash, she considered taking them all at once. The ringing roared. Put her mother in the mirror across from her. She was just like her. Longing, sick, dying for a love she couldn't have.

Abby chucked the pills into the toilet. She told herself she didn't need them, but then she dropped to her knees and fished out a handful. She popped one in her mouth, slunk against the tub, and buried her head into her hands.

It still wasn't bottom.

Bottom came a few days later at another poorly attended home game. She drank too much the night before at a party with T.K.'s friends. She assuaged the hangover with a few cocktails and an oxy that she swiped from the host's bathroom. It was, shamefully, the reason she didn't completely cut herself off from T.K. as she did the others. Her real estate and Hollywood friends often had plenty to spare.

As she stumbled into the dugout for warm-ups, she heard the words swirl around her teammates. Stockholm. Canceled.

"What?" she asked them.

"They're cutting softball again this year."

Abby went rigid. "They can't do that."

"Apparently, they can. I mean, they've done it before. It's up to the host city and the Olympic committee."

"That's bullshit!"

Something snapped inside. Something deafening. This ringing wouldn't stop. It drilled into her skull and sent her hands over her ears. Her teammates moved around her, wide-eyed, their mouths moving to ask if she was okay before she squeezed her eyes shut.

It was over. Everything she had done that horrible summer meant nothing. The pain, the pills, the loss. And of course it happened here, at UCLA. Her mother not in the stands but in her. Every horrible thing kicked up a storm as she grabbed her bat bag.

"Fuck this," she said.

"Where are you going?" one of her teammates asked.

She stomped for the parking lot, determined to run. She didn't care where, as long as it promised a drink and a dark place.

It took her several clumsy minutes to fish her car keys out of her bag, and when she finally got them, another person's hand swiped in. "Hey, I don't think you're good to drive," her coach said.

Abby jerked back. "I'm fine."

He snatched the keys from her. "Not like this. Why don't you come back and sit for a minute?"

Abby reached for the keys. A few of her teammates circled around, offering their support, but this wasn't her team. This wasn't Coach Whitley or the Eagles. This wasn't Mick or Jill or T.K. And it certainly wasn't Kate.

"Give them to me!"

She lunged, and the team boxed her out. Abby pushed them away. She couldn't make out what they said in the ringing. She barely made out shapes or colors as she lost her breath. Except for her bat. The one thing she knew how to do.

Abby swiped it like a sword and, with nothing left to take aim at, she cracked her own windshield. If they wouldn't let her meet the end she desired, then she'd create another. She smashed the headlights, her mother whispering in each one of them. The breaking and crunching metal of the same crash that took her life. And the ringing roared—of that phone call, of the horn honking from her mother's head slumped on the wheel, of her scream in the morgue.

She wouldn't know the other snippets until the police report. Fortunately, even when the team tried to stop her, she didn't swing at or hurt anyone. But she hurt their cars. She took all her drunk, high rage out on the entire parking lot, bashing a dozen until the police finally came. It wasn't until the cuffs snapped on her wrists that she could see again.

Three hours later, Abby sat in a downtown Los Angeles precinct. They'd taken her prints, snapped her photo, locked up her belongings. She shook in a cell, surrounded by a dozen others who scowled or cried or shuddered just as violently as she did.

"Cruz," an officer said. "You can have your call now."

Abby's teeth chattered as she followed them to a phone bank. "I think I'm in withdrawal," she said. "I need something."

The officer didn't look at her. "Make your call."

Abby knew two numbers by heart. While she should call Isla, she only wanted one person. One person if this was her end. And with how shitty she felt, she thought it just might be.

Her fingers shook as she dialed Kate. Tears filled her eyes, and she gritted her teeth. The ring was back. Not her mother's call, ruining the life she knew, but her own call, ruining what she recovered in the wreckage. She gulped, imagining Kate on the other end, learning the news in the middle of the night.

"This is a prepaid call from an inmate at the Los Angeles County Corrections Facility."

There was no answer, and she was grateful. The voicemail recording sounded, a brief glimmer of Kate that made her throat contract. She clutched onto the wall, knees almost buckling as dizziness threatened to take her down.

"Hey, it's me." Her voice broke, and she did her best to cough away the accompanying rasp. "I know I shouldn't call, but I thought I'd cash in on that free legal advice." Another unbearable tremor hit her. "I uh, I guess I really did it this time. Withdrawal's a bitch but I don't know if I'm going to come back from this one. I've just never really been this scared." Abby pressed her forehead to the wall. Someone shrieked behind her. More people getting booked and shouting for their phone calls. "I wanted to call in case this is it and I wanted to let you know I love you. I love you and I want you to be happy. I want you to have the life you want. All of it." She stopped and pulled the phone away for a tiny whimper. "I'm so sorry for always pulling you down with me. I don't mean for this to be another case of that, but I just don't know. I don't know what's going to happen, so I wanted to tell you that." Abby sniffled. "I'm sorry for all of it. You were always right about me. I don't want you to worry. I'm going to call Isla next, but I needed to tell you first." She didn't know how to finish it, so she blurted out the end before she wept. "Okay. Bye, Kate."

She spent the night in jail, twisting and turning on a thin mattress in the holding room. She threw up more than once, pissing off her cellmates. The officers weren't impressed, never sent medics for her, even though she was sure she was on the verge of seizing. She bargained with God, prayed that if she lived, if she got out, she'd turn everything around. God or no God, she promised herself she would.

"Cruz, someone posted bail."

Abby limped out behind the officer, reeking, shaking, exhausted. As she rounded the corner, expecting Isla, she came upon a few officers laughing as they posed for a picture with someone. That someone being Audie.

"Dad?" Abby whispered.

He opened his arms, and she collapsed into them. "Are you okay?"

"No," she whimpered. "No, I'm so far from okay."

"I know." Audie rubbed her back.

"Why am I like this?" She sniffled into his shirt before pulling back.

Audie cupped the side of her head, his copper eyes melting. "You're not like this," he said. "This is just the bottom. This is when your new life starts, yes?"

Abby sniffled, tears streaking her cheeks. The next four words built in her like a second chance, like a revelation, like a prayer. The key to a new life. The one she'd denied since her mother's death. "Will you help me?"

"Always," he said.

As she walked out of the precinct, leaning into Audie for help, the ringing stopped. It was an end. Just not the one she expected.

AFTER THE HURRICANE

Hurricane Maria hit the island during her third week in rehab. Solace Ridge didn't allow patients cellphones or internet access, and Abby rarely made it to the common room to watch TV, so she learned of the news from the kitchen staff who had family caught in the storm. Her heart sank for her former teammates from the Puerto Rican national team and their families, many of whom had welcomed her into their homes, cooked for her, taken the field with her, and unwittingly comforted her during that first year after Insley.

The counselors denied her access to the outside world, even after she pleaded her case, offering a therapy session instead. Abby rolled her eyes and stomped back to her little room with the twin bed. By then she'd made it through detox—a full week of hell complete with vomiting, bone-deep aches, chattering teeth, and sweat-soaked sheets. The delirium spiraled into hallucinations of her mother, father, and Kate, convincing enough that she fought each night to reach out and grab them.

Now, with that evil behind her, she sank into the low place she'd poisoned herself to avoid. One in which she conferred with her loss and loneliness. While it was far preferable than prison, Abby found the four walls of her blank room oppressive, her skin crawling as she paced, did push-ups, punched at the mattress to release everything that hadn't already escaped through tears.

Abby plopped down to her desk after learning the news and swiped up a pen. She ripped a sheet out of her journal, sucking in a scared breath before meeting it with ink.

Dear Kate,

But just like every other day, she stopped. She talked to her in her head constantly, and while she had plenty to apologize for, each time Abby put pen to paper it came up short.

A gentle knock saved her from agonizing over more. "Abby, you ready?"

She wasn't, but she trudged to the group therapy room anyway, where a dozen families awaited their recovering loved ones, including Audie and Isla. She wrestled with relief and shame that they showed up. Their absence might've been easier. An excuse to stay angry and avoid the guilt that they'd flown to Arizona to be with her, especially Isla with two little boys back home.

When the therapist called their small, strained, unconventional family up to share, Abby kept the hood of her sweatshirt raised and slouched in her chair. Isla and Audie sat across from her, their pity-sheened eyes too much for her to bear.

"I'm proud of you. I know this wasn't easy, to come here," Isla started things off. "I love you, and my biggest regret is that I didn't see the signs sooner. Or that I ignored them or that I didn't pay enough attention. You're the closest family I have." Her words caught and Abby realized she'd never seen her this close to tears. "I wanted a little sister so badly growing up, and I remember when you were born, how cruel it felt that I didn't get to be with you. That we were kept apart for so long. Now, I feel like I failed you. That I should've been there sooner or more. I've just never been good at family, you know?"

"It's not your fault, Isla." Abby wiped tears, always amazed at how deep their reserve went. "You've done more for me than anyone else. Always making sure I come out the other side. You're the best big sister I could ask for. I'm sorry I'm constantly testing that, making you worry and bail me out. I'm done with it. All of it. I promise."

They both sniffled and nodded, neither of them prone to large emotional displays. A shared, meager half smile did the job just fine.

"Audie, do you have anything you'd like to say?" the therapist asked.

He stroked his mustache and, before he even opened his mouth, Abby's knee bounced in preparation for a fight.

"I suppose I should start with an apology," he said. "I haven't been around for much of your life, but now—"

Abby hissed. "Not around for much of my life? If only it'd been that simple. Instead, it was the drunken drop-in or the hours of waiting at the window for you not to show. And then you wonder why I pushed you away just like Mom did!"

"I'm sorry—"

"Now you get to show up here like the hero? Like the guy everyone assumed you must be when they learned who my dad was? What a fucking joke."

Audie flashed his teeth. "Abby, *no seas malcriada.*"

She threw her head back and rolled her eyes. "*No me digas cómo comportarme, pendejo.*"

"Okay, maybe let's stick to English," the therapist said.

"I had my own problems! I'm an addict too," Audie said.

"*Y un tramposo,*" Isla murmured.

"I wish you just stayed away! From this, from all of it! If you hadn't shown up at nationals, I wouldn't be here." Abby trembled as the floodgates unleashed. In group sessions and individual therapy, she'd prepared for this moment, written down what she'd like to say, and how she might say it. This wasn't even close. "You fucking ruined my life, over and over, for what? Why are you even here, when you didn't show up for us when it actually meant something? Why couldn't you show up for her?" Abby met his gaze through tears as her anger dwindled into tired despair. "Quit acting like you're a good guy and just let me go already. You've done it before."

She returned to the pool house after rehab. The churning ocean and sand that had once brought her comfort felt foreign when she walked along the beach. She dug up her mitt and ran her hands over the leather, found her bat and adjusted her grip on the handle, but that too stirred nothing inside. Rehab hollowed her out the same way grief had once emptied her, only now she quietly mourned for the parts of herself lost in recovery.

While it did nothing to console her, Abby watched the coverage of Puerto Rico, heart aching at the flooded streets she'd once considered home. She scrolled on her phone and donated money, but it always came up short. And while she knew there was one person who understood better than anyone, she avoided Audie.

It was no easy task with them both in San Diego. In fact, that first week after rehab, she found him manning the coffee station at the nearest AA meeting.

"You've got to be kidding me." She turned for the exit.

"Hey, no! Stay." Audie followed her outside, weaving past the meeting members smoking beneath palm trees. "Abby, hold on a minute."

She shook her head. "Isn't there some rule against family members at the same AA meeting? How am I supposed to talk shit about you while you're sitting across from me?"

"I will go then," Audie said.

"No, this is your meeting. I'll find another."

She found her way to a small circle in a nearby church basement. She always thought it funny they stashed them there, like they had to be hidden away.

"My name is Abby and I'm an alcoholic and an addict," she said when the meeting leader asked her to share. "I like to say I'm a second-generation alcoholic, maybe even a third, I'm not sure. My dad is at a meeting down the street and my mom . . . my mom died because she couldn't beat it." Abby stared at her untied sneakers on the concrete floor. "And when you grow up like that, I guess chaos starts to feel normal. Comfortable even. At least, it has been for me."

Abby got her ninety-day chip before Christmas. She'd be lying if she said the time passed anything but agonizingly slow. There weren't enough meetings or therapy, surfing or reading to fill the days. She was lonely, but she struggled to speak with Isla. She didn't want to burden her, didn't know what to say, didn't think she'd understand.

It left her wrestling again with the urge to talk to Audie. He came by the house to visit his grandsons, always sure to stay clear of her. She envied his newfound steadiness, his purpose, his five years of sobriety—hated it even. Hated that she and Isla missed out on his best years. He worked for the Padres as a hitting advisor and went dutifully to the ballpark every day—a far cry from when his teammates had to pull him out of bars to attend practice as a player. And after the hurricane hit, he organized aid trips to Puerto Rico.

"I have some old teammates in San Juan," Abby said to him in December. He'd come to Isla's for dinner, before he shipped back out. "If I give you some names and addresses, do you think you can check up on them?"

Audie set aside his fork and dabbed his lips with his napkin. "How about you do it?" he asked. "Come with me."

Abby surveyed his gaze and knew he was serious.

"Are you sure that's a good idea?" Isla asked. "You're leaving tomorrow, aren't you? And Abby, you're only a few months—"

"What time do you leave?" she asked him.

Audie smirked. "In ten hours."

They didn't talk on the flight and as Abby peered out the window, she wondered if Isla had been right about it being too soon, because she'd never wanted a drink more when she saw the damage. It looked like something apocalyptic below. Mazes of dirty water and mud, houses in a thousand splinters, crushed beyond repair.

It was worse on the ground. They wore neon vests and distributed water and food, but it wasn't enough. It was gone in seconds and there were still more empty hands. When they shoved and wept, Abby stiffened in alarm, unaccustomed to such desperate despair, but Audie was there in the fray.

"It's okay," he said. "I'm right here."

Her eyes prickled with tears, but she didn't let them fall. Not as she encountered so many who'd had homes and jobs and running water and electricity and kids to take to school, and then lost it all in the unjust flash of a storm. When they passed out hot meals, she could barely take the whimpering children on mothers' hips and the elderly, shuffling along without anyone to care for them.

That night as they slept on cots in a tent, she wondered how it could ever get better. She wondered how much suffering she'd been oblivious to while she chose her own torment. When the tears quietly rolled to her pillow that night, she found solace in not crying for herself.

It would take months for the electricity to come back on. Years to rebuild everything lost. Abby grew accustomed to sleeping on floors, in aid vehicles, and under tarps. During that trip and the several that followed, she learned to patch roofs, lay foundation, and run pipes for plumbing. She was tired every night but every day felt a little lighter. She wasn't just rebuilding a community, but something in her too.

In between shifts, she explored with Audie. He took her to the shuttered factory where he once worked, the same one he quit for a life-changing tryout with the Padres. He showed her his childhood home too, or at least where it once stood. It was mud and a few pieces of plywood now.

"My father—your grandfather—was nasty when he drank." Audie kicked a rock while they wandered through the washed-out streets. A few people recognized him and waved, but it was no longer because of his baseball career. It was from his humanitarian work there. "I always told myself I'd never be like him, but then I was."

"A curse," Abby whispered.

"*Tal vez.*" They stopped on the side of the road to peer out at the ocean. Wind hushed up from the water and passed over them. "It never really leaves you."

She didn't ask what. She just nodded. "I know."

Audie frowned. "She would have been proud of you."

Abby drew back, unprepared for the subject. Unprepared for the ache that split through her chest. "Of what?" She scoffed and continued ahead of him. "I got arrested and went to rehab."

"Especially of that."

He laughed, and she laughed too, relieved to lighten the mood. As he walked alongside her, with the same stride, the same swing of his arms, she felt the warmth of childhood. Of the days when she'd longed to be just like him and chose to wear his number for Little League. Of the days when her mother smiled and the three of them went to the beach or baseball field. She realized that while she'd avoided all the bad, she'd kept herself from the good memories too. She'd worked through her issues in every kind of therapy and group setting imaginable, but this was what held her back.

"They had me write her a letter in treatment," she said.

"Did it help?"

Abby shrugged. "I told her I understood, maybe better now, but also that I didn't. It's weird because I hate her more now, but I love her more too and there's nowhere for it to go." Her throat knotted as they turned into another destroyed neighborhood. "Some days I look in the mirror and really feel it—how much I'm like her—and then I hate myself too."

"No." Audie's eyes flashed with anger, but not the kind that she knew from childhood. A broken, moral anger like he'd plucked it straight from the surrounding ruins. "Don't hate yourself. Don't hate her. She was beautiful, funny, smart—just like you, mija." He bit his lip. "But there was sadness there. You know she ran away when she was young. She had a hard life, and I never knew how to help her. I couldn't get out of my own way long enough to."

"Well, now she's given me a hard life too." She kicked at debris. "Maybe not like this, but she made shit really hard, you know?" The tears loosened in her throat and she let them go. "And I still want her back because she was my mom. Because she made everything so much better too. Sometimes I wonder who I would be if she was still here." Abby wiped her eyes. "Why couldn't she hold on and we get to?"

"We don't get to know," he whispered.

Audie didn't hug her, probably because she kept walking, and maybe because it wasn't their way. He just didn't stop walking alongside her.

"I still forgave her." Abby sniffled.

He squeezed her shoulder. "And yourself?"

She didn't answer.

He invited her to join him at work that spring. It was the first time she had stepped on the field since her arrest, and that too healed something inside. And it wasn't just any baseball diamond. It was the one with her father's number flapping on a flag in the outfield. The dirt she had once tottered on as a toddler. It was San Diego's team, but it was also her family history. Another sliver of home.

She watched batting practice with him along the first-base line, soothed by the rhythm of hits echoing through the empty stadium. Abby nudged him as a rookie dinged bloopers to right field. "He's off-balance," she said.

Audie's eyes widened. "What?"

"On the breaking ball." She spit a few sunflower seeds over her shoulder. "I mean, he's making contact, but it's weak. He should shorten his swing."

"And how do you know?"

Abby furrowed her eyebrows. "Because I can hear it. Can't you?"

A week later, the Padres organization sent her to scout school. While she cringed at the clear nepotism, she also couldn't deny it was a perfect fit—she spoke multiple languages, had lived and played in various countries, and most importantly, she could hear it. The game struck again. She could almost feel it.

Those first few months on the road presented new challenges.

Missing flights, renting cars, adjusting to little sleep and shitty meals. The temptation of bars or a drink at the airport nearly broke her more than once, but she called her sponsor, found a meeting, muttered the Serenity Prayer with her teeth gritted. And each time she made it through another day, another game, another city, she proved something to herself. That she could be steady, that she could be patient, that she could be more.

"My name is Abby and I'm an alcoholic and addict." She stood at the head of her AA group when she accepted her one-year chip. "For a long time, I used to believe that I was cursed. Maybe it's the ballplayer in me, but I wore it, carried that shame like a fucked-up badge of honor. Because there's something secretly glorious about curses. I'm sure the Red Sox and Cubs are happy about their World Series rings, but I think sometimes they miss the curse. That splintered, broken, unlucky part that becomes who you are. It's a lot easier to blame your mistakes or a poor performance on a curse. To say it's out of your hands. But it's not. It's in my hands now. It always was."

A year later, when she spotted Kayson Cannon, Abby knew it was time. He played like his entire heart lived in it, the same love she recognized in Kate. One she hadn't seen since. She just didn't know if she was ready.

So like the many other instances when she didn't know what to do, Abby picked up a bat. She tested its weight in her hands, took a practice swing, gazed out at the immaculate grass where so many greats had taken the field. She hadn't hit in two years. Not since she smashed a dozen cars, landed in jail, and didn't know if she'd ever pick a bat up again. If she'd ever feel it in her chest. But as she sauntered onto the dirt where Audie was wrapping up with a player, it surged in her.

"Hey, Dad, you got time for one more?"

He snapped his head to her, eyes stretched wide. She hadn't called him that since he picked her up from the precinct and before then, not since she was a little girl.

"*Claro que sí,*" he said with a smile. He tossed her a few balls, and she smacked each one. Not as powerful as before, but her body fell back into the old ways, no longer numb or empty.

"You are hitting lefty now?"

"Easier on the knee," Abby said between swings. "There's a kid out of Insley."

"He good?"

"I think so." She sliced another ball with a grunt. "I don't know if I should go back though. If I'm ready. Maybe they should send someone else." She paused. "What do you think?"

He smirked as he rotated a baseball in his hands. "I think we go where the game calls us."

Audie tossed her a dozen more pitches, and she wondered how many times they had missed this chance. But as the stadium lights droned, as the players filed out, as everything fell quiet except her breath, except the ball, she thought perhaps it was because the game hadn't called them back yet.

The bucket of balls emptied.

"A few more?" he asked her.

She adjusted the bat and nodded. "Yeah," she said. And it felt like forgiveness. For her and for him. And for the first time in a long time, she knew exactly what came next.

THE CASE

The partners thought she'd have an interesting perspective when they assigned her *Watterson v. First Foundations Charter.* Kate never asked why and would long wonder if it was because they knew of her religious background, her dissertation on Title IX, or something else that she often worried was written across her face, though never spoken aloud. Either way, she dutifully dove in, invigorated by the notion that everything led her to this case—for more reasons than one.

Marcus Watterson, a teacher at First Foundations Charter, filed a lawsuit against his employer for wrongful termination after they claimed his views didn't align with school values. He claimed the "views" in question were his sexuality. That, and just a few months prior, he'd agreed to be the advisor for a new LGBTQ student alliance club, which the principal and governing board shut down for the same reason.

The students protested with rainbow pins and flags, backed by Marcus, who used it as a teaching moment about the First Amendment. Little did he know the lesson would stretch beyond the classroom. When he and a handful of students and parents confronted the governing board about shutting down the club, the board said they were filing for religious exemption. They let Marcus go a week later.

Kate took on the case despite her lack of courtroom experience. Cortell & Griffin didn't leave her or their reputation out to dry, of course, providing a full team and resources, but this constituted a plunge into the deep end. A make-or-break-your-career moment that both exhilarated and terrified her.

She needed the case for other reasons too. Mick's wedding was just a month behind her, meaning Abby was just a month behind her. Their last conversation tormented her most nights as she tossed and turned and prayed for conflicting solutions—to stop worrying about Abby, to stop loving Abby; for Abby to call, for Abby to never call; most of all, for Abby to save herself, since she no longer could.

Ryan took Abby being her ex surprisingly well. He chalked it up to curiosity and youthful mistakes, though diminishing what they once had stung, even if it made him feel better. Still, if she spoke too long with a female colleague or another woman at church, she'd catch his watchful gaze across the way with his brow stitched.

She couldn't say for certain whether that or the new high-profile case inspired his proposal, but the timing was suspicious.

"We should get married," he said over dinner.

Kate's eyes widened as she slowed her chewing. "Yeah?"

"Yeah. We can go pick out a ring next week. It'll be fun." He smirked as he pointed his chopsticks at her left hand. "It'll be sized in time for opening statements."

It was so nonchalant and unromantic, the two of them discussing it over takeout during the rare hour she broke away from case prep, that Kate wasn't sure he really meant it until they were hovering over glass jewelry cases downtown. In his defense, she had always said she didn't want an over-the-top proposal. Blake unsuccessfully popping the question on New Year's Eve in front of her entire family still haunted her. This reverse approach, while passionless, suited her. No fuss or overthinking. She didn't know when she'd have time to plan a wedding, but at least it gave her an excuse. An excuse for what was difficult to pinpoint. An excuse to drag it out, to avoid it, to stall long enough for her to figure out what was going on inside or ignore it long enough that it might go away.

But it never went away.

It surged after Abby's voicemail from jail. It left her sheet-white and trembling, heart contracting like she too might die from years of unaddressed pain. She called the precinct back to no avail, then Isla, who brought her up to speed. She found comfort in her clipped tone, despite the circumstances. It'd been years since Kate talked to her.

"She's fine. I mean, whatever that is right now, but she's with Audie. I'm driving up for her arraignment. It's drunk and disorderly, destruction of property, and resisting arrest. Honestly, I don't think she would've gotten the last one if she hadn't called the officer a fuckwit."

Kate pressed her forehead to the wall, the only thing keeping her standing. "Oh, Abby . . ."

"She's not going to get hard time. I'll make sure of it. At least she was smart enough to not hurt anyone," Isla said above the hum of the road.

"Just herself," Kate muttered through tears.

"I knew she was drinking a lot, but I didn't realize it was this bad." Isla paused. "You saw her at the wedding. How did she seem?"

Kate released a jagged breath. "She's still taking whatever pills they gave her after her knee surgery. I don't know for how long." She broke on the last word and sniveled into her hand. "I'm really scared for her."

"She's going to be fine. We're going to take care of it, okay?"

"Okay. Okay, I think I need to go."

Kate hung up, tripped to the bathroom, and heaved into the toilet. She felt as sick as she did five years ago when Abby had left. Sicker now, knowing exactly where she was, and unable to go to her. Sicker because Abby had broken her heart twice, leaving her with nothing to do but pray beneath the shiny, soulless church lights for the hollow place in her chest to stop growing. To pray that she might learn to live without part of herself.

She dried the tears, firmed her chin, and put on a starchy dress with a decades-old cardigan. Marcus Watterson was in the conference room when she got to the office. "I'm so sorry to keep you waiting," she said.

"Are you okay?" he asked.

Kate nodded as she pulled out her work, unable to meet his face, which would reveal just how incredibly far from okay she was.

She didn't have an office, so the conference room had served as her headquarters for the last few months. Out of place at the table covered in boxes and case files was a bright yellow softball, smudged and worn from hits and dirt. The ball from her last home game at Insley.

These days it served as a fix for fidgeting hands, the frayed red laces soothing frustrations or prompting inspiration. She grabbed it to hide her trembling fingers from Marcus. And maybe, to feel closer to those days at Insley. Closer to Abby.

"Let's pick up where we left off a few days ago," Kate said. "Isn't it true that the school's policies are rooted in its religious beliefs, which were clearly communicated when you were hired?"

Marcus didn't answer. He was her star witness. In his mid-thirties, well-spoken, with a solid teaching reputation. He was easy on the eyes, but in an unassuming, genial way that people expected from educators—bald and mustached with round wire-frame glasses, friendship bracelets from former students on his wrist, a collar always beneath his chunky sweaters.

The silence continued as he stared at her with big, concerned eyes that made her squirm. Kate furrowed her brow. "And then, as we discussed, you'll explain that it wasn't considered part of a religious doctrine when you started—"

"My husband and I are praying for you," he said.

Kate's mouth fell. "I'm sorry, what?"

"I didn't mean to offend if you're not . . ." Marcus's voice trailed, and he squinted at her. "Oh, or you mean me?" He twisted his face and drew back. "It's the twenty-first century. You can be gay and Christian too. I assumed since you took on this case that you were—"

"No! I didn't think that you couldn't be both." Kate stopped as she replayed his last sentence. Heat flooded her cheeks. "What did you assume about me? That I'm . . ."

"That you're open-minded about sexuality and religion," he said.

"I am!" Kate blurted, almost too loud to be convincing. She was just relieved he didn't assume what she kept suppressing. Granted, it shouldn't have mattered based on her desperate proclamation. "Of course I am."

"I suppose it would be interesting to take this on if you weren't," Marcus said with a half smile. "You know, I think that's one of the reasons First Foundations hired me. Not being gay, but that I'm a Christian."

"Really?" Kate prepared to write it down on her legal pad before he shook his head to stop her.

"They weren't outright about it then, not an overtly religious institution, but they wanted to promote a certain set of values that aligned with the Church. Compassion, gratitude, respect, community service, and family. They never mentioned God or Jesus or Christianity, but I saw their eyes light up when I mentioned singing in my church choir. They must have misheard or glazed over when I mentioned my husband." He paused for a brief chuckle, but Kate couldn't bring herself to join in. "Either way, I believed in what they were doing. A place for kids who struggled in a traditional classroom setting or had a passion they didn't have the opportunity to express. Kids who might just need a fresh start or to find their tribe. The outcasts, the tough cases, the misunderstood."

" 'Give me your tired, your poor; your huddled masses yearning to breathe free,' " Kate said.

"Exactly. Like Jesus himself." His smile faded. "Then they decided to be more like the Church. Prioritize keeping certain people out. Forget about how it started by letting everyone in."

Kate stared at the ball in her hands, brushing a thumb along the seams, eyes on fire. It wasn't just a reminder of Insley or of Abby, but of just how far the game led her. Putting her here, across from Marcus, fighting for him even when she didn't know how to fight for herself.

She cleared her throat. "Let's get back to the cross-examination, shall we?"

Isla texted her the next day and assured her that Abby was okay. She'd get off with fines, community service, and a treatment center. Kate didn't message her back, and while the update brought relief, she didn't sleep any better. It didn't close the hole in her chest.

As if to atone for making zero headway in wedding planning, Kate agreed to pre-marriage counseling with Ryan. It was a requirement for their pastor to officiate the ceremony. And while Kate always assumed their large church, with its band and bright colors, the smiling faces and youthful congregation, was less oppressive than the one she grew up in, the first session squashed her delusions.

"Marriage, of course, is more than the flashy wedding or the perfect dress or all those pictures you post on social media," Pastor Greg said to the circle of couples. They responded with canned laughter, just like during his sermons. "It's a sacred covenant. A gift from God, reserved for a man and woman to enter into chastely for the procreation of children and the continuation of His church. It's also an opportunity for you to fulfill your God-given roles. A man to become a husband, a leader, and protector, and a woman to become a wife, who follows and nurtures."

Ryan squeezed her limp hand, and Kate fought every twitch in her face to resist scowling.

"Kate, we're all keeping a close eye on your case," Pastor Greg said, before they left.

"Oh, really?" she asked. "I didn't think it would be of any interest."

"It is for a lot of our congregation. They want their children to have a Christian-based education." He raised an eyebrow, the corners of his mouth twisting grimly. "From what I understand, the ruling could have a major impact on how our schools receive federal funding."

"Your schools?" Kate repeated.

Ryan grabbed her arm. "Let's go," he said. "Thanks, Pastor."

"Did you hear that?" she asked him.

Ryan shrugged as they stepped outside. "You have to expect it. I don't mind you playing in the middle, but you can't be surprised that there are sides."

There weren't just sides, but a pseudo-war. Conservative groups like the Family Defense Council and Religious Liberty Alliance financed and effectively pushed First Foundations Charter into refusing the settlement Kate initially brokered. It was as if they wanted to make a statement, stretch the boundaries of the law, and clear the way for others to follow. And it wasn't as though Marcus and his students were paying for Kate's obscenely expensive billable hours. LGBTQ rights groups rallied behind them, raising funds for their legal fees.

It kicked up a whirlwind of media attention. Demonstrations and cameras crowded Kate and Marcus as they climbed the steps to the courthouse. Opening statements weren't for another month. All this for a meeting with the judge and pretrial motions. It caught Kate so off guard that she stammered through an interview with the local news, not sure if she should look straight into the camera or at the reporter.

The next day, a media coach magically appeared in the conference room, sent by her bosses. Then Charlotte Pruitt, a senior partner and the only woman at the firm to achieve such a rank, opened the door. "Come with me," she said before stalking off.

Kate braced to be berated for her poor performance. Instead, Charlotte led her to a town car waiting outside and took her to a swank shop where security guards stood at the door and sales associates greeted them with champagne. Charlotte scanned her up and down once, guessed her size exactly, uttered a few things to the saleswoman, and said she'd take her to a proper tailor next. Kate followed her every command, though when she said she didn't know if she could afford it, Charlotte rolled her eyes.

"Charge it to the firm."

Kate gulped and nodded. As she studied herself in the mirror, she wasn't the girl who left Deer Park or the one who feared her family. She was a lawyer. She was powerful. She was exactly who she wanted to be but had never admitted to herself.

Charlotte's smile flashed behind her in the mirror. "You see, I don't buy this Dorothy misses Kansas, modest little lamb act."

Kate turned around, surprised but unperturbed by the woman's accurate read. Charlotte sipped her champagne and nodded at the spot next to her on the couch.

"I'm onto you. I was from the start when we hired you," Charlotte said. "You've taken very specific steps. Berkeley, the clerkship, always at the top, always the best. You are a competitor." She raised an eyebrow. "You could've joined a nonprofit or the ACLU, but you chose Cortell & Griffin, where just down the hall from your admirable cause there's a senior associate defending a corporation for false advertising and insufficient drug label warnings."

Kate blushed. Embarrassment hit her, not because this was who she wanted to be, but because she denied it, as if her dreams and wants were too big, too immodest, too impure.

"It's okay to want both," Charlotte said. "Because you can, as long as you know who you are. You decide who that is and what you want, and you take it. There's a reason we chose you for this, Kate."

"Why?"

"Because you know how to win."

While Charlotte meant her academic and career achievements, Kate thought of softball. She thought of captaining their small, scrappy team to a national championship. She'd worked tirelessly, willing them to the top, but she also hadn't done it alone. None of it would've been possible without Abby during that magical senior season. Abby crushing home runs, Abby lightening the team's mood, lifting Kate at her lowest, and encouraging her to reach her highest. Perhaps that's why it wasn't the new suits or long months of preparation that steadied Kate ahead of the trial. It was another letter.

Dear Kate,

I apologize for the delay in this long overdue letter. By now, you know that I'm okay. I'm so incredibly sorry that you had to worry. I asked Isla to tell you where I was as soon as I could, but my phone access has been restricted, and truthfully, when I got it back, I didn't think calling was the best for either of us. I'm writing to you 90 days sober.

Rehab, as you might expect, has left plenty of time for self-reflection, therapy, talking about feelings. All of my favorite things. I've had to face a lot of guilt and shame, my lesser qualities, my tendency to isolate or self-destruct when shit gets hard. I've also spent plenty of time reckoning with how that affected you.

In AA, we have twelve steps, and making amends with those we've hurt is a big part of them. I owe you more than a letter, but I'd like to start here.

I'm sorry for the times I pushed you away when you were the only one who showed up. I'm sorry for all you put in me, and I couldn't give back. I'm sorry for the times I caused fights on the field and off it, for the times I ran and made you fearful, for the times I selfishly couldn't get past myself to be more for you. I always wanted to give more and be more. I just couldn't figure it out. No one really showed me how. But I'm trying now.

I fell in love with you back in college because you're the kindest, realest, smartest person I know. The crazy thing is, everyone knows you're all these things, but it doesn't make them jealous or covet. I think that's what it means to be a light in the world. To simply give when everything else is dark. You've given me so much of that light, taught me about it, shown me what it means. I never meant to dim it.

It's no excuse, but I often doubted why someone with as much to give as you chose someone as empty as me. You were a light that shined in me and showed me something in myself. Something that I always wanted to be. The problem is that I rarely gave you light in return. Didn't know how to make mine glow without you. I like to think I'm figuring that out now. Just maybe, one day, I'll have some light to shine in you too.

We pray and talk a lot about God or a higher power here. Believe it or not, I've even given the Bible a shot. Too much time on my hands obviously. I've told you before, God never made much sense to me. I believe more wholeheartedly in the Church of Softball, but you're right. They are strikingly similar in that requirement of surrender. In bowing to the unknowable. The Serenity Prayer almost sounds like an ode to the game itself. "God, grant me the serenity to accept the things I cannot change, the courage to change the things I can, and the wisdom to know the difference." Is that not the field's mantra?

I gave the Book of Job a try. I still don't completely understand it, though I do feel bad for that poor bastard. Perhaps I see myself in his suffering. He even has three annoying friends to pull him from the rut. His plea for death, his misery, losing everything, only to keep going against his will resonates too.

I think the part I like the most, the one I understand best, is the epilogue. "The Lord blessed the latter days of Job more than his earlier ones." I pray that it's the same for us. That your days ahead are better than what I've put you through. That you get everything you deserve and the things I couldn't give you. I pray for it. If you only knew how often I talk to God about you.

As for me, I'm trying to take life slower. I always told you I never imagined a future for myself or knew what I wanted.

But now I at least know a few things that I want to be. I want to be someone who doesn't need saving. Someone who doesn't have to say sorry as often. Someone who one day might be worthy of someone like you. Though I doubt I'll ever find another you.

I love you, Kate. I always have. You're always going to be the one. But I also know that doesn't mean I get to have you.

I hope you're happy in your marriage and career and that one day I'm a wistful memory, an old teammate, a long-lost friend. And maybe we'll even be able to smile about it.

Don't forget to breathe.

Love,
Abby

It arrived the night before opening statements. Kate couldn't blame her for poor timing, because she had no way of knowing. She read it once in tears, once in anger, and once in relief. She read it over and over, Abby's voice in her ear like winds of the past. Her belief in Kate radiated through, championing her once again, even from afar. An unconditional love that Kate hadn't experienced in another.

She pulled down the other letters too, her shoulder twinging as she reached for the top shelf in her closet. The same ligaments she'd strained during college but never severed. The pain had flared over the last months as she crouched over her laptop and the conference room table.

She rubbed out another spasm as she fumbled through the letters. Her same Abby. Healthy, safe, new. Kate frowned at how badly she wished to know this side of her. How badly she wanted to respond. But there was the trial, and there was Ryan, and despite the many strides she'd made for the case, she wasn't quite ready to fight for all she might want. She'd fight for Marcus and the others instead.

Police held back protesters when they arrived for opening statements. Kate waded through the middle, rainbow flags on one side, Bibles on the other. She still didn't like the cameras, but she answered a few questions, poised, rehearsed, looking at the right places. If she was anything, it was coachable.

Her hand trembled as the proceedings started. She'd served as co-counsel several times but never taken the floor as lead. Never had she faced the judge solo, mind going blank as she tried to remember her opening statement. And while Ryan watched on, it was Abby's voice, the lines in her letter, reminding her to breathe.

"Your honor, at the heart of this trial is a simple question: Can an institution use its religious beliefs as a shield to deny others their constitutional protections? The defense will claim that the Constitution guarantees their right to freedom of religion. But it also guarantees the right to an education, to free expression, and to love openly. Those are the rights First Foundations Charter violated when it discriminated against the teacher and students behind me, stripping them of their dignity, and most importantly, their sense of belonging . . ."

She chugged through the rest of her opening statement, and her hand finally steadied during the defense's rebuttal. The preparation, years of it, snapped into place. Even through the stumbles—the objections she lost, the redirect she missed and her co-counsel reminded her of, the cramp in her shoulder that never ceased—she felt stronger, more certain, more like the version of herself she always hoped to be.

"You're like actually going to be famous," Mick said over the phone.

They'd barely talked since the wedding. Kate blamed the trial but also hesitated because it felt like a step too close to Abby.

"No, I'm not."

"Well, if there's anything Shupe or I can do to help with wedding planning, just let us know. We're on standby," Mick said. "Have you guys set a date?"

"Not yet."

Kate chewed her lip. Ryan had asked her the same question a thousand times, and while she threw out summer or the coming fall, she leaned on the trial's end as a caveat.

"Listen, I know this isn't your favorite topic, but have you heard from Cruz?" Mick's voice cracked.

"No. Why?" Kate hadn't reached out to Mick or Jill or T.K. about the letter. Not about Abby's arrest or rehab either. It didn't feel like her place. She prepared to sound surprised when Mick shared the updates.

"Uh." Mick huffed into the phone. "We got in a big fight."

Her mouth fell. "Oh. About what?"

She sniffled. "It doesn't matter. I just. I don't know if she's mad at me still or if I should call her. I just feel bad."

"You should call her." Kate's hand went to her chest, rubbing at her heart. It hurt for Mick, hurt for Abby, and hurt even more that she couldn't fix it. "I'm sure she's forgiven you for whatever happened. You two are so close."

"I don't know. It wasn't good."

"She seemed to have a lot on her mind at the wedding," Kate said. "Maybe she's feeling better now."

"Yeah. What happened between you two, anyway?"

Kate swiped the softball from the clutter and squeezed. "I really don't want to talk about it. I prefer not to talk about her at all, if that's okay."

"Yeah, of course. Of course, Hutch. I'm sorry." Mick changed back to her jovial, upbeat tone. "You know, I'm planning an alumni game at Insley. You should come. Shupe can't because of the new baby, but T.K. said she will. Seaborn, Palamino, and Brookheimer too. I invited everyone."

Kate shook her head, defaulting to her well-worn excuse. "I'm sorry. I can't with the case and everything else."

"Right. Well, let me know if you change your mind."

But as she hung up, she wondered if Abby would be there. She reread her letter, searching for her between commas and lines. She contemplated writing back, pen hovering above a blank sheet on her legal pad before pushing it aside.

Kate hunkered down for the last weeks of the trial. She was getting better at answering the reporters and quipping back at the defense. She held her chin higher, her breathing came steadier, like that sweet spot on the field, certain of the next move.

"And how did it make you feel when the school shut down the LGBTQ alliance club?" Kate asked the student on the stand. She didn't particularly like having the kids testify, wishing to protect them from every question, aching when their voices shook as they tried to sit tall.

"Like I had to hide who I was. Like I had this secret that I shouldn't share at school. No one told me I couldn't, but I just felt it."

"Objection. Subjective," the defense said.

"Your honor, testimony goes to show the impact the school's discrimination had on their psychological and emotional state, as well as their ability to learn."

The judge nodded at her. "Overruled. You may continue."

Kate stepped closer to the teen, who sat wide-eyed and mute, and placed a hand on the wood railing. "Go ahead," she said. "How did it make you feel?"

"That I was less-than. That something about me, something I couldn't change, was wrong and shouldn't be shared."

Kate paused to let the answer sink in for the judge, for the defense, for all those watching in the galley. But the brief moment she turned away in the quiet, pretending to fiddle with notes on the counsel's table before she asked the next question, was because of the hole in her chest, widening, deepening, never closed. A sharp pain shot through her shoulder, but she turned back around, cleared her throat, and carried on.

But it stuck with her. It stuck with her as she hovered over another pre-marriage counseling assignment. A letter to her future children. Another one she couldn't write. All trial long, she'd stepped into herself, and that night, when Ryan came to pick her up, she didn't step back out.

"I don't want to go anymore," she said. The testimony, the letters she still hadn't written, to Abby and to her nonexistent children, swirled inside.

Ryan's eyes narrowed as he walked into the apartment. "Why? We have to."

"No, we don't," Kate said, steeling herself to tell the truth, at least the part of it she knew for certain. "I can't raise my kids in a church like that. In a place where they might feel the need to hide who they are."

"We've been going for years now, and suddenly you act like this is new." He stared at her for a beat. "Why do you go if you don't agree with it?"

"Because it's what I've always known. Because I thought it was good. But I started working on this case and—"

"No. No, don't blame it on the case." Ryan's jaw hardened. "This is about you."

Sweat sprang along her back like a warning signal to hit the brakes. "What do you mean?"

He breathed hard through his nose. "Are you still in love with Abby?"

"No." Kate said it fast but airless, so that she wasn't sure if it made a safe landing. Ryan stalked past her. "What are you doing?" She followed him to the kitchen table, where he swiped Abby's letter from the mess like he'd done it many times before. Bile soured in her throat. She willed herself to keep her feet planted. To be the same person who battled in court.

"Why do you have this letter?"

"Because she sent it to me! I didn't write her back." Kate's chest galloped. She wanted to rip it out of his hand. Her last piece of Abby. A lifeline she wasn't sure she'd accept, but wasn't willing to lose. "You've obviously read it, so you know it's part of her steps. Why are you snooping?"

"Because I don't trust you! I feel like I don't know you or what you want, and that's terrifying for someone you're supposed to marry!" Ryan glared as if despising both her and the emotions she made him feel. "I don't . . . I don't know if I can do this with you."

"Ryan—"

"You know what's really fucked? The first thing I loved about you was your heart. Your kindness. But this isn't kind, Kate." He shook his head. "This is you, stringing me along."

Kate frowned. She hated hurting him, but her own frustrations bubbled beneath. "Why did you propose to me at the biggest turning point in my career? So that you can be disappointed when I don't set a date or make a guest list? So that you can still be the center of attention?"

"Oh, that's rich! You are the center of attention!" Ryan roared, and she flinched. "On the news, in your fancy suits. This case has fucking changed you. That's for sure. And it's just another excuse to put a pause on us."

And finally, after all the suppression, not just with Ryan, but years of it, Kate thundered back. She fought, unlike the child her parents had punished with the Bible or the young woman still scared of them decades later, losing out on love, on life, on who she really was. Because how could others trust her to fight for them when she had never won a fight for herself.

"I didn't ask for this attention! I didn't ask for any of it! Not even for you to propose! But if it's that important to you, if you really meant it, why don't you come down to the courthouse and we'll get it taken care of. I'm there every day anyway! Then I can be Mrs. Eckhardt in time for closing statements!"

"No. You don't get to put this on me." Ryan's throat bobbed as he inched into her space. "I know why you don't want to go back into that church. I know what letter you want to write." He turned and yanked open the door. "You're not as kind or perfect as you think you are. I'm done letting you hide it behind someone else's trial."

Kate closed her eyes as the door slammed in her face. She didn't cry. She didn't feel any relief either. Instead, she felt shitty and heavy, because Ryan was right about her excuses. If he'd proposed later, after the trial, Kate wasn't even sure she'd say yes again. Because the case was changing her.

She walked between the protesters the morning of closing statements, and they felt like pieces of herself screaming at each other. This was it. The championship game all over again. She swore that when she glanced at the defense table she saw her parents, then shook them out of her head. Just like when she glanced into the sea of the prosecution's supporters, she imagined Abby, with that knowing smile, reminding her to breathe.

She addressed the judge and clearly outlined the case. She hit the right beats, the emotions, the discrimination, and the law. But then, as her speech neared its end, her voice caught. She wasn't ready for it to be over. No more case to hide behind. She'd done it. She was here, being exactly who she wanted to be. So close to knowing who the rest of that was too. So close to taking it—just as Charlotte advised—that she could taste it. It put tears in her throat and behind her eyes.

"First Foundations Charter started by opening its doors to the very people it's now working so hard to keep out—those who think differently, create passionately, love fiercely, and may not be understood." Kate's gaze found Marcus, who smiled and nodded. "I understand the school's desire to guide its students by a certain set of values. Values that they believe are inherently good." Kate paused and swallowed. "But when those teachings hurt people, when they become tools of exclusion, when they make children feel like they must hide part of who they are in order to be accepted, is it really good anymore?"

Her voice wavered like it did under the shiny, spiritless church lights, like it did at the kitchen table with her parents, like it did every minute she wasn't herself.

"First Foundations Charter is desperately trying to gain religious exemption so that they may pick and choose who can learn, just as they pick and choose what verses they might follow or what version of God's love may be celebrated or persecuted." Kate stood taller for the finish. She stood not on the beliefs of her childhood, but the ones she sought herself in law school, suddenly more confident in her findings than ever before. "But the Constitution is crystal clear. It requires no baptism, no conversion, no denial of self. It is guaranteed that all of us are treated equally and given, without question, a right to life and liberty, and a chance to belong. Something no school, no courtroom, or God might take away."

When the gavel sounded and the judge left to deliberate, Kate closed her eyes and released the breath she'd been holding in for a year. Her co-counsels shook her hand and congratulated her. Marcus and the students hugged her. She made a brief statement for the cameras gathered in the marble hallway, but then hurried for the exit.

She felt reborn, sturdier as she walked past the competing crosses and rainbow flags. But it didn't stop the tears as she left the case behind. The tears from the trial's pressure, from the long nights, from the fight with Ryan, from the decisions that awaited her, tears both overjoyed and overwhelmed. Tears because she didn't know who to call. Because she didn't want her parents, and she didn't want Ryan. She only wanted one person, just like so many times before. All she had to do was decide and take it.

Instead, as she stepped down the concrete stairs, vision blurry with emotion, her heel lost traction. Her legs slipped out from under her and she fell with a thud. Right onto her shoulder. Kate groaned and nearly broke into another sob. She'd finally severed those ligaments, but she didn't feel broken anymore. She laughed as she stared up at the clouds, the tops of skyscrapers leaning into view, a plane leaving streaks in its wake. And for the first time in a long time, she knew exactly what she wanted. But for now, she'd wait.

PRESENT DAY

"Abby?"

She stared ahead, shoulders clenching at the voice behind her. One she hadn't heard in two years. She knew a reunion was possible when she agreed to scout at Insley. That she might very well come across another name on the list of people she owed an apology to. Abby clutched the plastic chip in her pocket as the reckoning drew closer, footsteps thumping above the cheers for the batter who knocked a ball into right field.

"Cruz, you are one unbelievable fucking asshole!"

Abby peered up at the woman in an INSLEY SOFTBALL windbreaker blocking her view.

"Hey, Mick."

She waited with her teeth clenched, braced for everything from more yelling to fists. In two years, she'd picked up the phone more than once to apologize for the awful things she said before hitting rock bottom. But then she never knew where to start, thought a face-to-face would be better, then would put it off until the next time guilt woke her in the middle of the night. Until two years flew by and she ended up here.

Mick surveyed her with arms crossed, as if the game and fans around them meant nothing. Then after a long sigh, she snatched Abby's hand and yanked her up.

"What are you doing? Come here."

Abby startled, then relaxed as Mick smacked her into a hug. A lump filled her throat. She squeezed her back, wishing it could make up for everything she'd ruined. When they released, Abby sniffled, thankful for the shield of her sunglasses.

"I can't believe you didn't tell me you were here," Mick said.

"I know. I came for work and—" Abby paused as her lips drooped. "And I didn't know if you'd want to see me."

"Of course I want to see you." Mick punched her shoulder. "You really are still an idiot, aren't you?"

"Some things never change." Abby forced a smirk even if it didn't fix the rest.

They sat down as the bottom of the inning started, squeezing next to Tanner, who grinned and scooted down.

"This is Tanner, another scout," Abby said. "Tanner, this is Mick. She's the head softball coach here."

"Nice to meet you," Tanner said. "Did you play with Abby?"

"Oh yeah, we go way back. Did she tell you she's the greatest ballplayer in Insley history?"

"She failed to mention that."

"Because it's not true." Abby scoffed, embarrassed but heartened. She didn't know how Mick still had a kind word to say about her.

"You guys here for Kayson?" Mick asked.

"Yep."

"He's a good kid." She raised a mischievous brow at Abby. "He plays like Hutch, don't you think?"

Abby swallowed. Of course, he played like her. That was the whole reason she was there. Why she never stopped chasing the game. *I miss you so much that I search for you in others.*

"Never noticed." She shrugged.

Tanner left after the next inning and Abby wished he'd stay as a buffer. It left her to do the heavy lifting.

"So, we going to talk about it?" Mick asked.

Abby wrung her hands, keeping her gaze on Kayson. It was enough silence for Mick to unleash her wrath.

"I mean, I know you do this. You disappear, and it was bad enough when you did it to her, but I've always stuck by you. What you said, cutting me out for two years? It hurt. I beat myself up at first, but now you come back, and you didn't even have the decency to tell me you were here? Are we really not friends anymore?"

"Hey, I know, I know. I'm sorry." She stopped Mick's flailing hands. "I'm really sorry."

Mick's face wilted. Her voice fell beneath the game. "What happened, Abby?"

The crowd cheered as the Eagles smacked in a few more runs. She drew in a ragged breath. "You think we could get out of here?"

"Thought you'd never ask." Mick punched her shoulder and Abby hissed, never so grateful for the tender spot it left on her biceps.

"This is seriously still your spot of choice?" Abby asked as they stood outside Sunny's. The bar hadn't changed in almost a decade. She swore the same beer residue coated the floorboards.

"I thought we could, for old times' sake." Mick shook her shoulders. "Plus, I wanted to show you something."

Tacked up on the wall, among the other immortalized Insley greats, was a photo of their senior fivesome. They sat on the bar in their letterman's jackets, Mick kissing a trophy in the center, Abby's arm draped over Kate's shoulder, Jill and T.K. raising drinks on Mick's other side.

"I think that was the last time we were all here together," Mick said.

Abby nodded, caught between a smile and a frown. "We'd won the regional title. Left for nationals a few days later."

"The four of us came back for graduation, but it wasn't the same without you."

Abby gritted her teeth and pivoted to the patio. "Let's sit outside."

"Sorry," Mick said as they plopped to a splintered picnic table. Abby took the spot across from her and stretched her legs across the bench. "I didn't mean to bring up old shit."

"I guess it's unavoidable," she mumbled. "But if we could ease into my failures, that would be appreciated."

"Well, maybe this will help." Mick waved at the server. "We'll do a pitcher of beer."

Abby shook her head and blushed. "Uh, just a Coke for me, please."

Mick's eyebrows shot up. "Yeah, scratch that. I'll do the same."

"You can drink whatever you want," she said when the server left.

"No, it's fine." Mick narrowed her gaze. "I've never known you to turn down a drink."

"Well, I turn them all down now." Abby pushed out a grim smile. "Two years sober."

Mick's mouth fell. She let her take it in, catch up on the math and new context. "When did this happen? How?"

Abby picked at her napkin as the waiter dropped off their drinks. "Not long after I was a total dick to you." She winced. "It was mostly booze, but I got tied up in painkillers after my injury. I messed a lot of things up, which we can talk about later." Abby sighed. "The main thing is, I'm here to say sorry to you."

"Oh, shit. Am I getting an amends?"

"Yeah." Abby furrowed her brow. "Why are you smiling?"

"It just, it seems official. I've never had one of these."

"Oh my God."

"Can I record it for Haley and Shupe?"

"No!"

Mick snickered. "Did you write me something?"

"No. No, I was just going to talk to you."

"Like a speech?"

"No, not really. Can you just try to take this seriously?"

"Ugh, fine. Go ahead."

Abby laughed at how things hadn't changed. Mick certainly hadn't. Her straw hair still pointed out with a cowlick at the back of her pixie cut and her hazel eyes favored green over gold. Her big smile, round head, and husky, huggable build never failed to remind Abby of a cartoon character. She wondered, now, sitting across from her, how she'd ever been afraid to come back. Worse, how she ever managed to hurt her.

"I had time to reflect on the last few months I saw you. The way I treated you before I got clean." Abby frowned. "First, I'm sorry for ruining your wedding."

Mick waved her off. "You didn't ruin my wedding. It was a little broken glass, and you already apologized for that."

"Well, I'm still sorry. To Haley too. And your folks. I'm sure they hate me."

"Are you kidding? My parents still ask about you every Christmas."

Abby cracked a smile at the memories, then let it fade at what she nearly destroyed.

"I'm sorry for our last conversation. I was really fucked-up and I shouldn't have taken things out on you." Her eyes prickled. "You *are* my family, Mick. Kate was Kate, but you were my first friend here. My best friend. You've always been there for me and I'm sorry I was too selfish to appreciate it, caught up in my own shit. Not just then, but the years before that too."

"You're hard on yourself." Mick reached across the table and squeezed her forearm. "But I accept your apology."

Abby sniffled. "I love you."

"I love you too, idiot." Mick stood to meet her for a hug. "You're a good person, Cruz. A good friend."

Abby slackened in the embrace, and when Mick clutched tighter, keeping her on her feet, the air settled deeper into her lungs. They'd shared hugs before, but none that Abby fully let herself go in. While she was the one tasked with mending the bridge, this was Mick mending her.

"I don't know how you can say that after everything." She dabbed a single tear as they retook their seats.

"Because you never stopped fighting, you know? And no matter how down you were, you still made us smile or hit one out of the park. In some ways, you were the best of us."

"No. That's Kate," she said before she could stop herself or the blush that came after.

"In her own way, yeah. Kate's our captain, our heart, but when shit hits the fan, when we need a clutch hit, it's always you. You know why?" Mick's eyes glowed with gentle admiration. "Because you've seen the shit. You've known loss and you persevered. Through this too."

"I don't know about that, but thanks, Mick." Abby fiddled with the straw in her soda. "I can't believe she didn't tell you."

"You're not a welcome topic of conversation." She shrugged and Abby ignored the punch in the gut. "So, you apologized to her too?"

"I did."

"Before me?" she shouted and tossed a crumpled napkin at her.

Abby chuckled. "You're my last one."

"You saw her then?"

"No. I sent a letter."

"You two and your letters." Mick rolled her eyes. "You know I invite her to the alumni game every year and she never comes."

"Really? I thought that would be her favorite day of the year."

"Me too. You should come though." She smacked the picnic table. "In fact, I'm demanding it as part of my amends."

"That's not how it works."

"Nah, I think it is," she said. "How long are you in town for? You should stay with Hales and me."

Abby shook her head. "I'm headed back to San Diego for a few days before I ship back out."

"No."

"Yes. You realize I have a job to do, right?"

"Well, then that's perfect, because I have a great player for you to scout." Mick ramped up at Abby's sigh. "Oh, come on. This was one shitty apology then. You save me for last, you don't even write me one of your little love letters—"

"Okay, okay, fine!" Abby laughed.

Mick grinned, reached across the table to ruffle her hair, and while Abby smacked her hands away, it was like two parts of herself harmonized. Like she was twenty years old at Insley again, but not so she could hide there. This time she'd fully come back to herself.

The latest prospect sent Abby to an elementary school. She followed Mick past the playground, dodging kids and strollers, to a small baseball diamond where a team of first graders in bright pink uniforms warmed up.

"Aunt Abby!"

Juniper spotted her first, skipping over with her bat. Abby kneeled to hug her as Mick scoffed. "What am I? Chopped liver?"

As Abby stood, Jill almost knocked her over with another hug. She squeezed so hard that Abby knew she didn't have to explain the last two years. Jill pecked her cheek, tears in her eyes when they released. "Mick told me."

Abby tilted her head and frowned. "I'm sorry."

"Don't be," she said. "Though I hate being the last to know. I mean, even after T.K.?"

T.K. appeared on cue, donning large sunglasses and a larger sun hat, out of place among the parents. "That's because I introduced her to some nice people, and what does she do? Sleep with half of them and pillage their medicine cabinets." She rocked Abby into an embrace. "Let it stand as proof that I am excellent at keeping secrets. In fact, I didn't talk about you once."

"Please, no one here is mistaking your narcissism for discretion," Mick said, earning a shove from T.K.

"I can't believe you're here," Abby said.

"You kidding? Mick sounded the alarm. I got on the first flight," T.K. said.

Abby smiled at the picturesque Saturday afternoon. The sun warmed her skin, and everything glowed bright around them. As she surveyed her friends—Jill in her pink hat, matching shirt, and mom jeans, T.K. in her heels and wielding a designer bag, Mick permanently in Insley softball gear, she hardly noticed a difference from eight years ago. Except that they were missing one more.

Juniper tugged her hand. "Why were you gone so long?"

"Sorry, Junie. I've been traveling for work."

Juniper pointed her bat at T.K. "She said in the car that you went to rehab."

Abby rolled her eyes.

"Oh my God, she repeats everything." T.K. scowled. "You don't have to be such a snitch, Junie."

"What's rehab?"

"Juniper Faye Farrelly, not appropriate," Jill said. "Sorry."

"No, it's okay." Abby chuckled. "It's like a time-out for adults, Junie."

"Why'd you get time-out?"

"Booze mostly. Some pills too. And I got arrested."

"Okay, let's spare the details, shall we?" Jill muttered to her.

"Abby!" Dylan joined them with Dylan Jr. atop his shoulders. "Where's Kate?"

Abby grimaced and the rest of the group recoiled too.

"Dill," Jill hissed, and smacked his shoulder.

"What?"

T.K. shook her head. "This is where Junie gets it."

"Well, no one tells me anything!"

"I've got an idea—how about I take DJ, and you do coach-pitch today so we can catch up?" Jill swiped the toddler from him.

"No, Jilly—"

"Hey!" Jill waved to the other parents. "Dylan is going to do parent pitch!"

Abby nodded at Juniper. "Come on, show me your swing."

After a brief hitting lesson with her favorite pupil, Abby slid into the bleachers with the gang. While she doubted any future MLB players skipped onto the diamond in their pigtails that day, she watched with the same reverence. Perhaps because beneath the bobbling heads with helmets too big, clumsy little hands struggling to swing and catch, Abby recognized the same love of the game. In fact, she might've very well been witnessing it take root as it had for her. She pictured her mother in the stands like she always did, only now it didn't hurt.

"So, I know it's not your favorite thing, but I think we should talk about it," Jill said.

Abby nodded, turning from the game. "Yeah. What do you want to know?"

Jill's eyes widened as she stopped bouncing DJ on her lap.

"What?" Abby asked.

T.K. scoffed. "Damn, rehab really worked."

"Told ya," Mick said.

"What is that supposed to mean?" Abby peeled off her sunglasses to squint at the trio.

"You've just never been one to share," Jill said with a grim smile, as DJ tugged at her hair. "Or let us help you. Like with this."

"I just never wanted to burden you guys." Abby's brow drew together. She nodded out at the field. "I never wanted you to look at me different than you did out there. That's where I always felt like I was enough."

"You were always enough, idiot." Mick nudged her.

"I don't know, I kept fucking up. Then I felt like you all were growing up, changing, and I was standing still. I didn't know how to ask for help. Plus, if I didn't ask, there was no chance of being let down."

"We would've been there," T.K. said.

"I know that now." Abby nodded.

A hit blooped to the infield and three players in pink raced to pick it up. The four of them chuckled at the chaos, the ball never reaching Juniper, who called for it at first base. The runner sat down to draw in the dirt after making it safe.

"You know, it's not all on you either. We could've been better too," Jill said as the clapping settled around them. "We knew you'd been through a lot when you came to Insley, but we never asked."

"I would've blown you off." Abby shrugged.

"Well, since you're not doing that now, there's something I wanted to say to you." Jill's eyes welled again, and Abby considered deflecting with a joke or shifting attention to the circus-like game. But she faced it instead like she never would've before. "Ever since I had Junie, I've meant to talk to you about your mom. I know the situation was different, but she'd never want to leave you, Abby. No matter how it happened, she didn't." Jill tilted her head down at DJ and then at Junie. "I look at them and no matter how bad things got for me, they'd never be the reason. And I know if something happened to me, no matter how low things got for Junie, you'd never give up on her. That's how we feel about you too."

Abby didn't bother hiding the tears. She let Jill wrap an arm around her and Mick pat her back while the game unfolded with giggles and nonsense before them.

"Thank you." She rested her head on Jill's and sighed.

T.K. sniveled. "Fucking Shupe."

Abby chuckled, rubbed away tears, and reached for T.K.'s water bottle. "Give me some of that."

T.K. quickly pulled back. "Oh, that's not water."

"Jesus." Abby rolled her eyes.

"What? This is a boring Saturday for me!"

Mick dug into the cooler at their feet, handing Abby a juice box. "Here."

"Can I have some of those orange slices?" T.K. asked.

"Hey, no, those are for the kids," Jill said, but they were already passing them around, sucking oranges into their mouths, passing out string cheese too. Abby leaned back and slurped apple juice.

"Okay, my turn," T.K. said as Jill swiped the "water" bottle for a drink. "Can we talk about Hutch? And what happened in Vegas?"

"Nothing happened." Abby slurped harder.

"Have you talked since then?" Jill raised a brow, shifting her eyes between T.K. and Mick.

"No, but she wrote her a letter," Mick said before Abby smacked her. She flashed her an orange slice smile in return.

T.K. groaned. "Not the letters."

"I think it's romantic." Jill smiled. "What did you say?"

Abby shook her head. "Nothing."

"Did she write back?" T.K. asked. "You know she's—"

"I'd rather not." Abby's cheeks burned, and while her heart fluttered at the mention of her, she wasn't ready yet. "Please."

"Oh, here's Junie." Jill smacked the shoulders nearest to her. "Let's go Junie!"

They cheered as she stepped up to the plate. She swung and missed the first pitch that Dylan lobbed in.

"That's okay!" Abby clapped. "Just keep your weight centered like we talked about!"

"Scoot up in the box!" Mick shouted.

"No, stay where you are! Just let it come to you!"

"Rip it, Junie, this pitcher is a cupcake!" T.K. shouted, earning a glare from Dylan.

"The ball's dropping early." Mick shook her head. "Scoot up, Junie!"

"No, don't!" Abby yelled.

Juniper turned back to them, eyes wide and exasperated by the conflicting advice.

"Choke up a little bit too," Mick said.

Abby smacked down Mick's hands as she demonstrated. "Don't listen to Aunt Mick. Connect on a straight line, okay?"

"I'm her godmother," Mick said. "She should listen to me."

"Well, I'm her hitting coach."

"Well, I'm an actual college coach now!"

"And I'm her mother!" Jill shouted over them. "Both of you shut up. Come on, June Bug, eye on the ball! Just have fun up there!"

Abby, Mick, and T.K. rolled their eyes at the advice. Juniper gulped and got back into position, and while it was nothing more than a children's game, Abby held her breath. The pitch came in slow and when Junie made contact, they all leapt from their seats. As she rounded the bases, the fans thundering, the players scrambling to the ball, Abby swore it was the best the game had ever sounded. Gentler. Softer. Slower. Full of love and almost perfect.

"She should be here," Abby muttered.

Jill smiled at her, Mick nodded, and as they lost themselves in high fives and hugs, Abby knew she was ready.

INSLEY

These days the table was full for family dinner. Two squirmy little boys, an old mustached man, a district court judge with the first traces of gray threading into his hair, and an effortlessly elegant law professor had already gathered when Abby slipped into the sixth seat. As she nodded at Audie across from her and smiled at Isla, who passed her the salad bowl, she wondered if they also thought this strange but warm mix of unlikely people was proof that they had achieved the impossible.

"Big game this weekend," Audie said to her.

While it was just the alumni game, while she was nearing thirty and well past playing competitively, it made her feel young. Like another one of those moments they had missed out on but now got to make up for.

"Just hoping I don't embarrass myself." Abby smirked.

Audie shook his head, waving her off. He leaned conspiratorially to the grandson nearest to him. "Your aunt was the best hitter I've ever seen. She hit a home run almost every game."

The little boy's brown eyes stretched wide. "Better than you?" he asked. The boys were old enough to understand Audie's legacy, recognizing his statue and records at Petco Park.

"No," Abby said.

"Much better." Audie winked. "You know why? Because she never gave up."

Abby shook her head at him but reflected his smile.

The sun set while she and Isla did dishes, while Luca took the boys up for bath time, while Audie kissed their cheeks before saying goodbye. Sleep seemed unlikely so Abby didn't try, lounging by the pool, the slither of ocean and sway of palm trees drowning out everything but her thoughts. Thoughts of going back, of playing, of Kate.

"What's that?" Isla asked over her shoulder.

"Just some houses T.K. sent over." Abby resisted slamming the laptop shut as Isla squeezed onto the lounge chair next to her.

"Are you moving?"

She shrugged. "It's been two years. Thought it might be time to get out of your hair."

"You're hardly in my hair. You're on the road two-thirds of the year."

"Well, the boys are getting older and I—"

"But you don't have to go." Isla frowned. "I don't know if I want you to go."

Abby's eyes widened. "This was only supposed to be temporary."

But that too reminded her of Insley. While she had moved because of Isla, she never expected to gain such a deep bond. For either of them to care when their roads diverged.

"Are you sure? It's a big step . . ."

"I'll still babysit."

"Oh, well, in that case, let me take a look." Isla clicked through the listings before Abby could stop her. T.K. had tracked down options in San Diego, Los Angeles, and "San Francisco?"

Isla raised a brow at her and Abby blushed.

"T.K. thought she was being funny," she said. Of course, it didn't stop Abby from browsing additional Bay Area listings on real estate websites.

"Is she going to be there?"

"Who?"

Isla scoffed. "Kate."

Abby gulped and closed the laptop louder than necessary. "I don't know. Mick told me she's never come before. And I haven't asked since then."

"What are you going to do if she's there?"

"Get on bended knee and recite a sonnet."

"I'm serious! She was supposed to marry that guy, and she didn't, right? Doesn't that count for something?"

"I don't know." Abby sighed and stared into the pool. "She never wrote me back."

"Well, weren't you the one who never wrote her back?" Isla smirked and Abby rolled her eyes. "I always liked you two together. Always liked her, honestly. Maybe better than you."

"That was no secret."

Isla smiled. "I hope she's there."

"Me too," Abby whispered.

"Part of me wants to go with you. Not for that, but back to Insley. There was always something magical about it." She gazed wistfully to the horizon, where the water met the sky. "Or maybe it's that my life started over there."

Abby smiled. "Mine did too."

"Have you forgiven yourself?"

"Almost."

"Good." Isla knocked her head to Abby's. "I love you."

"Love you too."

Isla patted her shoulder before standing up and backing toward the main house. "Text when you land?"

"Always."

"And tell Kate hi for me. Tell her we're proud of her."

"I will."

Abby arrived at Insley a day early—in part because Mick insisted, but also because she longed to return to the field. While she'd indulged in a few hitting sessions with Audie, she hadn't truly played or picked up a glove since getting clean. She couldn't imagine a better place to wade back in.

She joined Mick at the Eagles' practice, smirking at the young college players who listened to her friend's every word, who called her Coach, whose ranks she swore they had been in just yesterday. Mick gave Abby a vivacious introduction to the squad, which she turned red at. She encouraged her to share pointers while she observed, and then when they took infield, Mick nudged her.

"Get out there."

"No," Abby said.

"Come on!" Mick shouted. "Just take a few!"

The players encouraged and waved her on, until Abby jogged out to shortstop, secretly biting down a grin.

Within minutes, dust covered her sneakers and joggers, sweat coated her back, and a throb radiated from her hips to her knees. Still, Abby crouched into position with her glove as a ball skipped toward her. She anticipated the hop, met it after the bounce, and cradled it like an egg before throwing to first.

"She's still got it!" Mick shouted from home plate. She hit another ball to Abby. "Show these kids how it's done, Cruz."

Despite stiff joints and frayed twitch muscles, Abby didn't miss a grounder. She couldn't dive or stretch like she used to, but her footwork, her reads, her throw, didn't lose their shine. In fact, this slower, less risky play brought something refined to her game, like gliding on water. A steadiness she had never valued before.

Soon, the players gathered around as she demonstrated a behind-the-back toss to second. She took more grounders, flipped her hat backward as the sun beat down on her neck. She felt twenty-two again, in love with the game. In love with its sound and its rhythm. It was like she regained a piece of herself every time she snagged a ball. Except for the piece of her still missing. That piece being Kate. Abby looked twice for her at second base, frowning ever so slightly at her absence.

"Hit one!" Mick drilled another grounder to her.

Abby scooped the ball, set her feet, and zipped a throw to first base.

"Again!"

She froze before crouching for the next grounder. For so long, she'd pictured her, what it might be like when she finally arrived, if she were to even come for the game, but she never imagined this. Kate, in the stands, like some strange but welcome dream, one that radiated with the kindness of the past and the thrill of all that had changed since then.

She didn't look like the Kate who had once taken the field, but Abby knew every version of her and would've known a million more. Chestnut tresses curled down her shoulders, sunglasses hid her eyes, and she wore a suit and heels—she must have come from work. Polished, strong, maybe even a touch stern, with her arms crossed. Abby searched for a smile, for a sigh, for a sign of what she might be thinking.

She only spent a half second gawking, but it was enough to put her in harm's way. She registered the ping of Mick's bat too late and knew without seeing it that the ball was destined for her shin. It hit bone before she could move, and Abby grunted, doubled over, and gritted her teeth.

"Fuck!" She hopped on her good leg, ripped off her glove, and slammed it down. "Mick, you motherfucker!"

The college players snorted.

"Dude, I'm sorry," Mick said, hustling over. "I thought you were paying attention."

"I got distracted." Abby glanced at Kate, who'd made it down to the chain-link fence and observed with a grimace.

"Oh." Mick patted her shoulder. "Sorry, I should've made you look cooler. Maybe she saw the other plays."

Abby shoved her. "Shut up."

She sucked in a pained breath through clenched teeth and straightened up. Dirt covered her untucked shirt and one of her pant legs was higher than the other. She tried not to limp, but ended up hobbling across the infield, her shin radiating with the promise of a fresh bruise.

It wasn't how she wanted to see Kate, but something else in her took over. Something carnal and lasting that trumped ego. And even still, when she reached her, Abby didn't know what to say. She stopped at the fence and let the chain-link barrier ease them into reunion.

"Are you okay?" Kate asked. "That looked really bad."

"I'm all right, but I think I already feel the laces." She smiled, unable to fight it, and Kate grinned back. Abby quietly choked on a breath and had to whisper the rest. "How are you?"

"What a surprise!" Mick opened the gate and threw her arms around Kate. "Who would've known?"

"You." Kate shook her head as they hugged.

"I must have gotten my days mixed up and invited you early."

"Oh, is that it?"

Abby rolled her eyes. "How could you *possibly* make a mistake like that, Mick?"

She shrugged. "I've got to wrap up practice. Just give me twenty minutes." Mick winked as she backed away. "Don't kill each other."

"She's still as subtle as a brick through a fucking window."

Kate laughed, lightening Abby's chest. It was enough to encourage her to stagger through the gate. Kate removed her sunglasses, revealing baby blues that glowed just as gentle and intelligent as when they first met. Perhaps one of the few things that remained while the rest of her had aged, growing from an angel into a goddess. Faded freckles, firmer cheeks, and a sharper jaw that poked out from her heart-shaped face. Her hair was longer, darker lashes, more makeup than Abby recalled, but it was fitting, natural. She smelled richer, but Abby still detected that fresh, cotton scent beneath it. She wore nicer clothes, a silk blouse and tapered trousers with a clearly tailored jacket that screamed subtle success, and jewelry too.

"Hey," Kate said.

"Hi." She chewed her lip as they stood across from each other. It'd only been a few years, but her nerves surged with greater potency. Abby pushed through the awkwardness. She had lost Kate enough times to not embrace her now. She opened her arms and Kate nestled into them. "I missed you."

"I missed you too," Kate said, but drew away quickly, taking a step back to restore space. "Did Mick tell you I was going to be here?"

"What do you think?"

"Right." Kate sighed. "I hope this is okay with you then. I can always meet up with her later or—"

"Don't be ridiculous. It's fine with me if it's okay with you."

"Yeah. Yeah, it's okay."

They watched practice for a beat, not daring to speak to each other. Abby discreetly fidgeted with her fingers, heat rising across her cheeks when she glanced back at her. "Well, uh. This is your first time back here?"

"Yeah, kind of crazy," Kate said, her throat bobbing. She kept staring at the field, but Abby couldn't stop looking at her. "It really hasn't changed."

"No." Abby shook her head. "Hasn't changed at all."

Kate cleared her throat, arms still crossed in front of her chest as she glanced around. "Should we sit?"

"Yeah." Abby gestured to the bleachers. She tried to remember her own advice. Just breathe. But it didn't stand a chance.

Kate accepted Mick's invitation as a sign that it was time. She was stronger, confident, maybe even close to healed, with the case a year behind her. She didn't ask if Abby was coming, but she never once doubted it. Just like when they turned double plays together, throwing into emptiness, certain that the other would appear.

While she had prepared for the possibility of their reunion, she wasn't ready to see her like this. Coasting across the dirt, flawless but free in form, shoulders and thighs still strong, the rest of her agile, casual but so certain it was as though she had sprung from the earth beneath the field. It transported Kate back to twenty, discovering Abby at shortstop, but now she could feel all of what she knew back then but didn't fully understand: she was watching something special.

Sitting next to her on the bleachers, breathing her sweat, aware of her subtle warmth, Kate struggled to ground herself. She'd grown more self-assured since Las Vegas and Mick's wedding, both in the courtroom and outside it, but now worried she'd stammer, blush, or go mute if she basked too long in Abby. Because while she was eager to see her, she was determined to not lose herself either.

"They seem so young," Abby said while they observed practice. The game's soundtrack filled the wistful, not quite comfortable quiet between them. A steady rhythm of the ball dinging off the bat, sliding through the dirt, popping into a leather glove. "You sure you don't want to get out there for a few before tomorrow?"

"Not after watching you take one off the leg." Kate smirked but kept her stare trained on the action. "I've never seen you miss a routine grounder."

"Maybe I've lost my touch."

Kate couldn't resist her gaze, that self-deprecating, rocky chuckle, like another tug of gravity. When she scanned her face more fully, a little dust on her forehead, Kate detected something new. An unfamiliar lightness in her copper gaze.

"What?" Abby asked.

She was too entranced to shift away. "Your eyes are just so clear."

A sheepish smile lifted Abby's face. "Two years clean."

She pulled out the plastic chip commemorating the milestone and offered it to her. Their fingers brushed together for a fraction of a second, but the heaviness in her stomach overpowered the flutter. Kate frowned as she ran a thumb over the token embossed with *two.* "I'm sorry I never wrote you back."

"Don't be. You didn't need to." Abby stared at her feet, letting practice fill the quiet for a beat. "I'm sorry I called you."

Kate had deleted the voicemail, but the pain had never left her. "Don't be. It broke my heart to hear you like that, but—" She steadied herself with a breath. "But I understand why you called. I'm just glad to see you healthy. Two years sober is amazing."

"Nah. It's nothing." Abby shook her head. "Especially compared to what you've done. American Bar Association Top Young Lawyers Award. Ninth Circuit Court of Appeals win. What's next, the Supreme Court? Showing up here looking like a badass, no bullshit attorney."

"I had a meeting in Portland. And look at you . . . all covered in dirt." Kate dampened the pad of her thumb without thinking and rubbed dust from Abby's chin. "I take it you and Mick made up?"

Abby's eyes widened. "She told you?"

"Well, not what it was about." Kate blushed and pulled back from fussing over Abby's mess. Old habits never died. "What was it about?"

She grimaced. "You."

"Over me?"

"I said about, not over." Abby winked. Kate stayed rigid, only to keep herself from smiling, which wouldn't have lasted long anyway when Abby continued. "She wanted me to get my shit together and stop you from marrying Ryan." Her gaze shifted to Kate's left hand. She reflexively grabbed her naked ring finger, though there was really no reason to hide it. "Apparently, you didn't need my help. Unless . . ."

Kate shook her head. "You had nothing to do with it."

"Good."

"Yeah, good."

They both turned to the field, shoulders inching back up to ears, identical sighs puffing into the pine-laced air. Kate clasped her hands together and squeezed in the silence, willing herself to keep going. To find out if they could pretend to be two people without history tangled between them.

"So, you're scouting now?" Kate asked. "I saw the *Sports Illustrated* article."

Abby threw her head back. A glimpse of old that Kate grinned at. "Well, that was just bullshit. You can't believe everything you read."

Kate, of course, hadn't just read the article, but memorized it. It highlighted Abby as one of just two female scouts in Major League Baseball and half of the first father-daughter duo in MLB history. Not just that, but her and Audie's humanitarian work in Puerto Rico. Kate had lost herself in the photos. The one of Abby absorbed in a game, jaw hard as though back on the diamond, not just watching but hearing.

"Do you like it?" Kate asked.

"Scouting? Yeah." Abby nodded. "A lot of traveling, but it's good for me. Keeps me out of trouble. I never stopped needing the game, I guess."

Kate nodded, a happy skip unhitching her chest. "And you like San Diego?"

"Yeah. I'm crashing at Isla's pool house, but I'm gone half the year anyway. It's good though. And I get to see the boys." Abby grinned and pulled out her phone. "They're obsessed with baseball." She leaned closer to share pictures of her dark-haired, amber-eyed nephews. "Leo's grown like three inches, and he really understands the game. He'll watch for hours with me. But this little guy, Milo, is an absolute rascal. Always wiggling and on the move."

Kate laughed. "Sounds like someone else I know."

"Poor Isla's going to have her hands full." Abby chuckled. "She says hi by the way. She's proud of you." She tilted her head. "And I am too."

"Thank you." Kate gulped through the weight of the day. Of reuniting. Of taking in the new pieces against the old. She didn't know if how far they'd come and how much they'd changed left her pining for the past or relieved of it. "You seem really happy."

"I think I am," Abby said. Her eyes, glowing with a purity Kate was still getting used to, flashed into hers. "What about you? Are you happy?"

Kate nodded. "Yeah," she said, unable to put her full voice behind it.

"Okay, okay!" Mick skipped up the bleacher steps. "I've heard no crying, no thrown drinks, not even a raised voice?"

"On our best behavior." Abby chuckled.

"Well, let's get out of here and eat," Mick said. "Haley's waiting."

Kate, while intrigued by the years and feelings yet to be explored, happily accepted the distraction. She used catching up with Mick on the drive from the field as a chance to regain her breath, though her friend didn't hide her mischievous twinkle. "Cruz looks good, huh?"

"Yeah." She shrugged nonchalantly but then peered in the rear-view mirror for a glimpse of Abby's car trailing behind theirs as if scared it might disappear.

Mick and Haley lived on the ridge in a two-bedroom house plopped on a few acres, with their five children: two German shepherds, a senile Labrador, a snipping Chihuahua that led the pack, and an angry cat that kept the Chihuahua's power in check. Mick had big plans to start a fruit orchard, much like the other properties in the vicinity, and Haley maintained an overflowing garden with sunflowers and roses in every color, bright tomatoes pulling down their vines. Each breath arrived thick with wildflowers in the dry heat. Large birds circled and chattered overhead, but all other motion ceased. Even the road and river waned like an afterthought.

After dropping her bags in the guest room and washing up, Kate found Abby in the kitchen, chopping alongside Haley.

"You cook now?" she asked.

"When I can," Abby said.

"She's being modest," Haley said as she poured Kate a glass of wine. Kate froze, glancing from the glass back to Abby.

"It's fine. Really," Abby muttered to her with a smile as Haley prattled on.

"When she stayed with us, I was in heaven. Cooked every night. I dream of that carbonara." Haley threw her head back. "Oh my God, and the eggplant dish. What was that?"

"Melanzane alla parmigiana," Abby said in perfect Italian.

Kate had to keep herself from staring too long, and while seconds ago she wasn't sure if she should drink in front of her, she gulped wine to subdue the jitters.

"I had to kick her out after that one." Mick entered with the pack of dogs behind her. "No one is allowed to make my wife moan except me." She wrapped her arms around Haley and kissed her neck.

"You've come a long way from ramen and hot sauce," Kate said with a smirk.

Abby grinned back. "Oh, there's still plenty of that when you're living out of hotels."

"Well, uh, do you need any help?" Kate asked.

Abby shook her head as she wiped her hands on a towel. "No, I think me and Hales got it."

And while Abby likely meant no offense, and while Kate definitely shouldn't have cared, her shoulders drooped. She didn't think Abby withholding or distant, but there was indeed something unfamiliar now. A steadiness in her presence. In her cooking, in her way of moving and speaking, in her smile, and, of course, those eyes. Eyes that never veered from Kate's as they ate dinner across from each other, the twinkling outdoor lights mirroring the stars above. They blushed when their feet touched and then darted away. And despite how long they'd known each other, Kate felt the intrigue of eating dinner with a stranger.

"Okay, so here's the thing," Mick said after dishes and dessert. "We only have one guest room."

Kate rolled her eyes and Abby shook her head.

"Don't do this to them." Haley smacked Mick's butt. "The couch pulls out—"

"I can take that," Kate said.

"No. I already snagged a hotel," Abby said.

Mick sighed. "You're no fun."

"And you're delusional. You really think the one-bed thing is going to work? What are you, twelve?"

Abby grabbed Mick into a headlock, and for all her new poise, this was what Kate remembered and missed. Her sarcasm, her edges and laughter. She chuckled as Haley scolded them for roughhousing and riling up the dogs. Enough to distract Kate from the twinge that came with Abby deciding to leave for the night rather than stay. The same twinge that had her walking Abby to the door after she said good night to the others.

"So, I guess I'll see you tomorrow," Kate said.

Abby nodded as she stood on the porch step, everything pitch-black behind her except for a splatter of stars. No buildings or headlights. Just a choir of owls and crickets. Just them, alone in the woods they'd once peered up at from the field.

"This was nice," Abby said.

"Yeah." Kate's mouth betrayed her, lips pursing with a smile she wanted to suppress.

Abby grinned. "What?"

"Nothing. You're just—" Kate paused and squinted at her. "You're just really mellow now."

Abby groaned. "Oh, you mean boring."

"No!" Kate chuckled, then shook her head. She leaned against the doorframe and crossed her arms. "No, it's nice. Calming. You were like this before sometimes. In college."

Her cheeks twitched with a half smile. "When we were together?"

Kate nodded, slow, remembering that same Abby from not so long ago.

"You're different too," Abby said.

"How?"

"Well, you're way . . . bigger."

Kate's mouth dropped. "Excuse me?"

"No. I mean, you take up more space," Abby said as the single porch light put shadows across her dimples. "It's nice. Like you were always supposed to."

Kate's heart filled her throat. The knee-jerk reaction to reach out tempted her, but she didn't. Not yet. Not when they were still so new to each other. She reached out with what weighed on her chest instead, from the moment she'd seen the clarity in her eyes.

"I'm proud of you. Really proud," Kate said. "And I think maybe I didn't tell you that enough."

"Maybe I didn't give you a reason." Abby frowned. "Especially the last time I saw you."

"No, but you did. All those years playing, never afraid, no matter where it took you."

"Even if it was just running away?"

"No. Don't do that." Kate shook her head, aching at how Abby shirked the kindness, especially with how deeply she meant it, how desperately she wanted her to know and feel it. "You didn't run. You played. You were the best, and I wish I could've seen it. I mean, I finally let myself look you up. Italy, Japan, Canada, Puerto Rico—who can say they went that far for it?" Kate swallowed an overly sappy knot, eyes glistening with pride for all Abby had been before and all she was now. "It was never just a game. It was always you. It's like no matter how bad things got, you never lost your faith. It's really beautiful." She finished with a whisper and a tear in her throat.

Abby's smile wobbled as she tilted her head. "Thank you." She leaned against the doorframe, opposite Kate, inches separating them, but neither of them reached. They just breathed for too many beats, until it didn't make sense anymore. "I better get to the hotel."

"You really don't have to. I can take the couch."

"No, I have some things to do in the morning." Abby pulled back, and Kate pretended she didn't care. "This is technically a scouting trip anyway."

"Oh, right. Kayson Cannon?"

"Oh no. He's old news. I'm looking at a four-foot, fifty-pound, right-handed first baseman." Abby grinned. "Junie Farrelly. Never too early to scout new talent."

"Smart." Kate laughed. "At this rate, you'll have fifteen years to convince the front office to draft a woman. That should be enough time."

"Ah, not a chance. Oceans will rise, but hell still won't have frozen over." Abby winked. "Maybe enough time for you to take them to court though."

"Don't tempt me."

When their chuckles ended, Abby didn't move. She didn't say good night. She lingered in the shadows, perhaps the first tell of the day that she too longed for more.

"Are we a memory yet?" Abby asked. "Long-lost teammates? Maybe even friends?"

Kate lost her breath at the lines from her letter. The one she never responded to but knew by heart. She shook her head. "I'm afraid not," she whispered.

"I didn't think so." Abby smirked as she backed away.

"I'll see you at the game," Kate said. "I'll be the one at shortstop."

"Oh, you think you're playing shortstop? I won't be giving it up that easily. I'm not a lovestruck college kid anymore."

Kate raised an eyebrow and grinned. "You sure?"

Abby paused on the walkway. "Not right now," she said with a smile. "Good night, Kate."

"Good night."

She waited until the door closed to breathe again.

THE ALUMNI GAME

She went to church twice, maybe three times a week, though she still didn't call it a spiritual awakening. The closest she came to that was the Serenity Prayer, with its message of surrender—the same message she learned from the field, of taking the good with the bad, of showing up and trusting it to come to you. The closest she'd ever come to a higher power, a way of life, or religion.

But when the AA meeting ended and Abby climbed the steps out of New Hope Baptist's basement, she thought maybe she'd had a spiritual experience after all. She walked into a tepid but windy afternoon, with a pale sun. Perfect weather for the alumni game, made more perfect by the light it cast down on Kate, who stood just out of the church's reach. The same spot where Abby had once waited for her.

"The CAC is going to want to hear about this," Kate said.

"How the tables have turned." Abby chuckled. Her cheeks burned in the shadow of this new Kate, even as she appeared to have stepped out from their past. She wore running tights and an INSLEY SOFTBALL T-shirt, chestnut hair loose in a ponytail. Signs of a morning jog, which she'd returned from ruddy and sweaty but no less enchanting. "Mick tell you I was here?"

Kate nodded. "Had to see for myself."

Abby looked away from all that light. That blue gaze, that big smile, that halo around her head. "Well, different kind of Sunday service in there," she said, grappling for composure or a laugh that might restore her cool. "Alcoholics, drug addicts, criminals."

"What part's different?"

"True." Her cheeks ached from smiling. "You know who would be really excited to see me come out of there?"

"Jesus," Kate said.

Abby laughed. "No. Blake Davis. Whatever happened to him?"

"He owns a car dealership in Ann Arbor. Married with four kids."

"Damn. I bet he got a great deal on a minivan." Abby glanced back at the church. "You want to go in for old times' sake?"

Kate's smile faded. "No. I'm doing less of the church thing. More of the God thing."

Abby raised her brow. "Well, this I need to hear."

They fell into a walk, no different from the ones to a study session or practice, mirrored steps and comfortable silence.

"Was it the case?" Abby asked.

Kate wrapped her arms across her chest as the wind picked up and Abby wished she had brought a sweatshirt to give her. She wanted even more to wrap an arm around her, but dug her hands into her pockets instead.

"No. Not entirely." Kate shook her head. "It was inspiring, of course. These kids, fighting for who they are. When they asked me to fight for them too, I was happy to do it, but there was part of me that felt unqualified." She didn't look at Abby, but ahead. "Not because of my experience, but because they trusted me to fight for them when I never fought for myself. When I never stood so confidently in who I was and what I wanted that I wouldn't dare back down. Now, I think maybe that's why I got into law. I could hide behind getting justice, fairness, and acceptance for others, without ever taking a risk to get it for myself. It was my own way of playing it safe. Or maybe running away from what I wanted."

Rather than sweep in with assurance, Abby waited. Despite her growth, beauty, confidence, a whip of fresh sarcasm, the new clothes, and big job, this promised to be the most profound. The truth behind the broken engagement. The truth beneath the rest.

"I guess it's a lot easier to know what you want when you know who you are. Instead of thinking that you know who you are after someone told you what you should want." Kate glanced over at Abby. "I think you always had that part figured out. Knowing who you are."

Abby shrugged and kicked a rock down the sidewalk. "Yeah, but the knowing what I want part, I could never fully wrap my head around. I had to travel the world to figure it out." She smirked. "I always admired that you had a direction. You had your eyes on this plan. And not just the plan you were told to want."

"Well, the law school part, sure. But the other part—marriage, a husband—I tried pretty hard to make that work." Kate's brow furrowed. "But then we had this pre-marriage counseling assignment. Ryan and I. Write a letter to your future children. All I could think was, what if they're like me? Like that was some sort of bad thing, but also, I finally just admitted it to myself."

Abby held her breath as Kate paused.

"I started panicking," she said. "Not because of who I was, but because I suddenly worried about raising my kids to feel the same pressure I did. To be perfect, to follow rules out of fear, to marry someone they didn't love because of it."

"You wouldn't do that," Abby said.

"But how could I stop them if I didn't stop myself?" Kate frowned. "It made me despise my parents all over again. I started thinking I'd keep my kids from them to protect them. Then I realized, what's the point of that? Isn't that who I'm getting married for? Isn't that who I'm having these hypothetical children for? If I erased them from everything, would I even want any of it?"

They'd reached the edge of campus, a place for Abby's eyes to wander while she contemplated what to say, because this loomed like the perfect pitch. Like the timing might finally have worked itself out.

Only now she wasn't quite sure how to swing away. They stopped at the library. Abby stared at the phrase etched in marble that belonged to the philosophers, but she always considered theirs: *Ad astra per aspera.*

"I told them," Kate said.

Abby swiveled from the library to Kate, her eyes expanding as if she might read from her face what her ears didn't believe. "What?"

"I came out to them." Kate raised her eyebrows. "I told them I couldn't marry Ryan because I'm attracted to women. I always have been, and I always will be."

Abby gasped. "Kate, I—" She struggled for the words, overwhelmed by an excitement she didn't think appropriate to express. "That was brave. I know how much that took for you."

Kate twinkled with a half smile, something playful but restrained, before striding onward. Abby stood stunned for so long that she had to run to catch up with her.

"How'd it happen? How'd it go?"

"Well, I rehearsed the phone call a hundred times. I can't remember everything I said, but I remember what they did." Kate tensed. "Mom said she always knew, but not in a motherly, intuitive way, but an *I always hated you for it* way. She said I was sick and threw every Bible verse at me to prove it."

Abby's empathy rooted so deep that she gritted her teeth, unable to unleash the storm inside. So, she didn't. She didn't stop walking, didn't speak or curse. She grabbed Kate's hand, and she didn't pull away. She laced their fingers together and squeezed tighter.

"My dad cried, hard, which was somehow worse." Kate's voice wavered. "He offered to help and pray for me—and I had to tell him I didn't want him to. I had to tell him I wanted to be exactly who I was while he begged for me not to be." She brought them to another stop between the trees. Her eyes glistened, that chin crease wiggled, but she didn't cry. "It doesn't make sense, but I always thought he might be the one to accept me anyway. I always hoped for it. I thought he understood me, maybe not all of me, but my heart. And it's a different kind of breaking to realize he never will. That who I love diminishes the rest of me."

"It doesn't," Abby whispered.

Kate smiled. "I know that now."

Abby wrapped her arms around her. A hug not for lust or want or even to get her back. A hug for the years Kate had carried on, silently hurting, fearing the worst, and then having it actualized. A hug for the abandonment that came with her self-acceptance. For all Abby's grief, she never had to face that version of pain. She wished to take it away, but then she understood that she didn't have to, because Kate was still here. Kate was standing stronger, fuller, braver than she ever had been before.

"I'm proud of you, but I'm sorry you went through that alone. I never wanted you to. Not even back then," she said.

"I think I had to." Kate pulled away and peered up at her. "I didn't want you to go through what you did alone either, but didn't we have to? Would it even have meant anything if we weren't trying to find our way back here?"

Abby couldn't answer, too lost in awe. As they stood within Insley's green confines, the mountain looming like a guard above, the river a moat for trouble below, together but alone, Abby knew she was right. This was the only way.

Kate smiled in the long silence, slowly backing away with Abby's hand, letting go of it when their fingers no longer reached. "It hasn't all been bad," she said. "Getting to know myself the last year. Doing what I want, relearning my faith, my relationship with God, meeting new people. Work is a whole different world, and dating—"

"Dating?" It knocked Abby back.

"Yeah." Kate narrowed her eyes. "What about you? Back to posing as a windsurfing instructor? Impressing everyone with your four languages?"

"Not four. My Japanese is shit." Abby blushed. "But uh, no. Crazy schedule and . . . and I don't want to, I guess." She chewed her lip. "It's been a while for me."

Since rehab specifically, too fearful, too busy, too jaded to try.

Mostly too stuck on Kate. Abby trained her stare on the pavement, mind spinning at missing her shot.

"Don't worry," Kate said. "You're still the only person I've been with."

Her head shot up. "Good. I mean, not good. Not that you can't, or it would be bad if you did. I mean, if you wanted to, I wouldn't—"

"And here I thought I'd be the embarrassed one." Kate smirked.

She gulped, heart back to racing. The reunion, the confession, and this smiling, teasing, gorgeous Kate overwhelmed her. Because she really wanted this one. There was nothing holding them back now. Kate was out, Abby was clean. But as the field came into view, their old teammates warming up, friends and family trickling into the stands, she felt the chance slipping away.

"Kate, I—"

"I've been thinking," she said.

Abby nodded, not sure what she'd say, but ready. "Me too."

"We can switch off at shortstop."

"Oh."

Kate tilted her head. "What were you going to say?"

Abby stretched a stiff smile. "That I should play there because of your shoulder."

"Actually, that's a nonissue. Surgery last spring," Kate said with a grin. "In fact, maybe I should play there the entire game, just for a proper test run."

"No way," Abby said. "Switch at second every inning?"

"How else are we supposed to turn two?"

Kate winked, and when her eyes met Abby's, with the field behind her, a new message came off the wind through the canyon. They'd finally come home to win.

For all the talk of the afterlife instilled in her as a child, the heaven she may not reach, and the home she no longer had, Kate stepped onto the softball field as though passing through the Pearly Gates.

She'd changed more than she ever thought possible since she last played on it. But so much in her and on the diamond was the same. The same dirt. The same steps between the bases, colors, and smell. Home. Homesickness. She found both in one breath.

Not just home, but family. Two dozen former Eagles, who came before and after her, answered the game's call. The underclassmen, though they were hardly that anymore with spouses and children, flocked to her. Palamino, Quong, Brookheimer, and Crosby nodded and beamed like the C stitched on her jersey still meant something.

As usual, she congregated with the fivesome. T.K. with her hair bleached platinum blond and a twenty-year-old boyfriend who helped her stretch. Jill, with her redheaded brood in tow. Mick, always the catcher and coach, tweaking lineups and talking shit. And Abby, playing with Juniper, who wore one of Jill's old uniforms like a dress. Kate did her best not to stare as she warmed up with Jill, entranced by Abby's gentleness, the way she kneeled to help Juniper and praised her for every catch.

"Hutch, did you hear me?" Jill asked.

"What?" Kate snapped her head back and threw the ball to Jill.

"How was last night?"

"It was fine."

"But like, Mick and Haley's place is small, isn't it?" Jill asked.

Mick glanced up from her clipboard and glared. "What's that supposed to mean?"

"That there's only one extra bed," Jill said with a mischievous glint. "And two out-of-town guests . . ."

Kate shook her head. "Abby stayed at a hotel."

"Damn it."

T.K. popped up from the grass, where her boyfriend stretched her groin in a way that offered far too much insight into their relationship. "After all that planning? Mick, how'd you fuck it up?"

"I didn't fuck it up!" Mick shouted.

"Clearly you did!" Jill huffed. "It works in the books."

"You guys need a new hobby," Abby said as she joined them with

Juniper slung over her shoulder. She eased next to Kate and lowered to a whisper. "Or maybe we just need new friends."

Kate grinned. "I don't know. They're pretty hard to shake."

She nearly drifted into the same daze from their walk. A place where only they existed. Only Abby existed, because only Abby looked at her with such reverence. While the long winter away had cooled her in some ways and took a minute for Kate to get used to, that had never changed.

"Welcome to the third annual alumni game!" Mick shouted from the pitching circle. Kate and Abby and the others gathered around. "A few ground rules for all you washed-up jocks. No pulled hamstrings or torn ACLs. If you're questioning whether you're fast enough, trust me, you're not." The assembly of aging softball players chuckled. "Don't try to be a hero out there. Losers are on permanent gear duty and picking up the winners' tab at Sunny's. Okay, those are the only rules. Let's play ball!"

While her last game was nearly a decade behind her, Kate took the field like she never missed a day. She felt the freedom of not yet having everything she wanted, but carrying nothing she didn't. And as she looked at Abby, she wondered if this was what she always knew, even back then.

"What?" Abby asked in the dugout as she put on her batting gloves.

Kate shook her head. "Nothing."

"Good. Don't fuck up out there." Abby winked.

"Me? The pressure's on you, *Hanmāgaru.*"

Abby hitched her jaw. "Don't call me that."

But it was too late, as the rest of the dugout broke into chants of Abby's nickname from Japan, imitating her commercial, pulling it up on their phones. She chuckled as Abby rolled her eyes and blushed.

Kate hit in the leadoff spot, just like always. She faked a bunt, then popped a flawless, out-of-reach blooper over Madison Quong's head. And as always, after Kate got on base, Abby knocked her in. She couldn't quite pull it over the fence anymore, but connected on a perfect line, the ball springing from the barrel to the outfield, still one of the most beautiful swings Kate had ever seen.

Kate scored, but Abby got held up on her way to second base as Jenna Crosby and Izzy Palamino tackled her to the dirt. The game devolved almost entirely into shenanigans, jokes, cheating, cheap tricks, howling laughter when Mick tripped rounding the bases and when T.K. swung so hard she fell over. That's what happened when at least a third of them had pins in their knees, others with kids at home, some not picking up a bat since graduation.

In the field, Kate and Abby took turns playing second and shortstop. Abby coasted, barely seemed to try. Kate couldn't decide if she looked younger now or back then. In two years, she'd become healthier, brighter, the shadows no longer rooting beneath her eyes.

"So, I have a question," Abby said to her.

It was the bottom of the final inning. Abby stood at shortstop, hat on backward, the sleeves of another baggy T-shirt rolled up to reveal the biceps she kept no less toned than she had as a professional player. Kate dug in at second base, just like old times, though without the expectations of an actual game, she let herself chat through the last outs.

"What?"

"The dating thing," Abby said. "What's that about?"

"What do you mean?"

Abby kicked the dirt. "Well, I mean, is it serious? Are you seeing anyone now?"

Kate cleared her throat, heat climbing from her chest to her neck. Dating had been an interesting experience at best, but uneventful. Charlotte Pruitt ran with a group of powerful women, many of whom were queer, who she gladly introduced Kate to, but she'd yet to find a connection despite a few promising dates. Marcus Watterson tried a completely opposite approach, thrusting her into gay bars and dating apps, but they had never worked before and didn't now. Kate, frankly, wasn't that invested, especially over the last few months, knowing that Abby might be at the alumni game.

"We should probably finish the game," she said.

"I think we got some time." Abby shrugged as Courtney Seaborn swung and missed. "So, you going to answer my question? Do you have a girlfriend? Boyfriend?"

Kate sighed and rolled her eyes, but the blush didn't leave her cheeks. "No one serious."

"Why not?"

"Well, I'm a bit of a workaholic. What about you?"

"Alcoholic, remember?" Abby drifted over to Kate with a grin. "Recovering, of course. All things are possible through our lord and savior."

Kate couldn't help but chuckle and shoved her. "Go back to shortstop."

"Same old Cruz!" Courtney yelled from home plate. "Still flirting with Hutch!"

"Same old Seaborn! Still not funny!" Abby shouted back.

"Shut up and go back so I can hit!"

"This is more important than the fly ball you're going to hit to left center!"

"You don't know!"

Abby turned and gestured to left field. "Brookheimer, take two steps to your left! And one in! Perfect!" Abby pivoted back to Courtney and gave her a thumbs-up. "Okay, we're all set. Go ahead, Court!"

"Screw you!"

Both teams, including Kate, doubled over in laughter.

"So, what was I saying?" Abby asked, completely unfazed by her audience. "Oh yeah, so it sounds like you're single and I'm single."

Kate smirked, her stomach flipping in a way she'd long forgotten. A way that no one had inspired before her and no one since. "And what are you going to do about it?"

Courtney smacked the ball. It flew high to left field. Brookheimer didn't have to move, simply put her glove up. Abby never turned to see it, not even as the Eagles cawed in hysterics and Courtney flipped her off. Instead, she closed in on Kate again.

"You know, San Diego is less than a two-hour flight away," Abby said.

"Oh, really? I would like to see Isla again. Those nephews of yours are pretty cute too."

"Well, you know where they get it . . ."

Kate scoffed. "Yeah. Your sister."

"What's going on? Do you two need us to stop the game?" Mick asked.

"No!"

"Okay, then maybe pick it up after this, Cruz," Mick said before addressing the field. "One out! Runner on one, infield turn two, outfield cut three!"

Abby grumbled and jogged back to shortstop. She worked the leather of her glove, spit, flexed her knees, and Kate swore they'd gone back in time. Her heart could hardly take it.

"You know, flights to San Francisco are pretty cheap too," Kate said, as Madison Quong went up to hit.

Abby grinned. "I heard they even have a baseball team."

"Yeah, me too. A little one, I think. Field by the water. Won some sort of trophy."

"That's the one," Abby said as the pitcher started her windup. "Maybe there's someone worth scouting up there."

Madison drilled a ball to shortstop. Abby glanced from Kate not a second too soon, jolted a step to her right to snag the ball on a skip with her backhand. Kate didn't doubt that she'd get it, never slowed on her route to second, the ball always stopping in Abby's wake. She squared to Kate, took a step, and flipped the ball from her glove. Kate caught it, tapped second base before T.K. reached it, and fired a bullet to first for the double play. Turning two—the only time they got it right.

Both teams cheered. Kate shivered as she approached Abby for a high five, but she never received it. Abby hugged her, lifted her off the ground, and Kate held tight.

"Hey," Abby whispered when she released her.

The teams cleared the field, shaking hands and exchanging high fives.

"Hey," Kate said back.

They stared at each other, in the careful distance. Abby's breath shook on the way out, and Kate tilted her head.

"You okay?" she asked.

Abby nodded, her brow quirking, so that Kate didn't know if she might laugh or cry. "I think I'm just overwhelmed by you."

Kate's throat tightened at the admission, at how far they'd come, and the unknown ahead. She longed for the right words to take what she wanted, but faltered at the ghost of their failures and the reality of their separate worlds. After tonight, another end loomed until the next alumni game called them back. For all her progress, she was still in the middle, unsure of how to have both the life she'd worked so hard to craft for herself and the part of her heart she'd never learned to live without.

"I'm uh, going to get my stuff." Kate cleared her throat.

The two of them slipped into the throngs of their teammates, losing each other in the catching up and goodbyes, the shuffle in and out of dugouts. Kate joined Mick, Jill, and T.K. in the parking lot as the rest of their teammates tore off ahead for Sunny's. Another breath of old times. The four of them long ago had come together as scared freshmen and hadn't broken apart since.

"Shall we?" Mick asked.

Kate furrowed her brow and glanced around. "Where's Abby?"

"What do you mean? She's not coming," Jill said.

"Why?" Kate whipped around to find her, sinking under invisible weight when she didn't appear.

"She's headed to Venezuela or the Dominican Republic or somewhere to scout some kid." T.K. sighed. "Can we go? I'm starving."

"What? No. I didn't get to say goodbye." Her heartbeat filled her ears at Abby slipping away, just like after the national championship. "She can't just leave like that without saying anything—"

Jill patted her shoulder, assuring her with a nod toward the field. "She's still here."

"Oh."

Her breath returned when she spotted Abby at home plate, peering up at the mountain. And in that brief flash of fear, she ceased to be in the middle. Kate knew exactly what she needed to do. The others seemed to as well, stretching wide grins.

Mick tossed her the keys. "Turn the lights off and lock up when you're done?"

"Yeah. I'll catch up with you guys later."

A gentle wind streamed through her hair, cooled the sweat from the game, left her shivering on the first steps back to Abby. Toward exactly what she wanted. She paused at the fence behind her, living in that moment before you knew if it was an out or leaving the park. Before Abby turned with the same gleam in her gaze that had greeted her eight years ago. A reminder to breathe and let go.

"It's never going to work, you know," Kate said.

Abby didn't turn right away, but Kate didn't mind the wait. She knew this was it, the same way she knew the sound of a ball meeting the bat before a double play. She wasn't playing the game scared or halfway. They were right where they were supposed to be.

COMING HOME AGAIN

She could've sworn it was just the wind. Abby closed her eyes when she heard Kate and smiled.

"What's not going to work?" she asked with her eyes trained on home plate.

"We're never going to be a memory or long-lost friends."

Abby slowly turned to face her. Blue eyes and all that light, even as the sun disappeared. She clutched the chain-link fence and leaned in so that her forehead nearly brushed it. So that she might've kissed her if it weren't for the final partition.

"You weren't really going to let me leave without saying goodbye, were you?" Kate's mouth twitched with a slight frown.

Her brow folded together. "I'm sorry. I'm just tired of goodbyes."

"Then don't go." Kate's eyes glistened when Abby found them again. "I know you have work and a new life, but I want to be part of it. I've always wanted to be part of it. Part of you."

Abby smiled. "You always were."

"Then stay?" Kate asked, her throat bobbing ever so slightly. "Stay this time. Quit going away. I know you're chasing the game or the next baseball messiah, but—"

"I'm not," Abby said with a slight laugh, if only to hide her blush. "I was chasing you. Looking for that love you played with on every field." She rubbed a thumb across Kate's hand on the fence. "I should've known I just had to come back here."

They met each other halfway, with unhurried steps, and when they stood across from each other, Abby knew the timing was finally right. Their foreheads met first. And when they kissed, beneath the stadium lights, it was slower. Kinder. Unlike the sloppy passion of Las Vegas or the timidity of their first. It landed full and strong, but tender, because that's who they were now.

When the same happy tears that made them laugh rolled into their kisses, when they could have no more of each other on the open field, when the sky fell dark, they sat against the backstop and stared up at the hills. Kate rested her head against her shoulder, and Abby held her hand.

"I can see it," she whispered.

Bickering, morning coffee, scrambling to work, long runs, surfing new coasts. A future without children. A future with them. Abby could even see that, despite never letting herself before. Blue-eyed and swinging a bat. She saw a band on Kate's finger, one on her own. She heard vows somewhere. A courthouse, a beach, anywhere with their friends. Their real family. She heard all the right things. No ringing. Just laughter, whispers, tears, and love, over and over again. She saw them at twenty-two and thirty-two. She saw them at fifty, seventy, a hundred.

"I see it too," Kate said.

She saw the field. Saw them on it forever.

ACKNOWLEDGMENTS

I'm so thankful for the opportunity to share this book. It was incredibly personal and healing, at times exhausting, and absolutely would not have happened without a great support team behind me throughout the process.

First, thank you to my agent, Jo Ramsay. You truly keep the train on the tracks—answering every question, soothing every anxiety, and, most importantly, bringing such a kind, thoughtful eye to the work we do together. Thanks for letting me lean on you. I couldn't ask for a better teammate.

Thank you to my editor, Alicia Clancy. I was nervous to put this one out there, but you completely dove in and understood the direction, which meant so much to me. Thank you for honoring the shift and risks, and for working through the changes to get this where it needed to be. I'm honored that you believed in it, and grateful for how seamlessly we collaborated again.

A huge thank-you to the entire team at Bantam Dell and Penguin Random House. I know there are far more people behind the scenes than I know to name making the magic happen. Thanks for treating every book with such care. The work you do is powerful.

I have an immense group of friends and family who do everything from encouraging me to making me laugh to keeping me humble—all equally important. I can't name everyone, but big thanks to Darby

Bozeman and Ellen Meny for reading this go-around. And thank you to my sister, Alley, for making life doable, tolerable, and more colorful in every way. You're a better friend and sister than I deserve.

This book is dedicated to my parents—thank you. They bonded over their love for the game and then shared that love with their kids. I can't count how many hours they dedicated to coaching me and my sister and our friends. They spent even more years in the stands, encouraging me as I grew up and continued to play. When I look back, those are my favorite memories and years together. Most importantly, the field is where my dad taught me the most important lessons about love, loss, and life. Thank you. When I see a field, I see all of us there together. I love you.

The biggest thank-you belongs to my wife, Emily. You're the reason I'm able to do this with my whole heart. Thanks for your patience, for being my first reader, for loving me on the low days, and most of all, for helping me feel it again. I love you.

© JESSICA HILL PHOTOGRAPHY

SAMANTHA SALDIVAR is a corporate broadcast producer who has worked at the Oregon NBC affiliates KGW in Portland and KMTR in Eugene, where she won a regional Emmy Award for Best Evening Newscast. During her studies at the University of Oregon's School of Journalism and Communication, she reported on college sports for campus television. She lives in Portland with her wife and is the author of *Play You for It*.

samanthasaldivar.com
Instagram: @saldivar.samantha